THE CROWN OF FOOLS

CANDICE WRIGHT

**THE CROWN OF FOOLS COPYRIGHT © 2021
CANDICE WRIGHT**

This is a work of fiction. Names, characters, places, and incidents either are the products of the author's imagination or are used fictitiously.
Any resemblance to actual persons, living or dead, businesses, companies, events, or locales is entirely coincidental.
All Rights Reserved.
No part of this book may be reproduced or used in any manner without the express written permission of the publisher except for the use of brief quotations in a book review.
This eBook is licensed for your personal enjoyment only. This eBook may not be re-sold or given away to other people. If you would like to share this book with another person, please purchase an additional copy for each recipient.

Cover design by JODIELOCKS designs
Editing by Tanya Oemig
Proofreading by Chantal Fleming

CONTENTS

Chapter 1	1
Chapter 2	7
Chapter 3	15
Chapter 4	22
Chapter 5	28
Chapter 6	33
Chapter 7	39
Chapter 8	44
Chapter 9	49
Chapter 10	57
Chapter 11	63
Chapter 12	68
Chapter 13	74
Chapter 14	80
Chapter 15	86
Chapter 16	92
Chapter 17	98
Chapter 18	104
Chapter 19	109
Chapter 20	114
Chapter 21	118
Chapter 22	123
Chapter 23	128
Chapter 24	135
Chapter 25	142
Chapter 26	148
Chapter 27	152
Chapter 28	157
Chapter 29	162
Chapter 30	168
Chapter 31	172

Chapter 32	179
Chapter 33	185
Chapter 34	192
Chapter 35	197
Chapter 36	203
Chapter 37	209
Chapter 38	218
Chapter 39	223
Chapter 40	232
Chapter 41	238
Chapter 42	244
Chapter 43	249
Chapter 44	255
Chapter 45	262
Chapter 46	270
Chapter 47	279
Chapter 48	285
Chapter 49	292
Chapter 50	298
Chapter 51	307
Chapter 52	312
Chapter 53	318
Chapter 54	326
Chapter 55	335
Chapter 56	342
Chapter 57	347
Chapter 58	357
Chapter 59	363
Chapter 60	371
Chapter 61	379
Chapter 62	385
Excerpt of Ricochet by Candice Wright	393
Also by Candice Wright	403
Acknowledgments	405
About the Author	407

UNITS

LA Chapter of Kings of Carnage

ORION DIESEL
HALO REBEL
GAGE LUCKY
LUNA AVA

Vegas Chapter of Kings of Carnage

BATES
SAINT
PRIEST
REIGN

The Chaos Demons

VIPER
ZERO
GRIM
MEGAN

For the boy who let me fall.
Because of you, I learned to fly.

No matter how bad your heart is broken, the world doesn't stop for your grief.

— Faraaz Kazi

1

Kat

I was fifteen the day I met my soul mate and twenty-two the day I buried him.

With my chin tucked against my chest, my shoulders bowed under the weight of my grief, I smooth my hand over the cool lacquered wood of Alex's coffin, fighting the urge to lift the lid and climb in beside him.

He's already taking my heart with him. Who cares what happens to my body?

Except, it isn't just me anymore I remind myself, my hand sliding down to rest over my still flat stomach.

Our child is nestled inside me, oblivious that their future has irrevocably changed forever.

They'll never know what it feels like to be held in their father's arms, never hear his deep laughter or his raspy voice sing them lullabies goodnight.

Alex is dead, and if it wasn't for this baby inside me, I'd follow him to the other side because I don't know how to live without him.

How do I carry on when my days always started and ended with him?

How do I breathe without him or stop myself from bleeding out as Orion's words repeat in a loop over and over in my head?

"I'm so sorry, Sunshine, he's gone."

Gone. The man I love, the man I breathe for, is gone but I have no idea how to let him go. How can I possibly say goodbye to the person who became my whole word?

"It's time, Kat," a voice rumbles from behind me but I ignore it. It's not time. I didn't say goodbye yet. Alex can't leave without saying goodbye, right?

Except he did.

Gone. Gone. Gone.

My legs buckle and I go down, but strong arms scoop me up and hold me tight as my chest cracks open and a wail of hopeless despair escapes before I can hold it back. The arms holding me squeeze me tighter, but I can't stop screaming as I splinter apart. Pieces of me float away like dust, pieces I'll never get back. All the parts that made him and me an us are stripped away, leaving me feeling naked and alone, laid bare for the world to see in all my tortured glory.

When soft music starts playing, I catch movement out of the corner of my eye and see the coffin, laden with flowers, slowly being lowered into the ground.

I start fighting the arms holding me, trying to get to Alex before he's gone.

"No, stop it. We didn't say goodbye. Please, let me go. We didn't say goodbye!" I scream.

"Shhh...hush Sunshine. You're gonna be okay," the deep voice soothes me, holding me tighter as my fighting begins to ebb and all my energy leaves me.

"No, I won't," I whisper, each word feeling like glass. "I'll never be okay again."

I wake up and roll over and breathe in the faint smell of aftershave, the nightmare dissipating as the early morning rays spill through the blinds. Alex's side of the bed is empty, making me frown and wonder where he's gone before it all comes crashing back with the force of a wrecking ball.

Day in, day out, I die a little more as his smell fades from our bed and his absence leaves me so cold, I wonder if I'll ever feel warm again.

It's been a month since we buried him. That day, and the many that followed, are mostly a blur, but I remember the pain. It's been my one constant since he died. It hasn't dulled or faded in any way. That spiel people give about time easing all wounds is bullshit. Nothing's changed. Alex is still gone and I'm still here alone, trapped in an apartment that reminds me of everything I've lost.

I stare at the empty space beside me where Alex should be and feel tears slide down my cheeks.

They blur my vision as they fall, almost letting me fool myself into believing I can see him beside me, a distorted vision of regret and sadness, but I know it's just a trick of my mind.

If he were here, I'd feel him, like I always could. We'd been connected by an invisible tether from the first day I saw him sitting on the steps of what would turn out to be my last foster home.

Twelve foster families had taken me in and returned me like a faulty toy, but I had never had a home until I had Alex.

A wave of nausea washing over me has me staggering from the bed on shaky legs and collapsing over the toilet bowl as I throw up what little is in my stomach.

It's the reminder I need that I can't just lie down in that bed and die too.

I flush the toilet and stumble to the sink, splashing cold water on my face before brushing my teeth, all while avoiding looking in the mirror. I don't need to see my reflection to know what I look like. I can imagine it reflects just how I'm feeling, which is hollowed out. Like one of those Russian Babushka dolls with its insides missing.

I shuffle down the hallway to the kitchen and fill the kettle, hoping some ginger tea might settle my stomach, before wandering over to the window and gazing down to the street below.

It's still early but with school out for the week, children are already playing outside, soaking up the sun. Cars pass as people head to work, careful to avoid the teenage skateboarder with a death wish whizzing by. Everywhere I look, people are going about their day as if nothing has changed, as if I'm not standing mere feet from them with a gaping black chasm of nothing in my chest where my heart used to be.

I grip the windowsill and take a deep breath, trying to let go of the anger coursing through me but it's impossible. How is this fair? How can the world outside my window keep turning even though mine has stopped?

Each peal of laughter I hear through the window feels like a slap in the face, a taunt that there is happiness out there to be had, just not for me.

Turning away, I take my bitterness with me to the kitchen, making my tea with unnecessarily forceful movements.

I toss the teaspoon in the sink and take the tea back to the bedroom with me, placing it beside the bed. Staring down at the messy purple sheets that Alex had a conniption over because manly men didn't have purple bedrooms, I feel a crack fragment the wall around my heart.

Alex gave in, he always did, telling me nothing was more important than my happiness.

All he needed was me.

He was my anchor and without him, I feel like I'm floating aimlessly, trying to find my feet again.

And suddenly I can't look at the sheets anymore. Ripping them from the bed, images bombard my brain, of Alex and me making love, of us laughing, of him holding me, of me holding myself together since he left.

I crash to my knees and scream at the injustice of it all. He should be here with me, dammit.

Stumbling to my feet, I move to the closet, yanking the door open. I grab the first T-shirt of Alex's I can find and bring it to my nose but all I can smell is laundry detergent. I toss it behind me and reach for the next but it's the same.

Panic wells inside me. What if I forget what he smells like?

Frantically I start pulling everything out until I'm standing in a pile of clothes. Spotting his favorite band T-shirt tossed in the corner I grab it and bring it to my face, inhaling deeply and sinking to my knees when his familiar scent envelops me once more.

I'm done, so fucking done with this life.

I curl up in the fetal position and sob, not even bothering to open my eyes when a crashing sound echoes from down the hall.

The apartment building could be on fire and I still wouldn't move, the motivation to try harder disappearing as quickly as it came.

The door to the closet springs wide but I don't move, I just look up through my endless tears to the giant watching me with sorrow on his face and tell him the only truth I know right now.

"I want him back," I croak out. "I'll give anything, do anything but please, please, please," I beg, in a whispered plea, "Just bring Alex back to me."

2

Conan

I'd been boarding up the bakery window, broken by some asshole, when Orion called me.

A neighbor had reported screaming coming from Kat's apartment and knowing where I was, he asked me to check it out.

Hopping on my bike, I head over straight away, not giving the bakery a second thought.

Carnage had already lost too many people in the last six weeks. I'll be dammed if I let anything happen to someone else.

I swallow hard, picturing Kat at Pike's funeral. I've never seen the light go out of someone's eyes before unless they were dying, but Kat, well I guess part of her died the day Pike did, and the world has been a little darker since because of it.

Standing in a sea of bikers who had seen and done awful shit that failed to scar them, one broken girl marked us all that day in a way we never foresaw. It was more than just the day we buried a brother—it was the day the light disappeared from the one dubbed Sunshine and in her place was a girl none of us recognized.

The apartment is thankfully only a couple of blocks from the bakery, so it takes me only minutes to get there. I climb off the bike and head over to the ground floor apartment I came to once before with Pike.

I bang on the door, listening for anything out of the ordinary but all I can hear is silence and that's perhaps even worse than screaming. Screaming means you're alive.

Fuck it. I know one hard kick would be enough for the door to give way, the lock's a fucking joke. My horror grows when I realize that won't be necessary as the handle turns under my palm and opens. I shove it wide, ignoring the slamming sound it makes as it bounces off the wall. I'm pissed at how easy it is to get in here, flimsy lock or not, anything is better than leaving the damn door unlocked.

I call her name, my voice echoing off the walls.

Nothing.

The apartment is completely silent except for the low hum of the refrigerator. My pulse picks up as I grab my gun from under my cut and make my way through the small living room, down the hall to the bedroom.

Looking around the room, I see the bed in disarray but no sign of Kat. I'm just about to head to the bathroom when I catch the whisper of soft crying.

I follow the sound, moving across the room, and yank the closet door open.

And there she is lying on the floor of the closet, softly sobbing with her arms wrapped tightly around herself as if she is trying to hold herself together.

I tuck the gun away as she looks up at me, her broken whisper as she begs me to bring Pike back slashes my chest. I almost look down to see if I'm bleeding, my reaction to Kat's pain is so stark it hurts to breathe.

Reaching down, I gently pick her up, holding her to my chest as her tears run down my neck and soak my T-shirt.

I move toward the bed but stop. There is something wrong with lying in a dead man's bed while his woman falls apart in my arms, so I sit on the floor instead. Leaning back against the foot of the bed, I slip my hand inside my cut and remove the gun, placing it beside me before holding her tighter.

I don't offer her words of comfort. I won't lie to her, not now. Carnage has tried to give her space to grieve but I don't think her being alone here is the right move and that's coming from me, a perpetual loner.

Eventually, her breathing evens out, letting me know she's fallen asleep, exhaustion winning out over sorrow. I hope in sleep she can find peace, if only for a little while.

I should put her to bed now. I should tuck her in, call Carnage and have them send one of the old ladies around to tend to her when she wakes, but I can't bring myself to move.

Gently, so I don't wake her, I tip her head back and study her.

She's beautiful, there is no denying that. With her peaches

and cream skin, plump pink lips, and long thick hair the color of spun gold, she looks like a princess from one of those Disney movies Luna puts on for Ruby but secretly watches herself.

As beautiful as she is, there is no hiding the dark shadows under her eyes or the way her clothing hangs off her once curvy frame.

She looks like a shadow of the girl Pike first brought to the club not too long ago, her sunshine lost in the dark, nowhere to be found.

I pull out my phone and fire off a text to Orion letting him know I'm here and that Kat's okay. Instead of replying, he calls me. I swear he does this shit on purpose, knowing how I hate wasting my breath on conversation when I can just text instead.

Thankfully, my phone's on silent so it doesn't disturb Kat as she sleeps.

"Yeah," I answer.

"What the fuck happened?" Orion questions through the phone, making me sigh.

"She's grieving," I answer, keeping my voice soft.

"Fuck. She can't keep going on like this. Pike's gone—" I cut him off with a growl.

"Do you think she doesn't know that? Tell me, Orion, if you had lost Luna that night, or Diesel or heaven forbid, Ruby; would you take kindly to someone putting a timeframe on how long you get to grieve?"

"I didn't mean it like that," he refutes.

"You did," I grunt out before sighing again. "I know you mean well, and you're just worried about her, but president or not, you can't fix everything, Orion."

"It's not just her though, is it? She's growing a kid. She needs to at least try because if she loses that baby, Conan, we'll lose Kat too. It's the only thing keeping her here."

I slide my hand down to the hem of her T-shirt and slip my hand underneath, feeling her warm skin against my palm.

My hand rests over the smallest of bumps. I had forgotten about the baby. With the chaos of the club being rebuilt and dealing with the fallout of that night, Kat has managed to slip through the cracks and mostly evade us all. But that stops now.

"I'll take care of it, Orion." I hang up before dialing Doc's number. When he answers, I give him Kat's address and tell him what's going on, relieved when he agrees to come over.

Reluctantly, I climb to my feet and carefully lower her onto the bed, pulling the comforter over her to keep her warm while I head to the kitchen.

It's small but functional with glossy white cupboards and light gray countertops. A small white table sits against the far wall with four mismatched chairs.

I rummage through the cupboards but don't find much beyond a jar of peanut butter and a few packets of ramen noodles.

The fridge is in an even worse state. Giving up, I order some takeout and text a prospect to do a food run to the grocery store.

With nothing else to do, I wash up the few dishes in the sink and tidy around a little. I take in the small living room—the cream walls, gray corner sofa and the pine coffee table in front of it littered with motorcycle magazines—and somehow feel I'm intruding. Like Pike's presence is in this room, watching me as I move through the small space they made their home.

Walking over to the bookcase, I take in the array of photographs lovingly displayed, depicting the history of their relationship before it was cruelly snatched away. They seem to have been arranged in chronological order, so I pick up the last one and stare at the image of Kat with her head thrown back laughing as Pike presses his lips to the hollow of her throat, his hands gripping her hips possessively.

I wonder if, given a second chance, Pike would make the same choices. Seeing Kat smile, the warmth radiating from her so clearly that I can almost feel it, I figure I already know what his answer would be.

Some people spend a lifetime looking for the kind of love these two shared. Some never find it at all, but then there are the few who are blessed to recognize their soulmates the second they lay their eyes on them.

Pike might have had his life cut short, but I guarantee many men would trade places with him just to experience the kind of love that's usually reserved for the pages of a book.

A knock snags my attention so I place the photo down and open the door.

"Conan. How's she doing?" Doc asks me as I step aside to let him in.

"Not good. This is the first time I've seen her since the funeral, but she looks like she's lost weight."

He sighs. "I took an oath to protect the sanctity of life but if Garrett were alive right now, I'd take him apart with my scalpel, piece by piece."

"I know," I grunt out, running a hand through my shoulder-length hair, reminding me that it needs cutting.

The Crown of Fools

"Where is she?" he questions, placing his bag on the kitchen table.

"Sleeping. You want me to wake her?"

"No, let her rest for now." He's interrupted from saying anything else by another knock at the door.

Opening it, I grab the food and pay the delivery kid, kicking the door shut with my foot before setting the bag on the kitchen counter.

"What you got there?" Doc asks, wandering over as the smell of chicken noodle soup begins to permeate the air.

"Soup, sandwiches, some fruit, and some juice. I've got one of the prospects doing some shopping because there is nothing here to eat."

"I hate to say this, but she might need a firmer hand." He pulls out one of the kitchen chairs and sits in it heavily, his weight making the chair creak in protest. Doc's not a small man, although to me everyone is small. At around 6'1" with broad shoulders and a bit of a belly, the fucker isn't easily intimidated but that doesn't stop me from staring the asshole down.

"Explain," I bark, crossing my arms over my chest as I continue to glare at him. I'm not sure where this need to protect Kat is coming from but fuck me, if there was ever a girl who needed someone in their corner, it's her.

"Easy, Conan," he placates, "I mean with regards to eating, going to appointments for the baby, and stuff. The old ladies pussyfooting around her isn't helping. I know she is going through hell but if she's not careful, she'll lose this baby."

"No, I won't."

I lift my head at the sound of a soft feminine voice and

freeze when Sunshine fixes her stunning violet-blue eyes on mine.

3

Kat

I want to lash out at them both. Who the fuck do they think they are, coming into my home and making their demands? I don't though. I bite my tongue and stare into the inky blue eyes of the giant who held me earlier.

He stares back, both of us watching each other in silence as a sort of knowing passes between us.

"You need to look after yourself, Kat, your baby needs—" I cut Doc off, but keep my eyes on Conan, borrowing a little of the strength he's offering.

"I'm doing the best I can. You haven't been here, Doc, so don't assume you know what's going on. I've been to the doctors, I've seen an OBGYN. I take my vitamins like a good little girl before I puke them back up again. The fridge and cupboards are bare because I've been too sick to get out of bed and go shopping for the last week. Apparently, my baby doesn't understand the concept of the word 'morning' in morning sickness."

He stares at me before heaving himself up from the chair which creaks loudly.

"We all just worry about you Kat. If you needed food you should have called. Any one of us could have gone for you."

I shrug. I've never had anyone to rely on before. It's always just been Alex and me. At this point, it's instinctual to do everything alone without asking for help.

"Sit," Conan orders, pulling a chair out for me, leaving no room for arguments.

I'm too wiped out to put up a fuss anyway. The sooner I do what they want the sooner they can leave me alone again.

Doc asks me a bunch of questions until he is satisfied with my answers, then takes my blood pressure before nodding.

"Alright, Kat, everything looks good. If the sickness becomes too extreme, go back to your doctor and they can prescribe you something to help. Eat little and often, okay? You need to keep your strength up."

He squeezes my arm before grabbing his bag and heading toward the door.

"I have to get going, I'm meeting someone across town. Call me if you need me okay?"

Nodding noncommittally, I close the door behind him. I turn and jump when I find Conan right behind me. For someone so big, he sure moves quietly.

I crane my neck to look up at him, his eyes searching mine, making me feel as if they can see right inside me, past all the bullshit and the walls I've erected to keep what's left of my heart safe.

I look away, feeling stripped bare. Before I can move, he raises one of his large hands, presses it to the back of my head, and tugs until I face plant against his chest.

I have no idea what the fuck is happening. I barely know this guy and yet, as we stand there in silence, I feel my tense muscles begin to relax a little. He doesn't try to fill the silence like most people do, he's happy to stand in the quiet with me. I didn't even realize how much I needed this, something to calm the discontent in my head, until now.

"Come, let's get some food inside you." His deep melodic voice rumbles over me, breaking the strange moment between us.

He lets go and indicates for me to go sit, so I do and watch as he places a container of soup with a spoon in front of me.

"Eat, Sunshine," he orders. I wince at the sound of the nickname on his lips. It's the name Alex gave me when we were still nothing more than just kids and it stuck. My stomach churns at the knowledge that I'll never hear him say those words again, but I beat it back knowing that I do need to eat something and the soup smells amazing.

"Thank you," I tell him quietly, taking a small mouthful. As the flavors explode on my tongue, I wait for the nausea to swirl like it usually does, but when nothing happens, I take another mouthful and another and before I know it, the container is empty.

"Good girl. Here." He hands me a bottle of juice and takes

the container away from me, tossing it in the trash before turning to watch me drink.

"I'm fine, Conan, you can go now," I mutter once the juice is all gone.

He walks over and takes the bottle from me without uttering a word.

I've never seen a man as big as Conan in real life before. At around 6'8", and looking like Jason Momoa and Dwayne Johnson's love child, he could probably pick me up one-handed without breaking a sweat. He towers over everyone and with his permanent scowl, he usually possesses an air of menace, but right now all of his intensity is focused on me, making me resist the urge to squirm.

"Go take a bath. I have a prospect bringing some food to fill your pantry and fridge."

I swallow down the bile at the word 'prospect.' Alex was so fucking proud of being a prospect for Carnage, and look where that had gotten him.

"I don't—" My mouth snaps shut as he stalks toward me.

Before I can ask him what the hell he's doing, he scoops me up, making me squeal, before carrying me to the bathroom.

Placing me on the floor once more, he looks around before facing me.

"No bath?"

"I tried to tell you before you went all alpha asshole on me," I grumble.

He grunts before turning on the shower and stepping back.

"Shower then. I'll wait for the food to arrive, then put it away for you."

I open my mouth to protest and end up shutting it with a sigh, shoulders drooping as I give in.

Pick your battles, Kat.

"Fine." I wait for him to leave before turning and locking the door behind me.

I make quick work of the shower, not entirely comfortable being naked with a strange man in my apartment. Climbing out, I wrap a giant towel around myself before dumping my PJ's in the laundry basket behind the bathroom door. Pulling the door open, I come to a dead halt when I find Conan outside the door.

With a squeak, I jump back, my heart racing a million miles a minute.

"I was worried," he admits in that deep hypnotic voice of his.

I should yell at him for crossing a line here but something in his eyes tells me he truly is worried for me.

I don't answer. What can I say? I could offer him false platitudes, that I'm okay, but we'd both know it was a lie.

A knock sounds at the door so he heads in that direction as I move to the dresser and quickly get dressed in sweatpants and a plain black T-shirt before pulling my hair up into a messy bun so it doesn't drip down my back.

I hear voices talking quietly so I pad toward the kitchen on bare feet, freezing when my brain matches the familiar voice to the face.

Linc. A guy who became good friends with Alex as they were both prospecting together. He'd been around here more times than I could count, eating dinner with Alex and me, laughing and joking, but I hadn't seen him once since the night Alex died.

He had turned up before I left to go to Ava's and surprised the shit out of me by kissing me. I slapped him and kicked him out, furious that he would do that to his friend.

In a bittersweet twist of irony, I never got to tell Alex what happened but hearing him here, now, in my kitchen, laughing at something Conan says has my blood boiling.

I storm into the kitchen, Conan's blue eyes and Linc's green ones flashing to me as I approach but my sole focus is on the backstabbing bastard.

He backs up and looks at me with pity in his eyes as I get within reaching distance but that quickly turns to shock when I slap him across the face.

My chest heaves as I place my hands on him and shove as hard as I can.

Surprise must be on my side because he goes back a few steps before Conan is behind me holding me back.

"How could you? Get out of my home and stay the fuck away from me."

"Sunshine," he whispers.

"Don't call me that!" I scream, bucking against Conan's hold, but the man has an iron grip on me.

"You took my last kiss. It wasn't yours to take, it was Alex's, and you fucking stole it from me!" I rage.

He looks stricken as my words penetrate, but I'm too far gone to care.

"Stop fighting, Kat, you'll hurt yourself," Conan rumbles in my ear, making me look up at him.

"Make him go away, please," I beg.

He looks from me to Linc before speaking and I know he'll take his club brother's back over mine because that's how it works.

"Go," he orders Linc, making me crumple in surprise and relief.

4

Conan

For the second time today, I tuck Kat into bed. After her confrontation with Linc, she shut down, crying silent tears until she fell asleep in my arms as I refused to let go.

After making sure all the shopping was put away, I leave my number on the counter and head back to the clubhouse.

The security measures have been stepped up, making this place nearly as difficult to get into as the Pentagon. With reconstruction still underway, Orion isn't taking any risks.

Climbing off my bike, I head inside. I make my way toward the kitchen, which had become a makeshift bar while the main room was being fixed. Even though there was a large room at the back of the building where the pool tables and televisions had been set up, the kitchen was industrial-sized and had been adapted over the years to cater to us all. Tables and chairs were scattered around and a long counter in the back housed enough alcohol to keep even the heavy drinkers happy.

I spot Linc sitting at a table in the corner, nursing a bottle of Bud as he peels the label off, oblivious to the room around him.

I pull out the chair opposite his and watch him swallow hard as he looks up and his eyes land on mine.

"You want to explain what that was all about?" I growl softly.

He sighs before taking a swig from his bottle. "Pike talked about me joining them when we were both patched in. Me and Jeeves, actually. We knew the rules about old ladies, but honestly, Jeeves and me, well, we weren't sure we were ready for that kind of commitment. We didn't want to play second fiddle to Pike, but there is something about Kat that just draws you in. Besides, who else would he choose, Dozer?" He sighs and finishes his beer, thunking the bottle down on the table.

Dozer is the newest prospect recruit, although we had a few more starting in a couple of days. He's an arrogant dick who thinks his shit doesn't smell. I'd be surprised if he makes it past his prospect probation. Kat wouldn't take his shit for thirty seconds, let alone take on a relationship with the guy.

"I picked Kat up that night and I thought, fuck it. The least I should do is see if there was any chemistry between us." He shrugs.

Although part of me understands where he's coming from, another part of me wants to snap his fucking neck. "So, you put your hands on her without permission and in a cruel twist of fate you erased the last kiss Pike gave her before he left that night and never came home."

"I couldn't have known how that night would play out. Fuck, if I could take it back, I'd do it in a heartbeat—"

"But you can't," I reply, rubbing a hand over my face.

"Irony is, that kiss just proved there was nothing between us but friendship, and I don't even have that anymore."

"Just stay away from her for now. She's working through her grief as best she can but it's still too raw. Maybe down the line, she'll get over what happened between you, but there's a chance she'll never forgive you. You'll have to live with that."

I stand and walk away, heading through the door at the back leading up to Orion's office and the bedrooms.

Wanting to fill Orion in, I knock on his door and swing it open when he yells for me to enter.

I'm not prepared for Inigo sitting on the sofa watching me with anger etched on his face. He's been avoiding me since everything went down, which is hard to do when you share a house, but he wanted space so I gave it to him.

"How's she doing?" Orion asks.

I sit in the chair in front of his desk and lean forward, resting my elbows on my thighs.

"Still breathing, but she's hanging on by a thread."

Running a hand through his hair, he sighs and looks at me.

"She won't let anyone in."

"She let me in," I tell him quietly. Not by much, but she didn't push me away.

"I don't want her getting attached to you if you're going to leave her too. She deserves better than that."

The Crown of Fools

"What the fuck?" Inigo curses, but I keep my eyes on Orion.

"I'll stay," I tell him.

"Simple as that?" His eyebrows rise in question.

"For her, yeah, it really is."

Inigo gets to his feet and stalks toward me. As soon as he's within touching distance, he pulls his fist back and punches me in the face.

He seethes. "You son of a bitch."

I climb to my feet, wiping blood from my lip with the back of my hand.

"Conan," Orion warns, but I ignore him and glare at Inigo.

"That's the only one you get," I growl out as he steps toward me once more, clearly not bothered by my tone.

"You were just gonna leave? You really don't give a fuck about me, huh? What, does Kat let you in her pussy to ease her grief? Do you let her pretend you're Pike? Do you call her Sunshine while you fuck her through her tears?"

His words cut off when I punch him. He falls back onto the sofa behind him. He'll live because, despite how much I want to hurt him, I don't want to kill him. I pulled the punch at the last minute.

"You wanna do this here, huh? Well alright, Ini, you asked for it. I was planning on leaving and going nomad well before the night of the explosion. I was going to leave so that you, Tina, and Half-pint could be happy."

"Jesus, did you really hate Tina that much?" he asks, his words laced with pain.

"Of course not. She was sweet but she didn't want me."

"Don't put this on her, you prick, you wanted out. Tina

agreed to be our old lady. You said—" I hold my hand up and cut him off.

"I didn't feel for her what you and Half-pint did, that's true. I liked her though. If she was who you wanted, I would have gone along with it for you. Tina though, she loved you and Half-pint. I know she did, but I terrified her. She wanted you two so much she was willing to make do with me."

"That's a fucking lie."

"It's not," Orion adds, making us both turn to face him.

"Luna overhead her talking to one of the other old ladies. She had no interest in Conan, said the man terrified her, but as long as he didn't force her to sleep with him, she could cope."

I feel my skin crawl at his words even though I already knew all this. That she thought I might have forced her still eats at me. I might not have been into her like Inigo, but I'd never done anything to warrant her looking at me like I was a monster.

Inigo looks from me to Orion, waiting for us to say something else. When we don't, his shoulders drop in defeat.

"You should have told me." His voice grits out, his anger still there but dialed down a notch.

"You loved her. You wanted the life she offered you. Like fuck was I going to get in the way of that."

He stares at me for a beat more before shoving past me and walking out, slamming the door behind him.

"Fuck," I grunt, sitting back in the chair.

"He's right. You should have told him like I said from the start." He holds his hand up when I open my mouth to argue with him.

"I get why you didn't, but Inigo is a grown-ass man. He is big enough and ugly enough to make his own choices, but you decided for all of you."

"If things had been different, he would have been happy. He'd have gotten over it eventually," I argue.

"But they weren't different and now he has to deal with losing his old lady, one of his best friends, and the idea that you could so easily walk away."

Well, when he puts it like that...

"Shit."

5

Inigo

I storm out of the clubhouse and climb on my bike, ignoring everyone as I pass through, pissed off at the fucking world at this point.

I wait for the prospect to open the gate, then tear out of the compound with no destination in mind, just riding until the sharp edge of anger fades to a dull ache.

For a forty-six-year old man who has always been confident in who I am and what I bring to the table, I find myself in uncharted territory, questioning every decision I've made lately.

I ride for hours, not wanting to go back to the house and face Conan and the ghosts that now haunt what I thought was a happy home when everything was built on a lie.

I don't know how I end up at the bakery but when I park my

bike in front of the now boarded-up windows, I don't question it.

Using the key Tina gave me, I let myself inside, not bothering to turn on the lights. Carnage paid the utilities through the end of the year until we can decide what to do with the place.

The smell wraps around me as soon as I step inside. It takes me back, dragging me into memories I try not to dwell on. Cinnamon and vanilla invade my senses, making me close my eyes for just a second. I swear I can feel Tina beside me, feel her warm hand in mine and her soft lips against my cheek.

I roar in anger and frustration and grab the nearest thing, which just happens to be a stool, and throw it across the room, watching as it crashes against the wall with a thud.

I don't know what happens after that but when I snap out of it, the bakery that Tina was so proud of is destroyed.

Unable to bear another second here, I head back to my bike, leaving my heart in the wreckage.

Numb, I ride for a few blocks before I pull over and hammer on the door of the only place I can think of that isn't haunted by ghosts, at least not mine anyway.

When the door opens, I stare at the woman in front of me, the desolation in her eyes mirroring mine, and I break.

I drop to my knees, unable to hold the weight of my guilt and regret any longer.

I'm losing myself, losing my fucking mind if I'm honest. My days used to start with cupcakes, now they start with whiskey. Everything blurs together—the happy, the sad, and the downright fucking tragic.

Hesitant hands slide through my hair, which is more silver than black, and I find my face pressed against a firm stomach with just a hint of a bump beneath it.

"Why?" I ask her, reaching up to wrap my arms around her hips. "Why them and not me?"

Her body trembles as she continues to stroke her fingers through my hair. It's a strange occurrence from the outside looking in—a man drawing strength from a woman young enough to be his daughter when he should be the one giving comfort, but as I tilt my head up to look at her, I see what others don't. This woman has suffered a mortal blow. She moves with effortless grace, wearing her grief like a veil, shielding others from the staggering pain she feels every waking second. She's dying, slowly and painfully as her body tries to survive despite her heart withering to ash and dust.

"Maybe we deserve to suffer," she answers softly, her voice hoarse with emotion. "Maybe we were never worthy to begin with. Our happiness acted as rose-tinted glasses, blinding us to the truth. Fairy tales are not for the likes of us. We were never the kings and queens, we weren't even the jesters. We were merely the footnote in someone else's story. A part of a movie that ends up on the cutting room floor."

"Sunshine," I choke out.

She looks down at me, her gaze vacant, like she's with me but also a million miles away.

"I've been thrown away my whole life, Inigo. I always thought there was something wrong with them, but maybe the problem was always me. Perhaps this is our punishment, a reminder that love and hope are fleeting. But for that one perfect moment, we came so close."

Her focus sharpens and this time I know she's with me, her tears dripping onto my skin and mingling with mine.

"Close to what?" I ask softly.

"Heaven," she whispers before she folds herself over me, cradling my head against her as I hold her tight enough to leave bruises.

I don't refute her words. My emotions are too raw for me to even try to speak. I just focus on breathing in and out, the echo of vanilla in my lungs fading as coconut and honey take their place, soothing the wounds that I'd let fester.

Tina's gone. Half-pint is gone and I'm still here, on my knees proving what a fucking pussy I am.

When Sunshine's weight gets heavy, I realize she's fallen asleep. I don't know why that brings me comfort. Maybe it's because I know from the dark circles under her eyes that sleep has evaded her or her dreams are dark and brutal like mine, leaving her permanently exhausted. Or maybe it's just because it rouses that part of me that lingers in the deep dark recesses of my mind, the part of me that craves to be needed. More than that though, having someone completely reliant on me stokes the flames of something I thought I'd buried when I met Tina. She wanted me for sure, but she never *needed* me. After meeting Luna, Reign, and Megan, I figured that was who women are now.

Men are an option they can take or leave, so I hid that part of myself, concealed it down deep, only letting it out in my imagination with my hand around my dick. But the craving for obedience, submissiveness, and a woman who would capitulate to my desires or face punishment for it, claws its way to the surface now I have Sunshine in my arms.

My dick twitches, making me feel like a fucking asshole as I carefully climb to my feet and scoop Sunshine up, kicking her door closed behind me.

I should put her to bed, but I can't make myself let her go so I move over to the sofa, toeing off my boots, before lying down and arranging Sunshine on top of me.

She nuzzles her head under my chin before settling so I reach up and snag the throw from the back of the sofa and tuck it around her to ward off the chill before closing my eyes, letting sleep pull me under.

Maybe in our dreams, our demons can play amongst themselves and let us finally get some fucking peace.

As my breathing evens out, I finally relax enough to drift off, wrapped in the arms of a woman who isn't mine to hold.

6

Kat

Hands gripping my ass rouse me from my sleep. Squirming, I grind down on the hard length pressing against my core.

The hands move, sliding under the material of my sleep shorts and underwear so I can feel his rough calluses against my skin. Hardworking hands, I muse as they grip me tight, pulling down harder against his cock as I rock against him. Fingers skate over my pussy, feeling how wet I am, how needy I feel.

When a thick finger dips inside me, I gasp in surprise. "Alex," I moan. The hands freeze and, at that moment, everything shatters as reality crashes back.

Feeling vomit rushing up my throat, I fling myself off the

man beneath me and run to the bathroom, dropping to the floor before throwing up as shame and remorse war for supremacy inside me.

"Sunshine." I turn my head and see Inigo looking down at me with regret in his eyes.

"Just go." I can't look at him, not after that.

"I'm sorry." He steps toward me but if he touches me now, I'll lose it.

"Get out. Please, please just go," I beg.

He stops, his shoulders dropping before he nods.

I watch him leave but I don't move from my spot even after I hear the front door slam. Staying huddled on the cold floor, I shiver as I try to hold on to the tattered edges of my sanity.

I don't know how to deal with what just happened. I woke up feeling what I thought were Alex's hands on me only to have it snatched away in the cruelest way.

Standing on shaky legs, I climb into the shower, not even bothering to take off my clothes. Pressing my forehead against the wall, I suck in painful breaths as the cold water rains down over me, masking my tears as I mentally berate myself for being so fucking weak.

When my tears finally run dry, I strip off my wet clothes and leave them in the bottom of the shower before wrapping a towel around myself. In a daze, I walk back to the bedroom, swallowing hard as my eyes fall on the bed. I choke on the guilt threatening to rip me apart at the seams. How could I have let another man touch me? Worse, how could I have let myself enjoy it?

Suddenly the walls that have become my sanctuary feel like they're closing in on me. I have to get out before I lose my mind and what's left of my sanity.

I pull on leggings, which are far looser than I remember, and a baggy black hoodie before braiding my hair so I don't have to dry it. Slipping on my sneakers, I grab my keys and phone and leave before I change my mind.

I walk until I end up at the park and stop, looking past the play area toward the benches down by the river. Walking toward them on autopilot, I stop at the one that was witness to my secrets and sit, wrapping my arms around myself.

It's much cooler today than yesterday, making the park quieter than normal, which is just as well. Happy people make my skin crawl right now and I don't want to lash out at anyone who doesn't deserve it.

The river looks dark and ominous as I watch it flow past me, reminding me of a time not long ago. Looking at the empty space beside me, I picture Alex sitting there with a look of shock on his face as he stares down at the white stick in his hand that clearly says the words *pregnant* on it.

It had been a gray day then too. He'd stared at that stick for what seemed like hours until the heavens opened. He shoved the stick in his pocket under his prospect cut before scooping me up and running with me.

"Gross, Alex, I peed on that." I laugh at him.

He looks down at me, water dripping from his lashes, love shining in his eyes, "I love you. Marry me."

I stare up at him, soaked to the bone, knowing with every fiber of my being that this man is the other part of my soul. There would be no me without him.

"Yes, a thousand times yes," I sob.

Blinking rapidly, I snap out of the memory as I turn to look away from the empty space, squeezing my hands into fists.

I'd been right. There is no me without him. My whole life was about Alex and now I don't know who I am without him.

I jolt when someone sits beside me. I almost shout at them for sitting in Alex's spot but bite my lip to keep the crazy from spilling out.

A large dog plonks itself near my feet, resting its furry head against my thigh while his big brown soulful eyes look up at me knowingly.

I reach out and run my fingers over his fur, finding the repetitive action soothing.

The man beside me grunts. "He's such a flirt."

I don't reply, not wanting to strike up a conversation with a stranger, too exhausted to fake politeness and pretend I'm okay.

He doesn't say anything after that, not for the longest time anyway. We sit quietly while I stroke his dog.

"Don't give up."

His words make me jump and I look at him sharply, taking in his large frame and dark hair threaded with silver. His lined face speaks of a life well lived and not all of it has been kind to him. He's older than me by twenty, maybe thirty, years. There is a quiet strength about him, whereas most days I feel like I'm falling apart.

"I don't know what you're talking about," I answer sharply because fuck him.

"You do. In the end, it won't matter what I say, but I recognize grief when I see it. I'm sorry you're in pain, but you didn't die, even if some days you wish you had. Whoever you lost, you must have loved them a lot. But answer me this, would they be happy watching you drown because of them? My advice, don't try to go it alone. Sometimes, even when it seems like it's the hardest thing in the world to do, you have to ask for help."

"I don't need saving," I spit out even though his words work their way into my brain, digging away at the knowledge that Alex would be so pissed at me right now.

"We all need saving sometimes," he answers before climbing to his feet and walking away. With a click of his fingers, the dog licks my hand and runs after his master, leaving me watching his retreating back.

He doesn't realize that I don't have anyone to ask for help, nobody to lean on when times get tough, or to hold me now my world has imploded because that person is gone.

I'm alone *again*. I almost had everything and now, I'm right back where I started.

My phone rings in my pocket. I'm tempted to ignore it, but then I might end up with unwanted visitors again and I just can't right now.

Checking the screen, I bite my lip when I see it's Carol, my boss. She's been pretty understanding about me taking so much time off, but I know she's running out of patience.

It seems everyone has an opinion about how long grief should last, but what is a socially acceptable length to grieve for someone before you get over them and move on with your life? A couple of weeks, according to Carol, making me certain she's never lost anyone. If she had, she'd know when you lose someone who you loved wholeheartedly, you'll grieve them for a lifetime.

7

Conan

I pour coffee into my mug, intent on drinking out on the back porch when the front door opens and slams closed.

I stay where I am, watching the doorway until a pissed-off looking Inigo storms through. Seems a night out doing god knows what with god knows who hasn't lessened his anger any. The thing is, I'm at the point where I'm over his bullshit. I get he's pissed, I even get why, but his acting like a little prick won't change anything. Tina and Half-pint are still dead. We either need to work shit out between us or one of us needs to move out.

"There any left?" he grunts, nodding to my mug.

I cock my brow before turning and grabbing a second mug, pouring Inigo's coffee, black, the way he likes it. Handing it to him, I watch as he sits heavily in the chair closest to him, cradling his mug with both hands as he stares at it as if it will have all the answers he seeks.

"You wanna talk about it?" I offer, even though talking usually makes me want to cut my own tongue off.

He looks up at me, a frown marring his forehead before he sighs and gestures for me to sit opposite him. He waits for me to take a seat, swigging his drink, impervious it seems to its scalding heat.

"I don't even know where to start," he admits, "I fucked up. I keep fucking up."

I sit silently and wait for him to continue.

"I trashed Tina's bakery last night. I drove for hours, thinking about what Orion and you said, and once my anger began to fade, I was able to look back and see the signs I'd missed before. I remember how she would tense up whenever you were around, how when we talked about the future she rarely mentioned your name. She even planted seeds about how you didn't seem to like her or want to be around us. She was purposely placing distance between you, whether malicious or for self-preservation, and I missed it."

"She loved you. She wasn't cruel in her actions, she was just stuck in a situation she had little control over. And with the threat of losing you and Half-pint dangled over her head if she couldn't somehow make it work with me, she did the best she could. We made our triad long before Tina came along. There was always going to be a possibility that we'd find ourselves in this situation. It's the risk you take. I didn't want us to end up like Joker, John, and King, but I refused to wreck what you three had. You wanted to settle down and if you missed your chance with Tina there might not be another. I mean, fuck, none of us is getting any younger." I shut up when I realize how insensitive that sounds after losing not just Tina but Half-pint too.

"You wanna know what the fucked up thing is?" His eyes lock on mine, waiting for me to judge him with his next words.

"I didn't love her." He drops the bomb, his tortured eyes full of guilt and regret.

"I wanted to, and fuck, maybe given more time I would have. I cared about her a lot and I would have spent the rest of my time on this earth being faithful to her and giving her a good life. But now she's dead and all I feel is fucking sick because there is a tiny part of me that also feels relieved. I knew I was just settling for the sake of it. I should have been man enough to admit it earlier, then maybe she would have left me. She'd have still been alive if—"

I cut him off. "Nobody knows what life has in store for them. You could have had an amazing life together or maybe it would have fizzled out. The point is, you would have never known if you hadn't given it a shot. Tina's death isn't on you. It's on the fucker who plowed into her."

The fucker is lucky he died at the scene or I'd have skinned him alive myself.

Inigo grips his hair and leans his elbows on the table. "I'm forty-six years old, Conan. I'm over the whole club bunny scene. I want someone to come home to. I thought Tina would be the one. She was sweet, shy, and timid. She drew me in like a moth to a flame but after she grew comfortable around me and the club, she came out of her shell, and I knew then I would have to hide a part of me to make it work. I wasn't bitter about it. Something had to give. I'm too old and jaded to believe that I can have my cake and eat it too. Everything stays the same unless someone is willing to change and I was willing to do that, or at least I thought I was..." His voice trails off but something in his tone makes me frown.

"Ini?"

"I went to Tina's bakery, had an epiphany about what a piece of shit I am, and trashed the place in a fit of rage. I hopped on my bike so full of self-loathing and I went to the one place I could think of where someone might get what I was feeling."

The hairs rise on the back of my neck.

"What did you do?"

"I went to see Sunshine," he admits, making my whole body tense. If he hurt her, I'll kill him.

"She helped. She comforted me while I lost my shit and when she fell asleep, I carried her inside and laid on the sofa with her. There is something about her that quiets the demons and I just needed to sleep."

"Okay," I reply, but I know there's more.

"We were both asleep, dreaming I guess, but by the time we woke up she was grinding down on my dick and my hands were on her pussy," he admits.

"Fuck!" I curse, remembering how she lost her mind over Linc kissing her. Christ knows what kind of state she's in now.

"I know, alright? Jesus, you're not telling me anything I haven't already told myself. I told you I fucked up. I left as soon as she asked me to." He stares at me, something moving behind his eyes.

"Tell me," I snap, knowing he's holding something back.

"There is something about her vulnerability that snaps the chains I keep locked around the darkness in me. I woke up moments before she did. I knew who was in my arms. I could have stopped before she woke up, fuck knows I should have, but all I wanted to do was thrust my cock so far inside her we'd both forget."

"Forget what? That's she's half your age, or the fact she's pregnant, or what about the fact she's struggling to swim through her own chasm of grief?" I growl, ignoring the whisper in my head that tells me I know exactly what he's talking about because I've felt it myself.

"I wanted her to forget that she's not mine. How I feel doesn't really matter because I can't compete with a ghost, now can I?"

"You need to stay away from her." I point at him

"You think I don't know that? I'm just as fucking surprised about my reaction to her as you are. Jesus, she's not much older than my niece."

I think back to what Doc said about someone using a firm hand on Kat and about Inigo's reaction to her and feel a stirring below the belt. Ideas and plans begin to form in my head, the potential of something different on the horizon. But first, Sunshine needs time to heal. We all do.

Inigo's right when he says we can't compete with a ghost, but maybe what we can offer is something else completely.

8

Kat

"Kat, can I have a word?"

I toss the cape that's in my hands onto the chair and nod, following Carol out the back of the salon into her office.

I've been back at work for a while now, the routine helps to keep my brain busy if nothing else. Even so, I was ever conscious that I was coming up to the three-month marker. Three months since I lost Alex. Three months since I lost me.

"Take a seat." She indicates the chair in front of her desk which I take gratefully after being on my feet for the last ten hours.

"There's no easy way to say this, Kat, but I'm afraid I'm going to need to let you go." Carol grimaces as I open my mouth in surprise.

"I'm sorry, what?"

"Look, you were off work for a long time. People adjusted to your replacement and now you're back and you're..."

"What Carol? What am I?" I snap.

"See, this is what I'm talking about. You're surly and unapproachable. You don't go out of your way to make people feel welcome anymore. I had a complaint made against you today."

I hold up my hand to stop her, trying to keep my temper in check.

"Let me guess, the complaint came from Mr. Jones. Did he tell you why I refused to finish his cut? He kept groping me for god's sake."

"You've had difficult customers before, but you've dealt with it."

I stare at her with wide eyes. "Are you serious? My partner died, and I've been sick thanks to my pregnancy, so I'm sorry if I don't want to join in with idle chitchat about inconsequential shit, but I do my job, and I do it well. As for today, nobody deserves to be sexually harassed in their workplace." I scowl.

"Mr. Jones is an important client," she grits out, making me want to pick up the stapler off her desk and launch it at her forehead.

"It's your job to protect your staff," I remind her, feeling myself begin to panic. I need this job.

"I'm sorry, Kat. I really am, but this is my business and I have to put our friendship aside and do what's best for the salon."

I can tell by the set of her jaw and the way she crosses her arms over her chest that she isn't going to budge on this.

I climb to my feet, which scream at me in protest.

"Friendship? Is that what you call this? Fuck you, Carol. With friends like you, who needs enemies?"

I turn and storm out, leaving my work station a mess because fuck her and everyone else here looking at me with pity.

I grab my bag and coat from the hook near the door and leave without looking back. Tears fill my eyes, but I refuse to give anyone the satisfaction of seeing me cry.

I hurry across the street, not even stopping to slip my coat on when it starts to rain. I just need to get out of here, away from prying eyes and sympathetic glances.

By the time I make it home, I'm soaked through to the bone, my clothes sticking to my frame, making me look indecent.

"Ah, Kat, just the person I wanted to see."

I cringe at the sound of my landlord's voice. David. Well, one of them. Our whole apartment complex was owned by brothers Paul and David. I didn't mind lean dark-haired Paul. He wasn't around much but when he was, he was always friendly and polite. David, the shorter ruddy-faced blond, however, made my skin crawl. He always held his creepy ick factor in check when Alex was around, but anytime he cornered me alone, I was left feeling I needed a shower afterward, his ogling and inappropriate comments making me want to puke.

"I'm sorry, David, but can it wait? I'm soaked and don't want to get sick." I move to head to my apartment door, thankful it's on the ground floor, when he grabs my arm to stop me.

"It's important and so far every other time I've tried to speak

The Crown of Fools

to you, you've blown me off. If I was less of a man, I might start getting offended," he tells me with a smirk, but I don't miss the underlying threat in his tone.

"I'm sorry, David, it's been a rough few months." I smile to soften my words, but fear it looks more like a grimace if the narrowing of his eyes is anything to go by.

"Yes, I'm aware, and it's one of the things I want to talk to you about. Usually, I would have spoken to Alex, but with him not here, you need to know that after our annual review, we've decided to increase the rent by $100 a month."

I close my eyes and take a deep breath before blowing it out. "Can I ask why? We've lived here for three years and you've never increased the rent so much before."

He frowns at me, dropping my arm. "Times are hard and without having all the units filled it's either increase the rent or kick you all out and sell the place. I'm sure you can understand why we wouldn't want to pursue that route. I'd like that to be kept as the last case scenario."

"I just lost my job, David. I...I need to find something else and fast. I don't know if I can come up with the extra right now," I admit.

He drags his finger up my arm and over my shoulder. I think of the fuss I made at the salon about the guy putting his hands on me and now here I am again with another man touching me. I want to scream at the unfairness of it all but no matter what I do, I'm trapped between a rock and a hard place.

"I can give you a little leeway, Kitty Kat. Never let it be said I'm an unfair man," he teases, making me swallow hard.

"Thank you, I have to go. I'll find a job soon and get the money to you as fast as possible."

He lets me go, watching me with a sleazy smile as I struggle to find my key in my bag.

"Just let me know if you can't find anything. I'm sure we can come to some kind of... arrangement." He grins.

I find the key and shove it in the lock and let myself in, slamming the door behind me with a *thanks* so I don't anger the dirtbag asshole. The last thing I need on top of being jobless is to end up homeless too.

Placing a hand over my stomach, I take some deep breaths to calm my racing heart.

"Don't worry, little bean. Mama will figure something out. I know I'm failing everything right now, but I promise, I'm trying." A lone tear slips over my cheek but I swipe it away.

No more tears. I need a plan.

9

Inigo

"It looks good in here. You guys are awesome." Luna smiles, taking in the now finished clubhouse.

"I'm just glad it's done and shit can get back to normal around here," Gage grunts out from beside her.

Luna rolls her eyes, smirking at me. "What Gage is trying to say is 'thanks, Inigo, you did a great job,'" she tells me with a deep voice, before squealing when Gage slaps her ass at her poor attempt at mimicking him.

I laugh at the look of indignation on her face before leaving them to it and heading to the bar.

"Inigo, my man. What can I get ya?" Jacob asks from behind the bar. Jacob is one of the new prospects and after just a few months it's easy to see the guy lives and breathes the MC lifestyle. Loyal to a fault, he never complains, no matter what shitty job he's given. He keeps his head down and his mouth shut, which is why I chose to sponsor him in the first place.

"Just a beer for now. I like to keep my wits about me with the Chaos Demons arriving soon."

They might be our allies now, but old wounds take time to heal.

He snags me a bottle of Bud from the fridge and pops the top before sliding it over.

"How busy are we expecting it to get tonight?" he asks, glancing over briefly at a couple of club girls laughing in the corner.

"With Demons and Ravens coming in, it will be fucking chaos," I admit, already feeling the beginnings of a headache coming on.

"Should we be expecting any trouble?" he questions quietly.

See, this is why I like this guy. He's always thinking about the club over anything else. It's why I know he'll make it through the new rigorous prospect hazing they all get put through.

"There's always trouble when you have men, alcohol, and pussy in the same room but for the most part things should be fine."

Truth be told, the only person likely to be here tonight who rubs me the wrong way is Bear, the VP of Raven Souls. The only reason he has that patch is because his father, Jim, was the president until he succumbed to lung cancer. The then VP, Blade, stepped up to take over as president since Bear had only recently been patched in as a fully-fledged brother a month before Jim died.

I'd liked Jim but his parenting skills left a lot to be desired. Four fucked up kids were proof of that. I'd never met the other sons or his daughter but apparently, they had been in and out of rehab and juvie and had little regard for anyone but themselves.

Bear might look like he has his head on straight compared to the other three but there is something off about him that makes the hair on the back of my neck stand up whenever he's near.

"You seen Conan around?"

"Last I saw, he was out back ripping shreds off the other prospects. Something along the lines of how fucking hard is it to build a bonfire?" Jacob laughs, likely glad it's not him out there.

I shake my head and tap the bar, heading out to find Conan.

Things have grown easier between us lately. I wouldn't say we are back to the way we were before, both of us have shit we are still recovering from, but we have stopped playing the blame game and that at least means we can be around each other without wanting to kill one another.

As I swing the door that leads to the back of the lot open, three prospects hurry past me looking like they've had the fear of god put into them.

I can't help but laugh when I catch sight of Conan's smug face. He enjoys terrorizing the little shits just a touch too much.

"I'm pretty sure Dozer pissed his pants," I yell out, making him shrug with indifference.

"If he can't handle what it takes to become a brother, then he knows where the door is."

I shake my head, but don't argue. The man's right. Being a Carnage brother puts a target on your back. If you're gonna cry over a few harsh words, then this isn't the life for you.

"You staying for the party?"

"For a little while, maybe. You know I hate this shit, but Orion wants me here, at least for a bit," he grumbles.

The man is antisocial to a fault.

"Find me before you bail and I'll come with you. I'm too old for this shit." Once upon a time I could drink all night and get up after an hour's sleep and you'd never know I had been on a bender. Now it only took a couple of drinks to give me a hangover that would last all fucking day.

I make my way back inside just as the Chaos Demons descend in all their arrogant glory. Viper leads the pack with Zero beside him and just behind them is Grim with his arm wrapped around Megan. I don't know if the man has a death wish, turning up here tonight after what he did to the club, or a huge set of brass balls, but I'll keep my mouth shut for Megan's sake.

Someone cranks up the music, making me wince as I head toward them.

Megan smiles when she sees me, moving to step away from Grim to hug me, but the possessive bastard yanks her back. Can't say I blame him. Megan's a gorgeous woman with those big old innocent eyes of hers and the riot of black curls that spill down her back and over her property patch. If she were mine, I wouldn't want her touching another man either.

For a split second, I picture my reaction to Sunshine

touching another man and feel a wave of potent anger rush over me.

"Hey, Inigo," Megan offers and I wince at the music once more when some asshat turns it up even louder.

Turning to the bar, I signal for Jacob to turn this shit down. He looks at the prospect near the sound system and shoves him aside before turning it down a little.

"You know what they say, Inigo, if the music's too loud, you're too old," Zero jokes.

I flip him off as Megan scowls at him, reading his lips before turning back to me and smiling.

"You need ears like mine, Inigo."

I laugh at her sass. Megan never lets her deafness hold her back.

Diesel steps up beside me and shoves me a little with a mock scowl. "Stop hogging my sister." He pulls Megan from Grim, ignoring him completely as he picks her up and spins her around.

I let them have their moment and make my way back to the bar with Zero and a couple of other Demons I'm not familiar with walking in.

"Yo, Jacob, another beer and whatever they want," I tip my head to the Demons.

Jacob nods as I sit on one of the free stools and turn to face Zero.

"Thanks for lending me Trip. He's a fast worker." Replacing Half-pint on the job site was fucking hard, but Zero stepped in and offered up Trip as a temporary fix. The guy's whole family works in construction and I have to admit he's damn good.

"I know you guys don't have much love for us, but you're Megan's family and that means something to us," he tells me seriously.

I sigh and reach out my hand. "Truce?" He's right. With all the healing we're still doing as a club, it's time to leave the past in the past where it belongs.

He shakes my hand and nods. "Truce."

Gesturing behind him, he points at his guys. "You guys met yet? This is Wizz, Kaz, and Scope. They served with me and Viper and were my brothers long before we came back home and took over."

"Thank you for your service," I tell them honestly. I'd always wanted to enlist and follow in my father and brother's footsteps, but an underlying medical condition meant it wasn't an option for me. In the end, it was just as well. My brother came home in a box, leaving behind his three-year-old daughter, Mercy, who reminds me so much of him sometimes it's like he's still here.

When my phone rings, I pull it out and smile. I swear she has a sixth sense or something.

"Please tell me you don't need bail money again?" I answer, making the guys near me look over with interest. The nosy bastards.

"Lord, you have got to let it go. It was one time," she mumbles, making me laugh.

"And it was an accident," she adds, making me laugh harder.

"You accidentally beat the fuck out of your professor's car with a bat for failing you?" I snort, rolling my eyes.

"He didn't fail me. Why on earth would you think that?"

"You told me he tried to give you a D." I frown.

Now it's her turn to laugh. "Not that kind of D, Uncle," she chokes out.

"What the fuck, Mercy?" I shout, standing up and making the guys beside me go on alert.

"Oh, calm your tits. It's sorted now. I reported him, told the lovely police officer how scared I had been, and then sent everything I had to his wife and mother, dick pics included. You gotta love social media," she says while my blood boils in my veins.

"Dick pics," I growl out, making even Zero take a step back.

"Deep breaths. Come on, breathe with me or you'll give yourself a freaking stroke. In with the good air, out with the bad air," she mutters, taking a deep breath.

"You're the reason I'm going gray," I curse, pinching the bridge of my nose.

"How rude!"

"What's up, Mercy? Did you just call to induce a heart attack?"

"I shall ignore that sarcasm. I just wanted to let you know that I'm not going to be home next month. I'm going up north with my roommate for a bit. She's nice, quiet. You'll like her as mentally she's around your age." I hear a scuffle on the other end of the line and laughter before Mercy speaks again.

"Anyway, I just wanted to give you a heads up, I know how much you miss me and my awesomeness," she teases, making me grin.

"Yes, how will I cope without your awesomeness?" I deadpan.

"It will be hard but if anyone can make it through, it will be you. Laters." She hangs up, leaving me torn between wanting to hug her and throttle her.

"You got a kid?" the guy called Wizz asks.

"No, Mercy's my niece."

"She really got arrested smashing up her professor's car?" the one next to him asks. Kaz, if I remember rightly.

"The fucker deserved it," I grunt out, reminding me of what she said.

"How old is she?" Zero asks, laughing.

"Eighteen. How she made it to this age without killing one of us I'll never know. She's like her dad used to be. Fearless."

I think of her and my mind quickly drifts to Sunshine even though I know it shouldn't. Hearing Mercy laugh and joke reminds me of the emptiness I saw in Kat's eyes the last time I saw her and something compels me to check on her.

"Alright guys, I'm out of here. There's something I need to do."

10

Kat

I pause with the towel in my hand, listening again, straining my ears to see if I can hear anything. I swear I'm losing my mind. Even though I can't hear a sound, goosebumps break out over my skin, making me tighten the towel around me. Moving toward the bedroom door, I snag the robe off the hook and quickly pull it on, feeling vulnerable standing here half-naked. It doesn't matter that I'm in my apartment and should be safe, too many people become complacent because of should-haves.

Growing up in the system fine-tunes your survival skills. You learn quickly to listen to your gut.

Moving quietly toward the kitchen, I scan the surrounding area before reaching for the knife block on the counter and grabbing the largest knife it holds.

Pulling it free, I move farther into the room, freezing when I see the front door ajar. My heart rate speeds up even more, making me worry I might pass out. With only me here to protect my baby, hiding under the bed just isn't an option so I head to the door and pull it wide. Finding an imposing figure on the other side has me reacting before my brain can consciously kick into gear. I lash out with the knife, ignoring the cursing. I try to slam the door closed only to find a boot preventing me.

"Jesus, Sunshine."

I pause at the sound of that voice. *His voice.*

Lifting my head, my eyes clash with Inigo's angry ones.

"Shit!" That's about the time I realize his white T-shirt is quickly turning red.

"Oh, fuck!" I yank his T-shirt and pull him into the apartment, kicking the door closed as I lead him to the kitchen.

"God, I'm sorry." I sniff, tossing the knife in the sink as if it burned my palm. Reaching under the sink, I grab the first aid kit and move back to Inigo, who is watching me warily.

"Wanna tell me why you just stabbed me?" he asks quietly, not a hint of anger in his voice considering I just slashed him with a knife.

"I'm a pregnant woman who lives alone. I heard a noise and found the door open, fuck I thought someone was breaking in. What the fuck were you doing?" I yell, ripping open the first aid kit and tossing the contents on the table.

"The door was open when I got here, Sunshine." His words cut off with a hiss as I shove his T-shirt up and survey the damage.

"Shit, shit, shit. This needs stitches. You're losing too much blood."

"Hey, calm down." He cups my face, so I have no choice but to look at him.

"I'm okay. I have von Willebrand disease, which means I bleed a little more than the average person. Trust me, I've had much worse."

"It still needs stitching. Let me get dressed and I'll take you to the emergency room."

"Sunshine, I'm fine. Call Conan. He's patched me up more times than I can count, okay?"

I nod when he passes his phone to me after pressing call on Conan's contact information.

I take it from him with shaky hands as he grabs one of the pads from the table and presses it against the wound.

"Where the fuck are you, Inigo? You said you wanted to bounce when I did but I've been looking for your sorry ass for the last twenty minutes," a voice growls down the phone.

"Conan?" My voice shakes a little, the shock of the last ten minutes crashing over me.

"Kat? What's going on? Why are you calling me from Inigo's cell? Oh, the stupid fucker!" He snarls, never giving me a chance to speak. "Are you okay?"

"I stabbed Inigo," I whisper while the man in question rolls his eyes at me.

"Good, the fucker probably deserved it. I'm on my way." He hangs up, making me stare at the phone.

"There is something seriously wrong with both of you," I conclude.

"That's probably true," Inigo concedes.

"I'm sorry. I was spooked. God, I could have killed you!" I bury my face in my hands. That would be all I need on top of everything else, having Carnage MC hunting me down for killing one of their own.

"Come here." He lifts his arm and I step into his hold without thought. It isn't until I have my breathing back under control and the shaking has stopped that I realize just how close we are and just how little I'm wearing.

"Erm...I'll just go and put some clothes on." I pull away before he says anything and hurry to the bedroom, throwing on the first thing I can find, which just happens to be an old pair of ratty sweats and a black tank top.

I just make it back to the kitchen when there is a knock at the door. Inigo beats me to it, opening it wide while still clutching the dressing to his stomach.

"You stupid fuck. What did you do?" Conan growls at Inigo, making me snort. The man is bleeding everywhere after being stabbed by yours truly, and yet he's the one getting yelled at.

"It was my fault—" I squeak when Conan stomps over to me. It takes everything I have not to hum fee-fi-fo-fum before I'm lifted off the floor and crushed to his chest.

"Are you okay?" he asks, pulling me back to look at me. I stare wide-eyed at the man holding me off the floor with my feet dangling and nod.

"No, don't mind me at all. I'll just stand here and bleed out quietly," Inigo drawls, making me feel bad.

Conan rolls his eyes and places me gently back on the floor. "Fucking drama queen," he volleys back, making me giggle and surprising us all. I slap my hand over my mouth, instantly feeling like shit.

"Hey, it's okay to laugh, Sunshine," Conan says softly, and logically I know he's right but inside I feel my heart break a little more. How can I still laugh without Alex here?

"I'm just going to let you fix Inigo up. The first aid kit's on the counter if you need it."

They don't try to stop me, thankfully. I move over to the sofa and grab the laptop off the table, balancing it on my lap as I scan for job prospects. I upload my resume for two cleaning ones because beggars can't be choosers, but even they want a year's worth of cleaning experience.

With a sigh, I check my emails to see if any of the others I've applied for have messaged me, but so far nothing.

I frown when I spot one from Karen from the salon. I'd been expecting Carol to forward me my last paycheck but so far I haven't gotten anything. If this is an email to blow me off, I am gonna be pissed.

Hey Kat,

I'm sorry to tell you this over email but I don't have your cell phone number. Three nights ago, Carol slipped getting out of the shower at home and broke her neck. It's a tragic accident and the salon is in chaos, but I just wanted to keep you in the loop. I don't have any access to the bank accounts so I can't fix the payment issue you are still waiting for. I'm so sorry. Until her son flies in from Canada and decides what to do with the place it will remain closed. We're all in the same boat now, unfortunately.

I hope this email reaches you well.

Karen.

"Fuck." I snap the laptop closed and rub my tired eyes. This is the last thing I need.

Feeling like an insensitive bitch, I manage to swallow the rest of the obscenities I want to shout out. As much as Carol was on my shit list, the woman is still dead and I certainly didn't want that for her. It just doesn't change the fact that I needed that money.

"Everything okay?" Conan's deep voice calls out.

No, not even a little fucking bit but I can't tell them that without them trying to take over. I might not know much about the MC lifestyle, but I understand enough to know that a single unattached woman has no business with an MC unless she is on her back or on her knees. It was different when I had Alex, but he was still only a prospect when he died, never getting the chance to make me his official old lady and offering me the protections that come with being one.

I look over at the two bikers in my kitchen and shake my head. I've seen and done a lot of things in my life but I have zero aspirations of becoming a club whore.

"I'm just fucking peachy," I mumble back, hoping like hell I don't have to swallow my pride as well as dick six months down the line when I can't afford to put food on the table and feed my kid.

11

Conan

I told the fucker to stay away, but did he listen? I'm glad she stabbed the asshole. Maybe next time, he'll think twice.

"Oh fuck off. I know what you're thinking, but it wasn't like that. I didn't come here to cause any shit. I just had a weird feeling in my gut and you know damn well I never ignore shit like that," he argues with me quietly, so Sunshine doesn't overhear.

I finish gluing him back together and wash my hands before facing him, some of the tension loosening with his words. I do get where he's coming from. Inigo tends to have a sixth sense when it comes to trouble. I can't even remember the number of times he's saved our asses because of a weird feeling he had.

"Fine, but maybe next time try calling her, then I won't need to patch your sorry ass up."

"Fuck off, asshole," he grumbles, pulling his T-shirt down over his stomach before cursing when he realizes how much blood is all over it.

"Hey, Sunshine, you got a T-shirt Inigo can borrow?" I shout out, watching as she looks over, taking in his once white T-shirt and wincing.

"Erm, yeah, sure." She climbs to her feet and hurries to the bedroom, emerging a few minutes later with a plain black one. She holds it out for him but when he tries to take it she seems to struggle to let go.

"Sunshine?" Inigo says her name softly, making her snap out of whatever trance she was in.

"Sorry. Here, take it."

He does gently, his eyes never leaving hers as he removes his cut and pulls the dirty T-shirt over his head before tossing it in the trash.

"I'll get it cleaned and back to you," he tells her, but she's not paying him any attention, her eyes glued firmly to his naked chest.

I watch her watching him, trying to gauge her reaction, but she's locked up so tight she's not giving anything away.

She doesn't look away though until Inigo pulls the clean shirt down and covers himself.

She eventually speaks. "Why are you guys here? I'm not trying to be a dick but I'm tired and I'd really like to just go the bed."

"I just wanted to check on you. Why was your door open?" Inigo asks, taking a step toward her as she takes one back.

"Inigo," I warn him.

"No, Conan, she's a pregnant woman living alone for fuck sake. Do you have any idea what could have happened to you?" he roars at her.

Instead of cowering when faced with a pissed-off biker, she stomps closer and pokes him in the stomach, making him hiss.

"I don't know who the fuck you think you are talking to me like that but you are not my partner and you are definitely not my daddy so I suggest you get the fuck out of here before I stab you again and this time you'll need more than the big friendly giant here to patch you up."

She turns and storms off toward the bedroom, slamming the door behind her. Her outrage and defiance have my dick as hard as stone and I didn't miss the way Inigo's eyes flared at the use of the word *daddy*. I know now is not the time and if we push this thing too fast, we'll break something that isn't strong enough to withstand the heat.

When Inigo moves to follow her, I grab his arm and stop him, my grip tightening when he glares at me.

"You go in there and that's it, game over. She's not ready and if you push this, she never will be."

"Fuck." He spins and storms off in the opposite direction, across the room, and out the door, slamming it shut behind him.

I shake my head, wondering how the fuck I'm going to keep a leash on him when he's acting like a dog with a bone.

The bedroom door opens and Kat walks out all fire and

indignation, pausing for a moment when she sees me still standing there.

"I thought you left." She looks around for Inigo, but when she doesn't find him, her shoulders relax.

"What the hell is wrong with that man?" She shakes her head.

"He was worried. He got a gut feeling that something was off and came here to check on you and found the door open and you brandishing a blade. You have to remember what happened to the last woman he cared about," I tell her softly as she wraps her arms around herself.

"He doesn't know me, Conan, nobody does, not anymore."

I step toward her slowly and unlike with Inigo, she doesn't step back. I grab her hand and walk her over to the sofa before sitting and pulling her onto my lap, ignoring her protests. I tuck her head under my chin and hold her tight until eventually she stops fighting me and relaxes, her hand fisting the front of my cut.

"A lot of people care about you, Sunshine. You're just feeling too raw to let anyone in right now. I get it, and it's okay, but you are not alone and if that means I have to use my size against you, I will." When she tenses up again, I realize how my words could have been taken.

"Not like that, Sunshine. Never like that. I mean when it comes to comfort, like this hug for instance. If I offered to hold you, you'd refuse even as I stood there watching you try to comfort yourself. Now, I have no problem holding a hissing and spitting mad kitten until she calms down. I won't hurt you, Kat, you have my word, but don't ask me to stand back and watch you drown because I won't do it. I'll dive in and drag you out over and over until you're strong enough to swim again."

She doesn't speak but she snuggles closer and I feel dampness on my neck from her tears, but I don't acknowledge them any more than she does.

"Rest. I've got you. I'm not going anywhere, Sunshine."

"Don't make promises you can't keep, Conan. Everyone leaves. It's the one thing I've always known. I guess for a little while, I forgot, but never again."

"Keeping people at arm's length to stop yourself from getting hurt will lead to a lonely existence, Sunshine. Alex wouldn't want this for you."

"Alex is dead, Conan. What he wants doesn't really matter, now does it?"

12

Kat

I woke up alone, thankful I didn't have to make stupid idle chitchat when I feel like death warmed up this morning.

After showering, dressing, and forcing a piece of toast down, I get ready to face the day.

Stepping outside, I pull the door closed behind me and make sure it's locked up tight before heading off with a handful of resumes in my bag. Most places like applications to be filled out online but some older family-run businesses liked the personal touch, or at least that's what I'm hoping.

By lunchtime, I'm all out of resumes but my optimism is at an all-time low. As soon as I disclosed I was pregnant, people weren't interested. It's not like I could hide it from them—my growing bump makes that impossible. Nobody wants to hire someone they have to train just for them to go off again in a handful of months for maternity leave.

Feeling disheartened, I head toward the park, making a beeline for mine and Alex's bench, needing to feel closer to him today.

I have to find something. I don't care what it is at this point, I just need enough to pay the bills and get some food in. The thought of the bills that will be piling up for the baby threatens to turn me into a blubbering wreck but I swallow it down and keep putting one foot in front of the other until I reach the edge of the kid's play area.

I can't give up just yet. There has to be something, someone who'll be willing to give me a shot.

My steps falter when I see someone sitting on what I consider my bench before I remember that it's not actually mine, and it's not like other people know about the memories this place holds for me.

I sit down without a word, keeping my eyes away from the guy beside me, hoping it will stave off their need to make small talk.

As soon as I sit, a dog runs over to me and places his head on my leg. I remember him. I look up at the person beside me and swallow when I recognize the guy from before.

"Hello again," he says with a smile, his handsome face revealing dimples that make him look younger than the late forties I guessed him to be.

"Are you following me?" I ask nervously.

He throws his head back and laughs, making the dog look at him briefly before turning back to press against my leg.

"If I remember correctly, I was here first. Perhaps you are following me?"

I flush at his words, feeling stupid. Of course, he isn't following me.

"Sorry." I sigh.

"Bad day?"

"Bad life," I reply.

"Now that can't be true. I know it doesn't seem like it now but things will get better."

"How can you be so fucking sure?" I snap before wincing. "Sorry, that was rude."

He laughs again, unperturbed by my outburst, and leans over to fuss with his dog. "I'm a grown-ass man. I'm pretty sure I can handle a few cuss words. My delicate ears won't start bleeding because of a few f-bombs."

"Good to know." I smile. It's small but it's real.

"I'm Wes," he reaches over to shake my hand, holding his hand steady until I slip my much smaller one into his.

"Kat."

"Kat, huh? Is that short for Kathryn?"

"Katia."

"Pretty. That's not a name I hear too often."

I shrug. What else can I say?

"Family name?"

"You are kind of nosy. Anyone ever tell you that?"

"It might have been mentioned once or twice." He grins as I bite my lip.

"I don't know if it's a family name or not. I was abandoned as a baby. It's the name that was stitched into the blanket found with me outside the fire station. Truth is, the blanket could have been stolen so who knows? The staff at the hospital decided to use it and somehow I ended up with the surname Jones. Not sure where that came from, but it's better than being called Jane Doe so I never complained."

"Wow, that's a really shitty story," he tells me straight-faced and I can't help it, I burst out laughing. Most people try to offer me words of comfort. It's damn refreshing for someone to call it like it is.

"Yeah, I agree with you there but at least I was left somewhere safe instead of a dumpster or something." Although some days it's really hard to remind myself of the silver lining.

"Very true. There are some awful people out there. I'm glad that your parent or parents at the very least did right by you there."

I shrug. I have no clue what their reasoning was. My mom could have been a junkie who had no interest in being a parent, or she could have loved me beyond compare and gave me up because she felt she had no other choice. As a kid, I prayed for the latter, fancying myself as a modern-day Annie, only when my mom came back we would live happily ever after. As an adult though, and an expectant mother myself, my heart breaks for the woman who, for whatever reason, made the ultimate sacrifice.

"I lost you there for a minute. You okay?"

"Sorry, I was just thinking about what it must feel like to give up your child like that. Was it an act of cowardice or a bittersweet sacrifice to protect me?" I shrug as he stares at me intently.

"Questions that leave an annoying itch in the back of your mind often drive us to find answers which were hidden from us for a reason."

"Better an itch than a wound. I guess I can see the logic in that. We always think we're ready to hear the worst and yet it never fails to shock me just how much the truth can hurt."

"Exactly."

"What about you? What's your story?"

He gives me a half smile, those damn dimples popping up again, making him look less threatening than I suspect him to be. There is something about the way he holds himself that gives off an *I will gut you while you sleep and step over your cold dead body* vibe, and yet I have an overwhelming sense that he won't hurt me.

"Ah, nothing exciting, I'm afraid."

I stare at him and wait until his shoulders drop and he looks at his lap just as the dog moves over to him and nudges his hand as if he understands his master's turmoil.

"I had a wife and kids once. Seems like a lifetime ago now. You move forward, keep putting one foot in front of the other but you never forget. And now all I'm left with are ghosts and regrets. So many fucking regrets." He sighs. I lift my hand and reach over, slipping my cold one into his, making him startle.

"Sometimes being haunted isn't a bad thing, Wes."

"How can you say that? You of all people?"

I don't ask him how he knows. I don't exactly hide my grief from the world. I wear it as a shield to keep people away and yet it doesn't seem to stop this man from trying to get me to lower it.

"Because the alternative is being alone. Part of me wants Alex to have moved on to a better place, to have found some kind of peace, but the other part?"

I look up at him when he squeezes my hand. "The other part feels abandoned. As if he left me here to deal with all this pain alone. He doesn't watch over me or hover at my side. I know this because there was never a time I didn't feel him. Now all I have are empty spaces where he should be. So yeah, Wes, I'd take your ghosts every time."

13

Kat

Luck was finally on my side when I managed to score a job at the local gas station. It isn't ideal, but I need the money and beggars can't afford to be choosers. The fact the owner keeps a gun under the counter makes me feel a little better—I just hope I'm never in a position to need to use it.

To say I'm not a fan of guns would be an understatement given the exposure I'd had to them, ranging from drive-by shootings to one of my former foster parents putting a gun to his head and pulling the trigger in front of me. I'd been terrified of them for years. Alex helped me get past it, making sure I knew how to shoot. He even got me a gun and drummed into my head the importance of being armed every time I left my house. He had a real fear of something happening to me while he wasn't around to protect me, and now I couldn't help but feel he somehow sensed the day would come when he would be gone. Nevertheless, a gun for me would always be the last resort. I'm all too familiar with the devastation they can cause.

I've been working there a month, alternating a week of days and a week of nights. The constant change in schedule means I am tired pretty much every waking second of the day.

I trudge through the entrance to my apartment complex and head to my door and find it ajar again.

"You have got to be fucking kidding me." I reach into my bag for my gun, for once glad Alex made me promise to carry it. I might only use it as a last resort, but that doesn't mean I won't use it if I need to.

"Oh hey, Kat."

I spin at the sound of a man's voice and find Paul, my other landlord, behind me.

"Woah, Kat, what's going on?"

I realize then that I'm pointing the damn gun at him. I flick the safety back on and point it to the floor.

"Jesus, I'm sorry, Paul. The door to my apartment is open again. I was just going to check it out."

"Open again?" He frowns, looking at the door in question.

"Yep. This has to be the fifth or sixth time. At first, I thought it might have been my baby brain, but I know it's not that now. Trust me, I've become OCD about checking."

"Let me take a look around for you. Stay here."

I nod, relieved, and let Paul check out my apartment, feeling exhausted and wanting nothing more than to collapse in my bed.

"All clear, Kat." Paul appears in the doorway, bending down

to check the lock.

"There are no signs that the lock's been tampered with, no scratches to say it's been picked, but I'll get a locksmith out to change it for you."

My shoulders relax, the tension melting away with relief.

"Thank you, Paul. That would be amazing."

"Don't mention it, Kat. I know I'm not around much but you have my number and David is always around."

I manage to hold back my grimace at his brother's name. As much as I like Paul, his flaw is how protective he is of his brother. As much as I can appreciate his loyalty, it makes me question his judgment.

"Go get some rest. You look dead on your feet. I'll text you and let you know when the locksmith is available."

I offer him a tired smile and a wave as he leaves, closing and locking the door behind me. Then for good measure, I shove one of the kitchen chairs underneath the handle. I might be acting paranoid, but I'd rather be safe and feel stupid than be dead.

Tossing my bag on the counter, I start stripping out of my clothes, leaving a trail as I make it to the bathroom.

I turn on the shower and stare at my changing body in the mirror as I wait for the water to get hot.

My breasts are large now, going up two cup sizes. I had to splurge and buy new bras. Thankfully, I have no one to impress, so I went for basic cotton over the pretty lace ones Alex used to favor me in.

My stomach has grown, moving me firmly past the *is she isn't she* category to the cute bump stage. At six months, I can still mostly hide it with a baggy top, but in anything fitted it is clear for all to see I am pregnant.

Sliding my hand over my bump, I smile when I feel fluttering beneath my palm. When I first felt it, I wasn't one hundred percent sure it was the baby, but when I felt it again, I knew. It was a bittersweet moment, reminding me of all the things Alex was missing out on but feeling that flutter made me feel a little less alone.

Pulling my hair up into a messy bun, I step into the shower and let the warm water soothe my aching muscles before climbing back out and drying off.

I dress in one of Alex's old T-shirts and slip on fuzzy socks before heading to the kitchen for something to eat. Too exhausted to cook, I end up with a PB and J sandwich, a banana, and a glass of milk.

Curling up on the sofa, I pull the blanket over me and channel surf for a little while before settling on an episode of *Cake Wars*. I'm not much of a baker, but watching these shows makes me wish I were. For me, it's all about that moment at the end of the show where they have to carry their creations to the table upfront without dropping them, but exhaustion drags me under before my favorite part.

I toss and turn, finding it difficult to get comfortable when a sound brings me fully awake. Feeling disoriented for a moment, I look around, wondering what it was that woke me before I hear it again.

I turn to the door and feel my blood run cold as the handle jiggles up and down.

Rubbing my eyes, I climb to my feet and slowly make my way to the door. The handle isn't moving now, but I don't take my eyes off it as I lean over the chair to look through the spy hole, only to find nobody there.

As much as I want to open the door and look outside, I don't. Call me crazy, but isn't it always the barely dressed woman doing stupid shit that gets her offed by some deranged killer in a horror movie? Yeah, I think I'll stay safe inside my apartment, thank you very much. Even so, I drag the kitchen table over to the door and use it as an extra barricade.

I snatch my bag off the counter and grab my gun before turning off the television and making my way to bed. A quick peek out the window shows a quiet street, with most people turned in for the night.

Just as I'm about to step away, I spot a Harley at the far end of the lot. I can just about make out someone sitting on it, but they're too far away for me to figure out who it might be.

Part of me is pissed. I have no doubt that whoever they are is responsible for checking my door earlier, likely seeing if I locked it and if I hadn't, I have no doubt they would have stormed in and yelled about my safety. Chances are it's either Conan or Inigo. They seem to be the only ones who bother with me now anyway. As lost as I've been in my grief, pulling away and hiding from everyone, a part of me still expected Carnage to push back. Alex gave his life protecting them, I'm surprised how quickly they gave up on me.

I should be used to it. I guess I bought into the hype Alex gave me about the MC, and what the brotherhood meant, how they look after their own. But maybe that's it. I'm not one of theirs.

I'm just the girl who got left behind once again.

14

Inigo

I pack up early today, leaving the rest of the crew to finish up. I stayed away from Kat for the last two months, knowing Conan was right, but if I don't keep myself busy, she manages to invade most of my waking thoughts. I don't know why she has such an effect on me. I still feel like a piece of shit feeling anything for someone when Tina hasn't even been gone a year.

"Yo, Inigo, the prick from the library is on the phone. He wants to talk about the estimate again," my foreman Stuart shouts out. He's not a Carnage member, but after working for me for ten years, he's a brother. He just prefers four wheels to two.

"Jesus fucking Christ. I don't know how many times I can go

over this again. I swear to god I'm this close to pulling his spine out his throat."

"Nice mental image there, boss." Stuart tosses me the cell before leaving with a laugh.

Instead of leaving early as I'd planned, I spend the next thirty minutes explaining to the dumbass from city hall shit I've already covered a million times. I need to get a secretary or at least someone who can deal with pretentious pricks instead of me.

I pull my personal cell phone out when it rings and answer as I make my way over to my bike before the next crisis stops me from leaving.

"I thought you were finishing early?" Conan says as a way of greeting me.

"Sorry, wifey, I'm just leaving now."

"Suck my dick. I just didn't want to overcook the steaks."

"I'm leaving now even if I have to mow down motherfuckers to do it."

He snorts at that. "Fine, but swing by and pick up some more beer. We're almost out and it sounds like you need one."

"On it." I hang up and climb on my bike, pulling out before anyone can stop me.

I head to the gas station on the way home because I know where everything is there and I'm too fucking tired and low on patience to be wandering around a store.

It's quiet when I pull up, which makes a change. Parking my bike, I head inside, thumbing through my messages on my cell as I make a beeline to the beer section and grab two six-packs before heading to the counter.

I pay the guy, who is more interested in the car show on the television than what I'm doing, and turn to leave when a familiar voice stops me in my tracks.

"Okay, I'm off, Jim. I'll see you tomorrow."

I make my way outside and wait next to my bike, knowing she won't be able to miss me when she passes by. I look around for her piece of shit car but don't see it. Maybe it's parked around the back.

A couple of minutes later, Kat walks out the door, her hand in her bag rummaging around for something, completely oblivious to me. I can't lie, it pisses me off that she could be so unaware of the hulking biker behind her that I snap.

"What the fuck, Kat? I could have done anything to you. Get your head out of your ass!"

She spins around with a can of mace pointed directly at me.

"You were saying? Don't worry, I'm well aware of how many assholes this world has to offer," she tells me with disgust before turning on her heel and walking away.

"Shit," I curse, running my hands through my hair.

She disappears around the back while I contemplate going after her but by the time I get my ass into gear, she's getting into her car. Not trusting her to not run me over, I make my way back to my bike and make a snap decision. Too many times now I've shown this girl what an asshole I am. I need to apologize before she cuts me out of her life completely.

Climbing back on the bike, I make sure the beer is safe in the saddlebags and won't get knocked around too much before heading over to Kat's place.

I take the long way back, giving myself time to come up with a game plan but the truth is, Kat's unpredictable so this could go either way.

I pull up outside her apartment and park next to her car before heading inside, pausing before I knock. I take a deep breath, hoping to fuck I'm not about to screw this up further.

Tapping lightly, I wait for a moment but I don't hear anything. I'm just about to knock again when I hear shuffling, then the door swings open.

Kat stands before me, her eyes flashing with fire, and I'm momentarily dazed, wondering if I've ever seen anything more stunning in my life.

Before she can flay me alive, I step forward and crowd her until she has nowhere to go but back.

"I'm sorry," I tell her, walking closer even as she continues to back up. "I'm a prick but I swear I never meant to upset you."

She stops when her back hits the kitchen counter, her eyes widening as I keep moving until I'm standing right in front of her.

"Inigo," she says my name with uncertainty.

"I'm sorry," I repeat, cupping her jaw. God, why am I always such a dick around her?

Her eyes search mine before they close, a single tear slipping free. I wipe it with the pad of my thumb before pulling her in for a hug. Something slips into place when I have her in my arms. It doesn't matter that I'm twice her age or that she's carrying another man's baby. Kat's mine, I just need to let her figure that out.

"Come have dinner with me and Conan. He's grilling steaks. It's a nice evening, we can sit out on the deck and talk a little."

"What do you want to talk about?" she asks with apprehension.

"Anything you want. Your favorite color, what foods you like and loathe, baby names. Honestly, I don't care what we talk about, Sunshine, I want to know everything."

"Why?"

"Because you matter," I answer honestly as she looks up at me, another tear slipping free.

"I don't—"

I place my finger over her lips to halt her words. "Don't say no." Something about my tone makes her eyes flash, but it's not anger I see. It's gone before I can get a read on it but I swear for just a moment, there was lust in her eyes. Maybe that's just wishful thinking.

"Fine." She shakes her head as if she can't believe she gave in. "But I'm only coming for the steak," she tells me with a small smile. My returning smile is far bigger. Her cheeks flush as she pulls away.

"I'm just going to get changed. I'll be right back."

I nod and watch her hurry down the hall to the bedroom.

I make my way over to the bookcase filled with photos. Something about these always draw me in. Seeing Sunshine radiate with happiness...well, it makes you want to bask in it. She's so fucking beautiful it's almost painful to look at her because how can she possibly be real?

I scan the pictures, noticing the most recent one is missing. I swallow, knowing the photo is likely next to her bed. That's okay. If I'm planning on pushing this thing forward, I'm going to have to accept that Pike will always be the fourth person in this relationship. Dead or not, he will always hold a piece of Sunshine's heart that is his and his alone.

"Ready," Kat's soft voice calls out from behind me.

I turn and see she's changed into a pair of black leggings and a light purple off-the-shoulder sweater that somehow makes her eyes look purple.

Her hair falls around her shoulders in waves and she's put a little gloss on her lips to make them shine. Watching her look at me as she bites her lip, her fresh face making her look so damn young, I feel that beast inside me raise his head. It takes all I have to keep myself from pouncing on her, slipping those leggings down over her ass before fucking her over the kitchen counter.

Soon, I promise myself, but it's not enough to get my dick to calm the fuck down and as I move toward her I know I'm going to end up with the zipper imprinted on my cock.

"You look gorgeous. Come on, let's get out of here, I'm starving."

I can tell by her sharp intake of breath that she didn't miss the double entendre. The fact that she slips her hand in mine and doesn't run screaming tells me everything I need to know.

Sunshine is mine.

15

Conan

I hear the door open and close, but I don't move from my spot on the deck. I'm not sure where the fuck Inigo went for beer, but I swear if I'd have had to wait any longer for food, my body would have started eating itself.

"I was starting to think you got fucking lost," I grumble when I hear him slide open the door. I stop talking when I look up and see Kat staring back at me.

"Hi, Inigo said to tell you to get the food going, he's just jumping in the shower. The beer is in the fridge. I didn't bring anything. It was kind of last-minute—" I cut her off, standing up and pulling her in for a hug.

"You're always welcome here. You don't need to wait for an invite."

I pull back and look down at her and see she has a little more color in her cheeks than the last time I saw her.

"You doing okay?"

When I let her go, she shrugs before moving to sit on the bench.

"Good days and bad days. I guess that's the nature of the beast, though. Most days the pain is down to a dull ache, my soul achingly aware that it's missing something fundamental to its survival, but I'm not dead, and I'm the only person this little guy has so, I have to keep on moving forward."

She rubs her hand over her stomach, the move making something in my chest ache.

"Little guy? You know what you're having?"

"Just a feeling," she says softly, looking down at her bump.

"May I?"

She looks up as I approach her. She swallows before nodding, moving her hand to make space for mine. My hands are so big that one of them almost covers her whole stomach.

I hear her breath catch, so I look up and see her eyes boring into mine. I've fucked my fair share of women, stripped them naked, touched and tasted every inch of them, but I've never experienced anything near this level of intimacy.

"I'm starving. Where's this damn steak?" Inigo's voice grumbles from behind me, breaking the moment. Jesus, how long have Kat and I been just staring at each other?

I stand up as Kat looks away.

"I've been waiting for you, dickface, now stop your bitching and help me out before Kat thinks we really are a pair of douchebags."

Kat laughs, making Inigo grin as he passes me a beer.

"Yes sir. You want something to drink, Kat?"

"Just water is fine, thanks. Can I help with anything?"

"Nope, you can put your feet up and watch us work. Seriously, we've got this."

"I...Okay." She looks uncertain, but relents, watching as Inigo and I move around each other like the well-oiled machine we are.

By the time everything is finished and plated, I'm about ready to eat my own arm.

"Oh my god, this is so good," Kat moans around a mouthful.

Inigo and I both look at each other as we try to discreetly adjust our aching cocks. Kat is effortlessly sexy at the best of times, but listening to her make those soft sighs and throaty moans could test a monk's restraint.

"So you're working at the gas station now? I thought you liked it at the salon," Inigo asks casually but I can see the tick of his jaw.

The gas station? What the fuck? I open my mouth to tell her how dangerous it is for a woman, especially a pregnant one, to be working in that shithole when Inigo kicks me under the table and glares.

"The salon had to let me go. Not that it mattered in the end as my former boss died shortly after I left. Her son closed the place down and put it up for sale."

"It's not the safest place to work Kat," I comment softly, trying to keep my anger in check.

"It was the only place willing to take on an unqualified pregnant woman. Besides, Jimmy's a sweetheart and there's a panic button and a gun if there is ever any trouble, but so far it's pretty quiet."

I curse under my breath, needing her to see that this is not a good idea. She must know what I'm thinking as her eyes flash with indignation.

"I need to be able to support myself and my baby. There is nothing else out there for me. Trust me, I've applied everywhere. It was either this or stripping and even that's not an option unless I go to one of the fetish clubs."

"Stripping?" I choke on my beer.

"Fetish clubs?" Inigo groans.

She sighs, placing her knife and fork back down. "Jax, the owner of Sinners—"

Her words are cut off by Inigo's screeching chair as he stands up.

"Sinners is a sex club!" he snaps.

"And here I was thinking it was a daycare!" She snarls back, climbing to her feet. "I know Jax in a roundabout way because he liked to bring his girls to the salon. Something about if you treat a woman like a queen, she'll treat you like a king. Anyway, he mentioned once or twice that if I ever wanted a change of careers to give him a call."

"I can't believe this. Do you seriously have so much fucking pride that you'd rather whore yourself than ask us for help?" Inigo yells, the warm air suddenly going arctic around us.

In a monotone voice, Kat answers. From her tone, I know we've fucked everything up again.

"I went to him looking for bar work, waitressing...Hell, I offered to clean the rooms but he didn't need anyone. Said he was overstaffed as it was and the only place he could fit me in would be the fetish room. Apparently, some people are into big bellies. We both knew I'm not that kind of girl but he promised to ask around and see if any of his friends had an opening somewhere."

She moves around the table and takes a step in the direction of the house but Inigo gently grips her wrist.

"I'm sorry."

"You keep throwing that word around and yet the more you use it the less it means."

"I don't want you to get hurt, and the thought of you working at Sinners makes me sick."

Kat shakes her head and pulls her arm free. "You don't get a say in where I work. You don't get a say in how I live my life and you sure as fuck don't get a say in what I do with this body. If I wanted to sell my pussy to the highest bidder that would be my choice to make. But you can relax in your castle of self-righteousness. I have zero plans of becoming a whore. Why do you think I don't come around the clubhouse anymore?"

"What? Are you serious? Kat, that's not how it is." I try to explain but she holds up her hand and stops me.

"I'm suddenly not feeling great. I'm going to call a cab and go."

"No, Kat, please. Stay, eat," I press, moving to her other side.

"Why, so you can tear more strips off me?"

"Sunshine, I'm an asshole. All of this shit, it's because of my own hang-ups. I know I keep taking it out on you but I'm stubborn and set in my ways. Can you just, I don't know, punch me or something instead of leaving?" Inigo pleads, making his bottom lip wobble. He looks like a fucking fish.

"What is he doing?" Kat asks me quietly.

"I think he's pouting. Or trying to."

"It needs a little work," she comments wryly.

"If you stay, I'll order dessert from the Icehouse down the road," Inigo coaxes.

"Ice cream?" Kat takes a step toward him.

"Whatever flavor you want."

"And waffles?"

"Anything. But please stay." He tries the pouting thing again, but he just looks ridiculous.

Luckily Kat takes pity on him. "Fine, I'll stay, but maybe you shouldn't speak for a little while. I like you a lot better when your mouth's closed."

Inigo gets a wicked gleam in his eye at that but Kat quickly places her hand over his mouth.

"Nope. No talking. I'm trying very hard not to kill you. You talking will likely push me over the edge. Feed me and we'll review the situation when I'm feeling less hangry."

Tucking her under his arm, he leads her back to the table and helps her into her seat before returning to his own.

Somehow, we managed to avoid bloodshed, so even though we fucked up again, I'm calling this a win.

16

Kat

"Oh god, that's good." I sip the hot chocolate Wes hands me as he sits down on the bench in his spot.

I pause with the paper cup to my lips, wondering when I started thinking of Alex's space as Wes's? I swallow down the lump in my throat, reminding myself that time moves on and I have to move with it.

"You okay?"

I look at Wes as he cradles his coffee in his hands and nod. "Yeah, I'm fine. Every now and then I have a little wobble, where it hits me for a second that Alex isn't on my mind twenty-four hours a day like before. I know that's good, healthy even, but it doesn't make it hurt any less."

"I get that, trust me. Only some days I'm not sure if I'm

grieving for the people I lost or my life that I thought I had all figured out. Most days, I don't...."

"Know who you are anymore." I finish for him.

"Exactly. The man I once was...I'm not him anymore. Fuck, I'm not making any sense."

"No, you are. Take me for instance. Alex gave me the nickname Sunshine when I was still a kid. He said that it didn't matter what storms we had to weather, I somehow always managed to find the light. When Alex died, all I saw was darkness. I wasn't his Sunshine girl anymore, so who the fuck was the girl looking back at me in the mirror?"

"You figure that out yet?"

"No, but when I do, I'll let you know."

"Okay, let's change the subject. How was work this week?"

I frown at him, knowing he doesn't like me working at the gas station any more than Inigo and Conan do. He's just less vocal about it.

"It's been mostly quiet. I've been on nights this week, so I don't get many people in. Anyone out and about in the small hours of the night tends to use the large gas station across town."

"How about those men you mentioned? They treating you right?"

I chuckle before taking a sip of my drink. "If you're talking about Conan and Inigo, then things are fine between us. We've become friends, I think."

"You think?"

I sigh. "I'm sure to them I'm nothing more than an immature kid. They're in their forties. I'm not really sure how much we have in common."

"Trust me, Kat, speaking from one old man about another, they don't see you as a kid," Wes says sharply, his eyes roving over my face, his expression a little darker and more mysterious than I'm used to from him.

"How can you be sure?"

"Katia Jones, you are perhaps the most beautiful woman I've ever laid my eyes on and I'm not just talking about on the outside. Your age is merely a marker denoting the years your body has been on this earth, but your soul tells a story of a dozen lifetimes lived. Most people will never experience a fraction of what you have even if they live to be one hundred. Do you really think those men care that you don't listen to the Beatles or remember life before the internet?"

"Who are the Beatles?"

He sucks in a sharp horrified gasp, making me giggle, the sound foreign on my lips.

"Just joking." I grin as he shakes his head at me.

"Smartass. Tell me you understand where I'm coming from here."

"I get ya. Age ain't nothing but a number, blah, blah. You're right. I'm sure they value our friendship as much as I do."

He frowns, looking at me oddly. "Jesus Christ." He hisses.

"What?"

"They like you Kat, but I promise you they don't want to just be your friend. You get that, right?"

"What? No, don't be stupid." I shake my head but my mind

flashes to all the stolen moments I refused to dwell on for fear of betraying Alex's memory.

Soft touches, the way they watch me or hold me just a tiny bit longer than they should. Lips brushing my cheek, forehead kisses, Inigo's hands in my panties— "Holy shit, they like me."

"And that is what we call a Eureka moment." He laughs, then his watch beeps. Looking down at it, he curses before looking back at me.

"Sorry to cut this short Kat, but I have to go. Same time next week?"

"Sure, I'll bring the drinks next time."

"Don't even think about it." Leaning over, he presses a kiss to my forehead before standing up and leaving in a hurry.

I sit quietly and soak up the last of the late afternoon sun while I finish my drink and think over Wes's words. I'm not sure what I'm supposed to do with this information. I mean, I care about them but I'll never be able to offer them anything more than friendship. Shit, maybe I'd have been better off not knowing.

My cell rings so I rummage around in my bag until I find it and see that it's Conan. I hesitate before answering but realize I'm being stupid.

"Hey, Sunshine, how do you feel about movies and pizza?"

"I'm a fan of both, why?"

"I'm sick of staring at Inigo's ugly mug. Wanna come brighten up the house?"

"Hmm....will I get to pick the movie?"

"As long as there are no sparkling vampires, sure."

I laugh but agree. "Okay, let me go home and put something comfy on, and then I'll be over.

"Don't be too long. I'm starving."

"Conan, you're always starving!"

"Babe, you've seen the size of me. It takes a lot to fill this body, trust me. Now hurry up and get your cute ass over here."

"Yes, sir!" I salute even though he can't see me.

He's quiet for a moment before clearing his throat. "See you soon." He hangs up as Wes's words whiz around in my head once more.

―

"I don't think I can move," I groan.

"I'm not surprised. You ate nearly as much as Conan. Are you growing a linebacker in there?"

"It sure feels like it some days. I think I might be making up for puking up everything I ate for the first four months."

"Here, lie down, place your head in Conan's lap and I'll give you a foot massage."

"Really?" I whisper in awe as if he had just offered me a Maserati.

Chuckling, he winks as Conan tugs me back. Placing a cushion on his lap, Conan lowers me until I'm comfortable, then nods at Inigo, who lifts my feet and places them in his lap.

I have a moment of self-doubt where I consider leaving but then Inigo presses his thumb into the arch of my foot and I groan long and loud.

Inigo's fingers pause as Conan goes solid beneath me.

"I'm sorry, but please don't stop," I beg, having never felt anything so amazing in my life.

"Fuck!" Conan curses.

Inigo's thumbs start moving again and I decide there and then this man can have anything he wants as long as he keeps doing what he's doing with his magic fingers.

"Oh sweetheart, you have no idea just what these magic fingers are capable of yet."

"Oh crap, I said that out loud didn't I?"

When he hits another spot that has me gasping once more, I decide to just close my eyes and roll with it.

I have no clue what movie goes on, I'm pretty sure I fall asleep before the opening credits are done. I wake up later to find myself sprawled over Conan with one of Inigo's hands resting high on my thigh.

Friends, Kat. Friends, friends, friends. Maybe if I say it often enough, I'll start to believe it.

17

Kat

I hated leaving work early but thankfully Jim managed to arrange cover for me. I guess it wouldn't do to puke on the customers.

Getting a stomach bug while pregnant is exactly as fun as it sounds. I swear my ribs and belly feel bruised from the inside out from the number of times I've been sick today. I just need a shower and about three days' worth of sleep.

I grab my keys from my bag, a little zing of relief moving through me at finding the door closed. Just like Paul promised, a locksmith had come and changed the locks for me and since then, everything had been fine. No more coming home to find it open and no more nights of sleeping with the chair wedged underneath it. Paul had even waved off my offer to pay for it.

Yes, it was an expense I couldn't afford, but then can you really put a price on peace of mind and safety?

I manage to get myself inside and to the bathroom before I'm sick again. Jesus, how can there even be anything left inside me to throw up?

Brushing my teeth, I climb into a hot shower, hoping the heat might make me feel more alive but honestly, at this point I feel like death warmed over. I don't think anything is going to help until whatever bug I have runs its course.

Climbing out on shaky legs, I feel as weak as a newborn kitten as I wrap a towel around myself and dry off.

I manage to slip on a pair of panties and a T-shirt before collapsing on the bed and passing out.

I don't know how long I'm out before I start to stir. The feel of lips on my neck and hands sliding over my belly pull me out of the haze, my internal warning system going on red alert.

My eyes snap open along with my mouth but before I can scream, a gloved hand covers my mouth as lips hover near my ear.

"This can go one of two ways. The easy way or the hard way. Personally, I'm a fan of the hard way but given your current predicament, I thought you might choose the easy way out."

His words make two very important details surface in my brain before all others. One, I know that voice—David my creepy fucking landlord—and two, the feel of something hard and sharp against my stomach registers as a knife, leaving me unable to move and fight back without my baby getting hurt in the fray.

I freeze, my whole body going rigid beneath his. I feel his grin against my temple before he licks me across the cheek.

"Smart girl." He sits up, straddling my upper thighs, keeping the knife pressed to my stomach.

"What do you want?" I ask him, even though I know. No sane man breaks into someone's apartment in the middle of the night to borrow a cup of sugar.

"I want you, of course, I always have but that fucking boyfriend of yours was always around. Now though, you're fair game and I'm an excellent hunter."

He's out of his damn mind, that's what he is.

"It was you wasn't it?" I growl, everything finally clicking into place. "You were the one messing with my door?"

He laughs, dragging the knife across my belly, circling my belly button before moving to my panty line. I beat back my fear, knowing I need to be clear-headed if I stand a chance of getting out of here in one piece.

"Funny story. As your landlord, I have the master key. I wanted to look around, make sure you had everything you needed, but leaving the door open that first time was an accident. I had no idea you would start leaving a chair wedged under your handle though. Most people would have just assumed they didn't lock it properly, but you're not most people, are you?"

I don't answer him right away, I just continue to glare but something niggles at me.

"Why did you keep coming back during the day and keep leaving it open? What was the damn point if you couldn't get to me when I was inside? Like you said, I wedged the door so you were never getting in while I was here, I don't understand why you—"

I stop talking when I realize it was all part of his plan.

"You needed me to feel safe again, to remove the chair myself, and the only way for me to do that was with a new lock in place. New lock, new key for you. So is your brother in on this too?"

He pushes the knife a little harder and I know he's cut me, I can feel the sting across my bikini line as the air hits it. I can't stop the tears from falling as I send up a silent prayer.

Keep calm, Kat, it's just a scratch.

"My brother doesn't know jack shit and you'll keep it that way or next time I'll fuck you with this knife after I've cut this baby out of you." He snarls at me.

There won't be a next time, I know that much. Either he'll kill me tonight or I'll kill him because as soon as I'm able to grab my gun, this asshole's brain will be splattered all over the apartment.

"Now, are you going to shut up and stay still?" he asks, keeping the knife against my belly while he waits for my answer.

I nod before turning my head away from him, hoping to block out whatever comes next.

One hand slides up and under my T-shirt, pushing it up until it exposes my breasts. I have no control over my body's trembling, but I turn back and force a neutral expression onto my face. I won't let him see how he's affecting me but I can't look away either, no matter how much I want to, not if I want to keep an eye on his hands. It will take one split second for him to raise his hand to punch my baby or slice the knife through my skin. If it comes to that, I'll fight like a hellcat even if he slices my arms to ribbons. This asshole will not hurt my baby. No fucking way.

He swirls a finger around one of my nipples before pinching it. I bite my lip hard enough to draw blood but I don't make a sound.

"I knew you wanted it." He flicks my nipple as if to prove his point. I don't bother to tell him it has nothing to do with his touch and everything to do with the temperature of the room because this guy believes his own hype. He would never understand how I'd rather cut them off than have his filthy hands on them.

When his hand slides lower, he cups my bump, a look of awe on his face that has bile rushing up the back of my throat.

God, not now.

Somehow, I manage to swallow it back down even as he moves his hand and reaches into his pants, shifting slightly so he can free his dick.

My body is strung so tight, I know my muscles will be in agony tomorrow if I survive.

Staring at my belly, he starts stroking his dick, his eyes never leaving the swell of my bump. He seems to almost be in some kind of trance, making every single hair on my body stand on end.

I pant as panic claws at me, stealing my breath from my lungs as I go against every instinct I have that tells me to fight back. With a guttural moan, he comes over my stomach. Any hope I had of holding back my nausea is long gone. As he leans over me, I puke and I don't even try to turn away.

"You cunt," he roars, falling backward. I'd laugh at the irony, that me puking is the one thing he finds disturbing here, if I had it in me.

He climbs off me as I turn my head to the side. The coward punches me in the temple and everything goes black.

18

Kat

Roaring wakes me up. Either I left the television on or I accidentally bought a lion and forgot about it.

"Come on, Sunshine, wake up for me, baby."

I fight to open my eyes as I'm jostled and feel myself being lifted. "Inigo?" I groan, my head throbbing. What the heck happened to me? I feel like I'm hungover, but I wouldn't drink with the baby. The baby—fuck.

I frantically run my hand over my belly and suck in a sharp relieved breath when a little foot kicks my hand. Pulling my hand back when I notice it's wet, I stare down at it, expecting to see blood, but I don't.

I see puke and sticky stuff I refuse to name because I'll puke again, but no blood.

"It's okay, Sunshine, everything is going to be okay."

I hear the shower turn on, and then I'm passed to someone else, someone naked.

I start to fight, still confused enough to not understand what's going on around me, but Conan's voice whispers in my ear.

"It's just me, Sunshine. I'm not going to let anything happen to you, okay?"

He steps into the shower with me in his arms, holding me close to his chest as I let the emotions I had held at bay pour out of me.

Moments later, I feel Inigo behind me, rubbing his hand up and down my back in a soothing gesture.

"Can we get you undressed, Sunshine? We just want to look you over and get you cleaned up, okay?" Inigo asks with a soft growl like he's trying to keep his own emotions at bay.

That's when my brain processes that I'm still wearing the puke-covered T-shirt and my panties are still on. The relief is palpable, making me suck in gulps of air so rapidly I think I'm going to hyperventilate. I had assumed the worst after being knocked out. To find my clothing in place and my baby safe and sound makes me feel ten times better.

"It's okay, Kat. Slow your breathing, darlin', nice and slow. It's just me and Conan here, okay? Let us look after you," Inigo coaxes softly.

I nod, not trusting myself to talk just yet. Conan lowers me gently to my feet but keeps his hands on my hips to steady me which is just as well because I'm not sure my legs could support me right now.

I feel Inigo reach down and grab the hem of my T-shirt and

start lifting it so I raise my hands and let him pull it over my head before tossing it away.

When Inigo's fingers hook in the edge of my panties, I tense again but he places a soft kiss against my spine as Conan lifts a hand and cups my jaw.

"Let us take care of you. Trust us."

I close my eyes and drop my head to his chest.

After a moment, Inigo continues sliding my panties down until they drop to my feet. I step out of them, keeping my head against Conan's chest and my eyes squeezed shut, concentrating for now on just breathing.

In. Out. Repeat.

I don't move as Inigo pours shower gel into his hands and starts rubbing them over my back and shoulders. When I don't protest, he continues to wash me from head to toe, never crossing the line from caring to crass.

By the time he's finished, I feel something I haven't felt for a long time—safe.

I feel the cold at my back when Inigo steps out of the shower, but before I know it Conan is passing me over to him as he stands waiting for me with a large fluffy white towel in his hands.

As soon as I step into his waiting arms, he wraps the towel tightly around me and just holds me.

I feel Conan step up behind me this time and with a towel in his hand, he starts squeezing the excess water out of my hair.

"Thank you," I croak out, grateful to them both.

"You don't have to thank us for taking care of you, Sunshine. Fuck, we should be thanking you for letting us."

"I need to brush my teeth," I mumble, feeling emotional and not liking it one little bit.

"I'll stay with you while Conan grabs you something to wear. Then we're going to take you to our place for a bit, okay? Then you can tell us what the hell happened."

I nod, knowing there is no point in fighting it. Besides, I have the mother of all headaches and I just don't think I have it in me to argue right now.

I take the toothbrush from Inigo and brush my teeth, conscious of him watching my every move. He doesn't pepper me with questions and I'm thankful for that, but the silence is a little unnerving.

"Let's get you dressed," Conan announces, walking back into the room fully dressed with a dress slung over his arm.

I move to step toward him and sway a little. Inigo curses and reaches out to steady me. "Careful, sweetheart, I don't want you to get sick again."

"I'm okay," I reassure them, which is a crock of shit, but if I say it out loud, maybe it will become true.

"You're not okay, Sunshine, but you will be," Conan growls.

I try to keep the towel wrapped around me from falling while tugging the dress on one-handed, but it's not as easy as I thought it would be.

"Here, let me help you there." Conan takes the dress from me and helps me pull it over my head. It's strapless and floor-length, in a bright orange, which covers everything but my shoulders. Without underwear or a bra, I feel naked.

As if reading my thoughts, Conan holds up a pair of black panties, but I shake my head, knowing I wouldn't be able to wear them without aggravating the cut along my bikini line. I know it's stopped bleeding and isn't deep, but that doesn't mean that it doesn't freaking hurt.

With my head clearer now, I know it was just a scare tactic. David was never going to hurt the baby because he was too fucking turned on by my pregnant belly.

I swallow hard, feeling saliva pool in my mouth but thankfully this time I manage to fight it back down.

"Come on, let's get you out of here. You need to rest."

Everything becomes a bit of a blur after that. Later on, when I think back, I only recall snippets—being helped into a jacket, hands carefully snapping the seatbelt into place, strong arms lifting me and carrying me into their home, and finally warmth.

I didn't realize how cold I was until I came here. It had seeped into my bones, bringing with it a detached sort of numbness. Being here surrounded by their scents and feeling that same wave of safety I felt when they held me in the shower, the walls around my heart begin to crumble.

19

Inigo

I ease Kat down on the sofa just as I hear Conan pull up. Not wanting to leave our bikes at the apartment, he had waited for a prospect to come and drive mine home with him. As much as I hate anyone else riding it, I was never going to leave Kat with a prospect, not when she had finally placed her trust in us.

Besides, bikes came and went, but Kat is once in a lifetime precious cargo and I'd be damned if I left her care to anyone besides Conan or me.

He opens the door and his whole body relaxes when he sees Kat on the sofa. He sits beside her and pulls the blanket off the back of the sofa, tucking it around her.

It might not be particularly hot out today but it's certainly not freezing so Kat's shaking is telling me how sick she is.

"Baby, why didn't you call us and tell us you were sick? We would have been there to help you." I squat down in front of her and place my hands on her knees, waiting for her to look at me. She lifts her head and the look in her eyes can only be described as anxious. Her usually tanned skin is almost completely devoid of color.

"You scared the shit out of us. I think it's time we took you to the clinic."

"No, I'm okay, freaked out but I'm okay. Please, I don't want to talk about it," she whispers.

"Talk about it? Jesus Kat, you were in a dead faint when we found you. You were so out of it you hadn't even locked your door behind you," Conan grits out, making my jaw clench.

"What?" she says looking at him then back to me, confused.

"You threw up while you were passed out, fucking hell you could have choked to death!" I snap then wince when she jumps.

"Shit, I'm sorry but I hate seeing you this sick. I'm so mad you didn't call."

She shakes her head as if trying to figure something out. "I...I what...I'm lost. You think I got sick and passed out. That's why you showered me, because of the puke?" she asks, her cheeks now flushed with a little color.

Her breathing picks up a little but her words throw me.

"Kat, what's going on?" Conan asks looking as lost as I am.

"I...I am or was sick. Just an upset stomach. I got sent home from work early. I had a shower and went to bed," she mumbles before looking at me again.

"I locked the door but that doesn't matter if someone has a key," she whispers, and just like that everything in me freezes.

"What?"

"I woke up with him pinning me down and a knife pressed against my stomach."

"What the fuck?" Conan bellows but Kat's lost in her own world.

"He said hard or easy. I wanted to fight so fucking bad. He held that knife and told me he would cut my baby out of me."

The urge to grab her and hold her to me is strong but I need her to get this out so I can find this man and kill him.

"Did he...?" Conan swallows hard but Kat's already shaking her head.

"He touched me and himself but he finished on my stomach, which is when I puked all over him. I...I think that's what stopped him from taking it any further. He was so mad he punched me and it was lights out."

I curse out loud and stand up, whipping out my cell and calling Orion.

"Yeah," he answers distractedly.

"Kat was attacked. I need a doctor. I can't take her to the clinic because they will ask her questions and I don't want anything leading back to her when I find this guy and carve him out a new asshole."

"Fuck, she alright?"

"No, but she will be."

"Doc has gone back to Vegas but—" I hear talking in the background before Orion says something then sighs.

"Got a Demon here who came to pick up Megan. He says he

was a medic in the Army. He's more than willing to come take a look. Said he would bring Megan if it will make her more comfortable."

My first instinct is to say no, he's a Demon after all, but this isn't about me, it's about Kat. Right now, she's all that matters.

"Send them to my place."

"He's gonna stop for his kit and be at yours in twenty minutes. Find out what you can and get back to me."

I hang up and turn back to Kat, who is now tucked under Conan's arm.

"I want someone to check you over." I hold up my hand when she starts to protest and bend down in front of her. "I need you to do this for me, okay? We'll be here with you the whole time."

"Okay," she says softly. "Are you mad at me?"

"Mad? Why the fuck would I be mad?"

She shakes her head. "I don't know, but I can feel how angry you are and you're looking at me like you want to wring my neck. I wanted to fight, I'm sorry—"

I press my lips to hers, surprising us both.

Pulling away, I take in her wide eyes and cup her jaw.

"I'm pissed, but not at you Kat, never at you. You did what you had to do to protect your baby. You were smart when you could have panicked, but you didn't."

"Oh, I was panicking on the inside. I thought I was going to die, that my baby was going to die. I thought I would have felt some weird kind of acceptance. We would have been reunited with Alex. We could have been a family again, but..."

I suck in a breath at her words, my heart stalling for a beat as Conan looks like he wants to destroy this room and everything in it.

"But what, Sunshine?"

"I realized I don't want to die. I want to live. Does that make me selfish? I promised Alex I'd always be with him."

"You can't go where he is darlin', it's not your time. Besides, Pike would be so fucking pissed at you if you quit now and you know it. He would want you to live, for you, for him, and for his legacy," I tell her, sliding my hand over her bump.

"He'll be there waiting for you, never doubt that, but not yet, Sunshine, not like this. I know you're struggling, trust me, I know, but Pike died, not you. Honor his memory the best way you can."

"How? How do I do that?"

"By living, Sunshine. That boy wanted nothing but happiness for you. Find a way to give it to him. He deserves that, but mostly so do you."

20

Kat

I nod, thinking his words over. I know he's right. I don't like it, not one little bit, but it doesn't alter the truth. Alex would be so mad at me for allowing my grief to define me, for letting it take away his Sunshine.

"I'm trying. Some days I'm okay, some days it feels like I'm breathing glass, but I am trying because you're right. Alex wouldn't want this. I barely even recognize myself in the mirror anymore."

"Baby steps, Kat. We'll get you there."

"I can't go back. Alex is in every room of that house, but I can't go back there now, not after this. Everything is tainted. I'll never feel safe there again," I babble. The thought of leaving hurts my heart but the thought of staying makes me feel like puking all over again.

"You'll stay here with us," Conan says from beside me.

"I couldn't—"

"You can and you are. We want you here. We need you close to us for our own sanity, Sunshine."

"I don't understand what's happening here," I whisper, acknowledging for the first time that something is happening with them. I don't feel for them what I feel for Alex, but there is something there, something buried deep that doesn't want the same thing I had before.

The girl who loved Alex died when he did. The hollow version of me left behind needs something different to fill the void, something darker.

Sunshine and flowers never brought me anything but heartache and pain.

I'd rather take the lightning and rain. At least that way there are no pretenses, no illusions of perfection, just chaos and calamity, but when the storm passes it brings with it a clean slate. A promise to start anew, to rebuild on the broken foundation something fresh, something different, something stronger.

"How about for now we just take everything one day at a time?" Inigo suggests softly.

I nod, knowing he's right, stressing myself out over every little thing isn't healthy.

"You said he touched you. Did he hurt you?" Conan asks quietly from beside me.

"Erm...he punched me in the temple and knocked me out," I admit. Conan hisses and Inigo curses loudly.

"And he cut my stomach. It's only shallow," I rush to add

quickly when I realize both of them are two seconds away from exploding.

"Let me see, Sunshine," Inigo tugs me to my feet and I feel Conan stand behind me, his large hands on my shoulders, offering me support.

"I...I'm not wearing any underwear," I remind them quietly.

"As much as I want to gaze at your pretty pussy, Sunshine, that's not what this is. Trust us, please," Inigo commands gently, gathering the material of my dress at my thighs and tugging it upward, exposing me to him.

I dip my head when I feel my cheeks heat, which is stupid because they've already seen me naked once today, but now that the shock is wearing off, I don't have the numbness to hide behind.

I'm not sure what I'm supposed to be feeling. Everything is a swirling mass of uncertainty right now, leaving me out of control and directionless.

My breathing picks up as Inigo drops into a squat and inspects my injury, his jaw tight, his eyes flashing with fire.

"I'll kill the bastard. Once you've been looked over, I want you to tell me everything you can about this guy and where I might find him. Let's see if he likes the way I play with knives," Inigo growls.

I reach out and slide my fingers through his hair, gripping it a little so I can tug and tilt his head back and see him.

"I'm okay, Inigo, really I am."

He growls but relaxes into my hand.

"I don't like that he touched you, that he got close enough to leave a mark on you."

"It will fade and you'll get him. I know you guys will, that's why I didn't mention calling the police."

"Damn fucking straight we will," Conan growls from behind me.

Pressing a kiss to the swell of my belly, Inigo looks up at me, his gaze locking mine in place, making it so I couldn't look away even if I wanted to.

"We won't hurt you. If nothing else, you know that's the truth. We have two spare rooms you can choose from and we can store anything you don't want to bring with you. Just say you'll stay."

I don't know what the future holds for me. Day by day has been my motto since the day I lost Alex but I can't keep burying my head in the sand and hiding from the world outside my door. I could have lost my child today. I could have died myself but we both survived and now it's time to do what I couldn't do then.

Fight back.

"Okay, I'll stay."

21

Conan

I turn my head as Megan and Kaz walk out of the guest bedroom.

"How is she?" I ask, standing up, Inigo moving to stand beside me.

"She's resting, which is honestly the best thing for her. I can't detect any issues of concern but knowing she took a blow to the head, I don't want to take any risks so keep an eye on her. If she starts getting dizzy or seems disoriented get her ass to the hospital. She mentioned having a stomach bug so watching for sickness is kinda tricky but if you think it's something more than this bug that's going around err on the side of caution and take her in. She's refusing right now, so I'm glad that will be your fight, not mine." He smirks until Megan elbows him.

"Be nice." She snaps.

"I'm always nice," he grins unrepentantly.

"The baby?" I ask with a growl.

"Moving around nicely. The cut is very shallow but I've covered it anyway. No stitches are needed. I doubt it will even scar."

My shoulders relax. "Thank you." I hold out my hand for his to shake.

"Don't sweat it, man. Orion has my number. If you need me again just call," he replies, shaking my hand firmly before shaking Inigo's.

"Appreciate it." Inigo nods before moving to hug Megan.

When he steps back, I tug Megan toward me and press a kiss to her forehead before dipping my head to make sure she can read my lips.

"And thank you for bringing some things for her. Our main concern was getting her here. We didn't really give any thought to packing a bag for her," I admit ruefully.

She smiles. "Men are not known for their multitasking. We better go. Conner is getting back from camp today and I've missed that little booger like crazy."

I laugh thinking about her younger brother. "Little? Isn't he taller than you now?"

She flips me off and shoves Kaz toward the door when he starts laughing at her.

When they leave, the silence descends. I shut the door and turn to make my way back to the sitting room when I find Inigo leaning on the door frame watching me.

"We need to talk," he says quietly, making me crack a grin.

"You breaking up with me?" I grin ruefully.

He shakes his head and grunts, pointing toward the kitchen. I follow behind him and sit at the table in the chair opposite his.

"I want Sunshine to stay here," he starts without preamble.

"We've already got her to agree to that."

"Permanently. Shit like this wouldn't happen if she didn't live alone."

"Shit. She's going to fight this. I might not know her as well as I'd like to but that woman is as stubborn as the day is long."

"She's already agreed to stay so it shouldn't be that hard to convince her to make it more permanent."

"Don't bank on it. She's sick, scared, and exhausted. As soon as she's feeling better, she'll either want to go back or start looking for somewhere else." I wipe a hand over my face.

"Why though? We have space and she'd have the protection of two bikers at her disposal."

"Look what happened to the last person she relied on." I remind him quietly. "She keeps herself at a distance from us all because she doesn't want to lose anyone else."

"Sunshine is the friendliest person I've ever met. She needs people around her now, not this self-imposed isolation she insists on."

"You don't need to convince me, man, but I gotta ask what your end game is here. I know you want her." I lower my voice.

"Don't sit there pretending that you don't," he taunts, "Yeah, I want her. Will having her here make that easier, fuck yes, but that doesn't negate all the shit I said before."

I sigh and lean back, taking in how serious he is. I try to

think back to what he was like with Tina and honestly, I don't ever remember him being this intense.

"Okay, we will figure it out. The first thing that needs dealing with is the fucker that thinks it's okay to put his hands on her. When I remove them it will act as a reminder the next time he even looks at a woman."

The evil grin that spreads across Inigo's face makes me chuckle.

We might be a little fucked up but we get shit done.

A scream breaks the moment and has us running to the bedroom, shoving through the door to find Kat thrashing on the bed. We each move either side of her, climb onto the bed and wrap our arms around her as if we've done it a thousand times.

"Sunshine, wake up, we've got you. Come on, sweetheart, open those gorgeous eyes of yours for me," I coax and take a relieved breath when they flutter open. She looks confused for a moment.

"Conan?"

"Right here. We both are."

Inigo squeezes her hip. "You were screaming," he says quietly.

"I'm sorry. I was right back there and his hands were all over me and I couldn't fucking do anything without risking my baby," she cries out, tears spilling free, "I hate feeling helpless." She admits with a croak.

I lean forward and press a kiss to her forehead. "You did everything right. You kept your baby and yourself safe until we got to you. Having control isn't always about fighting. It's knowing when to play to your strengths and when to hold back."

"Thank you both for taking care of me. I know I've been a bitch, I just..." Her voice drifts off as I cup her jaw.

"It's your armor, something you wear to protect that battered heart of yours. We're not little boys, Sunshine. We won't cry and moan because you hurt our feelings. We're men who have dealt with loss and heartache and honestly, if we can't handle you when your world is falling apart then we don't deserve to be a part of your life when you're rebuilding it." I tell her softly.

I help roll her to her back so she can see Inigo too, her eyes wide with uncertainty as she chews her lip looking at us.

"What do you want from me? The truth."

"Everything you're willing to give." Inigo replies instantly. "Nothing more, nothing less than all that makes you, you."

"I don't even know who that is. Some days the girl staring back at me in the mirror is a complete stranger."

"Let us help you figure it out, but don't ask us to leave you alone. We will do pretty much everything for you if you asked it of us but don't ask us to leave you."

"Don't let me fall in love with you. You can take whatever else you want, but my heart is off-limits. I just can't do that again," she whispers.

I look over at Inigo and watch him swallow before he leans over and presses a soft kiss to her lips and for the first time since she arrived here, he lies to her.

"Okay, Sunshine. Your heart is safe from us."

22

Kat

"Oh my god, this is the best thing I've ever put in my mouth," I groan, greedily taking another mouthful of the delicious chicken soup Inigo made me.

I look up when I realize that except for the television playing the evening news, the room has gone quiet.

I find both men staring at me with unbridled lust which quickly has my eyes dropping to my lap and the bowl of soup resting in it. I will myself not to squirm, but with the feel of their eyes on my body and these pregnancy hormones running rampant, I wouldn't be surprised if I spontaneously combusted.

"You keep making those noises, Sunshine, Conan and I might take that as a challenge." Inigo growls.

I squeeze my thighs together as I feel my core slicken before guilt stabs at me, effectively dousing my libido in ice water.

"Sorry," I mumble, continuing to eat the rest of my soup.

My brain and body are in a constant battle right now at opposing ends of the spectrum.

"Nothing to be sorry for. You up to telling us a little about the prick who hurt you?" Inigo asks, coming to sit beside me.

"Um, I don't know much. David and his brother Paul own the building complex I live in. Alex used to deal with David so I didn't have much to do with him but even so he always gave me the creeps."

"Gave you the creeps how?" Conan questions, sitting on the coffee table in front of me.

"If you're asking if he gave off an *I'm going to break into your apartment and spunk all over your belly vibe* the answer is no," I snark at him before sighing.

"There was just something about him that made my skin crawl. He was always a little too friendly, a little too helpful, stood a little too close, and watched me a little too long, you know? When I lost my job, he pretty much implied I could pay my rent in sexual favors. After that, I avoided him like the plague."

"He did what?" Inigo booms, making me jump.

"And you didn't tell us?" Conan curses before I can answer.

"Do you want me to carry on or do you both need a minute?" I ask them, lifting the tray from my lap and placing it beside me on the sofa.

"Need a minute? What I need is to understand how you could blow something like this off? If you had just said something, this could have all been prevented!" Inigo roars at me. The angrier they get the calmer I become. It's an odd dichotomy but I learned in formative years how to stay calm and defuse a situation instead of escalating it.

"Victim shaming, hmmm.... I see the misogyny is strong with you MC types so let me stop you now before you cross a line that earns you a knee to the dick."

"I live alone. I have been dealing with a fucking lot and I have no family or friends to lean on and before you spout off shit about Carnage, you need to remember what I am and what I'm not."

"Explain," Inigo barks, making me want to growl but we can't both imitate junkyard dogs.

"Alex was only a prospect. Prospects don't get to make their women old ladies until they receive their own property patches. Even pregnant girlfriends aren't exempt from the rules."

They both look at me like they want to say something but I carry on talking.

"I'm not a club whore, I'm not an old lady and honestly, as much as I like everyone at Carnage, I don't really know anyone. We were friendly but still too new to call anyone real friends. The only person I've ever had to rely on is myself."

"Bullshit. If you had called any one of the old ladies, or fuck, any of the brothers for that matter, they would have been there in a heartbeat."

"Yeah? So tell me then, where is everyone? I'm not saying I didn't push people away, especially at the beginning because I could hardly breathe let alone speak and pretend I was okay, but I was drowning and nobody bothered to offer me a hand, bar you two, and even then I wasn't sure if it was because of me or because you worried I might spill shit about Carnage."

"Jesus? Is that really what you think?" Conan groans.

I shrug. "What else was I supposed to think? Like I said, I pushed but nobody pushed back. Maybe it's easier this way. I'm less of a reminder about how fucked up things became."

Inigo drags a hand over his face. "Do you blame the club for Pike's death?"

I shake my head. "I was mad at everything and everyone, to begin with, but it was Pike's choice to be there. Nobody made him do anything if he didn't want to. That doesn't mean I don't struggle sometimes, knowing that everyone else got their happily after." I look up at Inigo then and grimace. "Sorry, that was uncalled for. I didn't know Tina well. I'm not sure she really wanted to get to know me, maybe because of my age or because I wasn't an old lady." I shrug, not wanting to sound like I'm putting her down. She might have been a little cold toward me but she was never mean. "I'm sorry you lost her."

He stares at me intently. "She struggled to warm up to new people. It wasn't a reflection on you Kat," he tells me softly.

"I know," I agree, glancing at Conan who looks at me with a kind of knowing. I have a feeling he had his own issues with Tina.

"Look, can we just agree to disagree here? The club is your everything. I get that, I do, but you don't get to judge me for the decisions I made as a person living on the outside."

I look away, needing to break from his intense stare that I swear sees more than it should, and focus on the news still playing on the TV. I frown at the screen as Inigo keeps talking but his words sound as if they are coming from far away.

"They don't see you like that, Kat. Fuck. Orion was livid

when I told him you were attacked. If Orion gets his hands on him he'll be—"

"Dead," I answer, pointing at the screen showing a photo of David, identifying him as the victim of an attack two blocks away from my apartment building.

23

Inigo

"What? Conan, turn that up."

David Cummings was found with multiple stab wounds and a single gunshot to the head. Police are asking for witnesses to please come forward.

Conan switches off the TV, cutting off the blonde reporter's voice.

"Talk about instant karma," Kat blurts out, making me snort. "I guess it's safe for me to go back then."

Shit.

"Stay, seriously. We have a spare room, you've just suffered something traumatic. At least give yourself some time to get over it. You don't want to put any extra undue stress on yourself or your baby, now do you?"

She sighs, her shoulders dropping. I don't know if it's in relief or defeat, but I'll take it.

"Okay, thank you."

"Look we have church in the morning. Megan brought you a bunch of shit, why don't you take a soak in the tub for a while and relax and we'll spend the rest of the evening vegging. Tomorrow, if you're feeling up to it, you could come with us. Everyone misses you, Kat. I can see you don't believe me so why don't you come and find out for yourself?"

She eyes me for a minute before slowly nodding. "Okay fine, but we're getting food on the way home, something greasy."

"Yes, ma'am." Conan grins.

"Come on." I reach down and tug her up the stairs and to the bedroom at the far end of the hallway.

"The room you crashed in earlier used to be Half-pint's. You are more than welcome to keep using that one if you want but —" I swing the door open wide "—you might like this one better."

I step aside as she walks into the room, taking in the pale green walls, the huge custom-size bed with its sage and white bedding, and the antique dresser at the foot of the bed with the ornate mirror above it.

"Wow, it's gorgeous."

"Over here is the walk-in closet. We can collect your things whenever you're ready, and this—" I walk farther into the room, pushing open the door on the far left "—is the bathroom."

"Oh my god. This isn't just any bathroom, Inigo, this is the bathroom of wet dreams. I want to live in here." She breathes excitedly.

I can't say I blame her. Decorated in the same greens and white as the bedroom but with gold fittings and fixtures, the bathroom looks like something out of a five-star hotel with its double-headed shower, big enough for four, and the star of the show, the sunken tub with whirlpool features that's honestly big enough to be considered a pool.

"You relax, and when you come out, we can watch a movie or two. Sound good?"

"Will there be foot rubs involved?"

Laughing, he nods. "For you darlin', anything."

"Then yeah, Inigo, that sounds perfect."

"Here, let me start it for you." I reach over and close the plug before turning on both taps. Pulling open one of the cupboards under the vanity, I pour a liberal amount of bubble bath before rummaging around for a handful of other girly products. Placing them around the edge of the bath so she'll be able to reach them easily, I turn back to her and find her watching me curiously.

"What?"

"This room, the bedroom, it was Tina's wasn't it?"

"It was for her, well for all of us in theory, hence the custom bed to accommodate Conan's humongous frame, but she never stepped foot through that door. It was going to be a surprise, but it wasn't finished before she died so she didn't know."

"I'm sorry, Inigo. I promise I'm not trying to be ungrateful. I just didn't want to intrude on any painful memories."

"Yeah, I get that." I chuckle, remembering I felt the same way in her apartment.

"Okay, don't take this the wrong way, but these things, they weren't Tina's, right?"

She points at the bath oils and shower gels.

I huff. "No, they're just something we picked up. Why, what's the issue?" Why does this woman make it impossible to do anything nice for her?

"I'm sorry. I promise I'm not trying to be a brat. I'm grateful for everything, I just don't want to smell like the woman you loved and lost any more than you'd want to walk around smelling like Alex, smells can be triggering for me." She admits, rubbing her hands together and making me feel like an asshole.

Tugging her into my arms, I hold her gently and breathe her in.

"No, don't be sorry. I wanted to do something nice for you, but it seems I fuck up everything."

"No, this is exactly what I need. Can I ask you something?"

"You can ask me anything, Sunshine."

"I've noticed a pattern. You go from pissed to protective and back to pissed again so often I almost missed it but...," She chews her lip, looking up at me.

"You want to take care of me." It's a statement, not a question but I nod anyway.

"I've been so used to taking care of myself I can be stubborn," she concedes, making me grin.

Slapping my arm, she huffs. "Okay fine, I can be very stubborn. I'm not used to having people take care of me. Conan doesn't react the same way as you so I guess my question is, do you want to take care of me or need to take care of me?"

"Anyone ever tell you how damn smart you are?"

She laughs lightly which, given the events of the last twenty-four hours, is a miracle in itself.

"Maybe, now stop deflecting."

"I think you already know the answer. I promise, we'll talk about this more and I'll answer any questions you have, but not today. Today is for rest and recuperation."

I know she wants to argue but relents with a sigh. "Okay, Inigo. I can live with that."

I step around her and turn off the taps.

"You good or do you need a hand?"

She opens her mouth, likely to tell me she's fine, but pauses before swallowing. "Can you help me get undressed? I'm still a little stiff and I don't want to risk slipping."

A swell of pride bursts within me as I step closer to her and press a lingering kiss against her forehead.

"I'd be honored, Sunshine."

Keeping my eyes locked on hers, I tug the material of her loose dress down over her breasts and peel it over her belly until gravity takes over and it drops to the floor.

Her breathing picks up but it has nothing to do with fear and everything to do with the electricity crackling between us and damn if that doesn't make my dick stand up and salute her.

"I'm going to pick you up now, okay?"

"Okay," she answers breathlessly.

I scoop her up in my arms and gently lower her into the tub, resisting the urge to suck one of her nipples into my mouth when she moans in delight.

When I take a step back, the bubbles cover her chest, thank god, because I'm holding on by a damn thread here.

"Will you wash my back?"

I don't answer, I just reach for the shower gel and pour some into my hands as she leans forward. I smooth my hands over her back, massaging the muscles as I go, feeling her relax.

"I've said it before, but I'll say it again, you have magic hands." She groans, and I know I need to get the fuck out of this bathroom now before I lose my ever-loving mind.

"Done. Now lay back and relax. I'll leave the door open so if you need anything, just yell."

"Thank you, Inigo. For everything."

I wink and get the fuck out of there as if the hounds of hell are chasing me. She sure as shit wouldn't be thanking me if she knew all the dirty thoughts running through my head.

I head straight to the kitchen and grab a beer from the fridge, twisting the cap off and drinking it down in one go.

"Looking a little flush there, Ini." Conan grins as he stirs something that smells of garlic and onions in the slow cooker.

"Our girl's upstairs, wet and naked."

He pauses, turning to look at me.

"I feel like I'm coming out of my skin. I swear, I only have to breathe in her scent, and images flash through my mind like a never-ending porno flick. I visualize Kat tied to my bed begging for relief, then it's of her bouncing on your dick while she chokes on my cock with tears running down her face. I...I'm losing my fucking mind."

"Well you better rein it the fuck in until she gives us the green light," Conan growls, tossing the wooden spoon on the counter before stomping away.

"Where are you going?" I call after him.

"To crack one off in the shower."

He grunts, making me snort before heading to the other bathroom to follow suit. I have to take the edge off somehow because I know it's going to be a long night.

24

Kat

I sip my coke, wincing when little bean decides to drop kick my spleen. It's quiet today with all the guys in church, the prospects busy doing whatever jobs they had been tasked with doing, and Luna at home with a sick Ruby who was the latest victim of the stomach bug. Thankfully it seemed to just be a twenty-four-hour thing.

I guess the guys were right. My worries about coming here appear to be unfounded.

I hemmed and hawed, but the guys promised me burgers. I'm pregnant, not stupid. At this point, there isn't much I won't do for burgers. Or just any food, now the shitty morning sickness is behind me.

"Why are you even here? If you're looking to join us girls, you'll need to get rid of that first." I turn at the sound of the husky voice and see a woman who likely would have been stunning ten years ago but now she looks like she has been ridden hard and put up wet one too many times. Her pretty ash brown hair is over teased as if she stepped out of an 80s rock video. Her deep rouge painted lips draw attention to the small lines bracketing her mouth from years of smoking, making her mouth look like a cat's ass. Even so, if she smiled more often and maybe toned down the retro Barbie look, she would be a stunner. Well if she stuck to only opening her mouth for blowjobs. You can change ugly on the outside, but nothing can change ugly on the inside, at least in my experience.

"I'm going to assume you aren't talking about me and my baby because we don't know each other, and that would be a really bitchy thing to say to a stranger, now wouldn't it?"

I roll my eyes and take another sip from my straw, hoping she'll get the hint and move the fuck on but no, she sticks around, and another girl moves to stand beside her. This one is about a decade younger and is totally working the schoolgirl vibe.

Waiting to see if this is going to become the next installment of dumb and dumbest, I'm pleasantly surprised when the younger woman, who is probably only a few years older than myself, tugs on retro Barbie's arm.

"Come on, Jan, you know you don't mess with old ladies," she says quietly, trying to defuse the situation, but Jan is on a one-woman mission and shrugs her off.

"She ain't no old lady. She got knocked up by a dead prospect, how path—"

Her words cut off when I stand to my full height and quick

as a flash, draw back my fist and punch her in the face, knocking her out cold.

I sit back down on the barstool far less gracefully than I would have liked as the noise level begins to increase with my actions.

"Erm, I'm sorry about her. She doesn't speak for all of us."

I turn to face the girl and offer her a small smile, clocking the other two club girls approaching to pick up their friend. I notice none of the prospects have stepped in. I'm not sure how I feel about that. As much as I can hold my own, I'm a billion years pregnant. If anything happens to my baby while I'm here, Conan and Inigo would string them up from the ceiling by their intestines.

"I'm sorry, I don't even know your name. I'm Kat," I tell her, letting her know I won't be judging her by her friend's actions.

"Melody. I'm new here," she says with a slightly lopsided smile that softens her whole face. Damn this girl is wicked pretty. I can imagine how popular she is with the boys.

"Nice to meet someone close to my age. I always feel like the baby," I admit. She laughs just as one of the two women who came to collect their friend shoves her aside.

"Hey!" I snap at her, but she ignores me for a minute in favor of glaring at Melody.

"Know your place." When Melody tries to speak, the bitchy woman holds up her hand. "It's on your knees, in case you've forgotten. Now, get out of here and tidy the kitchen up like you were supposed to before I tell Gage you haven't been pulling your weight and he kicks your ass out of here."

Whatever Melody was going to say she swallows down and turns away, heading to the kitchen.

"And you. You think your shit don't smell, but I can assure you that you're no better than the rest of us. You ain't no old lady and around these parts that makes you a whore."

I stand back up again with a groan because that shit isn't easy anymore.

I look down at her and grin but there is nothing friendly about my smile. I also revel in the fact that I tower over her.

"I am not now, nor have I ever been, a whore. Not that I think there is anything wrong with that. A woman should get to decide what she does and who she does so no judgment from me but—"

And big mouth bitchy mcbitch face has to jump in and ruin my monologue. "You lost your golden ticket so now you're trying to hook your star to Conan and Inigo. I think you're disgusting. They lost the woman they loved and you're tempting them with your stretched out pussy."

"Woah, woah, woah. Back the fuck up there. First of all, Alex, or Pike as he was known here, wasn't my golden ticket. He was my whole fucking universe. Don't comment on shit your tiny brain can't even comprehend. Second, nothing about Conan or Inigo has anything to do with you so I suggest you keep your nose out of their business." I step to her until my bump prevents me from moving closer.

"And lastly, stretched out? Seriously. I've only ever had one man inside me. One. Do you really want to compare dick traffic right now? Do you even remember how many dicks have parked inside you?"

"You're a bitch," she snaps.

I beam a smug smile in her direction. "Why, thank you. Now if you'll excuse me, I just remembered I need to be over there doing nothing." I step to walk around her but she grips my wrist.

Big fucking mistake.

I lift my hand to grab her, only someone else gets to her first, yanking her back and making her totter on impossibly high heels.

"Don't," the familiar voice snarls out.

I look up and smile at the stunning redhead, Dee, one of the old ladies I had met a couple of times. Her old man had been a nomad for years but decided to settle down when he met Dee at a diner and the rest, as they say, is history.

Thankfully, the slap-happy bitch is smart enough to know better than to mess with Dee so she bites her tongue and scurries off after her friends.

"Hey, stranger." Dee leans in for a hug, pulling back with a laugh when a little foot boots her.

"How you doing?" she questions, sitting on the stool next to mine. I climb back up, vowing to not move an inch until the guys come to get me. Moving this pregnant body around is getting much harder.

"I'm okay." I give her my standard answer but this time I don't bother to muster a smile.

"Really. Wanna try again and this time with a little conviction?"

I sigh and rest my head in my hands. "I miss him, Dee. I miss him every single fucking day. Maybe losing him was my punishment, a way of showing me what I already knew, that I just wasn't worthy of him.

"Bullshit, Sunshine. You were like two peas in a pod. How can you possibly think you were unworthy?"

"Because when I look at Inigo and Conan, I see more than just overprotective bikers. I feel more than I should. My soulmate is dead in the ground and already I'm feeling something for not just one but two other men. What does that make me?" I whisper, fighting to keep the emotion from my voice, but as my feelings for Inigo and Conan evolve and grow, so too does my guilt.

"Oh, sweet girl, it makes you human. I didn't know Pike that well, me and Rusty were too busy being in our honeymoon phase to notice much beyond each other, but what I did see made it clear that he was a good man who thought the sun rose and fell with you. He would want you happy, both of you." She reaches out to pat my belly.

"More than that though, he would want you safe and protected and I can't think of two better protectors than Inigo and Conan. I mean, talk about go big or go home." She chuckles, making me choke on my sip of coke.

"I have no idea what I'm doing, Dee." I admit, feeling so out of my element.

"I'll let you in on a little secret, Kat, none of us do. We've just spent so long winging it we make this shit look easy. Let me ask you this, is how you feel about Conan and Inigo likely to stop in a year from now, or maybe two?"

I shake my head. I know damn well it won't. I don't know whether it's the years I spent in foster homes being shuffled around with next to no possessions of my own or what, but once I care about something and make it mine, I tend to keep it forever.

"Then why waste time waiting? You know better than most just how short life can be. You deserve to be happy, Kat, and if that means being the filling between two slices of hot daddy bikers I say nom-fucking-nom. Who gives a flying fuck what anyone else thinks?"

I wouldn't quite put it that way but there is something about Dee's words that resonate with me. I can't think of anything else but what it might be like between us.

Nom-fucking-nom indeed.

25

Conan

We leave church and head toward the bar. Hearing laughter, I follow the sound and find Sunshine sitting at the bar with Rusty's old lady, Dee. I have known Rusty for years, despite him flitting from club to club as a nomad. He was a grouchy fucker even if he is loyal to a fault but since Dee came along, the man has practically turned into a teddy bear. Not that I'd ever tell him that. I like my spleen where it is.

"It's nice to see a smile on her face," Halo says from beside me, his eyes on Sunshine.

I don't reply. I hang back and watch her gesturing wildly to Dee as Inigo approaches her.

"If you guys are going there, I have to know you're all in. She's been through enough. If you hurt her, I'll hurt you.

And, Conan, I don't care how big you are and neither will my ax."

I try not to bristle at his words, knowing he's only being protective of her, but there will never come a time when he needs to protect her from us.

"It's serious. We'd make her our old lady tomorrow if we thought she was ready."

He blows out a breath, looking at me intently.

"You love her." The guy always was perceptive as fuck.

I nod before turning to see her looking up at Inigo with a soft smile on her face before she scans the room, finally stopping when her eyes fall on mine. I watch her shoulders relax and feel a strange thump of righteousness in my chest at her reaction.

"She needs you guys. I can see that, but I think you guys need her more."

"I know. We still have a bunch of shit to figure out. She's working through the loss of Pike, Inigo is dealing with what happened over Tina, and me, well I'm all kinds of fucked up. I'm just waiting for her to realize she's too fucking good for two bikers old enough to be her fathers," I admit.

"Somehow I don't think she sees you that way," Halo says quietly as Sunshine smiles for me.

"But then again, you shouldn't knock having someone call you daddy while you bury your cock inside them and spank their ass. You know what? I'm gonna go home and check on Luna." He turns and walks away, making me snort at the randy bastard.

Looking back at Kat as Inigo holds out his hand for her, I

can't help picturing her on her knees in front of me, looking up at me with those sweet innocent eyes of hers.

Yeah, Halo might be on to something there.

"Hey there, Giganto, you're off with the fairies there. You okay?"

I blink out of my daydream and see Kat standing in front of me and looking at me with a worried expression. Inigo stands beside her with a smirk on his face because the fucker knows exactly where my mind has wandered off to.

"I'm good, starving though. This body needs a lot of fuel to run optimally." I wink, making her blush.

I reach to take her hand when Orion comes flying into the room making his way over to us. My blood runs cold at the look on his face but it's not me he's heading for, it's Kat.

"Kat, sweetheart. Shit." He grips his hair as Gage appears behind him, looking angry as fuck.

"What is it? Are...are you kicking me out?" she asks quietly.

"What? Fuck no. You're welcome here anytime, sweetheart. No, it's not that." He reaches forward and takes both her hands in his and looks her in the eyes. I can see my club brothers closing in and even Dee seems to be making her way over, each of them offering their silent support even before we know what's happening.

"Your apartment building is on fire," he tells her softly, keeping his voice even. Inigo hisses, both of us moving closer to her. Her brows furrow like she can't quite process what he's telling her. I see the exact moment that clarity hits because she starts shaking her head as she snatches her hands free from Orion's.

"No," she snaps, looking around wildly for escape.

"Sunshine," I murmur, reaching for her.

"No, fuck no. I need to go." She turns to run past me but I catch her before she can leave.

"No, Conan, let me go. Please. I have to get my things. Please, everything I have of Alex is in that building. I can't lose him again. Please, please let me go."

"I can't, Sunshine," I growl, her tears breaking my heart.

"Let me go!" she screams, fighting me.

"Enough!" Gage roars, making her freeze.

He steps forward and dips his head, cupping her jaw.

"You'll hurt yourself and your baby so calm down or I'll have Kaz come over and give you something to knock you out," he warns her.

"But Alex," she chokes, her words a whispered plea as she tries to make us understand that it's nothing about the building and everything to do with the last memories of the man inside.

"I'm sorry, Sunshine, it's gone," he tells her.

I see her wobble and know she's about to go down. I reach for her and scoop her up in my arms and carry her out of the bar and upstairs to the room I use when I stay here.

I climb onto the bed with her and pull her tight against me as she breaks down in gut-wrenching sobs that hurt me just to hear.

Inigo pushes the door open and without a word, climbs onto the bed behind Kat and presses against her back. We surround her with our heat, letting her know she isn't alone anymore. There isn't anything else we can do beyond keeping her safe and protected while she mourns one more thing she's lost.

Eventually, her sobs quiet, her chest hitching painfully with each breath as she tries to speak.

"Shh... it's okay, Sunshine, everything is going to be okay." I soothe her, looking over her shoulder at Inigo who looks devastated for her.

"How is it going to be alright, Conan?" she questions, her voice barely above a whisper. "We had no family, no distant relatives. Every memento from our life together was in that apartment. Every photograph," she sobs, "when I close my eyes, it's harder and harder to see his face but I always had the pictures of us to remind me, but now they're gone. I'm so scared that one day I'll wake up and his face will just be a blur. You all knew him as Pike and that's the man you remember. I'm the only person who remembers the man he was before Carnage. If I forget Alex, it will be like he never existed at all." She dissolves into tears again.

"No. Take a second, Sunshine, to just feel. I know it hurts but give in to the pain for a minute. Breathe through it and tell me what you feel," Inigo growls, sliding his hands over her bump protectively.

"Scared, angry, hurt." She sniffs before taking a deep breath.

"I know you are, Sunshine, but that's all you're focusing on, the things you lost. But you need to remember the things he left behind."

I place my hand beside Inigo's on her belly and swallow in awe when I feel the baby move under my palm. I swear it never gets old, but at this moment when Kat's being dealt another blow, it feels even more important.

"Alex is right here. His baby will be a reminder to the whole world of the man who helped create him. Don't you see, Sunshine, he will never be gone, not really, and no photograph will ever compare to looking in the eyes of the child you made together."

26

Inigo

"How's Kat doing?" Orion asks as we take our seats.

"Better for the most part. She has moments when she just zones out but considering everything, I'm in awe of her ability to bounce back."

"Well, she has you guys at her back now, which helps. She's finally figuring out that she doesn't have to do everything alone."

"Amen to that."

"Where is she today, anyway? Luna was hoping to see her. She's starting to get a complex." Gage adds from beside Orion.

"She's going to pop round to see her later but she has a thing she does every Friday. A ritual of sorts, if you like, where she goes to the park and meets her friend to reminisce about

Pike. Her friend lost their partner and kids too so I think it's good for them both."

"Friend? Anyone we know?" Gage asks as Conan sits beside me.

"I never asked. I think it might be someone from her old job at the salon."

"Ah, that reminds me. I wanted to run something by you both," Halo pipes in from beside Gage.

"What's that?" Conan leans back in his chair lazily.

"Tina's bakery. As you know, it's paid up for the rest of the year but I was thinking, what about if we turn it into a salon? It would mean Sunshine would have something better to go back to when she's ready. One of the club girls, Melanie or something, is a stylist Luna was telling me. It would be a legitimate club business and at the minute it's just sitting there doing nothing."

"I'll talk to Kat but I don't have a problem with it." It's time to put ghosts to rest and it's a nice legacy for Tina to leave behind.

"Okay, next order of business. The fire marshal confirmed arson," Gage begins, drawing the attention of the rest of the room.

"Shit. I really wanted to be wrong." I swipe a hand down my face.

Diesel leans over the table. "Anyone else hurt?"

"All the other apartments were empty," Gage replies.

"That's fucking lucky," Rusty throws out and he's not wrong.

"What are the odds of that?" Conan questions with a frown.

"Pretty damn high when you consider the fact that the only

rent agreements on record that I could find were for Pike and Kat and a ninety-year-old woman who has been living in an assisted living facility for the last four months."

I whistle. "All those empty apartments? They must have been hemorrhaging money."

"Or maybe the apartments were a front for something else," Diesel muses.

"Like what? What are you thinking D?" Lucky chimes in, watching him.

"I don't know, but with the demand for cheap apartments in that part of town being so high, there is no way they would be that empty unless it was by choice."

"I'll talk to Kat, see if she remembers anyone else. What about the other landlord, the brother. Paul was it?"

Rebel speaks up. "He's in the wind. I ran a check on him and nothing pinged, but there is nothing on file for either Paul or David before 2016."

"How is that possible? They didn't just appear out of thin air."

"New identities I assume. Could be for a number of reasons but given what we know, I doubt any of them were good."

"Fuck, keep digging, Rebel," I tell him. He nods and I know if there's something to find, he'll find it.

"Maybe it was for an insurance claim. Think about it, all those empty apartments and yet it doesn't burn down until the one night Kat's not there?" Diesel points out.

"Whatever the reason, I want to know. I don't like being in the dark when shit goes down in my town," Orion orders. "Now, what's next?"

Church flies by quickly after that. When we're done, it's almost dinner time, so I send a message to Kat and see what she wants to eat.

When her reply comes through, I must grimace because Conan frowns.

"What is it? Is Kat alright?"

"She's fine, but this pregnancy has a lot to answer for. She wants pasta for dinner with gravy and anchovies."

Conan gags. "What the fuck? I'm not cooking that."

I quirk a brow at him because we both know it's bullshit. He'll make her anything her heart desires. "Fine, but I'm not eating that shit."

"Thank fuck for that. I'm not a picky eater, but I've gotta draw the line somewhere."

"Let's pick up shit we need on the way home. I want to spend some time with our girl before she's back at work tomorrow."

"I hate her working there. I'm so fucking glad she finally agreed to leave, even if she insists on working out her two-week notice."

"She's stubborn as fuck, I'll give her that, but I think the pregnancy is really starting to take its toll on her now. Just think, if we can get her to agree to turn Tina's bakery into a salon, she'll never have to go back there again. You sure you're okay with this?"

"Yeah, Conan, I'm sure. It's time."

27

Kat

I stare at the clock and huff when I realize it's only been five minutes since the last time I looked.

I'm so ready to be done. Inigo and Conan hate me working here, but I put my foot down, needing to keep myself busy and wanting to put some money away for when the baby arrives. Now though, at thirty-eight weeks pregnant, I'm ready to admit defeat.

I conceded to working days as it was safer. The guys flat out refused to let me work the night shift. I'm smart enough to pick my battles, but now I've finally reached the point where it's just too much. My back has been killing me all day, thanks to my huge belly throwing off my center of gravity, and the stupidly uncomfortable stool behind the counter doesn't help. My ankles are swollen and if I don't get some ice cream inside me within the next thirty minutes, I'm likely to lose the will to live.

With only twenty minutes remaining of my very last shift, I'm already imagining one of Inigo's foot rubs after I devour the last tub of chunky monkey ice cream I'd strategically hidden behind the other tubs in the back of the freezer.

It has been quiet today, which made the time move even slower than usual, but I was determined to see it through to the end.

I look up from the baby magazine I had been leafing through when the little bell above the door jingles.

Two bikers walk through, laughing with each other. I check out their cuts and see they're prospects for the Raven Souls. The gas station isn't exactly local to them. I don't think I've ever seen a Raven in here or around the town before. I know they are allied with Carnage, so I leave them to it and carry on reading the magazine, skipping over the article about episiotomies.

Fuck no! The thought of giving birth is terrifying enough without having to worry about ripping from hole to hole.

I shove the magazine aside and frown, wondering why I started reading the damn thing in the first place. I always end up reading something that freaks me out.

A six-pack of beer hits the counter heavily with a handful of chocolate bars, startling me out of my thoughts.

"Twenty dollars on pump six," the older of the two bikers tells me. He's thin to the point of emaciation with greasy dark hair and eyes, although his pupils look like pinpricks right now. I look away quickly and ring up his things, feeling nervous for the first time since they walked in. I might never have done drugs myself, but I've lived in some shitty places where shooting up was the norm. I know a druggie when I see one and this guy screams trouble.

I take his cash and hand him the receipt and wait for his friend to approach. This guy is a skinhead, so it's hard to make out the color of his hair, maybe a dirty blond. He walks with a cocky swagger and a smirk like he's God's gift to women, yet somehow I doubt that.

"Pack of smokes and twenty dollars on pump two. Hey, you look like a fun girl, how about me and my buddy here give you a pump too?" He wiggles his eyebrows at me while laughing.

Yes, so fucking hilarious.

"I'll pass, but thanks," I tell him firmly, not wanting them to think for a second I'm encouraging them or playing hard to get.

"Fuck you, bitch. You think you're too good for us?" he snarls while his friend watches me as he scratches his arm. His overreaction sends a bolt of awareness through me.

"No, I think I'm too pregnant for you and my husband would likely have something to say about it." I keep my tone even, not wanting to anger them any more even though I want to reach over the counter and shove my fist into his windpipe.

"Fuck, yes. Pregnant bitches are greedy little sluts. We can make you take both our cocks in your pussy at once and we can stretch you out. Get you nice and ready for delivery while I deliver my load inside you. It will be like baptizing the kid with my jizz." He laughs as he reaches for my arm and yanks hard, pulling me partially over the counter. His dirty fingernails dig into my forearm making me cry out, but he doesn't let go.

The Crown of Fools

"Drag her in the back and I'll lock up," he orders the tweaker, who moves to step around the counter, making my heart race into overdrive. Any calm I still felt disappears with his words. The last time some asshole put his hands on me is still all too clear in my mind. I was helpless then but I'm sure as fuck not helpless now.

I reach under the counter with my free hand and pull the gun kept there, pointing it at the loudmouth asshole.

"Get the fuck out now or I'll shoot your dick off."

He lets go of my arm as if it burns him before reaching for his gun.

"I really wouldn't do that if I were you. I tripped the silent alarm, the cops are on their way and I'm a defenseless pregnant woman who will easily get off with killing you both in self-defense. Try me. I dare you."

I know my mouth is running away from me but god-fucking-damn these asshole men who think they can just take what they want without consequence.

"You stupid bitch," the cocky one sneers before laughing, all the while the tweaker stands silently watching the scene as if it's a movie.

"You're lying. You're just a little pussy who hasn't got the balls—"

I shoot him in the dick.

"Now who doesn't have any balls?" I taunt.

"Fuck, I didn't sign up for this," the tweaker curses, looking to his friend on the floor, then to the door, before making his first smart choice tonight and running.

The ping of a bullet whizzing past my head makes me jump and pee myself.

The guy on the floor tries to focus on me through his tears, cocking his gun once more but I'm not taking any freaking chances. I aim and fire, this time hitting him in the chest.

I keep my gun pointed at him until he stops breathing and his eyes stare at a fixed point on the ceiling.

Only then do I reach for my phone and with shaky hands hit speed dial one.

"You finished early, Sunshine?" Conan greets me as I stare at the puddle of blood forming around the guy on the floor.

"I just shot and killed a Ravens prospect," I tell him, my voice eerily calm.

I think I'm in shock.

"What?" he roars down the phone. I wait for him to calm down, listening to him barking at whoever is with him. I hear bikes start up but most of my focus is fixed on the claret red of the pooling blood on the floor.

"Hold on, Sunshine. I'm comin', darlin'. Just hold the fuck on."

With one hand I grip the counter and do as he asks, I hold the fuck on until I can hear the rumble of bikes outside the gas station instead of over the phone. Only then do I allow myself to look away from the man I just killed.

28

Inigo

I have no idea what to expect when we pull up outside the gas station, but all I care about is getting my eyes and hands on Kat and making sure she's okay. Everything else I can deal with but I can't lose Kat, not now.

I'm off the bike as soon as it stops, with Conan hot on my heels and half of Carnage at my back.

"Kat!" I roar as soon as I'm through the door, coming to an abrupt halt when I see the Raven member dead on the floor in a pool of his own blood.

"Fuck!" I bite out.

"Over here." I hear Kat's soft voice call out with a wobble.

I rush to the counter and make my way around it, stopping when I see Kat on the floor with her hands wrapped around her belly and the gun beside her leg.

"Jesus, Sunshine, you okay?" I squat beside her and cup her jaw, making her look up at me. Her face is pale and her eyes look glassy but otherwise, she looks uninjured.

"I'm okay," she answers as a tear escapes and runs down her cheek.

"Let's get you up so I can look you over, then you can tell us what happened, alright?"

A movement behind me has me turning to look over my shoulder. Conan stands there staring down at Kat, his jaw tight, his hands fisted as he tries to hold himself in check.

"I...I wet myself," Kat whispers so softly, I almost missed it. Her face flames red with humiliation as another tear slips free and fuck if that tear and her whisper don't make me want to pick that motherfucking prospect up and shoot him again.

"None of that matters now, Sunshine. Let me help you get cleaned up and then you can tell us what happened." I reach for her hand and help her to her feet, keeping my eye on her face as she winces.

"Kat?" Conan's voice calls from behind me.

She looks over at him, a frown marring her gorgeous face.

"Shit," Conan curses when Kat gasps and grabs her stomach.

Conan shoves me aside before scooping Kat up.

"What the fuck?" I growl at the asshole as he moves to the door.

"She's in labor. We need to get her to the hospital, now," he snaps.

It takes a second for me to place the pieces together, the wince of pain, wetting herself. Fuck. Her water broke, but she was so caught up in what was going on she hadn't put two and two together.

"Wait," Gage stops them from leaving. I move up behind Conan, ready to have my brother and woman's backs, but Gage softens his voice as he looks at Kat.

"Hold on for two minutes for me, okay? I need to know if anyone else is coming in, if this place has cameras, and where's the gun you used?" he questions. Thank fuck one of us is level-headed. My only concern was getting to Kat. I never even thought about the fallout.

"Jimmy will be here in—" she looks at her watch and swallows "—ten minutes. Erm...the gun is on the floor behind the counter and the camera is a fake. The only one that works is the one facing the pumps," she answers before hissing again.

"Alright, go. We'll get this sorted and meet you at the hospital. Don't talk to anyone about what happened here," Gage orders, giving her arm a squeeze before moving over to Halo and Orion who are checking out the dead prospect.

Conan doesn't waste any more time, heading straight out the door to the cage Orion made Jacob drive over.

Opening the back door, Conan climbs in with Kat still on his lap. Fumbling in his pocket for his keys, he tosses them to Jacob in the driver's seat.

"Call one of the others and have them come pick up mine and Inigo's bikes and take them back to the compound."

I pass my keys to him too and when he climbs out of the car, I take his spot in the driver's seat.

"Any damage to either of them and I'll hold you responsible," Conan yells out before I slam the door.

"What's going to happen now?" Kat asks as I pull out of the gas station and make a beeline for the hospital.

"Right now, all you need to worry about is meeting your baby. We'll deal with everything else later, but right now let's just focus on you," I reply, looking at her in the rearview mirror.

"Thank you for coming. I was so scared and for a minute, I was right back at my apartment with David. I..."

"Shhh...none of that matters now, Sunshine. Save your energy," Conan tells her, his voice gruff with emotion as he tucks her head under his chin and holds her tightly.

We make it to the hospital in record time and after a nurse takes her to a private room and helps her change into a hospital gown, we're allowed in.

"Katia tells me you're both her birthing partners." The nurse smiles, showing us inside.

"No way in hell she's doing this without us," I tell her emphatically.

"Sounds like she's in good hands." She turns to look at Kat. "You have a little ways to go yet. Try to rest. I'll come check on you in an hour."

"Okay, thank you." Kat nods, blowing out a breath before the nurse leaves, closing the door behind her.

"You ready to become a mama, Sunshine?" I ask with a grin, moving to sit beside her as Conan sits on the opposite side of the bed. In sync, we each grasp one of her hands in ours, letting her know she's not alone.

"I'm scared. What if I'm a horrible mom? I don't even know what I'm doing."

"Are you kidding? Sunshine, you were born for this. You

fought your way through hell and back for that baby. You loved him even when you didn't love yourself. It's instinctual, love always is. It's why you can't measure or quantify it with words. Trust me, this little guy will be the most loved up baby on the planet.

"Guy?" she asks with a soft smile.

"Just a feeling." I wink.

And four hours later, I'm proved correct when Alex Marley Jones enters the world screaming his head off, looking like a tiny version of the man who made him.

29

Kat

Sleeping soundly in the little hospital-issued bassinet beside me, I can't seem to tear my eyes away from my son.

My son. I have a son.

"Look at the perfection we made, Alex," I whisper into the empty room. I take a moment to try and process everything that has happened in the last twelve hours but it's impossible.

The door cracks open, showing Inigo with two paper drinks cups in his hand, followed by Conan, Orion, and Luna.

"Here, I got you a hot chocolate. I think you earned a little sweetness. You did good, Sunshine. He's perfect," Inigo tells me, handing me one of the cups before placing a kiss on my forehead.

Conan moves to my other side, kissing my cheek before leaning down over Alex, a look of awe on his face.

"Hey, Sunshine, congratulations. Welcome to the sore boob club," Luna says, making me chuckle.

Orion squeezes my foot before pulling up one of the chairs and tugging Luna into his lap.

"I hate doing this shit now, Kat, but I have a body on ice. If I could wait I would."

I hold my hand up to stop him. Orion can be a bit of a hardass but he's been nothing but nice to me, especially after what happened with Alex.

"I'm so sorry. I didn't think about what this would do to the club. Actually, when they first turned up, I dismissed them as a threat because of the alliance between both your clubs."

"Wait, them?" Orion's eyes widen which is when I realize up until this point I had forgotten all about the second guy.

"The tweaker. He ran when I shot cocky in the dick." Now it's Luna's turn to snort. Orion frowns at her but wipes his expression completely when he looks back at me.

"Start from the beginning, Kat," Orion orders and so I do, telling them everything from the moment the prospects entered the gas station until Carnage showed up.

"Jesus Christ, this is a cluster fuck." Orion groans, making me bite my lip.

"I'm sorry." I fidget, wondering what's going to happen to me now. Conan and Inigo press closer, offering me their protection, a fact that doesn't go unnoticed between Orion and Luna.

"Way I see it, the two biggest problems we have are the prospect who ran and whatever his version of events are and the fact that you aren't an old lady," Orion says matter of factly, making my hackles rise.

"Are you saying that because I'm not an old lady, I'm not offered the same protection so I should have let them do whatever they wanted to do to me for the better of the club?" I hiss.

"No, that's not what he's saying, Kat," Luna jumps in, elbowing Orion. "But he is telling you what a lot of other clubs will think, including the Ravens. MC's tend to be run by a bunch of sexist misogynists. Carnage is better than most, but as a general rule it's very much a man's world and in this case, they'll expect retribution. If you were an old lady it would be a moot point because nobody fucks with an old lady and expects to get away with it, but you're a bit of a gray area."

"Fuck that. Sunshine is our old lady, not my problem that those Raven fucks didn't know that. They should have asked," Conan growls out, making me jump.

"Wait, what?"

"That could work." Orion rubs his hand over his chin.

"Make it work or I'll go burn down the Ravens clubhouse my damn self. Nobody touches our old lady and lives," Inigo hisses.

"What the heck? I feel like I've missed something." I look to the men on either side of me but both are focused on Orion.

"You sure this is what you want?" Orion asks them both but by this point, I've had enough.

"Will somebody tell me what the fuck is going on?"

Luna grins at me as Conan reaches for Alex when my voice wakes him.

"Looks like you just landed yourself two old men. No pun intended." Luna chuckles.

"Luna," Orion groans, standing up and wrapping his arm around her.

"Oh come on, that was a good one."

"We'll leave you to talk. I'll come back tomorrow and let you know what the plan is."

He drags a protesting Luna out of the room, closing the door behind him.

I look at Inigo for answers before turning to Conan, my heart melting at the sight of the beast of a man cradling my son as if he's the most precious thing in the world.

"You both just claimed me? Why would you do that?"

"Jesus Christ, Kat. Why wouldn't we do that? You're ours. You have been for months, you just weren't ready to hear it or accept it. I get that this seems out of the blue for you but for us, it's been a long time coming." Inigo rubs his hand over his short beard.

"We made no secret over how we felt, Kat. You needed time and we gave it to you. Hell, we would have waited as long as you needed us to, but this forces our hand. Ravens will be gunning for you, being our old lady offers you the ultimate protection," Conan adds quietly.

"I thought you wanted to fuck me!" I blurt out, face flushing.

Inigo reaches over and tangles a hand in my hair, tipping my head back so I have no choice but to look at him.

"Make no mistake, Sunshine. I want to fuck you until you're raw, but if I just wanted sex I could get it anywhere."

"I'm not Tina," I whisper, feeling everything spiraling out of control.

"I know. And I'm not Alex. Doesn't change a damn thing though. You're ours. Get used to the idea because that's not going to change."

"You can't just—"

His mouth slams down on mine, silencing my words as he destroys my defenses with each stroke of his tongue. He kisses me until I'm boneless before pulling away.

"I get what I want, Sunshine. You'd do well to remember that. You're young, you're used to boys, but you're dealing with a man now, baby," he snarls.

I reach up and surprise us both by slapping him.

"You insult Alex's integrity again and I'll geld you. Let's see how much of a man you are then." I sneer.

"Inigo," Conan barks. "Outside, now!" His voice roars as he places Alex gently in my arms when he starts crying.

Inigo opens the door, slamming it against the wall as he storms outside.

"Feed your little guy and I'll go deal with your big one. He's an ass but it's a front. He wants you to want him as much as he wants you."

"He might want to rethink his approach, Conan, because now the only thing I want to give him is a black eye."

He grins at me. I'm starting to think the guy is certifiable.

"He deserves it. Give me five and I'll be back and we can talk. I'll answer anything you want, but just keep yourself open to the idea. As much of a dick as Inigo can be, he's right about the Ravens. This really is the best way to keep you safe." He presses his lips to mine and kisses me. His kiss is much more leisurely and less demanding than Inigo's but not any less confident. He might be trying to ease me in but that kiss feels like I'm being branded.

Nothing I say now will change anything because as far as they're concerned, I'm already theirs.

30

Conan

I shove Inigo up against the wall and growl at him.

"What the fuck was that?" I seethe.

"Fuck off, Conan." He shoves at me but I don't move.

"No, fuck you. You want to stand there spouting off shit about acting like a man to our girl, then fucking act like one. She has had a fucked up day, barely getting a chance to process one thing before something else is exploding in her face. But instead of giving her a break, you act like a fucking prick. She didn't deserve that and you know it. We knew going into this it wasn't going to be easy. It will always be an uphill battle to win Kat over because she knows exactly what it's like to lose everything. You might be twice her age, Inigo, but right now, you're the one acting like a fucking child. Go and cool off and when you come back, it better be with an apology because being our old lady means I'll protect her to my dying breath, even if that means protecting her from you."

I shove him away and push my way back into Kat's room, closing the door behind me quietly so I don't disturb Alex, freezing when I catch the vision of Kat feeding Alex before me.

Kat flushes, trying to use the hospital sheet to cover Alex suckling her breast but I move toward her and place my hand over hers, halting her movements.

"Don't. You have never looked more beautiful to me than you do right now."

She gasps, looking up at me. She searches my face. I don't know what she's looking for but she must find it because when I let go of her hand, she lowers the cover back down, focusing instead on Alex.

She watches him with such awe and devotion it's hard to picture the scared woman from a few hours ago who worried about what kind of mother she would be.

I know I want to see her like this again and again, carrying and nurturing mine and Inigo's kids until our house is filled with them.

"Kat?"

"Hmm?" She tears her eyes away from Alex and looks up at me.

"We can make you happy. We'll keep you and Alex safe, and I swear to God, you'll never be alone again. Say yes, be ours, but not because of the Ravens, say yes because you feel this thing between us too."

I want her, fuck I want her more than I want air, but I want her to want this too. I can do slow and I refuse to force her into this—all that will build is anger and resentment. Inigo knows this too, only the emotionally stunted asshole pushes back whereas I learned early on that you catch more flies with honey.

"Are you really sure this is what you both want? It's so much more than you signed up for."

She has no fucking clue how much Inigo and I would have sacrificed just to tie this woman to us.

"I've never wanted anything more than I do this. Say yes, Kat."

"I already did. I mean, I wasn't expecting to become your old lady when we decided to see how this played out but I understand why it has to be this way. I'm not mad or disappointed, but I stand by what I said before. I'll give you what I can but my heart is not up for grabs. You'll end up hating me because of it, both of you will, and yet, I can't walk away. Even before all this went down with the Ravens, I couldn't leave and that scares the shit out of me."

"It scares me too, Sunshine. You already met your soul mate, what the fuck could you ever see in an old fucker like me? The thing is, Kat, I'm selfish enough to keep you anyway. I'll take whatever you give me because even a piece of you is better than a life without any part of you at all."

The door opens as Kat covers herself and lifts Alex over her shoulder, tapping his back lightly.

The nurse checks on them both, asking Kat questions, which she answers quietly.

"Okay, well I don't see there being any issues with you going home tomorrow. The doctor will be around after breakfast, he can discharge you then. Do you have someone to collect your things? I know you came here in a bit of a rush but I figured you wouldn't want to go home in our stylish nightwear with your booty hanging out," she teases, making Kat laugh.

"It would be a little drafty, but yes I can get someone to bring our things."

"Excellent. I'm going to leave you to say goodbye then. Visiting hours end in thirty minutes but you can get your things dropped off at the nurse's station and I'll make sure you get them."

"Thank you." Kat smiles, relieved. The nurse nods and leaves, closing the door behind her.

"Is there anything in particular you want me to bring?"

"There are two bags sitting next to the dresser in my room. If you can shove my charger in one of them, then I'll be good to go. I've been preparing for this just in case, I just didn't expect it to go down quite like it did.

"I know, Sunshine, but for the record, I'm so fucking proud of you. This could have gone very differently if you hadn't have kept your head earlier. Instead of watching you bring new life into the world, I could have been saying goodbye."

The thought makes me sick to my stomach, but it also gives me a new appreciation for Kat's strength. If I feel like this now, god, the pain she must have felt losing Alex would have been staggering.

31

Kat

"He's so small, I'm afraid I'll drop him." Wes looks down at Alex in his hands with a spooked expression on his face.

"You've held babies before," I remind him softly, not wanting to dredge up painful memories.

"Trust me, my boys were never this small. He's perfect, Kat, well done."

"Thanks. I'm not gonna lie, being a mom is the most amazingly terrifying thing I've done."

"He's lucky to have you, don't you ever forget it."

I look up at Wes and grin, his eyes dropping to my mouth quickly before he looks away.

"How are you dealing with everything else? The robbery at work and shit?"

The Crown of Fools

I hadn't been able to explain to Wes the whole truth about what went down at the gas station, but I'm not comfortable outright lying to him either. As far as he knows, it was a robbery gone bad and I had been protecting myself.

"Surprisingly, I'm doing okay. It's hard to explain how I feel because I'm not one hundred percent sure myself. I remember everything that happened but when I think about it, it's like it happened to someone else, or I'm watching a movie or something."

"Compartmentalizing, lots of people do it, particularly professionals in fields such as medicine and policing. People would be having nervous breakdowns left and right if they couldn't."

"Huh, I never thought about it like that but it makes sense."

"What about afterward? Any panic attacks or nightmares?"

"Are you a shrink now?" I tease, even though he already told me he was in imports and exports until he took early retirement.

"Hush now, I worry that's all. You seem to be a magnet for trouble."

"Hey," I nudge him gently as he has Alex. "And for your information, no and no. Not gonna lie, it helps to have Inigo and Conan around. Not only are they amazing with Alex but they've been my rocks."

"I'm glad. You deserve to be happy, Kat."

I sigh and look out over the river. Alex is three weeks old and even though I am now officially Inigo and Conan's old lady, nothing has progressed past kissing. One, because my body is still very much out of commission and two, because I'm a nervous wreck just thinking about it.

"What's on your mind, Kat, maybe I can help?'

"Sex. I was thinking about having sex with not just one but two men and how that might work."

When he doesn't answer, I turn to look at him and find his eyes flashing with heat. He coughs and stands, placing Alex back in his stroller, but as he sits back down I catch sight of a very erect dick straining against his pants.

"Oh god, I'm sorry, I wasn't thinking." I feel my face flush with embarrassment and maybe a hint of arousal but I ignore that. I have no idea what to do with the two men I have without adding a third to the mix, not that that's an option.

"It's fine. I eh, just wasn't expecting that."

I shake my head, hoping the ground will open up and swallow me whole.

A finger under my chin has me tilting my head back and staring into Wes's cerulean blue ones.

"You're afraid?" he asks so softly, I strain to hear him.

"Not afraid, nervous. I've only been with one man and we had only just begun to discover a world beyond vanilla sex. I have no idea what they expect from me or if I'll even be any good at it. I have a feeling that Inigo, in particular, might have certain tastes but—" He places a finger over my lips to stop me from speaking.

"You have nothing to worry about, Kat. I'd stake my life on the fact that those men would rather chew off their own arms than hurt you. You're all consenting adults so what you do behind closed doors is up to you, nothing to be ashamed about.

Now as for delving into something a little...less vanilla shall we say? My advice, don't worry about it. If that's what they are looking for then they will teach you and guide you so you can see what you do and don't like and take it from there. Trust them to know when to push and when to pull back. I have a feeling you might discover a whole new side of you, you never knew existed."

"Thank you. No matter what I throw at you, you always manage to talk me down. I'm so glad you sat beside me that day. I never knew how much I needed you."

Pulling me toward him, he tucks me against his chest and wraps his arm around me.

"Trust me, the pleasure has been mine. You've helped me as much as I've helped you. My friend is sick. He's one of the only ties I have left to the life I once had and he's dying. Right now, you're the only thing keeping me sane."

I squeeze his arm and lean my head on his shoulder as we watch the water rush by.

"You should get home before it gets late. I know they'll worry about their...what is it they call you again? Oh, that's right, Sunshine."

I huff out a laugh at that. "I think angel of death might be more accurate these days."

"What's that now?"

"I don't know, just me feeling sorry for myself but I can't help but question if I'm somehow cursed with the number of people that have died around me lately."

"Coincidence, Kat, trust me."

"I know, but first there was Alex. Then my old boss died

when she fell, followed by my landlord." I hedge, remembering at the last minute he doesn't know about what went down with David. "Add in the guy from the robbery and then Jimmy the guy who ran the gas station and I swear, it's making me paranoid."

"How did Jimmy die?" Wes asks with a frown. "He wasn't a part of the robbery was he?"

"No, he had a heart attack while I was in the hospital with Alex."

"Falls and heart attacks happen, you know that. None of it was your fault."

"I guess. Maybe it's just my guilty conscience. After all, everyone who died, except for Alex, affected my life negatively in one way or another."

He turns me a little to face him, a frown marring his face.

"What do you mean they affected your life negatively?"

I chew my lip, realizing I might have said too much.

"Kat, it's important. You can trust me. I won't breathe a word about it to anyone."

"My old boss fired me and I never received my last paycheck. The guy at the gas station that I shot, threatened to rape me. Jimmy refused to pay extra for working security cameras. He sent me a voice mail apologizing but I didn't get it until after he died. My landlord," I cough and rub my hands together, stalling.

"He attacked me and then—"

"Someone attacked him." Wes finishes, looking alarmed.

"Hey, I'm okay, I promise. Conan says I've got Teflon skin."

My words don't comfort him. When his eyes meet mine again, I see a sort of resignation in them.

"Time to get you home. I don't want you out here alone."

"Don't worry, the guys have a prospect following me. They think they're so sneaky but I've caught him a time or two in the distance."

His eyes widen at my words as he looks around. "Come on, I'll walk you to your car and help you get Alex settled."

"Wes, are you alright? You're kind of freaking me out." He seems jumpy and if there was one thing I knew about Wes it's that the guy is never jumpy. He's calmness personified.

"Yeah, I'm fine, Kat." He flashes me a grin but it doesn't quite touch his eyes.

We don't speak as he pushes Alex's stroller toward my car. I don't ask him how he knew where I'd parked, the guy seems to have an innate sense about things.

He carefully lifts Alex out of the stroller after I open the back door and he straps him in while I fold up the stroller and place it in the trunk.

Closing it, I stand there for a minute, rubbing my arms as a chill works itself into my skin.

The door closes and Wes walks toward me, stopping just in front of me.

"I'm not going to see you again, am I?" I don't know how I know it but I do.

"I have to go away for a little while, but this isn't goodbye, Kat."

I feel the tears slide down my cheeks and I don't even bother trying to stop them.

"Why?" I choke out.

"There are things about me you don't know. Things in motion that—" He stops talking and sighs, stepping forward and wrapping his arms around me.

"I'll be back. I promise, Kat. I swear it on my life. I'm not sure I could leave you if I tried."

Tipping my head back, I look up into his pretty blue eyes and nod.

"Don't be just another person who lets me down. I'm trusting you, Wes."

His lips press against mine for a moment, then with a sad smile, the man who became my best friend, turns and walks away.

32

Kat

I hum softly as I rock Alex gently back and forth, soothing him back to sleep. The house is silent, not even the hum of the refrigerator can be heard from here. It's almost enough to make me feel like we're the only two people in the universe.

It's been four weeks since I last saw Wes and although I miss him, I've decided to just let it go. Whatever it is he's doing isn't about me, I need to be supportive. He'll come back when he's ready and if he doesn't, then he isn't the man I thought he was.

I wait until I know Alex is out for the count before laying him back down gently in his bassinet.

I stand and watch him for a moment, taking a mental snapshot and filing it away in a memory box for when he's grown and flown the nest.

Switching on the monitor, I tiptoe out of the room, pulling the door closed gently behind me.

Turning, I suck in a shocked gasp when I find myself pressed up against a hard naked chest.

"He asleep?"

I open my mouth to answer but my brain is focused on all that hard muscle pressed against me so the only sound that comes out is a whimper.

"You done fighting it?" Inigo crowds me, pushing me against the door. I look up into his eyes, as they burn so hot I swear I can feel flames licking over my skin.

I nod, not trusting myself to open my mouth again without embarrassing myself but my nod is all the permission he needs. Hands at my hips lift me up and without hesitation, I wrap my legs around his hips. He turns with me in his arms and leads me to my room, the heat of his hands scorching me through my clothing, or lack thereof. Finding myself pressed against Inigo in nothing more than one of his T-shirts and a pair of panties, I somehow feel both naked and overdressed at the same time.

He walks us over to my bed and lays me on it before stepping back to gaze down at me.

He doesn't say anything, he doesn't need to. His eyes and actions say more than words could ever convey.

I watch hungrily as he pops the button on his jeans and lowers the zipper before shoving his jeans and boxers down his legs, leaving him naked. My gaze drifts from his face, over his chest, down his stomach, to his happy trail, before leading to his hard cock.

My mouth waters at the sight and a tingle pulses between my legs that I try to alleviate by rubbing my thighs together, but Inigo is having none of it.

"No, you don't, Sunshine. This pussy is mine now. You don't touch it unless I say so. Any pleasure you get will come from my hand, my tongue, my cock. The only time that changes is when Conan joins us."

I nod because I want that dick inside me and if we argue he'll withhold himself. Besides, what he doesn't know won't hurt him.

"Oh, I see what you're thinking there, Sunshine. Do it, I dare you. I'd love nothing more than to blister your ass, and then when it's burning, I'll fuck it hard and fast until you're screaming my name."

"Fuck." I think I just came.

"Oh, you like the sound of that don't you, my dirty girl?"

I still don't speak. There's a possibility I've been rendered mute because, for the first time in my life, words fail me.

Leaning over me, Inigo's large hands slide up my thighs, hooking my underwear with his fingers before roughly pulling them down my legs and tossing them aside. Without preamble, he spreads my legs wide before staring down at my pussy, looking ravenous.

I squirm under his intense gaze as lust slams into me full force. I've only ever been with one man. Alex and I grew up together. We learned what each other liked and our sex life had been amazing but our experiences were limited to what we knew, which wasn't much beyond what we heard people talk about and what we saw in movies.

I might not know much, but I instinctively know that my experience with Conan and Inigo will be vastly different. They have twenty years on me. They've discovered what they like, what they don't, and how to please a woman in a hundred different ways. Most of me is curious and excited to see what else there is to experience but a small part of me worries about how they'll feel if I fail to meet their expectations. I'm not a virgin obviously, but that doesn't mean I'm not sexually naive in a lot of ways. Hell, if they ask me what I want, I'm not sure what I would say. I'm open and willing to try most things but too scared to ask in case I back myself into a corner I can't get out of.

A slap to my pussy has me screeching as I try to pull away but Inigo holds me in place.

"When you're in this bed with me, I want all parts of you. Not just your pussy, but your brain. If you're with me, you're with me and no one else," he scolds.

The slap itself, although shocking, didn't hurt but I never expected to feel a rush of wetness because of it either.

"I wasn't thinking of anyone else," I reply softly because I know he's talking about Alex, not Conan.

"What were you thinking about then, Sunshine? Because I have to say it's not good for a man's ego when he's between his woman's thighs and she's mentally somewhere else."

Sliding down so he's lying on his stomach, he pushes my legs open as far as they'll go before dipping his head and inhaling deeply.

My skin burns hotly with mortification and something else, something more primal as I lift my hips without thought.

"You want me to lick this pretty pussy, Sunshine?"

"Yes," I hiss when he draws back to look at me.

"Tell me what you were thinking," he orders. I want to scream but I know it will be pointless. I might be Miss Independent outside this room but lying half-naked before Inigo, I know he's the one in control right now.

"I'm nervous. What if...what if you decide I'm not experienced enough to satisfy you? Well, not just you but Conan? I don't know what I'm doing and I'm so far out of my element that I'm freaking out and getting stuck in my head," I babble, revealing far more than I planned.

Instead of looking disappointed, Inigo looks like the cat that got the cream. Okay, just thinking that analogy makes my stomach cramp with need because if I play my cards right, I'll be the Kat he licks the cream from.

"Your innocence is what makes me lose my mind, Sunshine. I've been with many women, all different shapes and sizes, different flavors, different tastes but there is only one type of woman I'm looking for."

When he doesn't elaborate, I ask. "What kind is that?" I mumble, not sure if I'm prepared for the answer.

"I want one who'll be malleable."

I tense, not sure I like the sound of that.

"I want someone to teach, someone who I can praise when they've been good and someone I can punish when they're being bad. I want you to do what I say when I say, no questions asked," he tells me before pressing two fingers against my lips.

"Suck."

I open my mouth and do as he asks, lathing his fingers with my tongue as I try to process his words.

Pulling them free, he presses them against my clit, swirling them around the hardened nub, making me cry out.

"I...I don't know if I can do that," I admit. I don't want to have my whole life controlled. I fought too hard to be strong just to let someone else come in and take it away from me.

He plunges those wet fingers inside me, making me thrust my hips but he pins me in place so I can't move.

"You can. In fact, you want to. You've been so strong for so long, let someone else take care of you," he urges as he strokes his fingers over a spot inside me that makes my back arch as he loosens his hold a little.

"I'm not weak," I cry out, making him stop and frown.

"Why the fuck would you think that? Giving your power willingly to someone else doesn't make you weak, it makes you brave. Plus, it's yours to give so if I ever abuse it, it's yours to take away. I'm not planning on locking you in a cage, sweetheart. In fact, I'm not planning on taking anything away from you. I want to give you something instead."

"What do you want to give me?" I ask before he twists his fingers and dips his head to suck on my clit. I come so hard and fast for a moment I forget to breathe. When the air rushes back into my lungs and white spots dance behind my eyes, I realize the power this man could have over me. With just two fingers, he has me ready to get on my knees and beg for more.

But begging isn't my style and I'm not sure how comfortable I am with it.

33

Inigo

I lick her clean, savoring the taste of her honey on my tongue before looking up at her flushed face and seeing the confusion in her eyes.

"Talk to me. Ask me what you want and I'll answer. I won't lie to you, Kat. I can't guarantee you'll always be happy with my answer but I won't lie to you."

"Can we do this when your face isn't inches from my pussy because I can't think straight knowing your tongue's that close to me," she admits, making me chuckle.

I climb up on the bed and tug the comforter over my lap as Kat sits up.

Reaching for her, I pull her onto my lap. I know she can feel how hard my cock is beneath her but she'll have to get used to it. My cock is always hard around her and that's unlikely to change anytime soon.

"This isn't helping either," she complains as she wiggles around in my lap.

"Keep rubbing that fuckable ass of yours over my dick and I'll fuck you before having this conversation. I'm already feeling like a saint for stopping as it is."

She huffs but settles down with her legs on either side of my hips and her hot pussy pressed against my abs.

She looks like she's struggling to find the right words but patience has never been my strong point, especially when I'm so close to everything I've ever wanted.

"Speak now, Kat. Ask me whatever you want before I shove my cock in your mouth and you can't speak at all."

"Alright! Yeesh," she snaps, making my lips twitch. That's gonna earn her a spanking.

"When you say you want control, do you mean in all aspects of my life or just in the bedroom?"

"That's not as easy to answer as you might think. Predominantly in the bedroom, yes, but there will be times it naturally bleeds into other areas. I want to take care of you. No, I need to take care of you. It's not about me thinking you're incapable of doing it yourself. It's about me wanting someone to trust me to take care of them in all areas of their life."

She swallows hard but doesn't pull away. "Can you give me an example of what that means outside of the bedroom?"

I look at her, take in her flushed cheeks and the way she bites her lip as she looks up at me under her lashes.

"You don't seem bothered by the bedroom side of things. In

fact, I bet your pussy is dripping at the thought of me taking complete control." She's panting and squirming now like she might come just from my words alone.

"I've not had the chance to experiment much in the bedroom and although I'm not one hundred percent sure of what you want, I'm willing to see if I like it because I know you'll stop if I don't like it."

"I'll push your boundaries, make no mistake about that, but I'll never force you to do something you don't want. You're right. As for outside the bedroom, it will mostly be things that seem innocuous to others but they mean something to me."

"Like telling me what to wear?" she asks apprehensively.

"I like you the way you are, Sunshine. I don't want to change you, but sure, if you come downstairs in a short skirt to go out in and neither Conan nor myself will be with you, then you better believe you'll be leaving with a red ass underneath a pair of jeans."

She rocks against me a little, my words not putting her off in the slightest.

"Why do I have a feeling you're gonna be a brat?" I groan when she squirms again and grins at me unrepentantly.

"I don't know what you're talking about. What else?"

I frown, gripping her hips to still her movements. "When we are out in public, I want you sitting in either mine or Conan's lap. If we tell you to do something and it's to do with your safety and protection, we'll expect you to do it with no questions asked."

She looks at me, her eyes softening a little. "What else?"

"Honestly, it's a million small things like that. If you agree to it, you'll learn what I teach as we go along. It will be a learning curve for us all."

"And if I'm bad?" she teases. I feel my cock weep in anticipation.

"Then you'll get punished, sweetheart. That could mean a spanking, or being denied an orgasm. What will never happen is Conan or I using our fists to hurt you, or using our words to make you feel small. You might not get pleasure from punishment but we sure as hell won't cause you any harm, that I promise. Just the thought of harm coming to you makes me feel physically sick."

"I...don't have to call you daddy, do I? I can get on board with most of this I think, but calling you daddy is where I draw the line. It reminds me too much of some of the so-called father figures who looked at me just a little too long in foster care."

"No, I don't need you to call me daddy." I grin before her words penetrate. "We will be revisiting this conversation about foster care though," I warn her, wanting to know the names and addresses of these men who made her feel uncomfortable.

"Hey, it's okay. It was a long time ago, and when Alex came along, he kept me safe."

She cups my tense jaw with both her hands, tips my head down, and looks at me.

"I want to try, but what if it just doesn't work? What if—"

I seal my lips over hers and wind my hands into her hair, cutting off the last of her words.

I already know she's naturally submissive, I just need her to get out of her head long enough to give it a try.

I yank my lips free from hers before grabbing the hem of her T-shirt and pulling it up and over her head.

"One day at a time. Baby steps, and I'll be there teaching you every step of the way."

"Okay," she agrees softly as I reveal her body. She looks like a fucking supermodel, her spectacular tits even bigger than before, thanks to her breastfeeding Alex.

"Good girl. You won't regret it. Now I want you to slide up the bed and lie down, spread your legs wide for me, and hold them open with your hands."

She does as I ask without complaint. I take her in and wonder again how the fuck I ended up here.

Moving closer, I bend and place a chaste kiss against the inside of one of her ankles. She shudders but doesn't move her hands away from her thighs which pleases me.

"Good girl, keep those hands there until I tell you to move them."

I wait for her to nod before trailing kisses up the inside of her leg and her inner thigh to her pussy.

Her breath hitches but I bypass where she needs me most and work kisses down the other leg ending at the arch of her foot.

"Inigo, please, I need you."

"Patience, Sunshine," I murmur, crawling up her body. My cock lays heavy against her slick pussy but I don't slip inside her, not yet.

I flick my tongue over one of her swollen nipples before sucking, groaning when the taste of her milk hits my tongue.

"Are you on birth control? Because I don't ever want there to be anything between us," I ask her, part of me hoping she isn't. I'm not getting any younger and despite having Alex, I want nothing more than to fill her with my seed and watch her grow round with my kid.

"I had an IUD fitted after Alex and I'm clean." She pants, her arms trembling now as she grips her thighs.

"I'm clean too. I'd never do anything to put you at risk. You gonna let me take you bare, Sunshine?" I groan, grinding my cock against her clit.

"Yes, please fuck me, Inigo."

"Hands and knees pretty girl, I want to see that ass."

I move back, giving her just enough space to flip over.

"Press your tits to the bed and get your ass up high. Don't come until I tell you to."

"Holy fucking hell. What the fucking heck have I got myself into?" She gasps, making me grin as I drag the head of my cock through her slick folds, bumping her clit over and over until she whimpers.

"You ready, Sunshine? I'm too far gone to be anything other than hard and fast. Can you handle that?"

"Do it. Fuck me, Inigo," she begs, moments before I surge inside her.

Cupping her ass, I plow into her over and over, the lewd sound of our skin slapping together spurring me on.

The heat coils and twists inside me like a ravenous snake begging for release.

"Inigo," she groans. I've been toying with her, keeping her on edge so much that the barest touch against her clit will likely send her over.

"Not yet, Sunshine. Not until I say so," I grit out, picking up speed. My thrusts are so forceful, I feel Kat inch up the bed with each push forward.

This isn't a declaration of love but a declaration of ownership. I'm calling the shots and Sunshine's just along for the ride.

But fuck, what a ride it is.

"Please, I can't," she whimpers, even as she thrusts back against me, the need to come riding her hard.

"Not yet, Sunshine," I growl, thundering into her before reaching around and strumming her clit.

"Now, Sunshine, come!"

She screams my name as a wave of sensation washes away all sense of reality for a moment before rushing back in. With a roar, I shoot my cum deep inside her, triggering tiny orgasmic aftershocks that make her pussy ripple around me, milking my cock.

"Good fucking god, Sunshine. I might never let you out of this bed again."

34

Conan

The house is quiet when I get back. Glancing at my watch, I note it's 3 am, so Alex would have likely already been up for his night feed and gone back to sleep again.

I'm not one for sentimental attachments, but Kat and Alex have changed that and I'm not too proud to admit I missed the little guy while I was gone.

I kick my boots off and shrug out of my cut, hanging it next to Inigo's on the coat rack beside the door.

Locking up, I make my rounds of the house, checking the windows and the back door too, just for peace of mind. It's been years since I left the military, but some habits die hard.

Creeping up the stairs, I peek in on Alex and see him fast

asleep, so I pull the door closed and head to Kat's room to check on her.

Pushing the door open, I pause when I spot Inigo lying beside her.

Damn, now I know I missed out.

He turns his head, sensing me.

"How did it go?"

"No problems. The streets were quiet tonight, which makes a nice change. The cargo was delivered and we were in and out in record time."

Some runs are easy but when you live in the gray area of life, you learn not to get too complacent. I nudge my head at a sound asleep Kat sprawled across his chest.

"Looks like you guys had a good evening."

Even in the darkened room, his grin is blinding. "You have no idea. Get in, she missed you tonight. She'd be happy to see you when she wakes up. Besides, it's time she gets used to how things are gonna be from now on."

"You talk to her, about what you want from her, I mean?" I question as I quietly strip off my clothes and toss them in the corner before carefully pulling back the covers and climbing in behind Kat without disturbing her.

"I did." He blows out a relieved breath. I know it's been eating him alive holding himself back.

"She's open to all of it. We just need to ease her in."

I grin myself now. "How was she?"

"Fucking spectacular."

I press a kiss between her shoulder blades, biting back a groan when she wriggles her naked ass back into me.

Slipping my hand over her hip, I let myself drift off to sleep, feeling content for the first time in as long as I can remember.

Hours later, I'm roused from a particularly hot dream by the sounds of a gasp beside me.

My eyes snap open as I turn to find Sunshine gripping the sheets with her head thrown back and Inigo on his knees between her legs.

Enthralled by the vision before me, I don't make a sound to alert either of them that I'm awake. I watch Inigo tease and torture Kat and her reactions to him. I don't see any hesitation, not even a tiny bit, which shows in how oblivious she is to me watching her.

"Come on my tongue, Sunshine," Inigo orders, and like a trigger, her back arches and her lips part on a silent scream as she comes.

"Christ, you're beautiful," I whisper, making her head whip around to face me.

And that's when Alex starts to cry, reminding us all that a day of fucking isn't in the cards for us.

"I'll go," I offer, knowing Inigo won't feel right unless he gives Sunshine a little aftercare after whatever went down between them last night. Besides, I'm a patient man.

"Conan?" Kat calls my name, unsure.

"Everything's good, Kat. I've missed the little guy. Besides, I'm all about delayed gratification. My dick might hate me for it now, but later when I slip into your slick pussy, it will have been worth it."

"Um, okay, he's probably hungry," she tells me.

"Then I'll bring him to his mama. Stop worrying, Kat, I've got this."

I climb out of bed and slip on a clean pair of boxers and a white T-shirt and follow the sound of Alex's cry.

When I open the door, the smell hits me.

"Fucking hell, little man, how can something so cute smell so fucking evil?" I grimace, but at the sound of my voice, he stops crying.

I lean over him and pick him up, feeling a wave of protectiveness rush over me. I never gave much thought to having kids before Kat but this little guy is quickly changing that for me.

Even so, if Kat decides she doesn't want any more, knowing I get to play a father figure role in this little guy's life will be more than enough.

"Okay, first things first. Let's get you changed, okay?" I coo as I walk him over to the changing table.

"You know, I've had to be persuasive with people before in order to get them to tell me things that perhaps they didn't want to tell me. I...use my toys to play with them until they finally spill their secrets but your dirty diapers could be a game-changer. One wave of this bad boy and they would admit to anything."

"Please tell me you're not talking about torturing people to the poor boy." Inigo appears in the doorway with a grin on his face. "Holy fuck, little man. What have you been eating?"

I smirk, his reaction just proves my point.

"Grab me a clean onesie. Sunshine okay?"

"She's in the shower. She won't be long. Any news from the Ravens?"

"Orion spoke to Blade. He's trying to calm Bear the fuck down but with the dead prospect being Bear's little brother, he isn't listening to reason right now. Blade's warned him that if he retaliates it will be the last thing he does, but I don't trust the fuck one little bit."

"What about the missing prospect, the tweaker who can corroborate Sunshine's story?" He grunts, about as happy about this whole thing as me.

"Still nothing. It's as if the guy disappeared into thin air. We have both Carnage and Ravens looking for him. He'll turn up eventually but until then, there isn't much we can do.

"Sunshine doesn't go anywhere without a prospect. I don't care if she's just popping out for tampons. I want eyes on her."

"I already spoke to Diesel. He's assigned Jacob to watch over her until shit dies down. Here." He hands me a little onesie with the words *lock up your daughters* emblazed on the front.

Laughing, I manage to wriggle the little guy into the suit as Inigo makes faces at him to keep him occupied.

"There, good as new. Now how about we see if your mama is free to open up the boobie buffet?" I tease, picking him up and laying him over my shoulder.

"Gotta say after sampling what's on the menu, I'm a big fan." Inigo laughs, shoving the dirty diaper into the disposal unit and tossing the dirty clothes in the laundry basket in the corner.

"Alright you smug bastard," I grumble, heading down to the kitchen to the sound of Inigo laughing.

35

Kat

"Hey, Kat, I have to head to the office and grab some blueprints. You mind if I take Alex? The guys have heard me talking about him and would like to meet him." Inigo stands in the doorway of the laundry room as I empty the dryer.

"Erm...Sure, if you want. I pumped earlier so there's a couple of bottles in the fridge and his bag is on the hook by the door."

I look down at Alex sitting in his bouncer and smile. "You wanna go play with Inigo, huh?" I undo his straps and lift him, feeling how much he's filling out already. I kiss his head and place him into Inigo's waiting arms. "My keys are on the counter," I add, looking up at Inigo.

"I'm not taking that piece of crap and I don't want you using it either. The truck is yours to use whenever you need it. Think of Alex's safety," he throws in before I can protest.

"Fine, you win this time."

He grins and presses a kiss to my cheek. "I'll get Conan to grab his seat, then we'll be off. Say bye to mama, little man."

Inigo lifts Alex's arm in a waving motion, making me smile. "Bye, baby. Be good for Inigo."

I get back to the arduous task of folding clothes, knowing Alex is in good hands and that this pile of baby clothes won't fold itself.

I finally pair up the last of the world's smallest socks when I hear Conan calling my name.

Leaving the basket on the dryer for now, I make my way through the house, wondering where the heck he is when I'm pounced on from behind.

I scream my freaking head off until I realize it's Conan. "You asshole." I shove him but it's like pushing a wall. Stupid giant. "You nearly gave me a heart attack."

"I'm sorry, Sunshine, let me make it up to you," he mumbles in my ear, making goosebumps break out all over my skin.

"What do you have in mind?" I ask, intrigued.

"I was thinking about spreading you out over the kitchen table and eating you until you scream."

I gasp and my stomach clenches. "I'm okay with this plan."

"Good, because I'm fucking starving," Conan growls before he grips my T-shirt and literally rips it from my body.

"Holy fuck, Conan!"

"It was in my way," he grumbles, shoving my shorts and

panties down my legs. Lifting me, he presses his lips to mine as I grind my bare pussy against him.

He walks us over to the table, leans down, and using one arm, he sends the contents crashing to the ground.

Placing me gently on top of the table, he groans. "Pull your bra down, Sunshine, I want to see all of you."

I do as he asks, tugging it down until my breasts spill free.

Conan's huge hands slide up the inside of my thighs as he pushes them wide. Bending, he buries his face between my legs and swipes his tongue across my clit before sucking hard.

"Ahhhh." I grip the edge of the table as Conan proceeds to school me in oral. Using his tongue to flick, lick, and stroke me into a quivering mess.

"Conan, please," I beg as he grins against me.

"What's that, Sunshine? You want more?"

I couldn't answer him if I tried because he chooses that moment to start fucking me with his tongue.

My orgasm crashes into me with the force of a freight train, making me scream loud enough for the neighbors to likely call the police.

"Bad girl, Sunshine," he growls, lapping away at me. "I never gave you permission to come."

"I didn't even know I was going to come until it hit me around the head like a two by four. Jesus, Conan, I'm going to need you to do that, like every single day for the rest of my life," I tell him in breathless awe.

"I think I can manage that, Sunshine." He laughs, tugging me into a sitting position.

"Can I return the favor?"

"There will never come a time when you have to ask permission to suck my cock, darlin'. You want him, and I'll stop whatever I'm doing for you, trust me."

I laugh until he opens his fly and pulls his dick out.

"Erm, what is that?"

Conan looks down at his dick and frowns. "What's what?"

"That!" I hiss, pointing at his cock. "Please tell me you got stung by a bee and the swelling is because of an allergic reaction."

He roars with laughter, but I'm not finding anything funny.

"Giant man, giant cock, babe. That's kind of how it goes." He shrugs casually while I just stare at it.

"Keep looking at it like that, Sunshine, and we'll move straight to fucking."

I hop off the table and move away from him, his laughter dying as he watches me warily.

Shit. I never meant to hurt his feelings. I mean, I really should be nice because if he swings that bat-like dick around I'll end up with a concussion. Fuck.

I assume a lunge position and stretch my leg before swapping to the other all the while reminding myself that I've just had a kid. How hard can it be?

"What are you doing?" Conan asks, taking a step toward me, frowning.

"I'm limbering up. I don't want to sprain my vagina."

"Sprain your—" And that's when he starts choking.

I'm not sure what's so funny. "You done?" I snark, hands on my hips.

He stops laughing at my tone, his eyes roving over my body, leaving a trail of fire in their wake.

"Oh, Sunshine. I'm just getting started."

Pulling out one of the kitchen chairs, he sits on it, gliding his hand up and down his anaconda. Er, I mean cock.

"I wanna fuck you so bad, Sunshine. You can handle it, I know you can."

"Oh god, help me. If I end up in the ER, please make up a really cool story."

"I'm not going to let anything happen to you, Sunshine. Are you okay with me going bare? I'm clean."

"Yeah, me too and I have an IUD. At the risk of sounding like I'm mounting a horse, can you help me on?"

He grins smugly, really making me want to headbutt him. I blow out a breath and grip his shoulders as he picks me up and holds me over his dick.

"Rub your clit for me," he orders, all humor gone from his voice.

I do as he asks, strumming my fingers over my clit as Conan lines up his cock with my wet slit and ever so slowly slides me down his hot, hard length.

I hiss as he fills me to full dick capacity, making me burn as my body adjusts to his size.

Once he's fully seated inside me, we both start panting and when I use the rungs at the side of the chair to push up, slowly gliding up Conan's cock, it's his turn to hiss and moan.

Yeah, payback's a bitch, baby.

Letting the rush of sensation rule me, I fuck Conan nice and slow until we're both losing our minds.

"Conan," I warn him when I know I can't hold back any longer.

His name spilling from my lips snaps the last of his restraint. He grips my hips and guides me up and down, harder and faster until he pushes into me as far as he can go and boom, it's game over. I clamp down around him and bury my face in his neck as I come even harder than I did the first time, this time dragging Conan right along with me.

"That, that..." Conan mutters, struggling to catch his breath.

"That was epic." I grin and wince when I feel him twitch inside me.

"I think though, at this juncture, it's important I let you know that you and I will never be attempting anal."

And that's when the big bastard starts laughing again.

What's so damn funny?

36

Kat

I take the card from the cashier and thank her just as my phone rings.

Grumbling, I curse myself for tossing it in my bag like I always do as I begin the game of *can I find it before it stops ringing.*

And the answer is no. I almost give up but when it starts ringing again, I know it must be something important.

Finally, my fingertips brush against it, making me shake my ass in a victory dance as I grin at the open-mouthed teenage boy holding the door open for me.

"Hey, Luna, what's up?" I ask, wedging the phone under my chin as I make my way to the car. Unlocking it, I pop the trunk and stow the shopping bags as Luna curses down the phone.

"Woah, slow down and move somewhere else. You're

breaking up and every word I'm getting is either fuck or shit and I'm guessing you didn't call just to cuss me out."

I hear shuffling as I slam the trunk closed and push the cart into the corral before Luna starts talking, far clearer now.

"Okay, I need a huge favor. I know this is the first time you've been out without your adorable boob ornament, but Ruby's daycare just called to say they've had a flood and she needs collecting early. Orion is on a job, Gage is on a run, and Halo isn't answering his damn cell. I have a flat tire, the prospect is changing it now but you're just around the corner from her and you already have a car seat, would you mind fetching her for me?"

"Of course not, can you give them a call so they know to expect me? I don't want to get there and get turned away."

"On it. Oh, and the password is footlong."

I snort at that. Now, why do I get the feeling it has nothing to do with a sandwich and everything to do with Orion?

"Thanks, Kat. I promise I'll watch Alex for you to make up for it."

"Please, it's fine. I filled my kid-free day with chores and shopping anyway. Not exactly a day at the spa."

I buckle up and switch to Bluetooth before pulling out of my spot.

"Even better, I'll get the guys to watch the kids and you and I can have a mommy day."

"Now that, I can get behind. I'll let you go so you can call the daycare. See you in a few."

I hang up and drive through town, turning in the opposite

direction I would normally take if I was heading back home, and make my way to Sunny Acres Nursery.

I turn on the radio and bob to the latest Bieber tune as I drive over the bridge. Traffic is still pretty quiet as it's too early for the rush hour crush. Even with the detour, I'll still be home before the guys with plenty of time to set up for tonight's surprise. I found a sexy little number online that looked like it would be sexy and yet flattering on my post-pregnancy body. Not that the guys don't like me just the way I am, but it's still an adjustment to look in the mirror and see stretch marks and a little pooch that I'm still trying to work off.

Pulling up outside the daycare, I manage to find a spot near the doors despite it being crowded as other parents come to collect their kids early, some looking happy to spend more time with their kiddos, others looking frustrated.

I head to the reception and let the woman at the desk know who I'm here to collect, show her my ID, and just about manage to hold back a smirk when I give her the password.

Grinning, she unlocks the security door and shows me to the room Ruby is in, listening to a story with a few of the other remaining kids.

They all turn at the sound of the door opening but when Ruby's eyes land on mine she squeals before climbing to her feet and running toward me. I drop into a squat and catch her as she plows into me. I wrap my arms around her small frame, lift her off her feet, and perch her on my hip.

"Hey, sweet girl. You have fun today?" She nods then pops a thumb in her mouth before tucking her head under my chin.

"It's usually nap time now so the last few are all tuckered

out," one of the staff members tells me as she walks over, handing me Ruby's backpack.

"If she's anything like my son, she'll be asleep before I'm even halfway home."

"Oh for sure. Can you let Mom know that she didn't eat much at lunch today? She was a little fussy and felt a little warm earlier but she perked up somewhat this afternoon."

"Sure, no problem. Thanks." I smile as Ruby waves goodbye, then head out front, waiting for the receptionist to let us out. I toss Ruby's bag on the backseat then fasten her in as her eyes already start to droop.

I grab Alex's blanket, kept in the car for just this kind of occasion, and tuck it around her. I close the door as quietly as I can before climbing into the driver's seat.

I wait for freaking ages to get out of the parking lot as parents who couldn't find a space park willy-nilly, blocking cars in and making it impossible for the flow of traffic to get past.

It isn't until I'm heading toward the bridge that I realize I have no clue if Luna wants Ruby dropped at her place or the clubhouse.

Calling her, I look in the review mirror and see Ruby fast asleep. There's a car almost on my bumper so I signal for them to pass me, not knowing yet if I need to turn off at the next junction.

"Hey, Kat. You get her okay?" Luna's voice comes through the car's Bluetooth.

"Yep, she passed out in the car seat before I'd even left the parking lot. I forgot to ask where you want me to drop her though—"

The Crown of Fools

My words cut off when I realize how close the asshole behind me is.

"Move dickhead," I growl, signaling again. Fucking tailgaters.

"What's wrong?" Luna asks, concerned.

"Nothing, just some asshole trying to climb up my ass. No lube no love asshole!" I yell before remembering Ruby's asleep. Luckily the kid grew up around the clubhouse and can sleep through anything. "So home or the clubhouse? Son of a bitch!" I bite out when the car behind bumps me.

"Kat? What's happening?" Luna asks, her voice losing its worried tone as she slips into her no-fuss business persona.

"The car behind me just hit my bumper." I shut up when the car hits me again, which is right around the time I figure out this isn't just an accident because the guy's an impatient asshole. He's aiming for me.

"Luna, I think he's trying to run me off the road." Now it's my voice that shakes.

"Floor it, Kat. Come straight to the clubhouse. I'll get one of the guys to call the prospect on you and see if he can get the fucker. I'm sending some guys to your car's GPS coordinates right now, I promise. Just hold on, okay?"

He hits me again, making the tail end of the car veer dangerously to the left. I struggle to correct without slowing down. My heart feels like it's about to beat out of my chest.

"Kat!"

I whimper when I hear Conan roar my name. He must have grabbed Luna's phone.

"Conan," I whimper, crying out when the car is rammed

again just before I make it onto the bridge. I oversteer but manage to right it before I hit the railing.

"I'm coming for you, baby. Just hold on." Before I can answer, a scream rips free as the car hits us with enough force to push me into the barrier.

There's nothing I can do to stop the inevitable and as the car smashes through the railing, I hear Ruby's terrified screams mix with mine as we plummet into the water below.

37

Conan

Her scream will haunt me for the rest of my life.

"Take Alex, I have to go." I place Alex as gently as I can in Rebel's arms before turning and running for the door, the sound of pounding boots behind me letting me know I'm not alone.

I head straight for my truck, which I brought instead of the bike because of Alex. Hopping in the driver's seat, I whip my head around when Luna climbs into the passenger seat.

"Luna—" I shut my mouth when she turns and glares at me, tears streaming down her face.

"Just drive, Conan," she spits out in a voice I don't recognize. "Don't tell me to wait here. That's my fucking baby down there." Her voice cracks as she swallows a sob.

I reach over and grab her hand as I fire up the truck and

make my way out of the compound.

"Head to the bridge. Jacob and Linc should be arriving there any time now."

"Why wasn't Jacob on her?" I grit out, fisting the steering wheel hard enough to make it creak.

"He called it in. Someone slashed his tires so Linc went to help him. When I called, they both jumped on Linc's bike and headed straight there. They'll be there before us," she answers in a whisper.

"Call your men, Luna," I remind her softly.

"I don't want to worry them."

I look at her and read between the lines. She doesn't want to call them because saying it out loud makes it real.

"Call your men, Luna," I repeat softly but firmly. She looks at me and nods her head, pulling out her cell as I take a deep breath and prepare to do the same.

"Call Inigo," I tell the Bluetooth and listen as it rings, ignoring Luna softly crying as she talks on the phone. If I focus on her, I'll never make it through this phone call. I squeeze her hand and suck in a sharp breath when Inigo answers.

"How goes daddy duty?" he asks with a chuckle.

"Inigo…" My voice sounds like I've swallowed gravel.

"What? What is it?"

"It's Kat. Head to the bridge, I'll meet you there."

"Head to the bridge? What the fuck are you talking about?"

"Kat's been in an accident, just hurry." I hang up, not giving him any more details, which makes me a prick but if he's riding his bike over I need him to keep his wits about him. Him getting in an accident won't help anyone.

"Orion's on his way back. Gage is swinging by to pick up Halo. He's at the gun range, which is likely why he didn't pick up."

She blows out a breath but quickly sucks in another and another and another making me realize she's on the verge of a panic attack.

"Luna, just breathe. We don't know what's going on right now. They could be fine by the time we get there, sitting there pissed off and waiting for us to get our shit together. Don't write them off yet, Luna."

"That's my little girl, Conan. I can't lose her. I just can't, but she's so small and she can't swim and—"

"But Kat can. She was on the swim team in high school and she will treat Ruby as if she had Alex in her arms. If there is any way for Kat to get Ruby to safety, she'll do it and she won't stop until her last breath." I try to comfort not just her, but myself too.

We remain quiet for the rest of the journey, so lost in our own terrifying thoughts we don't have any words of comfort left for each other.

When we pull up, it's pandemonium. The bridge is blocked off with emergency vehicles and motorcycles are laid down in the road where brothers had rushed to help.

I barely have the truck stopped before Luna is out and I'm right behind her, shoving law enforcement officers out of the way as they try to stop us.

We run around the edge of the bridge and slide down the embankment, me grabbing Luna's arms to stop her from falling too fast. We both freeze when we hear the unmistakable cry of a child screaming. Our heads whip up, then Luna sobs and virtually collapses as Linc emerges from the water with a crying Ruby wrapped in his arms.

As if someone presses fast forward, we rush to the river's edge as Jacob's head appears from the middle of the river, gasping for air but empty-handed. The current tugs him as he tries to get his bearings. I look around and can't see Kat or the car anywhere. Rusty rushes into the water and grabs hold of Jacob as he slips and the current tries to pull him in. Using all his strength, Rusty drags him to the bank as I search for Kat's blonde hair. As soon as we reach them, Ruby practically launches herself into Luna's arms. Luna starts sobbing as she holds her daughter tightly and drops to her knees.

"Where the fuck is she?" I yell at Jacob, who is coughing and spluttering.

"I tried man, I swear I did, but the seatbelt's jammed. I came up to find a knife or something to cut her free but the current's too strong. I couldn't—"

I roar in anguish, tearing into the water, shaking off hands that try to restrain me.

"Let me go. I have to find her."

"The current's too strong, Conan, you won't make it," Rusty yells behind me, refusing to let go.

"Then I'll die trying," I yank free just as I hear yelling.

"Conan!" I look up toward the sound of Inigo's frantic voice and see him pointing to the other side of the bridge.

I focus on where he's pointing and just there, on the side of the embankment is a body.

"Oh god no. Fuck no!" I lift my feet and let the current drag me, ignoring the shouting around me. Once I make it under the bridge, I swim against the current, using every ounce of strength I have to make my way to her. It seems to take me forever to pull myself out of the water but the second my feet touch solid ground, I run as if my life depends on it because it does. Nothing matters now but Kat. I've waited my whole life for this woman, I'll be damned if I let her leave me now.

I hear people trying to get to us, but this side of the bridge is cut off by foliage and is almost a sheer drop, making it treacherous.

I drop to my knees beside Kat and with shaky hands roll her over.

When her eyes flutter open and a look of confusion crosses her face, I almost burst into fucking tears.

"Jesus Christ, Sunshine." I yank her into my arms and rock her, holding her tightly. Hearing her breathing, feeling her heart thundering against my chest all act as a reminder of how fucking lucky we are.

I say a silent thank you to Pike, knowing he had a hand in keeping her safe and guiding her back home to me.

"Conan. Answer me goddammit. Is she alright?" Inigo's shout catches my attention as someone drops down beside us.

"She's okay!" I yell back and swallow down a lump in my throat at the cheer that sounds out from those gathered around.

"Let me take a look at her, Conan." My eyes move to Lucky crouched beside me.

I pull back a little, tipping Kat's head back so I can see her eyes.

"You scared ten years off me. You won't be able to sit down

for a week by the time Inigo and I have finished with you."

She snorts, turning a little as Lucky places a hand on her head.

"Ruby?" She asks looking up at him.

"She's all good, Kat, thanks to you. Jacob and Linc told us how you made them get her out first."

She blows out a breath, her body beginning to shake.

"I had the windows open so as soon as we hit the river, the water started to pour in. I tried to get to Ruby but my seatbelt was jammed. I managed to stretch far enough to hit the release button on her straps. She was so scared." Kat sniffs, shock making her shake even harder.

"The water had filled the car halfway by then so I tugged on Ruby's foot and the water helped me pull her to me. I didn't know what else to do. I couldn't get her out, Conan. I thought we were gonna die."

"Shhhh....it's okay, Sunshine. You're both safe now."

She wipes her hand across her face. When she struggles to sit up, I help her but I refuse to let her off my lap.

"I sang to her. It was the only thing I could think of that might calm her down but then Linc and Jacob were there." She blows out a breath and cries quietly as I smooth my hand through her hair to comfort her.

"You passed her out the window and made Linc and Jacob take her first," Lucky suggests.

She nods. "Jacob wouldn't go, though. He tried to get me out but the seatbelt wouldn't budge. I...I think...he was crying. He didn't want to leave me. Don't tell him I told you that, okay?" she mumbles, snuggling back into me.

"I won't tell a soul." But fuck, I owe that man an apology.

"We need to get her out of here and into some warm clothes. As much as I don't want to take her back into the water, it will be quicker than waiting for emergency services to rig something up," Lucky explains.

"One step ahead of you." Rusty emerges from behind us with Linc right on his tail, each of them holding on to a long strip of rope.

"It's damn good to see you, Kat." Linc swallows hard before looking away.

"Thank you, Linc. I'm sorry, for everything. But thank you for getting Ruby out."

He nods, looking too choked up to speak.

"Come on, let's get you out of here, Sunshine. There's a man on the other side of this bridge losing his damn mind." Rusty grins.

"I'm surprised he didn't follow us over," Linc replies as Lucky stands and pulls Sunshine to her feet so I can get up too.

"Gage wouldn't let him risk himself. He has some blood disorder and Gage said Kat would be pissed at him if Inigo ends up in the hospital playing hero." Rusty chuckles, making Kat laugh.

"Damn straight. Besides—" she looks around at us all before whispering "—I'm already surrounded by heroes. I think I'm covered."

Looping the rope around Kat's waist, Rusty ties her in securely, not that any of the four of us will let anything happen to her now we have her.

Linc and Rusty lead us back as I swim with Kat under one arm and Lucky supporting her other side.

It's slow going but the rope helps guide us back and stops the current from dragging us any farther downstream.

The second we make it to the river bank, Inigo is on us, practically ripping Kat from the binds of the rope and scooping her up into his arms.

"I'm okay, Inigo. I promise...but I could really use a hot chocolate about now."

Surprising the fuck out of everyone, Inigo bursts into laughter and as I look around at all the people here, I see them smiling too, knowing that fate had been kind to us this day.

Placing her gently on her feet, Inigo keeps his arm around her as EMTs rush over to check her out.

I give them a minute, searching out Gage in the crowd. Finding him arguing with Halo, I stomp over, people scattering to get out of my way.

"Conan, how's she doing?" Gage questions when he spots me as he's looking for Kat in the crowd.

"Cold, wet, and in shock but otherwise she seems okay. What I want to know is how the fuck this happened? Someone ran her off the road in broad daylight, and I want to fucking know who," I snarl, ready to murder someone with my bare hands.

"We don't know, brother, but we're on it. Linc and Jacob were first on the scene but whoever rammed into Kat was gone."

"Fuck, fuck, fuck!" I shout, gripping my hair.

"Go back to your girl. Leave this to us and tell Kat—" Gage

pauses for a moment, sucking in a deep breath "—tell her I owe her. Anything she wants, it's hers." My shoulders drop. I'm such a prick, I forgot what he must have been going through.

"How's Ruby?"

"Scared. Physically though, she's fine. Orion took her and Luna to the ER to get checked out."

I slap him on the back and make my way over to Kat. She's still in Inigo's arms but when she sees me approaching, she pulls away and steps into my embrace, perhaps sensing that I'm hanging on by a thread.

"Can we go home? I just want to hold my boy and snuggle with you guys."

"Abso-fucking-lutly."

"Kat." We both turn at the sound of Jacobs's voice. Kat pulls free from me and heads straight for Jacob, wrapping her arms around him as he grips her tightly, looking at me over her shoulder with red-rimmed eyes.

"Thank you, Jacob. Thank you for coming back for me." Kat whispers but loud enough for Inigo and me to hear. We both nod at Jacob, letting him know without words he just bought our respect and gratitude, but his face shows only confusion.

"Kat, I tried, I couldn't find you. The current dragged the car downriver."

"I couldn't see once the car filled with water but....what are you saying?" she asks, pulling back to look at his face as Inigo and I draw closer.

"I'm saying I didn't get you out, Kat."

"But, if it wasn't you, then who saved me?"

Who indeed?

38

Inigo

To say we were beginning to irritate the shit out of Kat is an understatement. Even though I know we're suffocating her, I can't pull back. Too many times in the last year the reaper has been hovering in the wings for his shot to take Kat from me. With nine lives, she's living up to her name but eventually, her luck will run out.

"Inigo, I say this as nicely as I can but will you back the fuck off?" she snaps at me, standing there with her hands on her hips, full of fiery indignation.

"I don't want you going out without me or Conan and as we both have church later, that's not an option."

Yeah, that didn't calm her down. If anything, it's like pouring gasoline on a naked flame.

"No. That's not gonna fly here, Ini. I've done everything you asked of me. I don't complain about having a prospect on me, even though in the beginning it was completely unnecessary. What I won't do, is let you lock me up in the house day in, day out so you know where I am."

She blows out a breath and slides one hand up my chest and wraps the other around the back of my neck.

"I know you're scared, Inigo—"

"I'm not scared, Kat, I'm fucking terrified. Why can't you see that I'm doing all this to protect you?"

"Ugh." She shoves at my chest but I refuse to back down.

"Maybe I should just fuck the insolence out of you."

"Maybe I should cut off your balls in your sleep," she sasses back.

We stare at each other for a beat before I have her shoved against the wall, with her legs wrapped around my waist and my mouth on hers.

"You make me so fucking mad," she complains, shoving a hand between us to unbuckle my belt and slide down my zipper. Freeing my cock, she tugs her panties to the side and places the swollen head against her wet slit.

As soon as she lets go and grips my shoulders, I surge inside her. I don't wait for her to adjust. I sure as shit don't make it easier on her. I fuck her hard and fast, part in punishment, part in desperate need for her to give in and just do what I fucking ask.

"I need you to stay home, Kat. I'll tie you to the fucking bed if I have to."

"No," she argues as I thunder into her harder and harder, even knowing I'll leave marks all over her.

"You agreed to this, to do as you were told."

"Within reason, Inigo, but for how fucking long? It's been six weeks since the accident. I'm going insane."

"For as long as it fucking takes. Do you hear me, woman? Nothing, not one single thing is more important to me than yours and Alex's safety."

I sink my teeth into her neck and she comes hard, dragging me over the edge with her.

"You can't just fuck me every time we disagree about something," she grumbles, but her voice is far calmer than before.

Gently, I place her on her feet but keep hold of her until I know she's steady.

"Is it so bad that the men who love you want you safe?"

She snaps her head back as if I slapped her, colliding with the wall.

"What? No, you can't. You promised." She shoves me and I stumble back. Shoving my still wet cock back in my pants, I growl at her.

"What the fuck do you think we're doing here, Kat? Conan and I aren't getting any younger. If we wanted a quick fuck we could get that at the clubhouse. What we want is a family and a woman who has our backs. I own you. You think you can let me inside your pussy but keep your heart locked away? Bullshit. Every part of you belongs to me and you fucking know it."

I pin her to the wall with her hands above her head, both of our chests heaving.

"Please, Inigo, I can't. Please understand."

"Too fucking late. I've loved you since that day on your

doorstep and you love me too. You just need to open your fucking eyes."

"Don't you get it? I can't!" She screams, tears running down her face. "If Alex were alive, I'd still be with him and only him. I would never have even looked at you or Conan because he was my whole life. How can I love you both now, knowing that to have you Alex had to die?" She gasps as if she's struggling to breathe.

She may as well have taken a sledgehammer to my heart.

I step back from her and wipe my face clear of all emotion.

"Say what you want about your precious Alex but know that while you're standing there with my cum coating your thighs, the guy was already lining up guys to be his second and third before he was even patched in. You might not have been willing to share Alex, but he had no problem sharing you."

I know I've crossed the line when her palm connects with the side of my face but her look of devastation hurts me more than a slap ever will.

"I don't believe you," she chokes out through her tears.

"It's one of the rules of Carnage. The brothers make a unit of their choosing and they share an old lady between them. Luna, Reign—"

"I thought that was just a personal choice. Dee only has Rusty."

"They're deciding where to settle, here or in Vegas, before making that choice."

The silence is deafening as we both try to recover from the words we throw at each other like weapons.

"Kat—"

"Just go, Inigo. You said your piece, shattering any illusions I had about Alex. Everything about him has been taken from me but my memories, and you just went and tainted them. I'm sorry I hurt you, that was never my intention, but you knew before you opened your mouth the damage your words would cause."

"Sunshine." I take a step forward but she wraps her arms protectively around herself.

"I don't want to hear it, Inigo. In fact, the sound of your voice right now is threatening to bring me to my knees so please, for the love of god, just go. Go to church and I'll stay home like the good girl you want me to be."

She slides away and turns to head upstairs.

"I'm sorry I hurt you, Kat, but I'm not sorry for loving you."

She looks over her shoulder, heartbreak written all over her face.

"I told you not to let me fall in love with you. I gave you everything I had to give, knowing it wouldn't be enough even when you both promised me otherwise. I guess we made liars out of each other. You broke your promise and I fell for you anyway," she finally admits, her eyes swimming with tears. "And I hate us both a little because of it."

39

Kat

The sound of breaking glass followed by a thump rouses me from my sleep. Finding the bed empty beside me, I roll over and place my hand on the empty pillow beside mine. The low murmur of voices lets me know the guys must be back and arguing. As much as I'd like to pretend this night didn't happen, I can't. When Inigo left, it gave me the space I needed to think. And with space came clarity.

I love them. I love them.

When I fell for Alex, I felt like I'd been struck by lightning. I knew instantly he would change my world but he was no angel. It's hard to remember that. When you grieve someone, you remember the good bits, all the parts you miss the most now they're gone, conveniently leaving out their flaws. But death doesn't turn men into gods and as time passes, I remember how many times he pissed me off and made me mad.

With Inigo and Conan however, I've spent so much time being mad, confused, frustrated, and pissed at them, I didn't notice I was slowly falling in love with them too. There were no lightning bolts this time. Their love snuck in like a thief in the night and stole my heart right out from inside me and now that I've had the chance to process it, I realize I don't want it back.

They picked me up each time I stumbled, held me together when I fell apart, guided me when I lost my way, and now it's my turn to eat humble pie and say sorry.

They say lightning never strikes twice and maybe that's true but that doesn't make the next storm any less devastating. Somehow, they pulled me from the wreckage of my past and cleared the way for me to have a future, I just have to have the courage to take that first step.

After this epiphany, I know I'll only toss and turn for the rest of the night if I don't go down and fix what I broke.

I quietly climb out of bed and quickly check on Alex. Seeing him still fast asleep, I pull the door closed behind me and pad silently on bare feet down the stairs.

The living room is empty so I head to the kitchen when I see the under-counter lights on. Inigo is sitting at the dining room table with his back to me when I walk in, his head hanging low. With a sigh, I walk past him without speaking and head straight for the fridge. Pulling the door open, I grab a beer for Inigo as a peace offering and the pitcher of apple juice for myself before taking a deep breath. I close the door with my elbow and spin to face him, ready to deal with this shit head-on. The sight of Inigo staring at me in horror has the jug and bottle slipping from my hands and crashing to the floor with a loud smash as the glass shatters.

I'm frozen on the spot, trying to make sense of what I'm seeing.

A raw red and swollen Inigo is tied to the chair with a strip of tape over his mouth. His head hangs heavy as he tries to lift it but it's taking more energy than he has.

Grabbing one of the knives from the block on the kitchen counter, I hurry around the table, hissing when a shard of glass cuts into my foot but I don't stop.

I drop to my knees in front of Inigo and cup his jaw, feeling terrified out of my damn mind. He looks out of it but he squints as he tries to focus on me.

Wincing, I pull the tape away from his mouth quickly, like a Band-aid, making him groan. He leans toward me a little, his head hitting my shoulder as he whispers, "Get out and call for help."

My blood runs cold. How the fuck did I not make the connection that there was someone else here? It's not like Inigo tied himself to the chair.

I move to free him when I hear a cry from Alex and an instinct I never knew I had has me shoving to my feet. I take off to Alex's room in a dead run, with the knife still gripped tightly in my hand.

Pushing Alex's bedroom door open, I stumble when I see a tall figure holding Alex in his arms. I want to scream but I'm so scared he'll do something to my baby that I fight my instinct to tackle him and snatch Alex away.

"Who are you?" I ask, my voice cracking as I try to keep it together.

The figure steps into the dim glow cast by the night light. "I'm a friend, don't worry. I need to get you both out of here. Somewhere safe." I'm about to throw myself at him and take my chances when I notice his Carnage cut and my legs go weak in relief.

"Jesus Christ, you scared the shit out of me," I growl, tossing the knife onto the dresser before hurrying over to them and extracting Alex from the guy's arms.

I breathe him in, letting the scent of talc and baby lotion soothe my jangled fears and racing heart a little.

"What's going on?" I manage to choke out after a moment, looking up at the older guy watching me. He looks vaguely familiar but I can't place his name.

"He's gonna hurt you. We have to leave. Put some clothes on and grab what you need."

"Inigo," I whisper, needing to get back to him to make sure he's alright.

The guy waves me off. "Go get changed. I'll take care of Inigo but be quick, we don't have much time."

I nod and grab Alex's baby bag from the dresser, shoving the knife inside it with an extra blanket and diapers. There is only so much I can do one-handed but I'm not ready to let Alex go just yet.

I wait for the guy to leave to help Inigo and run to my room, reluctantly placing Alex in the middle of my bed while I shove on one of Conan's huge sweatshirts that's so big on me it could double as a dress.

I don't give a fuck, I need the comfort right now and my main concern is getting Alex and Inigo out of here before the asshole that hurt him comes back. I wrap Alex in one of the blankets and hold him to me, rocking him gently as he fusses.

Grabbing the changing bag, I sling it over my shoulder and head downstairs to the kitchen where I can hear arguing again.

I frown when I see Inigo still tied to the chair.

"I thought you said we had to hurry?" I question as they both look at me.

"Run, Sunshine, RUN!" Inigo roars before the other guy draws back his fist and punches him in the face, knocking him out.

"What are you doing? Stop."

He steps toward me, his face set with a frown. "Let's go!" He reaches for my arm but I step back.

"Not without Inigo," I whisper, realizing belatedly that something is really, really wrong. The man is wearing a cut and I foolishly let that lull me into a false sense of security.

"No can do. He doesn't deserve you. I thought he could but he proved me wrong. I'll keep you safe, Kat. I've been doing it for the last few months because everyone else keeps failing you. Not me though, Sunshine. I'll never let you down. Not again."

I shake my head, so confused.

"I don't know what you're talking about. I don't know who you are. How have you been looking after me?"

I edge sideways, not wanting to get too close to him but I'm limited where I can go. Where the fuck is Conan?

"All those fuckers that tried to hurt you or made you cry. They don't understand that you've been through enough. But I helped, Kat, I made it better, right? I've atoned and I'll keep doing it. I won't let anyone hurt you ever again, sweetheart," he whispers, advancing on me. With the door at my back, I have nowhere else to go.

I whimper when he runs a finger down the side of my face.

"I know you're confused but I swear to you, I won't hurt you or Alex. All I want is to protect you. That's why I had to get rid of them all, especially David." He spits, his saliva hitting my face. "How dare he touch you? You're too precious and pure for his brutal hands. I'm sorry I didn't get to you sooner."

He pets my head like a child before smiling down at Alex. His words start slotting into place, forming the grim reality. I wasn't far off with the angel of death comment I made to Wes, only I'm not the angel, this guy is.

"You killed them all? Carol, David, Jimmy...the missing Raven prospect?"

"I had to. I needed to protect you. Those prospects—" He sucks in a sharp breath, shaking his head.

"Too close, too close." He hits his temple with the heel of his hand. "It was a trick you see, a test but you bested them. I had to kill the one who got away so he couldn't do it again. Ravens are poisoned. Carnage has gone soft letting them live but I've fixed it. It's all gonna be good now."

Inigo groans, making the guy turn to him and glare.

"He made you cry. He always makes you cry." He pulls a gun from the back of his pants and points it at him but I yell.

"No, stop, please don't hurt him. This isn't what I want," I cry, sucking in deep sobs as Alex starts to wail too.

The man looks at me like I'm crazy but his gun wavers.

"If you do this it will hurt me. I barely survived losing Alex but if you shoot Inigo you might as well kill me too. I love him. I'm begging you to leave him be. Please, I can't lose anyone else I love," I implore him because something tells me this man doesn't want to hurt me. The look of horror on his face at the prospect drives the point home.

"He made you cry," he reminds me. His words are almost childlike with confusion.

I don't recall meeting this man even if he does look familiar. The top label on his cut lets me know he's from the mother chapter of Carnage so perhaps I've seen him from a distance at one of the club parties. All I know is something isn't right. This man doesn't seem to be firing on all cylinders. I don't know if he has mental health issues or if something has happened to him but I don't sense evil, only pain and confusion.

"People who love each other fight sometimes. Yes, he hurt my feelings, but I hurt him too. We would have fixed it though because that's what people in love do when they wound each other. They tend to them, hold them, say their sorries and if they are worth their salt they learn from their mistakes. We're human, we make mistakes. It's part of who we are but if you do this you won't be human anymore, you'll be the latest monster in my nightmares."

"But..." He pauses and lowers the weapon, his eyes flickering as if he's remembering something before he focuses back on me, his weathered face looking tortured as a single tear rolls down his cheek.

"Something's not right. I can feel it but I can't figure out what it is. It's why I need to get you safe. Something's coming, something big. I promised him, I swore on his grave I would keep you safe but everything keeps getting muddled," he admits, touching his head.

"That's okay, we can figure it out together, alright? Will you untie Inigo for me? It will prove to me that I can trust you, that you don't want to hurt me."

He nods and moves behind Inigo, placing the gun on the counter between us before grabbing one of the knives and cutting through the rope.

"Will you let me call Conan? Inigo needs help but he's too heavy for me. I'm sorry, what should I call you?" I ask gently, praying I haven't just stepped into a minefield by admitting I don't even know his name.

"So many names, so many enemies." He shakes his head, looking tired. "Chester. You can call me Chester."

"Okay, Chester, will you let me call Conan now?" I ask softly, swaying slightly as Alex drifts back off to sleep.

"He can't help. He's not there."

Not where? Fuck. If he's hurt Conan I'm going to lose my mind. Think, Kat. First things first, I need to get Alex and Inigo somewhere safe.

"Okay. Would you be able to help me get Inigo upstairs to bed so he can rest?"

He nods slowly before tugging an unconscious Inigo up and tossing him over his shoulder in a fireman's lift.

I swallow down the bile, reminding myself that his docile nature right now doesn't make him weak. Inigo is not a small man by any means and Chester is carrying him as if he weighs next to nothing.

As soon as he makes his way past me, I grab the gun off the counter and shove it in the waistband of my sleep shorts, covering it up with the massive sweatshirt.

I never thought things would turn out like this, but whatever happens, I refuse to lose anyone else I care for tonight.

40

Conan

"They'll figure it out," Orion says from behind me.

I spin on my barstool to face him and sigh. "I know. But damn, when they go off at each other, it's like watching a storm in motion. I'm glad I missed it."

"Passion like that just means the make-up sex will be all the sweeter."

I snort. Guess I can't argue with that.

"Blade called back. He's got shit going on so he's in and out of the club right now. Said he can do a sit down now if you're up for it otherwise it will be another couple of weeks."

I look at my watch and see its quarter after twelve. It's not unheard of for bikers, in particular, to do business at night but it's not the norm either.

"Where does he want to meet?"

The Crown of Fools

"The clubhouse, but I told him to make it that diner between both clubs. Most of the guys have been drinking and I'm not walking into their clubhouse without reinforcements, not while things are still so up in the air."

"Fuck it, let's just get it over with. I'm sick of it hanging over our heads. Who's coming with?" I drain the last of my coke and place the now empty glass back on the counter.

"Gage, Halo, and Rebel. They were in my office when he called, and volunteered."

"It's not like you three to leave Luna and Ruby alone, not since—"

Not since Ruby and Kat were run off the road.

"Oz and Zig are with them," he grunts, making me chuckle.

They love their sister and are deathly protective of Ruby but they go out of their way to annoy the guys.

"I didn't realize they were in town. So you guys have been hiding out here, huh?" I grin as he scowls at me.

"I'm the president, I hide from no fucker," he growls, motioning for me to follow him.

"Of course you don't. That's why all three of you are here instead of in bed with your woman."

"Fuck you. You have no idea how much effort it takes to stop myself from stabbing tweedle-dee and tweedle-dumb."

I shake my head and follow him into his office where the others are waiting.

"Okay, let's get this sorted. I want to get back and make sure Inigo and Kat haven't killed each other yet."

The guys all witnessed Inigo storm in earlier and proceed to ignore everyone as he glared from the corner nursing his beer.

It took me hours to get him to tell me what went down and by that point, I didn't know if I wanted to pat him on the back for finally being honest with her or punch him in the face for handling it with all the class of a drunk frat boy doing a sobriety test.

"My money's on Kat," Gage grumbles.

"Mine too. If Luna taught me anything, it's to never underestimate a pissed-off woman. Don't be surprised if you go home and find Inigo handcuffed to the bed, begging for mercy." Halo grins.

"Not much of a punishment if you ask me. I'd be tempted to piss her off more often." Rebel smirks.

They all look at me with amusement.

"None of you better be picturing my woman naked or I'll cut off your dicks and send them to your old ladies," I snarl.

"Easy man, if I was thinking of another woman naked, Luna would sense it. She's some kind of witch, I'm sure of it. Anyway, you wouldn't need to do anything because Luna would slice and dice me before you ever got the chance," Gage says, looking proud.

"Ava's far sweeter. She wouldn't hurt me but she's way too good at hiding. I spent far too long hunting that woman down to have to do it all over again," Rebel throws in.

He's right of course, they both are. We've all hit the mother lode with our old ladies which is why it hits so hard when one of them is in danger.

"All right fuckers, focus because we need to leave now if we're going to get there in time. We're going in armed, wearing club colors as we'll be in neutral territory. I've called Chaos and they are sending Scope. He's the best sniper around and I want someone on them as insurance in case this blows up in our faces."

"You think it will? I mean I get that they have a dead prospect and one in the wind but the kill was justified."

"From what I can gather, Blade has ordered Bear to drop it but the VP is pushing for retribution."

"It was his brother. I get it, but the guy was a nasty piece of shit. Brother or not, it was a clean fucking kill and Bear is smart enough to know it so why the fuck is he forcing this?"

"That's a question I plan on finding out," Orion grumbles.

The diner is virtually empty given the late hour, with only an odd trucker or two and an older waitress who looks like she'd rather be anywhere than here. We make our way to the booth in the far corner and order coffee.

"Let's hope this doesn't take all night. I'm not in the mood to be dealing with any bullshit tonight." I grunt.

"Just chill, Conan. I know you're pissed. We all are, but Blade is usually a pretty level-headed guy. He isn't the one dragging this out. In fact, I actually think something else is going on."

"Like what? I don't want Kat getting dragged into anything else," I snap.

"I think there is dissension in the ranks. The Ravens have been around for years. Our association with them might be new but we've never had issues, even when Joker and King were in charge. We just kept out of their way and they kept out of ours. Their club is a legacy club though. Unlike ours, there is no vote. If the person in power has heirs they automatically ascend when their time is right, even if they aren't a good fit for the club. It's fucking stupid but it's a bylaw they've had from the beginning to protect the original member's bloodlines. The problem is, family don't often recognize a bad seed when they have one, choosing instead to bury their heads in the sand," Halo continues.

"Like with the VP," Rebel guesses.

"Exactly. His father was the president before Blade but Bear and his siblings were too young when he passed to sit on the throne. He will, however, become president when Blade's reign ends."

"Blade's around the same age as me, trust me, he's not going to be hanging up his cut anytime soon," I point out.

"There are more ways to lose the throne than to step down."

"You think the VP is planning a coup?"

"I think he's sick of waiting and he wants to take the club in a direction Blade has been vehemently opposed to."

"How the fuck do you know all this?" Orion asks Halo, who shrugs.

"Let's just say I know a guy on the inside."

"Well, that doesn't sound suspicious as fuck, Halo," Gage growls.

Halo just sighs and shakes his head. "I'm not hiding anything, assholes. I just don't gossip like you bastards do because shit like this getting out can get a man killed. G told me. I actually know him from back in the day. We grew up in the same neighborhood. Both of us had blood ties to different MCs so we didn't hang out but we had mutual respect for each other.

"When the two clubs became allied we reminisced a little and after the shit that went down with Ava, we talked more often. He let it slip about the growing animosity between the president and the VP."

"None of this has anything to do with us though. Its club business until it spills over and threatens Carnage," Gage adds, and he's right unless it affects Kat.

"Maybe the VP is using Kat to drive a wedge between the two clubs and to divide the Ravens," Halo says out loud what I was just thinking.

"Well, then I guess it's a damn good thing we're meeting them here isn't it, instead of their clubhouse?" Orion grunts, looking out the window at the empty parking lot. The question is, where are the fuckers?

41

Kat

After following Chester up the stairs, I indicate for him to place Inigo on the spare bed in the nursery. This used to be Half-pint's room. When the guys insisted on turning it into a nursery, we kept the bed because it's nice to have somewhere to curl up with Alex when I'm doing a night feed. I'm so damn grateful we decided to keep it.

"I'm just going to pop Alex down because he's getting heavy," I whisper, not wanting to wake Alex or spook Chester. When Chester doesn't stop me, I gently place my son in his crib and send up a silent prayer to his father to keep him safe.

I turn and find Chester staring down at Inigo, his face so void of expression he almost looks robotic. The hairs on the back of my neck stand up on end when he turns to look at me. He jolts as if seeing me for the first time.

"We have to go. It's not safe," he tells me, walking toward me. I fight the instinct to step back. Instead, I walk toward him. I slip my hand in his, tugging him out of the room, wanting him as far away from Alex as possible.

"You have to tell me what's going on first. I'll be upset if you hide things from me." I try to keep my voice stern but it wobbles as I close the door behind me and lead Chester back down the stairs.

"Don't be sad now. I've fixed everything. You and Alex can come live with me. I'll look after you. I promise I won't let anyone hurt you again. I don't like it when you cry, Sunshine," he admits, which ironically enough makes me cry harder.

He might not mean me any harm but he'll hurt everyone around me if he sees them as a threat, of that I have no doubt.

"Let me call Conan first and he can come patch up Inigo. Then we can leave. That will make me happy. You want that don't, you Chester?"

"Can't call him. Poison in the Ravens nest. He'll be gone soon which will leave you exposed. Gotta keep you safe."

"Who'll be gone? What are you talking about? Chester, focus. Tell me what's happening."

He looks at me, his glazed expression shifting into focus as he looks around the room in surprise.

"They went to make sure there was no blowback on you for the prospect's death but they don't know that it's a trap. The VP is planning to take out the president and he's going to use Carnage to do it. Only those loyal to him will survive and then he'll declare war on Carnage."

I try to process the words he's saying but it sounds like something from a B-rated movie.

"Who went to Ravens, Chester?" He doesn't answer for a minute so I shake him.

"Conan, Orion, Rebel, Halo, and Lucky. All the king's horses and all the king's men," he rambles as I finally begin to understand what he's getting at.

"But why? Why take out Carnage? They're our allies."

"Because the VP's brothers are dead. One for me and one for you.

"His brother? The prospect was his brother? Fuck! Why didn't the guys tell me? Wait, you said brothers. You mean the other prospect?"

He frowns, shaking his head. "No, Bear ordered him to take you out. You weren't supposed to come out of the water but I got you out. I saved you and then I snapped his neck."

"You saved me?" I whisper, shocked.

"I'll always save you. I promised."

But if he wasn't the other brother then—

Chester's eyes flash to mine. "He touched you, cut you, terrorized you. He had to die."

"David? David was Bear's brother? How? I mean, wouldn't Carnage have known that?" I cry.

"Everyone has secrets. Fingers in pies. Spies who watch and wait," he replies cryptically. "He tried to kill you. Everyone is always trying to kill you. You're the prize."

"What about Paul. Did you kill him too?"

He frowns. "Spies have eyes and fingers in pies."

He's lost it. I swear to god this man is crazy.

"Chester, think. Where is Paul?"

"Waiting for Carnage. We killed his brothers, Carnage will pay."

I feel vomit rush up my throat but force it back down. "Paul is Bear?"

Chester nods, frantically looking around the room at all the windows as if he expects someone to jump through them any minute.

"When is this meeting taking place? How much time do I have, Chester?"

"No time, too late. They left. Now we have to go before they come for you." He looks frantic now, tugging me toward the door.

I swallow down the hysteria bubbling up in my throat.

Swiping my phone from where it's charging on the counter. I try to dial Conan, but Chester snatches the phone from my hand and drops it on the floor, stomping on it until it shatters under his foot.

"They can track us. They're watching. Always watching," he warns, tightening his hand around my arm as we hit the hallway.

I can't leave with him. I've watched enough crime shows to know that getting in a car and being moved to a secondary location rarely ends well.

"Chester, we have to stop. We need to call Carnage and get them to the Ravens."

"No, it's too late. We have to leave now, I'm sorry."

I bite my lip hard enough to draw blood as he reaches for the door. I struggle against his hold, spotting the security panel on the wall near the door. The next time he tugs me, I don't resist hitting the panic button before stumbling into him.

"Come on, hurry." He yanks the door open before freezing solid. Shoving me back he slams the door again, leaving me completely confused.

"Alex, we need to grab Alex." He squeezes my arm hard enough to make me cry out but he's so stuck in his head he doesn't hear me. I fight against him but he's too damn strong as he drags me toward the stairs.

"Stop, please stop. Don't make me do this. I'm begging you please, Chester," I scream as I'm stumbling, smacking my shin on the bottom steps.

He doesn't stop, doesn't even offer to help. He's so hell-bent on his mission to get Alex and get us out of here, he has no idea he's hurting me. Which means he could hurt Inigo or worse, Alex. I have to stop him. He might need help, he might otherwise be an okay guy but I won't bet Alex's life on it.

I pull the gun from the waistband of my shorts and yank Chester's hand hard, knocking him off balance slightly.

"What?" he spins, eyes wide with panic.

"Forgive me," I whisper before pulling the trigger. The loud bang makes my ears ring but it doesn't stop me from firing a second shot or a third.

I have to make sure he can't get up because I'm the only thing standing between him, the man I love, and my little man.

Chester might be someone's brother, father, or son but to me, he's the person who holds the future in the palm of his hand.

I watch as he stares at me wide-eyed before collapsing to the floor, crumpling at the bottom of the steps as blood pours from his wounds.

He coughs, spraying himself with blood as I drop to my knees, ignoring the pain that ricochets through my body and the tears on my face.

"I'm sorry," I whisper, meaning it. I never wanted this.

"Pocket" he gurgles, becoming agitated so I search his pockets finding them empty until I get to the front pocket of his shirt. I pull out the contents and stare down at an envelope and the last photograph taken of Alex and me. The one from my bookcase in my apartment

I look at him. So many questions swirl in my head but he won't get the chance to answer them.

For just a moment, clarity appears in his eyes that I hadn't seen before. A knowing he fucked up beyond redemption and that there is no coming back from this.

Gripping my hand with the last of his strength he splutters before whispering, "Thank you."

And then he's gone, taking what's left of my Sunshine with him.

42

Kat

I hid the letter and photo in the kitchen drawer before scrawling a note for Inigo in case he woke up. I couldn't wait any longer and I couldn't risk him stopping me.

I'd taken a chance. I'd tried to do the responsible thing but that fucking prospect with a god complex, Dozer, shot it all to shit.

If I survive this, fuck if the rest of the kings survive this, I will beat that fucker into a pulp myself. I need help. The club's president is in danger and that dickhead wouldn't let me in because I didn't have my cut on.

The only comfort I can draw from this suicide mission as I fly down the highway in Chester's car, is that the alarm company would have sent the police to the house, meaning Alex and Inigo will be safe, and the trunk of this car is filled with an arsenal that would likely have me tried and convicted as a small arms dealer if I get pulled over.

I've never been to the Ravens clubhouse but I know I can't waltz in the front gate, especially if whatever their VP has planned is already underway.

What I do know about the clubhouse is that it's nothing like your average biker compound. I remember hearing a conversation about how it was once a Wild West ghost town that had been revamped for tourists before being used as a paintball site. The Ravens acquired the site and renovated it so it had small apartments for its members and the clubhouse itself was once the saloon. It sounds like it's a bigger space and more spread out than Carnage. Although that means potentially more members and more people to stop me, it also means more weak spots in the security. I mean, if they're fighting among themselves then hopefully they aren't thinking about an attack from outside forces.

Please god, let it be true. I want to make it home to my boy tonight.

The closer I get to the Ravens territory, the more off the beaten road I seem to head until all I can see through the night are hills as far as the eye can see.

I glare at the GPS, convinced it's fucking with me but then I see it, a wooden sign from an era long ago citing the faded words I might have missed if it wasn't for the car's high beams illuminating them- *Ravens Nest 1890*.

I guess I know where the club drew its inspiration regarding their name. I don't know if it's genius or idiotic. After all, I'm a nobody and I found the place easy enough.

I turn the lights off, not wanting to draw attention to myself, and follow the dirt road by the light of the moon until it forks. To the left is another sign, although I can't make out the writing now without the lights on. To the right is a pull-off area likely used by people who realize at the last minute that they've gone the wrong way. It's a dead end, not because of the dilapidated half-wooden structure that might have once been a building blocking the way, but because of the six-foot razor wire fence not far behind it.

One of these things is not like the other.

The fence is out of place, ironically letting me know exactly where I need to go.

Pulling the car up behind the wooden structure, I switch off the engine and suck in a deep breath to calm my nerves.

I have no business being here. I'm a mother now for fuck's sake but even knowing that, I can't turn back. I've already lost one man, I can't lose another, especially when I know how lucky I was to be given Inigo and Conan in the first place. How many people can say they found true love after burying their soul mate?

I suspect Alex might have sent them to me, knowing exactly what I needed before I did. He was always good at that.

Either way, I'll be damned if I stand back and lose one of them without trying my hardest to save him first. I had no control last time everything went to shit, and Alex bled out while I waited for him to rescue me.

Now, it's my turn to do the rescuing or die trying.

Climbing out of the car, the interior light flicks on, illuminating the area around me as I scurry around the car and pop the trunk.

Thanks to foster father number nine and his crazy prepper lifestyle, I'm way more familiar with these weapons than most girls my age. But then, some days I feel as if I've lived a thousand lifetimes already.

Dragging the clothes out of the bag I found in the corner while searching for a phone, I assess the pros and cons of wearing them when I know they'll swamp me. Conan's black sweatshirt covers the pink and white PJ shorts and tank beneath it easily without being cumbersome. The tactical pants from the bag might be practical in theory, but they're no good if I trip over them and end up shooting myself.

At least I had the foresight to slip boots on instead of flip-flops before I made my mad dash to Carnage.

Picking up the black skull cap, I put it on and tuck my blonde ponytail inside it. I grab a wicked-looking hunting knife and cut the straps off the backpack. Using the buckles, I fashion the straps into loops and slip my foot into one and slide it up my leg, tightening it around my thigh. The other, I slide up my arm and tighten around my bicep.

Taking the knife, I slip it back into its sheath and slide it through the strap at my leg before taking a smaller one and shoving it in the side of my boot.

Next, I strap a small gun to my arm and I take the shovel, trying not to think about why it's in the trunk in the first place. Lastly, I snatch up a Colt and tuck it into the waistband of my shorts. I'm about to slam the trunk when I spot an RPG. More importantly, an RPG with a strap. I might die tonight, but fuck it, this thing might just level the playing field.

Before I can second guess myself, I slip it over my shoulder so it crosses my body and the weapon itself sits flush against my back before slamming the trunk shut. If I even stop to process everything, I'll remember I'm just a hairdresser and run screaming for the hills.

Hurrying over to the fence, I move along the length of it before finding what I'm looking for—a disturbed spot in the soil, as if an animal had borrowed its way underneath it, which is likely exactly what happened. Using the existing hole, I place the shovel in the dirt and use my foot to shove it in as hard as I can before pulling it back out and tossing the soil behind me.

I work as quickly as I can, praying one of the weapons strapped to me doesn't go off and that I'm not too late.

It takes me about ten minutes to make the hole big enough to squeeze through and by this point, I'm dripping with sweat. I take off the weapons and work them through first because even I'm not stupid enough to try to slide through with a grenade launcher strapped to my back, though at this point, stupid is irrelevant. I passed that point a while ago and am now well on my way to crazyville.

It's a tight squeeze, but I don't have time to dig any longer.

I hiss when the fence catches my bare leg and gouges me as I climb out the other side. I feel blood trickle down my shin, but I ignore it.

There will be more injuries to deal with before the night is over.

43

Inigo

The smell of disinfectant stings my nose. I open my eyes before snapping them shut again with a groan as the bright light feels like a lightning bolt to my brain.

"Inigo?"

I open them again, but slowly, giving myself time to adjust. I'm never drinking again.

As everything comes into focus it takes me a moment to realize that it's not Conan saying my name and I'm not at home.

"Diesel?" I squint and realize I'm in the hospital. "What the fuck is going on?"

"That's what I'd like to know. The panic button was hit on the alarm. When the cops showed up, Alex was in his crib screaming his head off and you were out cold in the bed beside him, after taking a beating by the looks of things."

"What? Where's Kat?"

"She's missing. I have guys out looking for her but so far nothing. I'm sorry," he tells me.

The haze begins to shift and a picture starts to take place. I had been riding home from the clubhouse, ready to fuck Kat into submission after our argument, when an old Taurus pulled out in front of me. One minute I'm airborne, the next I'm being dragged into the car.

"Fuck. It's Kermit. He has Kat. He knocked me off my bike before dragging me home. He wanted to take Alex and Kat with him."

"Kermit's dead and if it wasn't you who killed him, then it was Kat. The question is, where the fuck is she? She wouldn't leave Alex and you unless there was no other choice," Diesel tells me something I already know.

"Where's Alex?"

"He's with Luna. They checked him out, but he's fine."

"What about Linc? He was on prospect duty. Didn't he see anything?"

"You texted him to tell him you were five minutes out and he was free to leave. Don't you remember?"

"I didn't text him, I don't fucking text anyone. Shit, I bet Kermit sent it to get rid of him. Where's my cell?"

"No idea, but if Kermit used it to send a text he likely tossed it out the window afterward. Think, Inigo. Did Kermit say anything? Did he give you any indication about what he wanted?"

My head is splitting, but I think back to the muffled words he was spouting.

"Something about fulfilling a promise to keep them safe. I don't know, he cracked me over the head with something. I'm missing chunks of time. I remember Kat and broken glass, then snippets of her holding Alex. It's all pretty vague."

"You're pretty banged up, Inigo. I'm surprised you were conscious for any of it with the nasty concussion you have.

"You've got a hairline fracture to your left leg and bruises over most of your body. Add that to the road rash and the fact you bled like an extra in a B-rated horror flick and well, you look like shit. You were out of it for a while so they took you down for a scan to check for brain bleeds but everything looked fine. We've just been waiting for you to wake up."

He shuts up when his phone vibrates in his pocket. Pulling it out, he glances at the screen with a frown before answering.

"Yeah?" He looks up at me as he listens to whatever is being said. "He did fucking what?" he roars, making me tense in anticipation. "Hold him. I'm on my way."

He ends the call and I brace myself for whatever he's about to say.

"I sent Jacob and Dozer to check out your place to see if they could find any clues. Jacob called to tell me that Dozer admitted that Kat turned up at Carnage about two hours ago and he turned her away because she wasn't wearing her cut."

"He what?" I growl, sitting up and moaning when my ribs pull.

"Lie the fuck down, Inigo. I'm on it. Jacob knocked him out

and called me to let me know he has Linc heading over with a cage to take him back to Carnage."

"I'm coming with you."

"Inigo, I know you're worried, but you are in no fit state to go anywhere."

"My woman is missing, Diesel. I already lost one, don't ask me to sit back and let it happen again. You either take me with you or I'll crawl back home on my hands and fucking knees."

"Fuck! You're a stubborn bastard. Fine. I'll get Lucky to bring a cage and some clothes. You owe me one, motherfucker. Let me find the doctor so you can sign yourself out. I'm sure he'll be thrilled," he snaps at me before storming out.

I drop back to the bed with a sigh, my body screaming at me to relax but it's impossible. I don't know what's happened to Kat, but I do know that woman would never leave Alex with me, not while I was in the state I was in. Either someone took her or someone else is in danger. Nothing else would have made her leave, but who?

Conan.

"Fuck!"

I reach for the nurse call button, cursing up a storm when pain explodes in my head and my chest. I press the button over and over until a harried nurse hustles through the door with Diesel hot on her heels.

"What the fuck, Inigo? Are you trying to give me a heart attack?"

"Where's Conan?"

"Relax, he's with my brother, Gage, Halo, and Rebel. They're meeting Blade to get this shit sorted with Kat and the prospects."

"I'm fine," I snap at the nurse who is fussing around me. She scowls and leaves, slamming the door behind her as she goes.

"What meeting? How come I didn't know anything about it? Kat's my fucking woman too," I growl.

"Remember who you're speaking to, brother," Diesel snaps back. "You were already on your way home before Blade called. Not to mention, your head clearly wasn't in the fucking game because you spent half the night bitching about Kat while fending off club girls."

"Does he know what's happened?" I don't apologize, still pissed. It shouldn't matter what mood I'm in. If it's something that pertains to my old lady then I should have been there too. If it had been Ava, it would have pissed Diesel off to be left out of the loop and we both know it.

"Luna is on it. She had to get Alex back and settled first. He was rightly her first priority."

"Shit. I'm sorry, I just. Fuck. When is it enough, Diesel, huh? I mean how much fucking more can one woman take?"

"Take it from me, Inigo, women are far more resilient than we give them credit for. When I think about what Ava went through?" He shakes his head and swallows. "I'm man enough to admit, I wouldn't survive what she did. She's the strongest person I know and you know something, Inigo? She has no fucking clue how truly formidable she is. None of our women do. What I want to know is when are we going to learn our lessons and stop underestimating them?"

"I need to protect her, Diesel, not because she can't do it

herself but because she shouldn't have to. My one job is to keep her from harm and yet I fail at every turn."

"Jesus. Do you want some cheese with that whine? You aren't failing her. You're a man, not a god. You can't be everywhere all the damn time. You protect her by giving her the tools to protect herself. In a world as fucked up as ours, that's all you can do."

I ponder on his words as the doctor comes in and tells me I'm making a mistake by leaving but he eventually shuts up and signs my release forms. I'm now the not-so-proud owner of a leg brace that will prevent me from riding, as if I wasn't pissed off enough. At least I can take it off to get dressed in the clothes Lucky brought me.

I've never been so relieved to see a pair of sweat pants. Having my ass hanging out of this stupid fucking hospital-issued nightgown is not improving my mood.

I'm sweating like a fucking pig by the time I'm done and my sanity is hanging on by a thread.

"Did Luna get ahold of Conan?"

"She's waiting for Orion to call her back. Don't worry, she'll call once she gets hold of them." Diesel attempts to reassure me but nothing is reassuring at this point and nothing will be until I'm back at home in my bed with Kat wrapped up tightly in my arms.

44

Conan

"Fucking pricks. I swear to god, I'm ready to take the bastard out myself. I get it, he has shit going on but a phone call to tell us he wasn't coming would have taken him two seconds and you know it." I fume at Orion. I toss a couple of notes on the table just as Orion's phone rings.

"Hey, Luna, give me five and I'll call you back." He hangs up before she can say anything else.

"She'll kick your ass for that," Halo laughs.

"I need to call Blade first. He knows I won't accept this no show as anything less than an insult."

"All I'm saying is, it's your funeral." Halo shakes his head and walks toward the glass door with Gage behind him wearing a smirk.

Orion tucks his cell under his chin before shoving the glass door open. I grab it from him before it closes and breathe in the cool night air, letting it wash away the smells of grease and coffee from the diner.

"Fucker's not answering." He sighs before dialing another number.

"What's up, cherub? We're just about to head back."

"What? Why didn't you call me?" he snarls, which is what stops me from mentioning she did indeed call him.

"I'll tell him. We're coming back now. Call me if you find out anything else." Hanging up the cell, he turns to me, a look of remorse on his face.

"Inigo got knocked off his bike. He's banged up but he's okay and on his way back to the clubhouse with Diesel and Lucky."

"That stupid fuck. Why isn't he going home? Does he really think Kat would hold a grudge especially when he's hurt?"

"Kat's missing, Conan. I don't know all the details but we need to go home now."

"Fuck! Alex? What about Alex?"

"Alex is fine. Luna has him at our place."

"Someone's taken her, haven't they? Level with me, Orion. Tell me what the fuck is going on," I growl, taking a menacing step toward him, which is when Halo and Gage appear out of nowhere, stepping between us.

"That's all I know, Conan. I wouldn't keep that shit from you."

My shoulders sag under his words. "Right. Okay. I'm okay. Let's just go." I make my way to my bike, which is parked next to Rebel's.

He lifts the visor of his helmet and looks at me with a questioning expression.

"Who the hell died?"

I blank him. If I try to speak now, I'll choke him and pound his face into the ground.

"Kat's in trouble. We're leaving now!" Gage orders from behind me. I ignore everyone and climb on my bike, making sure the Bluetooth in my helmet is on.

"Call Kat." I wait but the automated voice tells me she is unavailable right now so I dial Inigo and get a similar response. What the fuck is going on? None of this makes any sense.

When the helmet rings, I hurry to answer it, praying its Kat but it's Halo's voice that rings out.

"Blade's calling in his marker. He's in trouble and so is anyone loyal to him. Whatever is going to happen is happening tonight. They need help getting the women and children off-site."

"I have to find Kat, Halo," I grit out, knowing what he's going to say.

"We're closer than anyone else. Everyone at Carnage is looking for her, but we are talking about innocent casualties here, Conan. We can't leave them to die. We owe them for helping us search for Ava."

"Fuck, fuck." I snarl. "Fine, but we'll be talking about fucking priorities when we get home. Carnage is my club, not the Ravens, and my loyalty is to Kat. If that makes me a selfish prick then so be it. But hear this, if anything happens to Kat because I didn't get to her soon enough you can take your goddamn patch back and shove the brotherhood up your ass."

I turn my bike onto the deserted road and head in the opposite direction.

"Conan," Halo starts, his voice cracking slightly.

"Fuck you, Halo. I would never have asked this of you, not if it was Luna, and you fucking know it."

I disconnect the call and increase my speed, needing to put a little distance between myself and the others before I say or do something I can't take back

I've been riding hard, letting the vibrations of the bike soothe me a little when my helmet rings again. I'm tempted to ignore it but when I see it's Diesel calling, I know it's fruitless. I know better than to ignore my VP.

"Diesel, tell me you have something."

"It's me." Inigo's hoarse voice sounds loud in my ear.

"Jesus fuck. I tried to call. Are you okay?"

"My cell got lost. I'm okay, Conan, I swear. My only concern right now is getting our woman back."

"You find out anything that might help?"

"Maybe. Dozer admitted Kat turned up at the clubhouse in just a sweatshirt, demanding to be let in. He refused because she wasn't wearing her cut," he snarls.

"I'll kill him," I snap.

"You'll have to get in line. Anyway, forget him for a minute and listen. He said she was rambling about ravens and bear traps. He thought she was drunk. He'd heard we'd had a fight before he went on gate duty not long after I left. He assumed I was still inside banging a club whore and wouldn't want Kat inside catching us and causing trouble."

"If he knew anything about the kind of men we are he

would know we wouldn't do shit like that. You are not a cheat and if you were I'd kick your ass myself, not condone it. Jesus. He'll never fit in with Carnage. I don't know who his sponsor is, but I want him gone."

"Half-pint was his sponsor. I think that's the only reason we let him get away with half the shit we did because Half-pint saw something in him nobody else did, but no more."

"So ravens and bear traps. Any idea what she might have been talking about?" I ask, pondering his words as I hang left and take the small side road off the highway and head toward the hills.

"I assumed ravens might be her referring to the Ravens club but she had no way of knowing you would be heading there. Hell, I didn't even know you were going."

"We didn't go in the end anyway. We were set to meet at the diner but Blade was a no show. Halo reckons he has some shit going on with Bear. Fuck! Ravens Bear trap! No way is that a coincidence. I'm thinking that the president of Carnage was supposed to meet at the Ravens clubhouse until there was a last-minute change of plans. What's betting Bear didn't know about the changes and instead of rolling out the welcome mat, he set a trap."

"But why? Even if he wants the throne he would have to know he would be declaring open war against Carnage."

"Not necessarily. What if he pinned everything on Blade and executed him as payment. To us, a president for a president. Most clubs would have considered that paid in full."

"Most clubs don't have Luna and a bunch of homicidal mercenaries who deal in vengeance."

"Ravens don't know about Luna though. To anyone outside of Carnage and Chaos, Luna is just another old lady and you know Ravens are more archaic in their nature than us. They'll never suspect a woman to have that kind of firepower she does."

"Even if you take Luna out of the equation, Diesel is Orion's blood brother—"

Inigo sighs before I can finish. "But as the new president, he would be expected to keep his personal feelings out of it and do what's best for the club, which would be to maintain the truce between us."

"I still don't understand how Kat fits into any of this."

"I don't know. That's the part I'm still figuring out. Footage shows her pulling up in the Taurus that hit me so I'm guessing that's Kermit's car. She yells and pleads with Dozer for a while before finally giving up and speeding away. My question is, why not call or go to Luna's or Ava's?"

"Jacob found her cell at the house smashed to pieces and neither Luna nor Ava has seen or heard from Kat. I'm telling you, someone has her, I just don't know who. Like fuck would she have left you guys otherwise. Nothing could drag her away from her boy or—"

He hisses before sucking in a sharp breath.

"What? Tell me?"

"We're making decisions based on what we think she might have known, but what if she knew that Bear was setting a trap and thought you were going to be at the Ravens compound when it was executed?"

"No. No, Inigo, because if that's true then I know exactly where she is."

"She's gone to Ravens hasn't she?" he asks quietly but it's not really a question. He's put the pieces together himself.

"Yeah, the same fucking place I'm on my way to now because the trap has been sprung and fucking chaos is raining down on them and what do you wanna bet our woman has just driven right smack bam into the middle of it?"

"I swear to fucking god if she gets a single scratch on her, I'm going to spank her so fucking hard she won't sit down for a week." He growls, but I hear the underlying worry in his voice. She has no fucking clue what she's walking into. Worse than that, she's putting herself in danger, risking Alex growing up without a mom after already losing his dad, and for what? Me? I'm not fucking worth it.

As humbled as I am, my overruling feeling right now is utter terror.

I push my bike to its limits, knowing that the second I get my hands on my girl, I'll never let her out of my sight again.

Even if that means handcuffing her to me.

45

Kat

Slinking my way through the shadows as the strap on my leg rubs the skin raw, I realize I likely look like a broken-down poor man's version of Lara Croft, but Lara had far less at stake than I do.

I freeze when I hear a scream and drop to a crouch behind the wall next to me.

I knew it had been too quiet. I'd chalked it up to the place being a ghost town, literally. I had hoped and prayed that Chester was just crazy but it's easy to forget that being crazy doesn't make someone wrong.

I move closer, keeping to the shadows, skating around the outer rim of the compound. The buildings are sparse here but I check through the windows of each one I pass, hoping I might get lucky and find Conan or one of the others but then lady luck never was much of a friend of mine.

When I hear shouting and cursing, I press my body flat against the edge of the building I was just about to pass. I use the term building loosely. This one is set much farther back than the others, which is why I came this way around, and is more of a barn than anything else. I swear I can smell hay even though I'd bet good money there hasn't been horses kept here for a few decades.

The voices are closer now and I can tell there is a small group of people heading this way. Four, maybe five, distinct voices and the sound of another groaning as if in pain.

This is bad Kat. Really fucking bad. Just go home and call the police, let them deal with this shit.

Except calling the cops is a cardinal rule you don't break in an MC and there is no guarantee they would get here in time to save Conan.

The door at the front of the barn slams open and bashes against the wall so hard I can feel it vibrating through the panel I'm leaning against. Cursing sounds out again, louder this time, followed by angry shouts.

"What the fuck, Bear. This wasn't how shit was supposed to go down. What happened to the fucking plan?"

"Shut up, Snake. Plans change. Stop being a pussy and help me hoist this heavy fucker up."

"Why bother? Why not just off him now and be done with it?"

"Because we don't have anyone to pin it on and we'll be the first people they look at."

"So what? By then it will be too late. You'll be the prez and I'll be the VP. They will do as we order or die for it."

"A president is only as strong as his club, Snake. We want them to follow us and protect us with their lives, not because they're scared of us. Men don't die for others if they haven't earned their loyalty. That's why I need those Carnage bastards here to take the fall. If the rest of the Ravens believe Carnage killed Blade before turning on the women, they'll destroy them once and for all, killing two birds with one stone. We'll rule this club with loyal, supportive brothers, and Carnage will be wiped off the face of the earth, leaving a space in the market for us to pick up the slack."

"Guns and protection? I don't know, man. I heard they had a new supplier, some guy called Gemini. He's really select in who he deals with and, I hate to say it but, we have nothing to offer him."

"Gemini is old news. He cut Carnage free years ago. Jesus, wake up and pay attention, Scuttle." Bear laughs, the sound grating on my nerves. He thinks he's so clever, but men like him forget to keep their ear to the ground when they have their eyes on the crown. In the end, the crown won't matter because nobody will willingly follow a fool.

"But—" the voice speaks up again, but a gunshot rings out, making me jump.

"Fucker always did talk too much."

"Easy, Bear. We don't have enough men on our side yet to start killing them when they piss us off," another says and I wait for Bear to shoot him too, for the disrespect. Instead, I hear him sigh.

"Fine. Lenny, stay and guard him. Pip, I want you to go back to the compound and start planting seeds. Tell them you've heard that Carnage members were spotted on-site and they took the president as retaliation for the attack on that slut Katia."

"On it, Bear." The door opens and closes again.

"Blade said they were supposed to be here an hour ago. Go call Orion and see what's up. Play dumb. Don't give anything away."

"I can, but Orion won't fall for it. He won't tell me jack shit. You? Sure, you're the VP. Not me."

"Fucking hell, fine. I'll go. Bring me a couple of fucking whores. They can put on a show while we wait."

I wait for the door to open and close again, holding my breath as I listen to the sounds around me. I can hear faint music if I strain myself, but I'm not sure which direction it's coming from. Scuffing boots on the ground reminds me of the man guarding the door. His boots draw closer to me. He's not even trying to mask his steps. Does he know I'm here?

I move around the side of the building in the opposite direction, trying to be vigilant, but I feel out of my depth here. I should keep going, but the man they have inside is dead if I don't at least try to help him. I keep moving around the building. When I get to the entrance, I slip inside and pull the door closed quietly behind me before the man guarding the place rounds the corner and resumes his post.

The sight makes me want to puke but I suck it down. There will be plenty of time to freak out later. Fuck knows I have a mental list of things ready that will haunt my nightmares for years to come.

Hanging by a hook on a chain high enough so that only the very tips of his toes touch the ground is a man I know to be their president, thanks to the title stitched into his cut. It's just as well. Even if I knew the man I doubt I'd recognize him, thanks to the beating he's taken.

And so it begins.

I came here to find my man and stumbled into a fight that isn't mine but I'll be damned if I just leave him there. Ever so slowly, I make my way toward him as if he's a wounded animal that might pounce at any second, but the man doesn't stir.

When I'm close enough to touch him, I reach up and slide my hand up to his neck and press my fingers against his throat, picking up the rhythmic beat of his pulse. I blow out a relieved breath and look at the chain holding him. It's attached to some kind of lever. The thing is, if I pull the handle down, he'll crash to the floor and I don't know if he's too hurt to withstand it.

"Do it," a rough voice whispers at me, making me swing my head around, my eyes clashing with the pain-filled bottle-green ones that are already swelling shut.

"I don't want to hurt you," I reply, my voice soft and filled with frustrated tears. I'm afraid I'm going to make whatever injuries he's sustained much worse.

"I can handle it. We can't be here when they come back. They'll kill me and do worse to you."

"What's worse than killing me? Oh. Never mind," I mumble, figuring out belatedly what he's alluding to.

"Why are you here anyway?"

The Crown of Fools

"Wait—" I pause with my hand on the lever, my eyes squinting with suspicion "—how do you know who I am?"

"Katia Jones. You killed one of my prospects. You're damned right I know who you are but you still haven't told me why you're here on my home turf, half-naked and armed like an extra from a spoof movie."

"I was thinking more Lara Croft," I mutter.

"Focus on the important shit, yeah?" he snarls at me, making me glare at him.

"I'm so sorry your rescue mission isn't to your liking. Perhaps I should leave you to it. Maybe some other sucker will come along and rescue you."

"Fuck. I'm sorry, okay? Just get me down."

I look at him and see the pain in his eyes and the lines of strain around his mouth as he grits his teeth.

"I can't release this without alerting the guard out front. I need a way to distract him," I muse just as the footsteps sound outside the door.

"Hide," the president hisses.

I duck into one of the disused stalls and watch as the door opens and a man about my height and build strolls forward. Blade lifts his head and glares at him, somehow managing to look menacing even in his current condition.

"Who were you talking to? I heard voices," the goon asks his president as if seeing him hanging there is just a normal thing for a Saturday night.

I want to wake up now and this all be a dream.

"Lenny, should have known you'd be in on it. Stupid attracts stupid. I was talking to myself. It seems the friends I thought had my back turned out to be nothing more than two-faced assholes."

"Fuck you. You've gone soft, old man. This club used to be great but you let it turn into a club for pussies and the only pussy I'm interested in is your mom's." Lenny snorts like he's hilarious.

"My mom's been dead for ten years, which you know. Never thought you'd be into necrophilia but I guess nothing surprises me anymore."

Creeping around the edge of the stall, I tiptoe as softly as I can around the perimeter of the room, using the surplus of tack and general junk stored in here for cover until I'm right behind Lenny.

How he hasn't heard the thundering of my heart I'll never know.

Blade catches sight of me but looks away quickly so he doesn't give my intentions away as I lift the knife from the sheath on my leg.

I try to center myself, knowing that if I do this, it will be something I can never truly come back from. I'm out of time and options. Even so, my mind and body revolt at what I have to do.

This Lenny guy being about the same height as me, maybe a touch taller, thankfully works in my favor. I wouldn't stand a chance if he was built like either of my men.

"You don't get it do you, Pres?" Lenny hisses the word in disgust. "You can be as cocky as you want but nobody is coming to save you. You're not walking out of this alive, but don't worry, I'll be sure to pass my condolences on to your sister for you."

Turns out his threat to some random woman is enough of a trigger to eradicate my nerves, leaving me with only steely determination.

"That's where you're wrong, Lenny. The only person dying in here tonight is you."

Taking that as my cue, I close the final distance between us and reach up to grab Lenny's hair. I tug it back, making him stumble in surprise, and drag the hunting knife across his throat, splitting the skin as easily as if it were rotting fruit.

And that brings my kill count to two tonight.

I can't even claim self-defense. I'm a stone-cold murderer.

46

Kat

I stare at Lenny numbly as his body twitches on the floor, his blood pumping out at such an alarming rate that even if someone wanted to save him they'd be too late.

"Hey, Hey. Look at me."

I lift my head and focus on Blade, who watches me with concern.

"He would have killed us both. You did the right thing." He tries to reassure me but all I keep thinking is, how did I end up in a world where killing people is suddenly the right thing to do?

"I need you to get me down from here. Can you do that? We need to get out of here before the others come back."

I focus on his words, my body moving mostly on autopilot as I step around Lenny's prone form.

I push the lever and watch with detachment as Blade collapses to the unforgiving ground with a pained groan.

It's that sound that breaks me out of my haze and has me rushing to help him. There will be time later for me to have a nervous breakdown. Preferably when I'm home and safe in the arms of the men I love.

"Hold on, let me help." I move back toward Lenny's body, ignoring his wide-open death-glazed eyes, grab the knife I dropped beside him, before scurrying back to the pres.

"What's your real name? It's getting really annoying referring to you in my head as *the pres*. I mean, I know Blade's your club name but why should you get to sound like a badass when I'm the one here saving you? Please let it be something lame like Barry or Sid," I ramble as I saw through the rope at his wrists until it frays and snaps.

As soon as his hands are free, he wraps one gently around my wrist.

"It's going to be okay. I promise. My name is Dredd," he tells me with what I'm sure was meant to be a wink. He can't quite pull that off though with two black eyes and ends up hissing for his effort.

"Of course it is." I sigh because Dredd is a perfectly normal name, isn't it? Damn bikers.

"It could be worse. My sister's name is Justice. My mom had an unhealthy obsession with that Stallone actor, in particular his movie *Judge Dredd*.

"What about you? You like to be called Kat?" he asks as I help him to his feet. He leans his weight on me for support, his shoulder thrown over mine as he tries to find his balance while favoring one side.

"My friends call me Sunshine," I answer as I scan his body to make sure he's not bleeding too badly from anywhere. Most of it seems superficial enough, you know if you don't count the possibility of broken bones and internal bleeding.

Get it together, Kat. You can do this.

He chuckles. "Sunshine? Really? Stormcloud I could see, but Sunshine?" He grins, which causes his already split lip to start bleeding again.

"Yeah, well, it's hard to stay upbeat and cheerful when the Fates keep raining on my parade."

"I hear that," he grumbles as we make our way to the door.

I lean him against the wall and crack the door open a little before peering outside.

"Fuck me! Is that an RPG strapped to your back?"

"Hmm...what this old thing? I never leave home without it," I answer flippantly while making sure the coast is clear.

"You are not blowing up my club," he growls as I slip my arm under his shoulder once more and help him limp outside.

"You are not in any position to be giving me orders now, are you? I have men I love and a little boy at home that need me to make it out of here in one piece. If that means blowing this place to smithereens, so fucking be it."

"I'm pretty sure I'm dying. That must be the only reason I'm considering bending you over and fucking you against that wall."

I sigh as if the man beside me is nothing more than a petulant child.

The Crown of Fools

"Given your age and the state you're in, you'd probably keel over and die. Honestly, I think I've killed enough men tonight, don't you? Which way?" I ask.

When he doesn't answer, I turn to look at him and find him watching me with a strange kind of intensity I can't decipher.

"What?"

"I won't always be injured. Besides, I'm pretty sure they didn't break my dick."

I shake my head and feel myself grin at his ridiculousness despite the current situation.

"Which way?" I repeat.

He sighs and points. I keep us to the shadows and follow his directions, realizing I should have been more specific when we end up around the back of what was once the saloon and is now the clubhouse.

Fuck me.

"You cannot be serious. They tried to kill you." I enunciate slowly as if he's stupid because he has to be for bringing us here.

"The club hasn't turned against me. I just have a rogue faction."

"Rogue faction? This isn't fucking *Call of Duty*. You have no idea who you can trust in there. You're not just putting yourself in danger here, Blade, but me too. I have a baby remember? I didn't risk everything to save you just for you to walk us into our own funeral."

"Hey." He cups my face with his hands and turns my head to look at him.

"Nothing is going to happen to you. I know you don't have any reason to believe me but I'm asking for you to trust me."

"Fuck! If I die, I am coming back and haunting your ass. I'll sing "Baby Shark" for an eternity and make sure you never get laid again."

"Don't talk to me about getting laid, my dick is already trying to bust out of my jeans. Here, help me get my cut off."

"Wait, what? Good god, man, I'm not having sex with you," I hiss, ready to punch him, injured or not.

"Well, not right now, no. I need you to put this cut on, trust me," he urges, his voice tight with pain.

"Not ever, asshat," I growl, helping him out of his cut. "Why am I wearing this?" I question, wondering why I'm entertaining this man's idea.

"Easy, because it will hide your rocket launcher," he smirks.

He waits for me to slip it on and given the man's size, it covers me nicely. I mean it's obvious something is underneath the cut, just not what.

"Now let me have that one?" I look where he's pointing at my Colt, now shoved in the strap where I had the knife, and back up at him with a smirk of my own.

"Yeah, I don't think so. Here." I pull the smaller gun from my arm strap and hand it to him.

"Oh come on. This gun's for pussies," he snaps.

"Well you'd better start purring then because I'm not giving you my—"

My words are cut off as I'm yanked forward into Blade's arms and his lips slam down on mine.

I try to object and pull away but he grips my hair tightly, keeping me in place and swallowing down my protests.

When his free hand slides up under my sweatshirt and cups my ass, I decide to bite the asshole's tongue off even if he isn't a bad kisser, but that's when I hear the voices talking just a few feet from us.

"No clue who she is but she's wearing his cut so she must be doing something right. Hopefully he tosses her our way when he's done. Those legs, man, look like they go on forever."

"Who cares about her legs? It's her pussy I'm interested in. I'm sick of loose snatch around here, though by the time the pres is finished, all pussy is loose," the second voice complains as Blade rips his lips free from mine, the effect the kiss had on him pressing hot and hard between us.

Oh boy. Abort. Abort.

"You fuckers wouldn't know what to do with a prime piece of pussy like this. Stormcloud is mine, you better remember that. Where's G? He was supposed to meet here," Blade casually throws out, keeping me pinned to him, his eyes never leaving mine even as he talks to the bikers behind me.

"Think I saw him inside. Want me to go find him?"

"Yes, Probe, you do that."

Probe? Eyes wide, I bite my lip to keep from snorting as Probe leaves us. Now that is an unfortunate name.

"What about Bear? I haven't seen him around all evening," Blade lies through his teeth, pushing his hard dick against me. I reach a hand between us and flick his nose like he's a bad puppy, making him hiss which he covers with a cough.

"I saw him heading up to your office about half an hour ago. I thought you were up there so didn't really think anything of it. Look, Pres, I know he's the VP, but something is going on with him."

"I know, Crane. Something is going down. I can't say right now, but I know you'll have my back when I need you. Just keep your ears to the ground. I want you to go back inside and keep your eyes open for anything odd."

"You mean like all the women being made to leave?"

"Yeah, exactly like that. If he makes them leave, find out—"

"No, Pres, I mean he made them all leave earlier this evening. He had Snake gather them up and walk them all out."

"Did he say why?"

"Some kind of meeting being called. Apparently, he has an announcement to make. He wants us all to stick around the saloon until otherwise notified, but without the club whores to occupy people, everyone is getting antsy."

"Go back inside and wait. Find Probe and make sure he doesn't mention seeing me. The same goes for you. I'll signal you when I need you. You carrying?"

"Always, sir."

"Good, keep it handy. It seems the officers are being restructured and I'll need all the loyal men I have to step up to the plate."

I stand there and let them talk. It's like they forgot I'm here anyway, my mind drifting to my boy. I hope and pray I'll be back before breakfast and I can just pretend today never happened.

"He's gone. You can relax now," Blade whispers in my ear.

"Relax! You just had your tongue down my throat and your hand on my ass. How the fuck am I supposed to relax?" I whisper-yell at him.

"I'm a cheat. A dirty, dirty cheat. I'm going to hell and it's all your fault." I punctuate my words with a poke to his chest.

"I'm sorry. I needed your identity to stay hidden and I needed you to hide the state I'm in."

"You were in the shadows, that's how come they didn't see your giant swollen head," I guess.

"Yeah, but the only reason they didn't come any closer was because of you."

I don't have an answer for that, which just pisses me off more.

"Come on, we don't have time for you to have a snit—"

"A snit? A SNIT!"

His mouth slams down on mine again, but he rips it away almost immediately when a scream splits the night sky.

We both turn toward the large barn behind the saloon as crying sounds out from more than one person, followed by the distinctive sound of a slap.

I pull away from Blade and head toward the barn. Blade reaches out and grabs my wrist, halting my movements.

"You can't go running in there half-cocked. You'll get yourself killed."

"I can't stand around here while someone else gets killed. I'm sorry Blade, I might for whatever reason trust you, but I don't know your men, and I refuse to wait around here for someone to save me or whoever's in there when I'm more than capable of saving us myself."

And with that, I yank my arm free and run for the barn where the sound of muffled sobbing fills me with grim determination.

47

Inigo

"What's taking them so long?" I growl, wishing I could pace but this stupid brace makes it near impossible.

I turn back to face the prospect strapped to the chair and hobble over to him. Pulling my arm back, I plow my fist into the side of his face, making his head snap to the side.

"We trusted you. If anything happens to my woman, I'll rip you apart piece by piece."

"I didn't know," he slurs. "I thought MCs were all bro's before hoes. I didn't think you wanted the drama of her catching you getting your dick sucked."

I punch him again, just because I can, and a third time because it soothes the beast inside me.

"First of all, refer to my woman again as anything other

than Sunshine and I'll cut out your tongue so you can never speak again. Second, you clearly have no clue how Carnage is run or what we're all about. We protect what's ours and nothing is more important than our women and children."

"Yeah? Then why do they always wind up kidnapped or dead? Doesn't seem to me like they matter that much or you'd do a better job of keeping the bitches locked up," he replies flippantly.

Sighing, I move to the table and select the two tools I'll need before walking back to Dozer whose eyes are wide.

"I see it's finally dawning on you now the predicament you landed yourself in."

"Jacob," I holler behind me and wait for the man to appear. "Open his mouth for me."

Jacob ignores Dozer's squeals of protest and squeezes his cheeks hard.

As soon as I see the pink of his tongue, I grab it with the pliers in my hand and grip it tightly.

"Hold his head steady," I order Jacob, who does so without question.

"You know we won't get anything else out of him if he can't talk." Diesel walks over from where he was leaning against the wall.

"He has nothing else useful to say. Even now, he's talking so much shit, I can smell it on his breath."

"It's your show, Inigo." He claps me gently on my arm, knowing I'm still hurting.

"Jnjncbsj," comes Dozers' muffled reply as I grip the pillars hard enough to make him bleed.

"I did warn you," I drag the scalpel into his view before grinning manically and slicing through the muscle he clearly uses too much.

Jacob lets go and steps back as Dozer screams before passing out like the pussy he is.

I slap him around the face to bring him around but he's out cold.

Jacob grabs Dozer's hair and lifts his head up but still nothing. It isn't until Jacob checks his pulse and shakes his head I realize the asshole went and died on us.

"Un-fucking-believable," I hiss, tossing the scalpel to the floor where it lands next to the pliers still gripping Dozer's tongue.

"Well, that was anticlimactic," Diesel complains.

"Probably had a heart attack from the shock," Jacob adds as we all look down at the dead bastard.

"Pussy." I spit before turning and walking, or hobbling, away.

"Where the fuck are your crutches?"

"Upstairs, Mom," I gripe, gripping the handrail.

"If you fuck up your leg, I'll let Luna kick your ass," he warns me, stomping ahead.

"Hey, you need a hand?" Jacob asks, coming up beside me.

"Fuck off. I'm not an invalid," I snap but there's no heat behind it.

"I don't know, old man, you're looking a little frail there." He laughs, hurrying out of the way when I reach up to grab the fucker by his neck.

I follow him up the steps at a far slower pace and make my way into the back room we use for church.

"Tell me what the plan is," I order, making Diesel scowl at me. I hold my hands up in capitulation. I know I'm skating on thin ice here. Worried or not, Diesel is still my VP.

"You know what the plan is but I'll go over it again for the others just in case."

He stops talking as a few other brothers enter the room, offering me a nod of respect, letting me know they have my back before taking a seat.

"Okay, we are working under the assumption that Kat is caught up in the middle of a hostile situation at the Ravens compound," Diesel begins.

"What the fuck?" A voice calls out but I don't lift my head to see who's speaking as exhaustion pulls at my battered body.

"We believe she went there to stop our guys from walking into a trap. I won't go into the specifics because the why doesn't matter. What does matter is getting Kat out of there alive. Orion, Conan, Rebel, Halo, and Gage are en route and should be arriving around now. G managed to get a message out to Halo earlier, letting him know shit was going down but he didn't give a lot of details. Normally we wouldn't get involved, but this situation is a little different for two reasons. The first, G only asked for help with the women and children. I have nothing but respect for a man who understands where his priorities should lie. Second, Blade and Carnage have a good relationship but Bear is a fucking tool and you all know it. If Bear becomes president of the Ravens, we'll be forced to cut ties with them because I wouldn't trust that man as far as I could throw him. The problem with that is Ravens have many chapters and they are still one of the most formidable MCs in the US. Having them at our back has kept other up-and-coming wannabe MCs and gangsters off our backs."

"We can hold our own, Diesel. Carnage isn't a bunch of pussies," someone says, clearly offended.

"Did I say we couldn't? No, I fucking didn't. We would kill anyone that tried to mess with us, but being at war means lives get lost. It's not just brothers now. We have old ladies and children to consider. We might have a *no woman no kids* policy but don't think for a second other outlaw MCs will give a shit about that."

The room goes quiet once more as they concede his point.

"The guys are going in. Their primary objective is to get Kat out. But also to locate and extract the women and children and protect Blade if they can do so without compromising the first two objectives."

"Should we send in more men?" Jacob asks, looking like he would volunteer if needed. Prospects aren't usually allowed inside church but given the circumstances, an exception has been made for Jacob and Linc tonight.

"We'll play it by ear. At the moment, stealth and the ability to move around undetected are needed but if that changes, I will let you know. Have faith in your brothers, they know what they're doing."

I nod along with the others. If there is anything I do know, it's that my brothers will always have my back.

"That being said, after what happened before with Garrett, I want to put the club on partial lockdown. Nobody rides alone and I want the women and children brought here for safety. I'll let Inigo organize you all and tell you who is collecting who. Anyone not given the job of collecting someone needs to make up the beds in the family room and make sure it's stocked for a few days."

I don't argue with him, relieved to have something to do to stop my mind from spinning.

Everyone talks quietly around us, making plans until Diesel's phone rings, effectively silencing the room.

"Conan, what you got?" Diesel asks before putting the cell on speaker and placing it in the middle of the table.

"We're at the Ravens compound and there is a silver Taurus parked and partially hidden about halfway between the compound and the exit, but no Kat."

"Okay, well at least we know where she is. What else?"

"It's quiet, D, too quiet. I'm not sure what's going down but whatever it is either hasn't started yet, or we've just walked into the eye of the storm."

48

Kat

I'm as cautious as I can be while running but when I hear the distinct sound of a child crying, I lose my collective shit and forget about trying to be quiet.

I manage to stop myself from yanking the door open and stomping inside only because I don't want anyone getting hurt.

I make my way around the building, looking for another way in when I spot a piece of wood that's been snapped off, giving me a clear, albeit small, view into the room.

Straight away I'm aware there is no other exit and when I see the fuel cans stacked up at the front of the barn partially hidden behind a huge bale of hay, I know why.

These people are going to burn to death and there will be no way for them to get out.

I scan the crowd sitting on the floor. There must be about

twenty women and two children—a boy and a girl of maybe nine or ten—huddled together behind them, the women using their bodies as best they can to keep them hidden.

Some of the women are wearing cuts, although I can't make out the details from here. Some are scantily clad, shivering in the night air. Club girls, I'm guessing. They don't usually mix well with the old ladies but right now they all seem to be banding together in one common goal. Protect the children and survive.

The man, whose voice I recognize and identify as Snake, stands at the front of the room with a club girl on her knees sucking his dick while he points his gun at the crowd of women all huddled in on themselves.

It's impossible to tell if the girl on her knees is under duress or an accomplice so for right now, I have to assume she could be a threat.

"Yo, prospect, get over here," Snake yells, gripping the woman's hair with one hand as he fucks her face harder but his eyes never leave the crowd of women. He's getting off on them watching, fear coating their features as they worry about what's to come.

"Pick whose next. Once my dick's hard again, I want to shove it inside a tight wet hole. Not one of the whores though. I've had all of them. I want one of the old ladies. Any will do, I'm not picky." He laughs.

I step back and freeze when a hand wraps around my mouth and an arm bands around my chest.

I lift my leg to kick back when whispered words at my ear register.

"It's me. Calm the fuck down."

Why do men think sneaking up on a woman is ever a good idea? And then to tell her to calm down afterward? I can only assume Blade's single at this point because no woman I know would put up with him.

When I don't fight, he relaxes and lets me go.

"The next time you run off, I'll tan your ass," he growls. I slap my hand over his mouth.

"You don't have rights to my ass. You're not my man or my daddy and you sure as shit aren't my president."

My shoulders droop in defeat as I suck in a breath. "I'm sorry for running though. I wasn't thinking at all. I just heard the crying and reacted.

"What's going on in there?" He tries to move me aside but I'm not sure he'll be able to look inside and not lose his mind.

"Snake has the women inside and two kids. He's holding them at gunpoint while one of the club girls is sucking him off. I can only see one other guy in there, a prospect. He must have been guarding them while the others snagged you because Snake was definitely there but I don't recognize the prospect's voice at all."

"Where the fuck is G?" he grumbles but I don't think the question is aimed at me.

As the light spills out from the crack in the slats, I notice Blade's skin seems pale despite the bruising and slick with sweat even though its's cool tonight.

"You okay?" I step closer but stop when a cry sounds from inside followed by a bellow signaling Snake's release.

Fucking delightful.

"I can't believe I'm gonna say this but, do you have enough strength to shove me against the side of the barn and make out with me?"

He somehow manages to look offended that I'm doubting his manly prowess.

"Easy, tiger, I want to lure one of them out but we will need them to come close enough to knock them out."

Blade shoves me against the barn and kisses me softly down the column of my neck, making me moan unexpectedly.

Focus on the plan, Kat. You can go to church and repent for being a dirty ho later.

"Ready?" I whisper. He doesn't answer, he just slides his large hand under the hem of my sweatshirt before slipping it over my ribs.

"No, stop, get off me," I shout, making him pause even though I don't fight him off.

He looks at me with horror in his eyes so I do the only thing I can to reassure him. I lean forward and place a soft kiss against his lips before smiling then I open my mouth and scream.

"No, fuck you, get off me." I shut up just long enough to hear Snake order the prospect to check it out.

"Get ready, big guy," I whisper as thundering footsteps approach us.

I figured I could bash the fucker on the head with the butt of the gun hard enough to knock him out but I never imagined Blade would go all commando and spin around grabbing the guy and snapping his neck with a sickening crunch before I could even suck in a breath.

Blade looks at me, his chest heaving in and out as he watches me warily, waiting for me to freak out.

"Two to one, I'm still in the lead." I smile even if it is a little shaky. Sucking in a breath, I take the gun and fire it into the dead prospect, making Blade look at me in shock because that wasn't part of the plan.

"Oh, thank you, mister, thank you," I gush to the dead guy who can't hear me.

"I just came to party but he wouldn't stop and I just want to go home."

I shuffle and bang against the barn knowing everyone inside is listening.

"What? Wait, what are you doing? Get off me. No, oh god please, not again. Stop, it hurts, no—" I cut off my voice abruptly while banging my head against the barn in a repetitive motion, hoping it sounds like I'm being fucked against it.

Blade looks like he's trying to hold back a chuckle until the door slams open and footsteps approach.

"Hey, fucker, I get first choice remember. I'm your VP now and you're just a—"

He rounds the corner and pauses in shock as he sees Blade standing beside me with his tiny gun raised.

I wave before the bullet hits him in the neck and blood shoots out, hitting me in the face.

"Ewww, ewww, god-fucking-dammit, Blade," I hiss, frantically wiping my face with the sleeve of my sweatshirt.

"Kat," he says softly. I turn to look up at him just as he falls.

I reach out and manage to stop him from bouncing his head off the ground.

Hovering over him I feel the panic start to take over.

"No, no, no. Blade." I slap his face but he doesn't answer.

"Hey!"

I whip my head up at the sound of the shout and aim my gun into the darkness.

A tall fair-haired man covered in tattoos and piercings steps out of the shadows and stops when he sees the bodies surrounding me as I hold the gun on him.

"Busy night, huh?"

"You have no idea, but those two kills are Blade's. He doesn't like being beat by a girl." I sniff, feeling the tears well up.

"You Sunshine?" He edges a little closer so I make sure I aim the gun at his head, just so he knows if he tries anything he won't be getting back up again.

"How do you know who I am?"

"I have some very pissed-off Carnage bikers looking for you," he tells me as he checks the pulse of the prospect and Snake.

"Who are you?" I ask, still not knowing if this man will end up being my third kill tonight.

"I'm G and that man in your arms is my best friend. You wanna let me help him?"

"G?" I remember that's who Blade asked for over everyone else.

"That's me. What happened?" I lower my gun, my arm shaking from keeping it up for so long. I let the gun drop to the ground beside me as I begin my story, not leaving anything out until my voice is hoarse and filled with unshed tears.

"I owe you a debt. You saved my president's life."

"I like him but don't tell him I said that." I sniff again as G moves closer, checking Blade.

"He's okay. His breathing is good and his pulse is steady. You really have an RPG?"

I laugh a little even as a sob threatens to escape. I slip off Blade's cut and pull the RPG free, laying it on the ground beside me.

"Nice. Next time though, you might want to try loading it."

"What?" I look at the thing and huff.

"Well, that's just typical. I feel I should tell you at this juncture I'm a hairstylist by trade. Plus the amount of times I've been shoved against walls tonight it's just as well it wasn't armed," I babble away, making him laugh at me.

"I could still beat you to death with the thing," I throw in, frustrated that he isn't impressed by my badassery.

"Katia" is roared, making goosebumps break out all over my skin.

"Conan," I whisper.

I climb to my feet and move slowly around the edge of the building until there, on the center path, illuminated by the old-fashioned street lights, are the Kings of Carnage and front and center, the man I love.

I take off at a dead run but I only make it a few feet before I'm wrenched back by a hand in my hair, ripping a pained scream from me.

"Well, well, well. If it isn't my brother's murdering whore."

49

Conan

It's only Orion and Halo holding me back that stop me from charging Bear when he viciously grabs Kat.

"Well, well, well, if it isn't my brother's murdering whore," Bear snarls loud enough for us to hear from here.

"Fuck you, Paul. I'm nobody's whore." She spits venomously despite the obvious pain she's in.

I take her in, her long tan legs bare, the only clothing she's wearing is one of my long sweatshirts which swamps her. The thing that worries me the most though is the blood smear across the sweatshirt and her face.

"Who the fuck's Paul?" Rebel asks, moving a little closer.

"Bitch, please. All women are the same. They're only good for two things, sucking and fucking. Isn't that right, Lil?" He shouts behind us as the barn door cracks open with a creak but I don't take my eyes from Kat.

"Men don't take what women would give them freely if they were real men to begin with. But you never were a real man, were you Bear?" A woman's furious voice yells behind us as a dozen more footsteps retreat away from us.

Who the fuck was in the barn?

I know my men have my back so even though it galls me not to turn, I refuse to look away from Kat for even a second.

"If you don't want to see this cunt die, I suggest you round up your little pussy brigade, Lil, and get them back in the barn and bring those brats too."

"No." Kat's voice rings out, filled with determination as she moves her eyes from mine to focus on the person behind me.

"Get them safe. If he kills me, he'll die here too. The only way he'll get out of this place alive though, is with me and he knows it. Go, you've been through enough."

I don't know what Kat's talking about, but a moment passes between the two of them before Kat's shoulders drop and I assume the other woman leaves.

"That was stupid. You think I'm alone here? I could slash your pretty little throat, finish what my brothers started, and these guys would be dead before they could raise their weapons." Bear laughs but it sounds...hollow somehow.

Brothers? Paul? Holy fuck! This is the missing landlord. But how?

I see Gage out of the corner of my eye scoping the place out for snipers, but shrugging when he doesn't spot anything.

"You could try, but we both know only one of you two are pussies and it's not Kat." Gage snorts. I growl when Bear yanks Kat's head back harder, pressing the barrel of his gun against her temple.

"Now, is that any way to speak to the new president? You'll bring down a murder of Ravens upon you." He grins.

"It's a murder of crows you dumb fuck and FYI, I wouldn't count on the rest of your men running to your rescue. Let's just say they got tied up," Kat yells.

"You fucking bitch. This is all your fault. First David, then Screech? Everything was going to plan before you came along." He hisses and spits in her face.

My hand slips inside my cut for my gun. I take a step behind Halo and use him to cover me pulling it free.

"I think we can safely blame your parents actually, because that is one fucked up gene pool. I mean David was batshit crazy. I'll admit, I was surprised to find out the repulsive prospect Screech was your brother, but I guess I can see the similarity. And to think I thought you were a nice guy. You're all as selfish and as fucked up as each other."

"It's called loyalty, you whore. Something you'd know nothing about."

"Kat," I warn her, needing her to stop antagonizing Bear before he says fuck it and puts a bullet in her brain.

He doesn't spare us any attention but he doesn't need to, he has Kat covering him so we can't take a shot.

"I don't think loyalty means what you think it does." She laughs and it's a sarcastic harsh noise designed to irritate.

"Were you loyal to Screech when you sent him after me? Yeah, too much of a coincidence for it to be anything else. Were you loyal to Carnage when you ran me and Ruby, the club princess off the road? Where was your loyalty when you beat your president black and blue and strung him up?"

Whispers sound around us as Raven members start to exit the clubhouse to see what's happening.

"Were you loyal to the prospect you shot who questioned your actions?" Kat continues, ignoring everyone around her. "Perhaps your loyalty was for the women and children you were planning on burning alive after you raped them?"

The crowd is snarling now, confusion rampant in the air.

Bear shoves Kat to her knees but presses his gun to her forehead so we still can't risk firing on him. If his finger squeezes the trigger it's game over for Kat.

"Where's Blade?" one of the Ravens yells behind me but nobody surges forward, thankfully.

"Dead. Drunk on a false sense of power." Bear grins manically before looking down at Kat. "Suck my dick, bitch, or I'll fuck you with this gun."

If I hadn't been staring at Kat in horror, I might have missed her reach for something in her boot. As it happens, I clock her movements and realize what she's going to do a second before she attacks.

Lightning quick, Kat uses her free arm to shove Bear's arm away and the hand now brandishing a knife lifts, embedding the knife in Bear's groin before she twists it viciously.

"I'd rather fuck the gun," she admits as he staggers a step to the right.

"Oh, and Blade is very much alive," she says with a smug smile, looking behind Bear's wide form as he teeters on his feet a second before his head explodes and he drops to the ground.

"Goddammit, Blade," Kat curses from her crouched position.

Everyone slows down for a minute as they take in the scene. Bear is dead on the ground with half his head blown off, Blade is just behind him being held up by G, a gun hanging by his fingers, and Kat stands up, this time covered in more blood.

As if someone presses fast forward everything speeds up and I charge through my brothers, heading for my woman.

She turns just as I make it to her, then she's up in my arms with her legs wrapped tightly around my waist.

"Holy fuck, holy fuck," I chant as she peppers me with kisses.

"God, I was so worried," she tells me before bursting into tears and tucking her head into the crook of my neck.

I try to keep calm but I came so close to losing her tonight that the grip I had on my sanity disappears now she's safe in my arms.

Leaning away from her a little, I wait until she looks up before bellowing in her face.

"Are you crazy? What the fuck were you thinking?" Everyone around us freezes but not Kat, she fires right back.

"What was I thinking? What was I thinking?" she screams. "I was thinking that the man I love was going to die. That the men Luna loves were going to die and I would have to stop her vengeful ass from dropping a bomb on this place. I was—"

I cut off her tirade by slamming my mouth down on hers and kissing her as if I'm suffocating and she's the air I need to breathe. I cup her ass and pull her as close as I can get without being inside her and I do it not giving one single fuck about who might be watching.

"Talking of crazy. Do you want your RPG back?"

RPG? I reluctantly pull away from Kat's lips and turn my head to find G and Blade watching us.

"You can keep it," Kat replies flippantly.

"RPG?" I frown.

"Looks like the score ended up in my favor, Stormcloud. Three to two." Blade chuckles.

"That's cheating! I already butterflied his wing-wang. Trust me, that man was dying on the inside before you shot him." She huffs. Huffs at the mother-fucking-president of the Raven Souls Motorcycle Club.

"Stormcloud? RPG?" I quirk my brow.

"How about you let G and Blade fill Orion and the boys in while we disappear for a minute and you can fill me in?" She waggles her brows at me and I can't help it. This woman might just be certifiable.

I throw my head back and laugh, the deep sound setting off the others around me.

"Fuck, I love you."

She presses a kiss to my forehead and whispers, "Right back at ya, shorty."

50

Kat

We did not get to fuck. Which was just as well, I suppose, because once the adrenaline wore off, the events of the evening crashed in and I...well, I crash too under the weight of it all. Thankfully, Conan was there to catch me.

Blade offered to put us up for the night after we had all been checked out by EMT's but I just wanted to get home to see Inigo and Alex.

The ride home somehow felt both longer and shorter than I remembered as my frayed nerves sapped the last of my strength.

I was dead on my feet, my face pressed against Conan's cut as we pulled into the gates of Carnage just as the sun rose, bathing us all in its pretty early morning pink and orange rays.

Conan helps me off the bike before climbing off himself and snagging my hand, tugging me toward the large main doors of the compound. Swinging them wide, Orion enters first. He hasn't spoken one word to me all night. Neither had Gage. Not that they are the chattiest of guys. Rebel and Halo had at least offered me head nods and hellos but right now, I felt very much like a girl being lead to the principal's office. When my eyes fall on Inigo's furious ones, I know I'll be on the receiving end of a spanking later.

My eyes drop to my little man, fast asleep, safe and sound, wrapped in his arms. I move toward him, needing to touch him, but come to a stop when Inigo twists and holds Alex away from me.

Sucking in a sharp breath, his actions causing me more pain than any words he might have said, I grit out, "Give me my son."

"You weren't bothered about your son earlier when you went to play Zena fucking warrior were you, Sunshine?"

"Inigo! That's enough," Luna snaps, coming in from the kitchen with a bottle in her hand. "Have you guys learned nothing since the whole debacle with Ava?"

She moves to Inigo and takes Alex from him before passing him over to me.

I suck in a sharp breath, breathing in his baby goodness, and let my tears flow down my face.

"He's okay, Sunshine. I promise. He's just getting hungry. If you'll let me, I'll take him into the family room, where Lucky is watching Ruby, and feed him. I swear to you I'll keep him safe until you come for him," she reassures me.

I kiss Alex on his forehead, his soft fuzz tickling my lip,

before handing him over and giving Luna an appreciative squeeze.

I follow her with my eyes until she leaves the room, noticing Diesel step into the room before the door closes. I turn my fire-laced gaze to Inigo but it's Orion who speaks first.

"You put yourself in danger tonight."

"Yup," I reply not looking away from Inigo. Conan steps up beside me and squeezes my hip. "Kat," he whispers as a reminder that this man is the president and deserves respect but I'm too pissed off, too tired, and too hurt to rein in my temper.

"Your men were going out of their minds!" Orion growls when he doesn't get more of a response.

"And?" I ask, turning to look at him briefly as his eyes flash with anger.

"And?" his voice rumbles deceptively low. A warning to say *danger lurks here.*

Well fuck danger and fuck him too.

"Did I stutter?"

Gage makes a shocked wheezing sound but I keep talking.

"Is Inigo's or Conan's pain more important than mine? Does having a dick make their fears greater? Do the balls swinging between their legs make their protectiveness more acceptable than mine somehow?"

"I don't see how—"

I cut him off, turning back to Inigo, who hasn't moved, hasn't reacted at all.

"I came down the stairs of my home to find one of the men I love beaten and tied to the kitchen chair. I walked into Alex's room to find a strange man with a gun holding my son." I hiss and the men in the room go from tense to downright rigid.

"It wasn't until I saw his Kings of Carnage cut that I realized I was safe," I tell them, lost in my memories of how relieved I had briefly felt.

"That was until he pulled a gun on Inigo. I knew then that I would do whatever it took to keep both him and Alex safe."

"What did Kermit want?" Conan asks gently from behind me, his hand sliding around the front of my belly, giving me something to hold on to.

"He told me to call him Chester and that he was there to save me. He wanted to take me and Alex far away so he could protect us." I stare at Inigo. "He wanted to kill you for making me cry. He killed David, Carol my old boss, and Jimmy. He hunted down the missing prospect and killed him too. He's the one who told me that Bear and Paul were the same person and that he was the one who drove us off the road."

I swipe at my tears furiously. "He was the one who cut me free and dragged me to safety that day."

"What the fuck? How do you even know Kermit?" Gage asks, his intense dark eyes burrowing into mine.

"I've never met him before in my life but he mentioned making a promise to Alex." I shake my head, unsure of the details.

"How did you end up at Ravens?" Orion turns the conversation back around, his voice calmer than before.

"Chester told me you guys were walking into a trap. He said you were all going to die."

Inigo growls, "So instead of getting help you—"

"Saved the day. Yeah, how fucking dare I, right?" I snarl, cutting Inigo off.

"I tricked Chester into helping me get you upstairs. I left you with the most precious thing in my world and then I tripped the alarm when Kermit tried to leave with me. I was going to try and talk my way out of leaving, but he wanted to go back for Alex. I just couldn't let him get my son so I...I shot him. He...he thanked me. I shot the man who dragged me out of that river and he thanked me. I don't think he was a bad man. Something was just wrong, you know? Anyway, I knew the police would come because of the alarm being tripped, but I didn't know how much time you guys would have left, so I shoved on some boots, left a note on the fridge, and drove straight to Carnage in Chester's car."

"There was no note," Inigo hisses, but his eyes look wild and I'm not sure the anger is all for me anymore.

"There was a note. I explained what was happening and that I loved you both." I sniff.

Turning back to Orion, who has moved to stand next to Gage and Halo, I continue. "I got here and the prospect wouldn't let me in." Even I can hear the anguish in my voice. "I wasn't wearing a cut so he turned me away even after I told him what was happening. I had no cell and no time left. I searched the car, looking for a cell, and found an arsenal instead. I just went on autopilot. I had already lost Alex. I couldn't lose Conan too. I had to warn him."

"There was no note," Inigo yells before throwing a chair that smashes against the wall. I pull away from Conan and edge toward Inigo slowly as if he's a wild animal.

"There was a note. I'm sorry I scared you, but I—"

He grabs me and collapses onto the chair behind him, pulling me onto his lap.

I wrap my arms around him and let him hold me and breathe me in much as I did with Alex.

"Jacob!" Halo calls. I turn when he approaches from the corner where he was standing with Diesel and Rebel.

"Go check Dozer's pockets." Jacob nods before walking away.

"Go on, Kat. What happened when you got to Raven territory?" Halo asks me softly.

I tell them about arming myself and digging my way under the fence before going in search of Conan but how I instead stumbled upon Blade.

"So instead of keeping to the shadows and staying safe, you risked yourself for a man you didn't know?" Inigo snaps, every muscle in his body is rigid beneath mine.

"Yeah, I did and, Inigo, you have to know I'd do it again. You talk about the possibility of me not being around to raise my boy, but what kind of man would he grow up to be if I taught him to turn the other cheek? To walk away when others were in danger just to save himself? I never want him to willingly walk into danger but I won't be raising a coward either."

He doesn't reply but his silence is answer enough. The men of Carnage are not cowards, they have to respect the choice I made even if they don't like it.

"I waited until all but one man left and snuck inside the barn. The president was pretty banged up, I wasn't even sure he was alive at this point. They had him hooked to this chain and

—" I shake my head, not wanting to think about the barn and what I did there.

"I couldn't get him down without making a noise, but I couldn't risk getting caught and not finding Conan or making it home to Inigo and Alex so..."

They all look at me waiting as I take a deep breath.

"So when the prospect came to mock Blade, I crept up behind him and slit his throat."

Absolute silence. I'm not even sure any of them are breathing anymore.

"I'm sorry, can you repeat that?" Halo says with wide eyes.

"I couldn't shoot him and attract any more attention, so I used the knife. I went for the one spot I knew would silence him." I reply quietly, wondering if I disgust them now.

"Oh, I like her." Gage grins, earning a growl from Conan, which just makes his grin even bigger.

"Okay, so then you manage to get the president down," Orion prompts, keeping me on track as Conan walks over and stands beside Inigo and me, offering me his hand. I reach up and grip it as Inigo holds me tighter so I don't get any funny ideas about moving.

"Turns out the president is a dumbass," I grumble, which now has Orion, Halo, and Gage all grinning at me.

"What? He is. I let him lead the way and he freaking led us toward the clubhouse instead of away and you talk about me not having any self-preservation." I huff, shaking my head before focusing back on the story. An image of the two children huddled together in the barn pops into view.

"Snake was in a large barn behind the saloon making a club

girl give him head while he held the other women at gunpoint. There were two kids in there. The women were trying to keep them out of sight but Jesus, they'll have nightmares for a lifetime."

I look up at Orion, who is not smiling now.

"He wanted to fuck an old lady, made the prospect with him pick one out. It was a nightmare, but the worst part was seeing the gas cans piled up at the front of the barn, knowing there was only one way in and out."

"He was gonna burn them?" Conan snarls.

I squeeze his hand and look up at him.

"Either that or use the threat of it to get the men loyal to Blade to comply." I shrug. Who knows how madmen think?

"We couldn't take that risk so Blade and I created a distraction. Snake sent the prospect out and Blade snapped his neck. When Snake came out after him, Blade killed him too before fainting like a freaking diva." I curse, hating how panicked and worried I had been.

This time even Inigo and Conan laugh.

"I would hardly call the president of the Raven Souls a diva." Orion chuckles.

"Well, he must hide it well. The man's a damn drama queen. Lucky for my sanity and his noggin, which I was two seconds away from cracking, G arrived and that's when I heard the best sound in the world." I look back up at Conan and smile.

"My giant, roaring my name."

"You know everything that happened afterward." I wave them off.

"Yeah, you turned Bear into a eunuch before Blade put a hole in his head." Orion shakes his head.

"Blade's a dirty cheat," I mutter, still feeling a little salty about...well, everything at this point.

"Look, I know you guys are pissed but don't ask me to lie to you and say I'm sorry because I'm not. I tried to come here first and get help. If I had a cell I would have called but I didn't and I couldn't just sit back and do nothing. I did what I could. Hate me if you want, but it won't change a damn thing."

"Sometimes I wonder if we should let women prospect for us," Halo mutters. We all look at him, me with a self-satisfied smile on my face, the others with a look of horror. I can't help it, I burst out laughing and don't stop until tears are running down my face.

"Jesus, don't even joke about it." Orion shudders which set me off again.

"Well as fascinating as this has been, I think I want to get my family home. We can talk about everything else in the morning," Inigo says and something in his tone sets off a swarm of butterflies in my stomach.

Gage winks at me, making my face heat. "We'll leave your punishment up to your men. I'll be sure to bring you a cushion tomorrow."

"This is why I like Halo better," I grouse, making Halo laugh as Conan tugs me to my feet.

"Go grab Alex, Sunshine. I just want a quick word with Orion."

I nod and hurry before anyone changes their mind and decides to stop me.

51

Inigo

"There were parts of her story she glossed over," Orion tells us the second Kat's out of earshot.

"I know, we'll get the rest of it out of her, trust me," I growl, looking forward to my interrogation process.

"I have no doubt. Look, everything worked out in the end but I can't have old ladies playing hero every time things go tits up."

Conan grunts. "You sure about that, Pres? Because from my count Luna saved Lucky and Megan. Megan saved Conner and liberated a bunch of women being forced into sexual slavery. Reign survived a serial killer and somehow keeps Bates in check. Ava *killed* a serial killer and saved Reign. I mean, I could keep going but at this point it's starting to make us look like pussies. The way I look at it, we fell in love with them because of who they are not in spite of it. If you insist on changing them, you might find the women we love disappear before our eyes, so I'd be careful what you wish for."

"I don't remember you ever talking so much in all my years here as I do in the last few months." Orion sighs, conceding my point.

"I only say shit when it's necessary. Just think about what I said, yeah? Because for me, beneath the fear and relief, I feel nothing but pride for that woman in there who willingly sacrificed herself to save us. We're not easy men to love so why would we want easy women? Fuck, we have a club full of whores who will bend to your every whim but is that really what you want?" Conan asks. "Carnage women are as formidable as their men. Why the hell would we want anything less?"

He shuts up when Luna and Kat appear. Kat has Alex over her shoulder with a blanket tucked around him, a soft smile playing on her face. You'd never know that hours earlier she stormed an MC compound with an RPG strapped to her back.

"Why indeed?" I murmur, watching the woman I love.

I thought I wanted someone moldable. Someone who would bend to my need. I do want that in the bedroom, but outside of that, how boring would our lives be if all the sassy stubbornness that gets me hard and earns Kat a spanking were to disappear, leaving a docile yes-no girl in her place?

I try to picture it and envision a meek woman, scared of her shadow, worrying herself sick when we go on runs and leave her at home. A woman who would crumble under the cattiness of the club whores.

Maybe Kat isn't the one that needs to change at all, maybe it's me.

"He doing okay?" I ask her as she stops in front of me.

"Yeah, he's oblivious to all the night's excitement," she answers warily.

"Come on then, let's go home."

"Take my truck. Ruby's car seat's inside. We'll crash here tonight. It's safe to say a lockdown is no longer needed but I don't want to wake Ruby up when she's finally settled." Halo tosses Conan the keys to the truck.

"Thanks, man." He nods at him before looking toward me. "Where are your crutches?"

I point at the wall beside the door to the basement just as Jacob steps up to me. I was so focused on Kat, I never even realized he had come back up.

"Here." He shakes my hand and passes me a scrunched up sheet of paper. I look down at it and close my eyes.

It's the damn note. Dozer must have swiped it.

"I'm glad you're okay, Kat. Kermit's gone and the mess has been cleaned up. You'll need a new rug, though." He winces at her apologetically.

She reaches over and squeezes his arm. "Thank you, Jacob. You have no idea how much I appreciate you doing that for me."

"Not gonna lie, it was mostly the newer prospects." He chuckles before his face turns serious as he looks past my shoulder.

I look over and see Diesel just behind us. He ruffles

Sunshine's hair affectionately before talking quietly so he doesn't disturb Alex.

"I don't know if the others mentioned anything but we managed to stall the cops for now, but they'll be back."

Orion groans. "Shit, I forgot about that."

"Nothing can be done now. Inigo needs to be in bed and, Kat, you look dead on your feet. I'll call the Ravens and see how they want to play it but I won't let you catch flack for saving Blade's ass. As for Kermit, it was self-defense so I don't envision any issues."

"I'm not so sure about that. He was a decorated police officer. He might have retired but his face has been splashed over the news as the hero who caught the Captain Killer," Jacob comments.

"Can it even be called self-defense if he didn't attack me? I mean look at me, I don't have a mark on me," Kat points out.

I try to reassure her. "We will figure it out, don't worry."

"Shit, Conan, can you take Alex for a minute? I forgot his bag."

She hands Alex to Conan before he can even answer, then turns on her heel and hurries back to the family room.

"Stubborn ass women. Didn't even occur to her that one of us would have grabbed it for her." Jacob laughs.

"That pretty much describes all the women here. Welcome to Carnage, Jacob. It's all downhill from here." I laugh, surprising myself.

"No kidding." Diesel snorts. "Seriously though, we need to get this shit straightened out with the Ravens before the cops come sniffing around later, especially now we have a trail of dead bodies and the only link is Kat."

"They won't be making her a scapegoat. Over my dead fucking body. It's because of these so-called fucking cops that Garrett was let out on some kind of technicality and killed her man in the first place. They started this. It's not Kat's fault she was forced to tidy up their mess."

"Maybe we should stay here and get shit sorted first. You could go sleep in your old room with Alex while we hash shit out down here." Conan looks at me, clearly worried, but I'll knock the fucker out if he thinks I'm going to let him get away with treating me like a fucking baby.

"I'm fine, Conan, and fuck you for treating me like I'm five. I wouldn't care if my arm was hanging off. My woman needs me and that's the only thing that matters."

"Oh get down off your high horse. I'm looking out for you that's all, brother to brother, just like you would do for any one of us, you cranky bastard," he snaps back.

I mutter under my breath, calling him an asshole but I can't refute what he says. He's right, which just makes me want to punch him in the face.

"Listen—" I start, but the words die on my lips when I see Kat return.

"What the fuck happened to you?" I roar.

This is about the time Alex starts screaming and everyone spins to see Kat's bruised and bleeding face.

52

Kat

And this is why I didn't tell them what I was planning. "Calm down, guys. It's all part of my plan. Can one of you take some pictures for me before I wash the blood off? Luna has iron fists, I swear."

"Luna did this?" Orion growls.

"Oh calm down, Adonis." Luna appears from behind me and links her arm with mine.

"Calm down? CALM DOWN!" he shouts while Luna and I roll our eyes at each other.

"It was my fault. I told Luna you fucked me in the basement last night."

Orion snaps his mouth shut as stunned silence blankets the room.

"No, no it was my fault. I admitted to wanting to bounce up and down on the baseball bat in Conan's pants so I could see how big he is compared to Orion," Luna admits.

"What, really?" Jacob asks, making us both scowl at him.

"No. Jesus, what is wrong with you all? The cops will be here later and I don't have a mark on my face after killing a cop and you think they'll let me walk away with a self-defense plea. Did you all start taking drugs?" I snark.

"She knew none of you would hit her, but she's right. They would take one look at her and scream foul play. This evens the playing field. Now stop being assholes and get me some ice for my knuckles. I swear to god Sunshine's face is made out of concrete."

They all just stare at us open-mouthed. Even Alex has calmed down and is watching us.

"Erm, Luna. I think we broke them."

She looks at them all and sighs before turning to me. "Quick, get your boobs out. It will reboot their brains."

"What? Why me? Get yours out."

"Fine, both of us together. On three. One, two—Eeek," I squeal, finding myself over Conan's shoulder a moment before his large hand slaps me hard on the ass.

"Hey, put me down, pretty boy!" Luna curses. I lift my head and see Luna in a similar position, tossed over Halo's shoulder. Catching my eye, she winks at me, threatening Halo's manhood —Gage and Orion's too—for not helping.

I lose sight of them as Conan bounds up the stairs with me, making me groan.

"I thought we were going home."

Another slap to my ass, making it sting.

"No talking," Conan growls.

"But—" Another slap before I'm tossed unceremoniously on the bed.

I'm about to shout when Diesel walks through the door with Alex in his arms, which is around the time I remember Conan had him before going all caveman on me. Jesus, I'm going for the mother of the year award here.

Inigo steps in behind him, using his crutches to balance.

"You want me to put him down next door?" Diesel asks but I shake my head.

"It's Inigo's room and it has a connecting door see?" Conan opens it and pushes the door wide.

"I have Jacob bringing up one of the portable cribs. You could leave this door open but it would give you guys some privacy to...talk." Diesel smirks.

"Do it," Inigo answers for me. I bite my lip to swallow down my words, realizing I've pushed them as far as I can tonight. I always knew there would be repercussions and now it's time to pay the piper.

I lie on the bed and don't move, fighting the urge to squirm at the knowledge of what's to come.

I shut everyone out and try to prepare myself, knowing they won't take it easy on me.

Jacob arrives with the crib. After setting it up, Diesel gently places Alex inside it before walking back through the adjoining door to me.

"Ava said to tell you there is one bottle left. If you want her to feed Alex when he wakes up she's more than happy to do so."

"God, I love that woman. Tell her I said thank you."

"No worries. Try to get at least a little rest." He smiles before leaving, pulling the door closed behind him.

The tension dials up from ten to one hundred in an instant. Any moment now, I expect my heart to beat right out of my chest.

"Stand up," Inigo orders, his words deceptively calm.

I climb off the bed, feeling nervous, but even beneath the wave of apprehension, I feel a frisson of heat.

Good girls don't get spanked, but they don't get fucked hard and dirty either.

"Strip." Conan moves to stand beside Inigo, both of them watching each movement I make.

Slowly, I bend down and unlace my boots, toeing them off before tugging the sweatshirt over my body and tossing it into the laundry basket in the corner.

I see Conan's eyes draw into a frown as he takes in the large scratch on my thigh made by the fence, but he doesn't speak another word until I strip off my PJ's and I'm completely naked.

"Go and get in the shower and wash away every trace of tonight from your skin. You have five minutes."

Not expecting that response, I hesitate, but Inigo's glare has me moving quickly into the attached bathroom and hurrying through a shower, which is tricky when you have long hair.

"Time's up," Inigo says as I switch the shower off.

"Sorry," I mumble.

"Did I say you could speak? No. Tonight, as part of your

punishment, you'll not be able to use your voice at all. Ideally, I would gag you, but with your face already bruising, I don't want to cause you any more damage.

"Instead, you'll need to heed my warning. If you speak, even once, you will not be allowed to come. I'll leave your pussy wrecked and weeping for release but I'll tie you to the bed so you can't even get yourself off. Do you understand?"

Not sure if this is a trick, I just nod.

"Good girl. Braid your hair then go into the bedroom and lie face down over Conan's lap."

I look at him, wanting to say a thousand things, but recognize this isn't about me anymore. I scared him tonight. He needs this and perhaps on some level so do I. After all, how can I be mad at someone who was terrified they would lose me, when I went searching for Conan for the very same reason?

Love makes sane people act like crazy fools. Too little leaves you lonely and directionless. Yet if you love someone too much, it can consume you until the lines blur between passion and obsession. Looking at him now, I wonder if it's possible to love someone to death. I willingly walked into the reaper's path tonight to protect someone I loved, willingly skating that line between responsibility and recklessness. Inigo needs me to remember that it's not just my heart, my ability to love, on the line. My heart is linked to his and when I walked into the fray tonight, I took his with me whether he was willing or not.

I nod and move back into the bedroom where Conan sits at the foot of the bed wearing only jeans. I walk toward him and wait for him to lean back a little.

"Lose the towel, Kat." Inigo says as he sits in the chair

Conan must have positioned to face the foot of the bed. He's so close, his and Conan's knees brush, giving me the illusion of me lying over both of them.

I see the lines bracket Inigo's lips as he leans toward me a little. He winces but I know he won't stop until he sees this through.

I blow out a breath and bend over.

53

Conan

I wait for her to make herself comfortable, forcibly keeping my hands pressed to the bed so I don't touch her. I know she's tired and I know Inigo's in pain but this needs to happen now if we stand any chance of moving past it.

I keep my eyes on Inigo, waiting to take my cues from him.

"We could have lost you tonight," Inigo scolds quietly, trailing his fingers down the bare skin of Kat's back, over the curve of her ass, before lifting his hand and slapping it hard.

Kat jolts but she doesn't make a sound.

"Good girl. Stay nice and quiet and take your punishment and I might let you come. You're lucky you're returning to me unharmed or your punishment would have been far worse." He finishes his sentence with another slap, the skin of her ass turning a sexy shade of pink. Watching Inigo work, feeling Kat's heartbeat thundering against my thighs, has my dick painfully hard.

"You see, the problem with your heroics, Sunshine, is that the body you endangered belongs to Conan and me. Our ass." *Slap.* "Our tits." *Slap.* "Our pussy." *Slap.* "And our motherfucking heart." He slaps her now in quick succession, alternating between cheeks until I know her ass must feel like it's on fire.

He's breathing heavily by the time he's finished, almost as rapidly as Kat is. With her squirming around all over my lap, I'm two seconds away from shooting my load.

"On your knees, Sunshine."

I help her up, sensing she's feeling a little wobbly and she squeezes my hand in a silent thank you. She kneels in the narrow space between Inigo and me, forcing us both to spread our legs to accommodate her.

"Take out my cock, Sunshine," he growls, gathering her hair in one hand. I try to think of something, anything to distract myself, but the carnal sight is nearly enough to send me over the edge.

"Now suck." He guides her mouth to his dick and she slides him inside without hesitation.

"Hands behind your back now, crossed at the wrist. Let your mouth and tongue do all the work. That's it, Sunshine, just like that."

His eyes slip closed for a moment, the pain that had been etched on his face clears as Kat worships his cock with her talented tongue.

I watch, unable to tear my eyes away until I'm practically vibrating with need.

"Stop," he orders abruptly, pulling her head back by her hair. "I think Conan needs some attention too. Same deal, Sunshine. Take his cock out, slip it in your mouth, then put your hands behind your back, okay?"

She nods, the movement small with the hand in her hair until Inigo releases her.

Turning around, her small hand reaches for my fly and pops the buttons. I lift my weight a little so she can tug my jeans and boxers down a touch, smirking at the look on her face when my dick springs free. That look of wonder never gets old.

"Fuck, baby," I curse when the heat of her mouth wraps around me and she sucks hard.

Like Inigo before me, I grip her hair, moving her head back and forth over my dick, forcing her to take a little more each time until she gags.

I pull free and hold her steady, waiting until her eyes meet mine.

"You good?" She nods. "Can you handle more?" She hesitates for a moment before a look of determination crosses her face. When she nods and opens her mouth once more, I thrust my cock between her lips again, keeping the movements shallow for a moment before taking it farther.

"Relax your throat for me, Sunshine," I coax, feeling my dick slip a little farther. When she swallows reflexively around me, I groan as white flashes behind my eyes.

"So good, Sunshine, so fucking good."

"Well done, Sunshine. Now I want you to stand up and bend over the bed. I want your legs straight and your tits pressed to the comforter. Understand?"

She pulls free from my dick, sucking in a deep breath before coughing and nodding.

"Good girl, Sunshine, you're doing so well. I think you deserve a reward," Inigo murmurs.

I move aside, so Kat can bend over, and take in the sight of her red ass displayed before us.

"Jesus, how did two old fucks like us get so lucky?" I question in awe as I stare at the arousal coating her inner thighs.

"We've been blessed for sure, which is why we know how much it would hurt to lose her." Inigo climbs to his feet, ignoring the hand I hold out for him, and pushes the chair aside.

"Eat her, Conan, but don't let her come." Inigo smirks, moving toward the desk where he slowly starts to undress. I'm not even gonna bother asking if he needs help because I don't fancy getting punched in the face.

Focusing my attention back on Kat, I shove my jeans and boxers to the floor before kicking them aside. Cock in my hand, slowly stroking up and down, I stand just behind her and smile at her ragged breathing. Punishment or not, she's as affected by this as we are.

Slipping a finger inside her, she grinds down on it and groans. I pull it free and slap her already tender ass, making her jump in surprise.

"No sound," I snap before shoving two fingers inside her, hard. Her juices run freely, coating my hand as I finger fuck her. When she starts rocking backward and forward, needing more, I squeeze a third finger inside her. It's tight but she always needs a little stretching before taking my cock.

Sinking to my knees, I pull my fingers free and lap up the mess she's made, reveling in the feel of her body trembling.

I grip her ass and spread her cheeks, giving me an unobstructed view of her delectable pussy, which I spend the next ten minutes feasting on. Each flick and stroke of my tongue over her clit has her gripping the sheets hard enough for her knuckles to turn white.

I pause as Inigo sits on the bed and removes his leg brace before gingerly scooting back against the headboard, shoving a couple of cushions behind his back for support.

"Time to fuck, Sunshine. Now, as I'm hurt, I expect you to do all the work. I want you to slide down my cock, facing Conan so he can watch your tits bounce."

She scrambles to do his bidding, so turned on now I'm sure she's a touch away from coming. But my feisty girl is strong, she can hold on a little longer.

Inigo groans when she skewers herself on his cock, easing her way down his hard dick slowly.

She whimpers but neither of us calls her out on it, both of us too entranced by the vision.

Inigo grips her hips but lets Kat do all the work lifting her ass up and down while trying not to hurt him.

I can't remember being as turned on in my life as I am right now. This moment should be immortalized so I can play it over and over again.

I move over to my discarded jeans and pull my phone from my pocket and flick it to video before hitting record. Turning, I focus the camera on Kat, her eyes closed, her lips parted as her tits bounce with each glide.

"Eyes on me, Kat."

Her eyes snap open and widen a fraction when she sees me recording her but she doesn't use her safe word so I keep going.

"Fuck, Conan, she's dripping. She likes you filming her. I bet she's fantasizing about you sharing this video with the brothers. How they would all stroke their cocks while staring at her pussy as she creams all over my dick."

My cock throbs at his words. Not that I'd share it with the brothers but fantasizing about it is another matter altogether.

"You like the idea of that, Sunshine?" I ask, using my free hand to stroke my cock.

"You like being watched, being desired?" Inigo's breathing is out of control.

"They can look but they can't touch, can they Sunshine? Why?"

She looks at me before looking over her shoulder to Inigo for permission. He nods with a smirk before she turns back to face me.

"Why can't they have you, Sunshine? Tell me," I command.

"Because I'm yours."

"Whose tits are these, Sunshine?" Inigo asks as his rough hands glide up her body and cup her breasts before pinching her nipples.

"Yours."

His hands disappear behind her and when she sucks in a sharp breath I can only imagine what he's doing to her.

"Whose ass is this?" he grits out, sounding like he's close to the edge.

"Yours, oh god, yours," she pants.

When his hand snakes around and starts strumming her clit, her eyes plead with me to let her come.

"Whose pussy is this?" Inigo barks.

"Whose?" I repeat, still stroking my dick when she doesn't answer quickly enough.

"Yours and Inigo's and you belong to me."

"Damn fucking right we do," I snarl as I climb up on the bed in front of her.

"Come, Sunshine, come while I paint your tits and Inigo paints your womb, branding you as ours."

Her back arches as she clamps down around Inigo who bucks wildly as I watch my cum shoot from the tip of my dick. The first strand hits her collar bone, the next her left nipple before I give in to the pleasure and lose focus as ropes of cum cover her.

Flicking the video off, I toss the phone on the bed, all of us breathing as if we've just run a marathon.

"I...wow," Kat stutters, a few tears slipping free and running over her cheeks.

"You okay, Sunshine?" I cup her face gently and kiss her lips before pulling back.

"Yeah, it was just intense. Jesus. I might have to watch that video myself."

"It might be a little shaky at the end there," I admit, making her grin.

"As fun as this is, if your cum drips all over me, Conan, I'm gonna be less than impressed," Inigo deadpans, making Kat bust out laughing.

I climb off the bed, scoop her up, and carry her into the shower.

Turning her away from the spray as the water heats up, I trail my fingertips gently over the darkening bruises on her face.

"You okay?" I ask, knowing her emotions have been put through the wringer tonight.

"I'm perfect, Conan."

"Yeah, Sunshine. You really fucking are."

54

Kat

Fingers trailing over my bare hip and up over my ribs stir me from my sleep.

My eyes flutter open and connect with Inigo's stormy ones.

"Hey," I reach up and cup his cheek, feeling tears spring to my eyes. "I'm sorry I scared you. Sorry you got hurt, and I'm sorry I left you to get Conan. I don't want you to think I was abandoning you. I swear to god, I was only going to Carnage to get help, and then everything got out of control. I love you so damn much. The only thing that kept me sane was knowing you were safe and you would raise my son as if he were your own and shower him with all the love in the world. I'm so sorry I couldn't tell you how I felt before...I...I..."

"Shhh...I get it." His deep voice rumbles over me. "I understand why you did what you did, I do, but it doesn't change the fact I could have lost you, Kat. I...fuck. I can't sleep. Every time I close my eyes I convince myself you'll disappear."

"I'm not leaving you. I promise I'm not going anywhere without you by my side. I tell you what, if it will help you sleep, you can tie my wrist to yours."

Heat flares in his eyes at that. "Yeah, you'd do that?"

"Tie myself to you? Yeah, Inigo, in every way that matters."

Lips on my shoulder have me turning to see an adorably sleep-ruffled Conan looking us both over.

"You both look like shit."

I laugh, but it makes the skin pull tight on my face.

"Come on, let's get cleaned up and downstairs. Inigo needs his meds and I could do with something myself."

I know Inigo's hurting when he lets Conan help him get up but I don't say anything, letting the man have his pride.

By the time we get downstairs where the others are gathering to eat, I feel a little more human, even if I do look like I've gone a few rounds with Tyson.

"How you doing, Inigo?" Conan asks quietly as we enter the kitchen.

"I'm okay as long as I don't move, talk, or breathe."

"I knew you were playing it up." Conan laughs, pulling a chair out for Inigo, who takes it gratefully.

I run my hand over his head before making my way to the far corner where Ava, Lucky, and Diesel are sitting. Diesel has one of his twins over each shoulder while Lucky has a sleeping Alex in his arms.

"Fuck, Sunshine, you look like shit," Diesel announces.

"So I've heard," I huff.

"Remind me never to get on the wrong side of Luna," Lucky adds, which means he and likely everyone else who wasn't around last night has been filled in on what happened.

"No kidding. How's he been?" I ask Ava and move to give her a quick hug. She holds on a fraction longer than necessary, making me sigh.

When I first started coming back around the clubhouse, I had a heart-to-heart with Ava, who blames herself for Alex's death. I don't hold her responsible, I never did, but I can tell she still struggles with it.

"He was an angel as always."

"I'm pretty sure ours are broken. All Alex does is eat, sleep, and poop. He's like an adorable puppy, but ours are like rabid dogs. I don't think I've slept a full night since they were born." Lucky shakes his head, lifting Alex into my arms as I just stare at him. "What?"

"Did you just call my son a puppy?"

"Did you just call our babies rabid dogs?" Ava hisses.

"Brother, think it, don't say it." Diesel laughs, which makes little King start crying.

"Yo, Kat."

I turn at the sound of my voice being yelled across the room and see Gage beckoning me back over to the table where I left Inigo and Conan. They've now been joined by Orion, Gage, and Rebel.

I thank Ava, who I've missed while she's been in Vegas visiting her brother, and wave to the guys before heading back.

I snuggle Alex closer, vowing to spend all weekend doing nothing more than cuddling my little man.

"You bellowed?" I tease.

"Yikes, you look like shit." I roll my eyes at Orion's words.

"Yes, so I've been told."

Conan slides his chair back and points to his leg, so I make my way over to him and sit in his lap and snuggle against him with Alex, feeling content despite the circumstances.

"The cops will be here soon. We need to make sure we have our stories straight."

"Did you speak to Blade?"

"Ah, Stormcloud, you could have just called me yourself," a familiar voice announces with amusement.

"Speak of the devil and he shall appear." I look behind me and see him approaching with G at his side. He grins, his black and blue face not quite as swollen now. When he sees the state of me though, the grin is replaced by a scowl.

"What the fuck?" He turns his glare to Conan and snarls, "You put your hands on her because I kissed her?"

"Oh boy." I groan as Conan goes rock solid beneath me.

"What did you just say?" Inigo snaps at him.

Blade looks from Inigo to Conan before focusing on me. "You didn't tell them yet?" he comments sheepishly.

"Haven't really had time to explain but thanks for making it sound far worse than it was."

"Okay, in my defense, the first time I was hopped up on gratitude and well, have you looked in a mirror lately?"

"First time?" Conan's voice rumbles dark and ominous like clouds rolling in before a storm.

"The second time was to keep her safe. I needed to hide who she was and keep my injuries from view. A couple of brothers were close, too close, and I wasn't sure I could trust them. Letting them think I was just making out with a club girl was the only thing I could think of, given the circumstances."

Inigo turns his glare on me but I glare right back.

"Don't look at me like that, mister. I wasn't allowed to speak, remember? And there has been no time this morning because of the police coming. I wanted to talk to you and Conan about it before the whole club found out but the fainting diva over there took care of that."

"Hey now, I resent that," Blade complains, sitting on the chair on the opposite side of the table from us.

"Everyone out," Conan snarls, gripping me around the waist as I move to stand.

"Not you, Sunshine, and not you, Blade. Inigo and I would like a word."

"Blade?" G murmurs from beside him. I didn't realize the six-foot-two tattooed man had moved, which shows how focused I am on this hot mess unraveling in front of me.

"We need to know what she's gonna say to the police, Conan." Orion tries to intervene but Conan turns his glare on Orion.

"Fuck, fine. Five minutes," Orion complains.

"Here let me take the little guy," Gage reaches for Alex who has no problem snuggling up against the big bad biker. I swear my son has yet to meet a stranger.

I sit quietly as everyone leaves, following Orion's orders. Ava squeezes my shoulder as she walks past, silently letting me know she'll be there for me when I need her.

And then there were four.

The silence stretches until I'm ready to pull my hair out. I'm too tender in too many places, not to mention sleep deprived, to deal with male posturing. I attempt to rise but Conan stops me again, my tender butt pressing tightly against him as he holds me still.

"Where do you think you're going, Sunshine?"

"For a tape measure so you guys can measure your dicks."

"You need me to show you whose dick is bigger, baby? Because I have no problem fucking you in front of Blade and reminding you," Conan growls in my ear. I feel a rush of wetness between my legs, which makes me blush. I know it's fucked up but I can't deny that my inner slut likes that idea a lot.

"You touched our woman?" Inigo hisses at Blade, who for his part leans back cockily in his seat looking every bit the president he is.

"She saved my life, I was protecting her. You weren't there, you don't know shit. I see her squirming in Conan's lap. I bet her ass is cherry red this morning. But tell me this, assholes. Did either of you ask her how she was doing emotionally before you dealt out your punishments? Did you ask if she was dealing with the fact she killed two men last night?"

"Two and a half," I add quietly, making him shake his head, his lip twitching.

"You telling us how to care for our woman?" Conan stands but I climb him like a spider monkey.

"Conan, calm down."

"Yeah, Conan, listen to your woman for a change."

"Blade, if you don't shut up I'll let Conan go all fe-fi-fo-fum on your ass, and president or not, you'll end up a smear on the floor against my giant."

Conan halts his movements and looks down at me, frustrated amusement clear on his face.

"He kissed me, yeah, but it was your dick in my throat just a few hours ago and Inigo's battering my cervix," I tell him quietly, although not quietly enough, judging from Inigo's chuckle.

"Shit. I really need to work on my indoor voice. Look, can we just figure out what I need to say to the police because three of the four of us really should be back in bed."

Conan huffs but sits with me back in his lap once more.

"Is that an offer, Stormcloud?" Blade teases as Inigo moves to stand but I pick up one of his crutches from beside the table and use it to poke Blade in the head.

He looks at me in shock. "You really aren't afraid of me at all, are you?"

"Should I be?" I look around at everyone's amused expressions.

"Most people are. Blade didn't get his name for knitting." Conan sighs.

I wave them off. I've seen bad men. I have no doubt Blade is capable of bad things but he isn't a bad man. Besides, if I was being truly honest, I'd admit I'm not as blasé about Blade as I'm pretending to be. It's sure as hell not fear I feel when his gaze lingers over me just a touch too long.

"So, the police. I got Luna to do this—" I indicate my face "—so that there would be no doubt that Chester meant me harm. What I need to know is what you want me to say next. I need to have a damn good reason to leave the scene of a crime like that."

"Let's stick as close to the truth as we can. It's easier that way and there's less chance of getting caught out. Tell them Kermit told you he had hurt me and that by the time anyone found me, I'd be dead. You panicked, rushing to get to me."

"But why would I do that? I'm not trying to be a bitch but nobody is going to believe I would leave one of the men I love and my son to rush off and save the president of a rival club."

"We're not a rival club, we're an allied club and you would rush off to save someone you loved. You proved that by looking for Conan here."

I frown, feeling like I'm missing something.

"Are you saying that Kat should pretend she's in love with you, which is why she rushed off to save you?" Inigo asks, his face looking as confused as mine likely is.

"Yeah, that's exactly what I'm saying. Nothing else will work and this way it keeps everything about Bear and the other now dead ex-Ravens, which don't forget, Kat had a hand in killing, hidden."

"Jesus, Blade. You know as well as I do the cops aren't gonna buy Kat being in love with you while being mine and Inigo's old lady. She would be classed as a traitor and that would raise more questions," Conan points out.

"Not if she had your blessing. Not if she were my old lady too," he adds quietly, his intense eyes on mine.

Inigo surges to his feet, not giving a flying fuck about his injuries

"What the fuck did you just say?"

"Look, something else is going on here, something bigger than all of this. If Kat goes down for Kermit's death it will start a domino effect like you wouldn't believe. I'm asking you to trust me," Blade adds softly, looking at me.

"Tying yourself to me will also give you Ravens protection, not just from my club but from all Raven Soul chapters. I'm not saying this lightly, and I know you'll need the green light from Orion, but we're going to need as many allies as we can get in what's coming."

"What do you mean? What's coming?" Conan growls, his body vibrating with anger.

"War."

55

Kat

"We'll be in touch, Miss Jones. Don't leave the state." The officer hands me his card as if I don't know where to reach him.

Blade yanks it from my fingers and tosses it back to him. "If you need any further assistance you can contact her lawyer."

The officer shakes his head before turning to leave, the detective who had attempted to play the good cop to the other officer's bad hesitates for a moment taking me in as I sit between Inigo and Conan, each of my hands clasped firmly in one of theirs. Blade moves to stand behind me with a possessive hand on my shoulder as Orion, Gage, Halo, and Luna stand to the left of us and Diesel, Lucky, and G stand to the right.

"We'll be watching." He smirks with a nod of his head, a threat clear in his voice.

"What a boring little life you must lead, detective, but go ahead, we have nothing to hide." Luna smirks back but hers is filled with so much confidence and charm even I almost believe her.

The detective turns to leave, following his partner's path out. Orion looks to Linc, who is standing by the door. With a nod of his head, he follows both policemen out, making sure they leave without snooping around.

I slump in my chair as Blade massages my shoulders.

"You did good, Kat." Luna smiles softly but it doesn't hide the worry on her face.

"Right, now they've gone, you'd better explain what the fuck is going on." Orion turns on Blade.

"Not until I get an answer from Kat, Conan, and Inigo. If they say no, I'll go back to my club and you guys can figure something else out. I won't risk my club, my people, without a guarantee that it will be worth it."

"Why? What the fuck do you have to gain from this? And even if they did agree, you still need my approval. Your club would never accept her."

"If Megan can win over the Chaos Demons then I doubt these three will have any trouble. Besides, the Ravens already love Kat. She saved their president, after all."

I've been sitting mutely as everyone talks around me, feeling shocked into a weird state of numbness. I've only just adjusted to being an old lady to two men and now I'm supposed to take on a third? And not just anyone but the president of the Raven Souls. How? Why fucking me? I look up when I realize it's gone quiet and everyone is staring at me. I look to Inigo and

Conan as Blade walks around us and crouches down in front of me.

"It's bad, isn't it? Whatever's coming, it's as bad as it gets?"

"Yeah, darlin', it is. I won't lie and tell you I don't want you. I've wanted you since the second I laid my eyes on you but it's so much more than that."

I look at Inigo and plead with him. "Tell me what to do and I'll do it." Turning to Conan, I feel a single tear slip free and roll down my face. "I can't lose you."

"That will never happen, Sunshine. They'll have to pry my cold dead fingers from you and even then I'll haunt your sexy ass," Conan promises, making a few of the men around us chuckle.

Looking up at Inigo, I wait for him to speak, feeling my heart crack with each second of silence that passes.

"You want him?" he eventually asks in his gravelly voice.

"I want you. I will always choose you," I whisper, feeling torn in two, stuck somewhere between love and duty but my selfishness could cost the lives of the very people I love.

Inigo reaches out and swipes another tear from my cheek with the pad of his thumb. "I'm not asking you to choose, Sunshine. I'm asking you if you could love him. Not now, maybe not this year. But is there a seedling there that has the potential to grow if he works to nurture it? Because I will not tie you to a man you have no interest in. This isn't the dark ages, I won't barter your hand for protection or alliances. I'd rather take my chances and go down swinging."

I look down at Blade on his knees, stare at his bruised handsome face, and remember how he was with me last night. How his lips felt on mine, how he tried to protect me even when he could hardly stand on his own two feet.

"Yeah, Inigo, I could love him," I whisper, the tears now running freely.

Blade takes the opportunity to lift himself and place a soft kiss on my lips before pulling back. "You won't regret it, Stormcloud."

"Kat?" I look up at the sound of Orion's voice. "Inigo's right. You do not have to do this."

"Do you trust Blade? Do you think he's lying or exaggerating about the possibility of war even if you don't know all the details yet?"

A look of resignation passes over his face before he masks it.

"No, Kat. Blade is a lot of things but a liar isn't one of them. Doesn't change the fact that I won't push you into this. Not now, not ever."

I offer him a watery smile. "But I have to, don't I? For Ruby and Alex and King and Elsie," I whisper, my eyes moving from him to Diesel, who has been remarkably quiet.

"Tell me how it would work," I ask, looking back at Blade.

"There are two options. You can split your time between here and Ravens, between Conan, Inigo, and me."

"Like fuck."

"Hell no!" Both Conan and Inigo curse at the same time.

Blade grins like he expected that answer. "Or, I can make Inigo and Conan dual members of Raven Souls as well as Carnage. It seems I need a new VP and this would be another way to tie the two clubs together. Your cut would need to reflect both clubs and Kat's property vest would too, with the addition of my name of course. You could all come and go freely then between clubs."

"What you're suggesting, Blade, is unheard of." Diesel looks shocked.

"Not many clubs share their women either but Carnage and even Chaos seem to make it work. Times are changing brother, it's time we changed with them."

"And the other chapters of Ravens?"

"I'm the mother chapter president. I get the final say. Either way, we took a vote this morning and after the shit storm with Bear and what the women went through, well, the vote was unanimous."

"What do you think?" I ask, looking between Conan and Inigo.

Inigo sighs, rubbing a hand over his face. "I've been a Carnage member most of my life. I..." His voice trails off.

"This doesn't make you disloyal. Fuck, who else can stand back and say they would do this for their club?" G questions.

"Don't you want to be VP?" Diesel asks G.

G shakes his head. "Fuck no. I like computers more than people."

"It should be Conan. Out of the two of us, he's the most level-headed. I tend to react first and think second," Inigo answers.

"Fuck you. I don't like people any more than G does." Conan groans but he doesn't say no.

"Well?" I ask.

"Fine. I'm in. For the future generation of Carnage, fuck yeah," Conan agrees.

"I'm in because I'll be damned if I let Conan and Kat go without me," Inigo grumbles, making Conan snort.

"I'm in but hear me now, diva. If this is some kind of hoax or trick or if you ever pose a threat to me and mine, I will carve your heart out with a rusty spoon and feed it to you."

"Duly noted." Blade grins.

"I like her," G adds, making Orion, Halo, Gage, Diesel, and Lucky look at me.

"Yeah, so do we. Treat her like gold because if you don't, Conan and Inigo will be the least of your worries. Carnage will bury you," Gage growls at him, making me sniffle.

I look to Luna, who has been surprisingly quiet.

"Luna?" She lifts her head and I'm shocked to see tears in her eyes.

"I'm sorry," she whispers. I climb to my feet and move toward her, wrapping my arms around her smaller frame.

"You have nothing to be sorry for. Yeah, it's new and different and, okay a little scary, but that's life. Right? And that's the beauty, Luna. A year ago I was slowly dying, and now? Well, now I have a chance to really make a difference here. Plus, Blade might be a bit of a fainting diva but beneath the kaleidoscope of bruises, I think he might be quite a looker," I tease, trying to lighten the mood.

She snorts before pulling back and wiping her eyes.

"Well, you certainly have a type. I mean their collective age is over one hundred," she teases.

"Some things are better with age—wine, cheese, cars."

"Hmmm...I guess I can see that."

"Look at it this way, it's like interviewing for an intern and the position going to the CEOs. I don't have to teach them anything, they're so overqualified it's ridiculous, and they have plenty of experience." I wiggle my brows.

Luna laughs now. "Well, when you put it that way, you are one lucky fuck."

"Oh, I know," I agree and turn us both so we are facing a sea of amused men.

"I'm gonna be okay," I whisper, squeezing her.

"I know. I never had any doubt about your ability to weather a storm, Kat. Just know you will always have a home here no matter what. You saved my daughter, rushed into danger to save my men…I…if I swung that way I would totally wife you."

At that, I burst into laughter, the uncertainty of the moment lifting.

Everything would be okay. It had to be, right?

56

Blade

I sit in my office and swill the whiskey around in the glass, the ice clinking together before I take a sip. I look up as the door opens and sigh.

"It's done?"

"Yeah, we're all still trying to figure out the logistics but yeah, they're all in."

"I have a house about halfway between the two clubs. It's a six-bedroom, five-bathroom monstrosity that I bought on a whim. It's more than big enough for you all."

"Jesus, they're still reeling from the last shit I just pulled and now you want me to dump this on them?"

"We are out of time, Blade. Besides, it will be worse if they find out you kept stuff from them later down the line."

"This has the potential to backfire spectacularly, then what?"

"Then we all die."

"Shit. Just go, they'll be here soon. I'll talk to them. Give me a few days."

"You got two," the asshole answers before leaving the way he came.

I down the whiskey and throw the glass at the wall in frustration.

I meant what I said about wanting Kat, and having Conan and Inigo here can only help after the chaos Bear created while I was focused elsewhere. But when they find out I've been hiding shit, they might walk right back out the door.

A knock at the door has me looking up but this time nobody enters until I yell for them to come in.

"Hey, G. They here?"

"Yep, just arrived."

"And the boy?" I question. I need to meet the little guy who is now going to be a big part of my life, but a Raven Souls party probably isn't the best place for that to happen.

"He's at Carnage tonight being spoiled by the old ladies, apparently."

"Okay, good. You have everything set?"

"Yep, boxes are already in church, all that's missing is you."

I stand and swipe a hand down my face. "Tell me I'm doing the right thing, G."

"I can't tell you that. I do know you're doing the best you can with the information you have. But saying that, I think there is something special about Kat. If there was ever a woman alive that could navigate the approaching storm without flinching, it would be her.

"God, I hope you're right."

I follow G downstairs to the clubhouse and spot Kat leaning against the bar with Inigo and Conan flanking either side of her. She must sense my eyes on her because she turns and offers me a nervous smile as I drag my eyes up her skin-tight leather pants and black Harley tank top.

Feeling my dick swell in my pants, I smile lazily at her before placing two fingers in my mouth and whistling.

The music shuts off and all eyes turn to me.

"Ravens, as most of you know, we are going to be facing uncertain times. Sometimes the only way to deal with change is to change yourself. So without any more fuss, I'd like you to meet Inigo, Conan—our new VP—and Kat, our old lady."

All three of them walk forward as if they don't have a care in the world but I can see Kat's hands tremble a little as they walk through the throngs of silent people.

Conan stands on one side of me, Inigo on the other while Kat steps in front of me. Taking my shot, because I'm the motherfucking president and I can do what I want, I scoop up Kat and slam my lips over hers as she wraps her legs around my waist. The room explodes into a cacophony of cheers and revelry.

Her taste explodes on my tongue as I take what I want from her, leaving her breathless before pulling away.

"Tonight marks a landmark occasion! G, hand me those cuts."

G steps up with a box under his arm, placing it at his feet when a shout draws our attention across the room.

"Wait!"

Silence once more. This time for the newcomers.

I stand Kat back on her feet and grip her hip possessively as Orion, Gage, Halo, and Luna walk through the crowd.

"You didn't think we'd let you have all the fun now, did ya?" Orion smirks.

I reach out and shake his hand as Inigo slides off his cut and hands it reverently to Orion. A poignant moment passes between them before I break it by taking the offered cut from G and holding it up. The burning deck of cards logo that represents Carnage is ever-present but it's encompassed inside the wingspan of a giant Raven. Two clubs joined together in a symbol of unity. Inigo's name is stitched into the left breast and underneath that are two badges, one depicting him as a member of Kings of Carnage and the other marking him as a Raven Soul.

"Welcome, brother," I tell him as he slips his arms in.

I repeat the process with Conan and finally, it's time for Kat's. Her vest has *Property of Blade, Conan, and Inigo* stitched into it, making mental images of the three of us fucking her wearing the cut and nothing else flash through my head.

As soon as she slips it on, a cheer sounds out across the room before everyone else joins in.

"Thank you for coming." Kat smiles at the Carnage guys.

"You might be part Raven now, Sunshine, but you'll always be all Carnage." Orion places a kiss on her cheek, passing the cuts in his arms to Halo before picking up Luna and tossing her unceremoniously over his shoulder.

"Hey!" Luna squeals.

"We got one night kid-free, cherub. Let's get a drink so we can leave and fuck."

"We can't leave, it's their coming out ceremony."

I laugh at that. "We're bikers, not debutantes, Luna. Go get your freak on."

"Go, quick before they change their mind." Gage slaps Luna's ass as Halo winks at us and they disappear into the crowd.

"Come on, let me introduce you to everyone. I know this is beyond weird but that doesn't mean it won't be the best thing that happens to us all," I murmur into Kat's ear.

"I'll hold you to that, diva."

57

Kat

Surprisingly, everyone was pretty accepting of us, even Conan and Inigo. I don't know if it would have been this way if the events of last Friday hadn't played out as they did, but it was the wake-up call the club needed.

They seemed to have bonded in their near tragedy, with no divide between old ladies and club girls. If anything, the men in the room seem to be struggling to take their eyes off the women and I suspect it's not for the usual reason.

The last time they looked away, they almost lost them all. That does something to a man's pride, especially when it's at the hands of men they trusted and called brothers. Still, it takes a certain kind of resilience to pull together instead of letting it pit you against each other and pull you apart.

I sit in Inigo's lap as he and Conan talk to Mac and Toot, two of the many club brothers I met tonight. Both of them look to be in their early thirties and are clearly related in some way if the chestnut hair and chocolate brown eyes are anything to go by. They had me in stitches earlier, regaling me with stories of Blade, much to his annoyance.

Now as Blade grabs me a drink from the bar, I sit quietly, taking in the room and coming to the conclusion I could like it here. There are bound to be bumps in the road. People are gonna butt heads and the clubs might take different stands on different issues, but we will work through it.

Looking at the old-fashioned clock hanging above the bar, I notice it's one am. Alex had slept through the night for the last week. If Ava was lucky she wouldn't hear a peep from him until morning.

I watch Blade as he heads toward our table with two bottles of beer in his hand, frowning and stopping for a second. Transferring both bottles to one hand, he pulls his phone from his pocket and his eyes go wide at whatever he sees.

Hurrying to the table, he places the bottles down with a thump.

"Everything okay?" I ask.

"Yeah, I just have to take this. Give me two minutes."

He disappears before I can question him further. I chew my lip, worry clawing at me as I look up the stairs.

Conan leans over and whispers in my ear, "Go, take the beer to him. We'll come find you when we're done."

"No, he's busy. I was just worried."

"He's not too busy for you, Kat, I swear," Inigo chimes in. "Seriously, just go."

"Alright, sheesh. But if he gets pissed, I'm blaming you." I stand up and hiss when Inigo slaps my ass.

Glaring at him, I snag the two bottles of beer between my fingers and make my way up to the office Blade pointed out as his during our tour.

The music from below is muffled now but the party shows no sign of slowing down. I don't pass a soul so everyone must still be down there having a good time.

I tap the door before pushing it open and freeze, gripping the bottles tightly before they can slip from my fingers.

"Fuck, Conan, she's dripping. She likes you filming her. I bet she's fantasizing about you sharing this video with the brothers. How they would all stroke their cocks while staring at her pussy as she creams all over my dick. You like the idea of that, Sunshine?"

The sound plays from Blade's phone while he slowly strokes his cock and I stand there, mouth open, gaping like a fish.

"If you're gonna open your mouth like that, Stormcloud, you might as well put something inside it. Get in here and lock the door." Blade's gruff voice makes my stomach clench.

I push the door closed and slide the lock into place before walking over to the desk and placing the beers on top of it.

Blade's eyes watch me as I walk toward where he's sitting on the sofa in the corner, his thumb hovering over the screen of the phone. He must have paused it as it's silent now.

"You look hot as fuck in this video, Kat, but nothing compares to the real thing. Take your clothes off, Stormcloud. I wanna see my old lady."

"Blade." I groan, nervous but excited too.

"Get naked, Kat. I want you on your knees looking up at me

with those pretty eyes of yours as you show me how well you can suck my dick."

The authority in his voice makes me obey without conscious thought. One day, I think I'll enjoy pushing my luck to see what kind of punishment he would dole out but right now, I want to show him what a good girl I can be.

Stepping out of my heels, I slowly lift my tank top over my head and toss it onto the chair beside the desk. I take a step closer to him before reaching around and unhooking my red lace bra and pulling my breasts free to the sound of his choked moan.

"Fuck me, your tits are spectacular." He hisses.

I bite my lip, acting coy before turning my back on him.

Sliding the zipper down on my pants, I slip my hands inside the waistband and slide them slowly down over my ass, bending at the waist to give Blade a show.

His muttered curse has me fighting back a grin as I step out of the pants, leaving me in nothing but a red G-string.

I sway my hips seductively as he snags a cushion from the sofa and places it on the floor between his legs.

"Kneel."

I slide my hands over his thighs, my purple-tipped nails digging into the denim of his jeans, and I arrange myself comfortably on the cushion.

"Get me out, Stormcloud."

I roll my eyes at the ridiculous moniker he insists on calling me.

Snaking my hand inside his jeans, I pull out his hard cock

and swirl my thumb around the drop of pre-cum gathered at the tip.

Flicking my tongue over him, I then drag it down his length to the base and back up again before opening my mouth and taking him inside.

"Good girl," he praises as I hum around him, working him in and out of my mouth at a leisurely pace as if we have all the time in the world and there isn't a party going on downstairs.

I hear Conan's voice and pause for a second, realizing he's pressed play on the video again.

He watches me on-screen bouncing on Inigo's cock. I work his dick backward and forward between my lips, my body on fire and my core slick to the point of dripping. The tiny soaking wet G-string does little to hide it.

"Jesus Christ, Kat, it's like you were made for me. Looking at you now, so fucking sexy worshiping your man, it's like you walked right out of one of my fantasies."

I release his dick with a pop.

"Well, it's about to get better." I channel my inner hussy and climb to my feet, slipping my heels back on to give me an extra few inches so I can accommodate his *extra few inches* a little easier.

I bend over the desk and wiggle my ass, fluttering my lashes in what I hope is a sexy way and not like I'm having an episode.

It must work because he's on his feet behind me with his large rough hands smoothing over my ass before I can speak.

"You need fucking, sweetheart?" His growly voice makes my skin break out in goosebumps.

"Yes, so bad." I moan as he slides a finger inside me before slipping it into his mouth.

"Mmm...you taste as sweet as I knew you would."

I watch with a clawing hunger inside my belly as he strips out of his clothes and squats behind me, dragging his tongue through my wets folds all the way up to my ass.

"Fuck, I could eat you out every day and it will never be enough to sate the hunger I have for you."

"Oh, god!" I gasp, dropping my head to the desk as he swipes his tongue over my clit, the hard bundle of nerves sending pulses of ecstasy through my body.

"More," I beg, earning a swat to the ass.

"You don't tell me what to do, Stormcloud. You're in my castle now."

He doesn't say anything else as he returns to eating me out like he has something to prove. Maybe he does. I'm spoiled, after all, with three men now willing to fulfill me in ways I only dreamed of.

A pang of loss stirs for a moment but I fight down the guilt that threatens to rear its ugly head like an ever-present entity inside me. I know this is what Alex wanted for me—to have people in my corner who would bend over backward to protect me and fill me with so much love that the loss of him dulls to an ache I can live with rather than a wound I'll slowly bleed to death from.

A stinging slap to my ass snaps me out of my head as Blade climbs to his feet.

"You don't get to check out when you're with me, Kat, not

now, not ever. If you don't want this tell me now and I'll get dressed and walk away."

"Really?"

"Fuck no, but it sounded better than *snap out of it before I fuck you so hard you won't be able to walk for a week.*"

"Hmmm...I don't know. If I had to pick, I'd choose option two, please."

"You aching for me, huh?" He reaches around me and yanks the drawer open, grabbing a condom and hurrying to slide it down his dick.

"I'll get tested and then I want you bare, yeah?"

"Okay, Blade," I whimper, wanting that too. I know how much I like feeling Inigo and Conan come inside me even if it can get messy as hell. I guess that's part of the fun.

"You want that, Kat, you want to feel my seed inside you? Or maybe I should paint your tits like Conan did in the video."

He dips his finger inside me again and uses my wetness to coat his latex-covered dick before nudging it at my entrance.

Leaning down over me, he presses his mouth to my ear and whispers, "Or, maybe I'll fuck your ass. Take you while Inigo takes your pussy, and Conan shoves his cock in your mouth. Make you airtight."

I shiver at his words but worry if wanting that makes me a slut.

As if reading my mind, he chuckles. "Do you think it makes you a slut, little one, wanting three dicks at once?"

"Maybe? I don't know," I reply breathlessly as I wait for him to slip inside me.

"I think it makes you our slut, Kat. That's what you really

want, don't you? You might look like a beauty queen on the outside, but in the bedroom, you'll be our dirty girl." And that's when he surges inside me, wrenching a scream from my body as my hips push flush against the desk.

"That's it, Kat, squeeze me tight." He growls as he fucks me savagely. I'm no longer an equal participant in this, all the power shared before transfers to Blade as I submit to him in all his brutal glory.

I do the only thing I can, I grip the edge of the desk and hold on for the ride.

"This what you wanted, baby, huh? Is it? Fuck, you feel good," he curses, his rhythm faltering for a second.

He pulls out of me and I mewl in protest. He picks me up and perches me on the edge of the desk before shoving his dick back inside me.

"Touch yourself, Kat, I wanna see your face when you come."

I pant, slipping one hand down to my pussy and flicking my fingers over my clit.

Dipping his head he sucks one of my nipples into his mouth, making me clench around him. He bites down, making me arch with need.

I gasp.

"You there, Kat, you gonna come for me?"

"Yes, yes, please let me come."

"Do it now, Kat, strangle my cock."

Anything else he might have said gets lost as I scream Blade's name loud enough to leave my throat hoarse.

It only takes a moment for him to follow, burying his head in my neck as he groans through his release.

"I'm forty-five years old and finally found peace. If I die tomorrow, I'll die a happy man with a smile on my face. When I face the devil, I'll go knowing that for the briefest time, I was lucky enough to find heaven."

"Blade," I whisper, cupping his jaw with my hands and bringing his lips to mine in a sweet soft kiss at complete odds with the wild fucking moments before.

"I could easily fall in love with you," I murmur against his lips.

"Darlin', I knew you were for me the second I opened my eyes in that barn and saw you standing there like a fucking warrior. I'm just waiting for you to catch up."

"I see that tongue of yours is good for more than just eating me out." I grin, feeling pretty fucking good right now.

"This old man might have a few tricks up his sleeve to teach you yet. How about we get you cleaned up and we find the other guys? I want to show them my smug face."

I throw my head back and laugh, feeling his dick start to harden inside me once more.

He pulls free, making us both wince as he slips the condom off and ties a knot in the end.

"I thought old men couldn't get it up again so quickly," I tease reaching down to stroke him.

With a growl, he pushes me back so I'm lying flat on his desk before his head is back between my legs again.

"Looks like you need a reminder about who's the boss, Stormcloud."

"I'm only young, sometimes it takes me a few tries to remember."

"A few, huh?"

"Oh yeah, at least three."

"Challenge accepted, sweetheart." He reaches up and puts his hand around my throat. "I hope you're ready to play with the big boys, darlin'."

58

Inigo

"Look, I get that you have your own place but it's too small for all of us and I don't want to be in Kat or Alex's life part-time. I told you before, I'm all in and this is part of it."

"This place is huge, Blade. Don't you think it's a little overkill?" I sigh.

"Not if we fill it with kids." Blade grins as Conan and Kat turn to look at him.

"You want kids?" Conan asks, looking surprised as he holds Alex's car seat in his hands, swaying it gently when the little boy stirs.

"Well yeah, I just hadn't found the right woman before now. Don't you?"

Conan looks at me then shrugs. "I'd love more but I'd also be happy with just Alex."

"Don't you think we're getting a little old?" I ask, liking the idea of a houseful of kids but hating the fact I won't always be young enough to run around after them.

"If it's good enough for Jagger..." Blade jokes.

"Do I get any say in this at all? You know, since it's my womb you guys are basically planning on renting." Kat folds her arms over her chest and pouts.

"You gonna deny me watching you grow round with our kid? Deny them? I've only just met Alex and I already love him but these two have been with him from the start. You know what kind of fathers they are. And with you as a mother? Jesus, any future kids will be hitting the parent lottery." Blade grins, making me snort. The smooth bastard.

"How have I never noticed what a conceited asshole you are?"

"The word you're looking for is awesome," he jokes, unlocking the door.

"The word you're looking for is diva," Kat throws in with a sing-song voice before squealing and hiding behind me as Blade lunges for her.

"Now, now, children, play nicely," a familiar voice sounds from behind us.

Turning, I come face to face with a fucking ghost.

"Shit!" Blade curses while Conan looks an alarming shade of pale.

"Wes?" Kat steps forward and wraps her arm around his

neck and sobs, leaving me feeling like I must be losing my mind. That's the only way to explain what I'm seeing.

"What are you doing here? Do you know Blade?" she asks, turning to face the three of us, her whole body freezing when she takes in our expressions.

"What's happening?" Turning she looks back up at him, her voice dropping to a whisper. "Wes?"

"Hello, Sunshine," he says softly, cupping her face.

"How...how are you here?" she whispers.

"Yeah, King, how the fuck are you here when you're supposed to be dead?" I spit, my anger so acute every single muscle in my body locks up.

"King?" Kat asks, confused before the name clicks and she sways on her feet.

"Orion and Diesel's father," she mumbles, taking a step back but he closes the distance once more by stepping forward.

"You son of a fucking bitch," Conan growls and I have no doubt if he didn't have Alex in his hands he would have charged King by now.

"I have to admit you look pretty good for a dead guy." I stalk forward and grab Kat, swinging her around until she's behind me.

"You don't understand, Inigo, let me explain."

"You're damn fucking right I don't understand. You were more than just my president, you were my fucking friend. I trusted you with my life," I roar, remembering the grief I felt when he died.

"I know, I'm sorry—"

I swing my fist and connect with his jaw, making him stumble back.

"Fuck your sorries and fuck you too."

I reach to grab him again but Blade stops me. "That's enough. Hear him out."

I turn to look at Blade and see it written all over his face. "You knew. You son of a bitch, you know he was alive all along."

"No, I didn't, not all along that is."

I swing and punch him too but Kat's hand on my arm stops me from doing it a second time.

"Enough, Inigo. Hear him out so we can leave," she says quietly and I can feel her shaking.

I turn and wrap my arms around her and use her to ground me. My woman needs me now and that's what she'll get.

I look up at Conan, who is staring at King with hatred and hurt in his eyes. "Call Orion. Get him and Diesel out here."

"I don't think—"

I glare, cutting Blade off.

"It's okay, Blade, it's time," King says sadly as he steps around us and heads to the door like he owns the place, which has me pausing and looking at Blade again. Blade has the decency to look sheepish.

A whistle from King has the four of us turning toward the sound of claws scrambling over the pavement, heading in our direction.

"Jesus Christ," I spit when canine King comes flying across the yard, stopping briefly in front of Kat to lick her hand before following King inside the house.

"Why, Blade? Why would you do this?" Kat asks him. He

reaches for her but she shrinks back, burrowing deeper in my arms.

"There is so much more going on than you know, so much more than I know. This is the only way to keep not just you safe, but all of you."

"So it was never about you wanting me?" I hug her tighter at the hollow sound of her voice.

"Fuck me. Is that what you think?" He stalks forward and pulls her free. I let go only so she doesn't get hurt in a tug of war but I don't step back, crowding him until he's said his piece.

"It might not have started out with you in mind, Kat, but this is how it ends for me, with you and these ugly bastards together. I never lied to you about my intentions or about how I felt. I told you there was more, I just couldn't reveal anything until everything else was in place. Honestly, most of this isn't my story to tell, it's King's. You guys can hate him all you want and perhaps he deserves it, but you have no clue why he did what he did and how many lives he saved by doing it."

"Somehow, I don't think Orion and Diesel will give a shit," I growl.

"Oh grow up and hear him out. What do you have to lose?"

He turns his attention back to Kat, who is looking up at him with tears in her eyes.

"You didn't know King. You know Wes. Don't judge a man by the ghosts of his past. He isn't the same person they all knew. Make your own choices but don't let their perceptions cloud your vision or dim your voice. Give him a chance as the friend he was to you when you sat on that park bench ready to give up."

Kat sobs and steps into his embrace and lets him hold her while she cries but I'm still stuck on his words.

I look at Conan, who is staring at Alex, deep in thought before his head lifts to Kat, his face wincing as he witnesses her pain.

"I'll hear him out. But Kat, we need to talk. Where the hell did you even meet King, to begin with?" Conan asks, moving behind her.

She turns in Blade's arms to look at Conan. "It was his dog who offered me comfort first. I was sitting on mine and Alex's bench at the park and I was barely staying afloat. I was just so damn tired of it all. Wes, or King, sat in Alex's seat. I was mad at first, but we got to talking and afterward, I didn't feel quite so alone."

"Was that the only time you met him?"

"No, but it was the only place. We never met anywhere other than the park, but he became my confidant because it was easier to talk to a stranger than to admit to either of you how weak I was. How much I was struggling," she admits quietly.

"Shit." Conan blows out a breath before reaching for her hand. "Let's go inside. Alex will be waking up to eat soon, and I'd like to get him settled before the guys get here."

"They're coming?" I question, trying to process everything.

"Yeah, they'll be here in about an hour."

"I hope to fuck this place has insurance," I grumble.

"What, why?" Blade asks.

"Because you better believe there's gonna be fireworks."

59

Kat

"He go back down okay?"

I turn at the sound of Wes's voice and nod, pulling the door but leaving it open a crack in case Alex wakes.

"He's fine, thanks." I wait for him to step back so I can pass but when he doesn't move, I stop and look up at him and wait for whatever it is he wants to say.

"My intention was never to hurt you or deceive you, Sunshine. Never that and never you, but sometimes a man is forced to make decisions he knows will make him a villain. But he does them anyway to save the people he loves, even if they end up hating him for it."

"I'm tired, Wes, or should I call you King?"

"King is good." He nods for me to continue.

"Okay, King it is. I don't really know what to say. I...guess I just don't know you as well as I thought I did."

"You know me better than most, Kat, and that's saying something. I might have held stuff back but I never lied to you."

I think about everything we talked about and put it into the context of what I've heard around Carnage about him and realize he's right.

"I'm just not really sure where that leaves us or where I even fit into the equation, to begin with. Should I feel grateful that you were there beside me in the dark or should I feel hurt because you followed me into the dark willingly, just to use me as an in?"

"That's what you think this is? Fuck, Kat, I could have found a thousand different ways to find my way back *in,* as you put it. Hell, I didn't even want back *in.* I left for a reason, causing so much fucking pain, but did it knowing it was for the greater good. Only none of it matters anymore." He closes the last of the distance between us and rests his chin on my forehead in a surprising move. There has always been a crackle between us, an awareness of some kind which I mostly ignored, but standing here like this feels intimate, which is both comforting and concerning.

Hearing bikes in the distance, I lift my head, our faces so close our lips almost touch.

"They're here," I whisper unnecessarily, suddenly fearful of what might happen to this man because there is no way we'll make it through the night without bloodshed.

"Maybe you should stay up here for a moment while we talk to them."

"It's gonna be okay, Kat."

"I don't want you to get hurt," I whisper, blinking back tears, my emotions giving me whiplash.

"I'll be fine. You're just going to have to trust me for a little longer. Go on ahead of me, I don't want them getting mad at you too."

I close my eyes, take a deep breath, and blow it back out before slipping a hand down and lacing my fingers through his.

"No. You kept your promise. You came back. Everybody always leaves but nobody ever came back before." I square my shoulders and squeeze his fingers. "I'm not gonna let you do this alone. You were there for me and no matter how much I want to kick you in the shins, I refuse to let you do this alone."

King swallows hard, his eyes searching mine before ever so slowly he dips his head and presses a kiss to my lips.

A cough has us pulling apart to find Blade at the top of the stairs looking between us before smirking.

"It's time," he says before turning and jogging back down the steps, not acknowledging the kiss at all. I'm not going to try to analyze that. If it had been Conan or Inigo, King's lips would have likely been ripped off and lying on the hallway floor.

Maybe he could see the kiss wasn't about sex or King's desire to get in my pants but his appreciation for my solidarity and gratitude that, despite what's to come, he will always have one friend in that room with him.

I can hear Orion and Diesel's voices as we make our way down the stairs, Orion's louder than his brother's as his shocked happiness rings out.

"I can't believe you found him. I thought for sure he was

dead by now. Luna will be so damn happy to see you, boy." King's panting sounds out and the jangle of his collar indicates that Orion must be showing him some fuss before we step into the entrance of the kitchen.

"What the fuck?" Diesel yells, spotting us first. Orion is crouched next to the dog but his head whips up at Diesel's yell. His eyes land on King and go wide.

"No. No! You son of a bitch!" He stands and charges, pulling back his fist and letting it fly but I've had enough of this bullshit already. Without using any of the common sense I was born with, I step in front of King and take Orion's fist to the side of my head.

Yeah, I've had better plans.

I drop to the floor when my head feels like it's about to explode and cartoon versions of birdies take flight.

Oh boy, that can't be good.

"Shit." King scoops me up in his arms as I hear grunting and the sounds of yelling but it seems a lot farther away than it should be.

When I lift my head, I see Orion on the floor with a split lip, Diesel standing in front of him like a sentry as Blade and Inigo fight to hold Conan back.

"I could have your cut for that," Diesel hisses at Conan as King sits me up on the counter. King grabs a bag of peas from the freezer, wraps them in a kitchen towel, and presses them against my head, making me wince.

"I could rip your heart out for that!" Conan roars, reaching for Diesel now. It takes a lot to get Conan to lose his shit but me getting hurt will do it every single time.

"Conan, I'm okay. Dial down the urge to grind his bones and come love on me a little," I call out weakly.

Getting punched fucking hurts. I'm lucky his fist glanced off the side of my head or I'd be out cold on the floor right now.

"I get that this is a shock but if she gets hurt any more than she already has been, sons or not, I will kill you both." King seethes, his voice sounding as lethal as a blade, surprising the shit out of everyone.

"We are not your sons. You gave up that right when you faked your fucking death. No fuck that, you gave it up when you screwed our mother over. I have nothing to say to you. As for you three…" Diesel looks from me to Conan to Inigo and shakes his head.

"It's a good thing you have the Ravens because you're not welcome at Carnage anymore." He takes a step to storm out but Blade blocks his way.

Hearing him kick us out of the club breaks my heart. Fuck knows what it must be doing to my guys and suddenly I'm pissed. So unbelievably pissed that the pain in my head dulls as a ferocious roar builds inside me.

"You asshole. You pathetic spoiled little boy. Oh boo-fucking-hoo, your feelings are hurt. So what? You're just gonna spit your pacifier out, stamp your feet, and tells us we can't play with you anymore? Grow up." That's rich coming from the youngest person in the room but I carry on, hopping off the counter, ignoring the protests of my guys, I stalk toward Diesel, albeit on shaky legs.

"You might be the VP of Carnage but you're acting like a little boy right now and that's dangerous. Man the fuck up!" I screech in his face, watching Blade out of the corner of my eye turn to hide his laugh.

"And you?" I spin and glare at Orion, who stares pale-faced at King.

"Are you seriously going to stand there knowing King is the only reason Luna is still alive and say nothing?"

I look back to Diesel and shake my head in disgust.

"You're right. Thank fuck for the Ravens because right now I'm ashamed to say I'm Carnage."

"You're not a member, Kat, but these two knew fucking better," Diesel growls.

"Not a member? Well, bless my soul. I'm glad you told me that. I thought for sure I was, at least in as much as an old lady can be. But don't worry, I'll be sure to let Luna and Ava know they're not members either. We'll go back to being pretty little arm trinkets." I step closer and poke my finger against his chest.

"Inigo and Conan found out about King about an hour ago, much like you did, and the first thing they did was contact you." I grin but I know without seeing it that's it's twisted and ugly.

"Don't ever question their loyalty again when they did everything right. And you?" I step back and look him up and down, showing him exactly how lacking I find him right now. "You turned your back on your brothers without giving them a chance to even speak and explain."

"Kat, it's alright. I was pissed too—" Inigo rubs his hands up and down my arms but I shake my head.

"Of course you were pissed, and I'm not saying they don't have the right to be, but there's being pissed and then just being a fucking dick," I snarl.

The Crown of Fools

"I'm so turned on right now," Blade mumbles from behind me but I ignore him when Orion steps forward.

I move in front of King once more but he quickly spins and places me behind him.

"Not a chance, Sunshine."

"I'm not gonna hurt her. Fuck." Orion rubs a hand over his face.

"I'm sorry Kat, I never meant to hurt you but you know better than to step in front of a man like that." He growls and I nod, conceding his point. He's right, I have an egg on the side of my head to prove it.

"Just let him explain and if you still want him out of your life then go for it, but if it's just pride stopping you from hearing him out then swallow it the fuck down. Do you know what I would do to have Alex walk back through that door? Rarely do you get a second chance when the reaper is involved but here we are. You're being given a chance to right the wrongs. Miracles might happen for you guys every day but not for me. I'm smart enough to know when to hold a grudge and when to let go. But then I'm just a woman, what do I know?" I sigh but not before turning my glare on Diesel.

"Look, can we please just sit? I'll tell you everything you want to know but Kat looks like she's two seconds from falling over and Alex won't sleep forever," King says quietly.

The room goes silent, everyone waiting for someone else to make a move.

Rolling my eyes and instantly regretting it when it feels like an icepick has been embedded in my brain, I stomp to the table and pull out a chair before collapsing on it and placing my head on the cool wood.

A hand at my back has me turning and pausing when Diesel leans over with the bag of peas I dropped earlier and presses them to my head.

He doesn't apologize. I don't think he trusts himself to speak, but the peas are his version of an olive branch. I snort.

The man needs lessons in humility but I let it slide.

We have bigger fish to fry.

60

King

I take a seat beside Kat, who reaches under the table with her free hand to grip mine tightly.

What this woman does to me.

Diesel and Orion sit opposite as Inigo and Conan sit on Kat's other side and Blade sits beside me. There's a clear divide with each half letting the other know exactly where their loyalty lies.

Oh, I'm not stupid. This show of unity isn't for me, it's for the woman sharing her strength with me and that's why she's so damn important. She has this unique ability to bring people together, despite losing a piece of herself when Pike died.

She'll never need me the way I need her. I'm far too old for her and come with more baggage than I'll ever be able to unpack but I'll be here, like a shadow watching over her, even if that's all I'll ever be.

"Speak and make it good, old man, because this is the only shot you'll ever get," Orion orders like the president he is but the boy forgot I changed his diapers.

Cocking my brow, I stare at my boys with their crystal blue eyes and dark hair so much like their mother's. The only thing they get from me is their height and their smiles, not that I've had much cause to use mine of late.

Not since the last time I basked in the warmth of Sunshine.

"To explain it all I need to go back to the start. It won't be pretty, and you might hate me even more after, but you deserve to know the truth.

"You know about the mother chapter of Carnage being infiltrated by undercover cops headed by Flex and Coil." I shake my head. It sounds like a terrible reality TV show.

"They, along with Kermit, were placed there to bring down the Serpents, a particularly nasty MC, but also to find out how a new lethal street drug was spreading through the US like a fucking plague.

"It proved to be a genius move and with their success, it was decided that a second club should be started. We could cover more ground and pool our resources if necessary, so that's what we did."

"Wait. You're a fucking cop?" Diesel spits, standing, the chair falling to the floor behind him with a loud crash, making Kat jump.

"Sit the fuck down and listen for once in your goddamn life, Diesel," I growl.

He glares at me for a minute. I can feel the hatred wafting off him in waves but thankfully he sits, which saves me from putting him on his ass.

"They had detectives and beat cops in Vegas keeping an eye on the drug scene but for LA, they had something else in mind."

"The guns?" Conan guesses. I nod.

"Yeah. Huge shipments were making their way over to US soil and we had no idea where they were coming from."

"So you're ATF?" Orion guesses but I shake my head.

"No, Orion. It wasn't just guns. We had reason to suspect a terror attack was being planned."

"Terror attack?" Diesel looks at Orion who looks at me speculatively.

"FBI?"

"CIA," I admit. "And so was your mother."

Utter silence blankets the room. The only thing keeping me grounded is Kat's hand still squeezing mine.

"You lie," Diesel hisses but there is no venom behind it. He wants me to be lying but he knows I'm not and that kills him.

"We were assigned identities. We went in as a couple with limited information to make our reactions genuine." I shake my head at my stupidity, back when I believed in the shit I did.

"We had the property secured and then it was just a case of recruiting members. Melly and I met Joker and John completely by fluke. We were at a biker rally trying to put out feelers when we found out a cartel that had been slowly encroaching on their territory had destroyed their previous clubs.

"We got talking, got them drunk, and convinced them to start a new Carnage chapter with us. What we didn't know was that the mother chapter had imposed the one woman to multiple men ratio. I mean, who does shit like that?"

Kat coughs beside me. I look at her and smile sheepishly.

Returning my stare to my boys, I continue. "We walked into the mother chapter to meet Flex and Coil, playing up the part where we accepted their terms for opening the new club, and that's when they dropped it on us.

"We couldn't back out without blowing our cover but I didn't want this shit for Melly. I told her to bow out, knowing there was no way she could get out of sleeping with them, and that was when she punched me in the face and broke my nose."

I finger the bridge of my nose and smile at the memory. "God she was so pissed. She told me she knew what she was doing. She was a CIA operative for god's sake, *her words*. And that's what sealed our fate.

"With the top dogs in place, it was easy to recruit others and before we knew it, our club was bigger than the mother chapter."

I stare at the table and think of the life that passed in the blink of an eye.

"But?...All these stories have a but." Kat sighs.

"Power corrupts. It always does. The CIA refused to pull us out, always moving the goalposts until eventually, all the lines blurred. By this point, I wasn't just the president of Carnage, I was the top dog over at the agency too. But when you make it to the top, the only place left to go is down.

"Melly wanted out. She'd given half her life to the job. We

had you boys and she loved you both more than anything, but she wanted out of the life and she wanted me to go with her."

"You refused," Diesel scoffs.

"Your mother was an operative, but I was one of the top dogs. You don't just get to walk away from that, Diesel. That's not how it works and you fucking know it."

"One day, I woke up and Melly was gone. What I couldn't tell you before was she left me a note saying she was done. She had nothing more to give. She had called her handler and he was pulling her out. It was just after John split and the cover story was going to be that she had left to go be with John. I was surprised they didn't fake her death, but then I supposed it meant that they could drag her back in if necessary. There wasn't anything I could do. She had made her choice. My handler told me to put up and shut up. She was happy and that's all there was to it."

Diesel looks torn at my words. I know he believed Melly's death was all my fault, and maybe it was, just not in a way they were thinking.

"So the phone call she made that you blew off saying she needed help?" Orion asks, not missing a beat.

"Her handler told me to expect it. Said she had been spotted by Joker and it was to reel him in. Melly had been tapped once more, but this time she would be under at Chaos. To say I was livid is an understatement. I ripped the clubhouse apart. It was the first time I realized I needed an out. After that, I was shut down when I asked about Melly and my sleuthing was considered insubordination, which meant I got demoted and conveniently, Melly's handler got promoted.

"What about the cancer? Were you even sick?"

I shake my head regretfully.

"Jesus. Everything about you is a lie." Diesel shakes his head sadly.

"No. How I felt, feel about you two, that was never a lie."

"So where did it all go wrong?" Orion asks with a touch of sarcasm in his voice.

"Everything that happened the day I shot Joker was real. I had no idea Melly was dead. I just reacted. I knew something was going on outside of Carnage, shit kept happening I couldn't explain, but I was being deliberately kept in the dark. I wanted out. I talked to a therapist at the agency. I told her I needed extracting as I was getting sick. There is a reason nobody takes undercover jobs for as long as I did. It changes you. You become the very role you were asked to play. I stopped being Wes and became King until I sat next to Kat at the park one day." I look at her and see her looking at me with concern on her face.

"I take it they weren't keen for you to leave," Conan questions.

"I was told to rest and they would get back to me. A week later, the therapist was dead and I received photos in the mail of you two with your eyes cut out."

"Fuck!" Orion curses.

"I'd been planting seeds before then, covering my tracks just in case, which is where the cancer came in. If I died, there would be no blowback on you two. I wanted to keep it as a last resort but then orders started coming in for girls."

"Carnage doesn't deal in skin," Diesel spits.

"The agency doesn't give one fuck about Carnage. They

wanted a scapegoat and a way to find the sellers, or at least that was what I thought. But the more I dug, the deeper I realized the dirt was."

"You could have told us. We would have helped."

I shake my head at Orion. "The next lot of mail I received was over one hundred photos of Luna. Some from the day she freed the dog, some from the time she ran, and some were taken from within the same room. I had pictures of the woman my son loved, in the shower, sleeping, and fucking you while you were all oblivious. There was a traitor in the club and I had no clue who, but I also had an ally," I admit, making everyone tense.

"Who?" Inigo looks at me and asks. I stare at him, hating that I'm tarnishing the memory of his friend.

"No. I don't believe you," Inigo snaps.

"Half-pint was at my place when I opened the mail. I wasn't thinking. It was after the shit went down with Joker and I knew my time was up. Half-pint wanted to warn you all, so I came clean to him. Told him everything and he offered to help me. To keep you all safe, he'd have done anything."

"But you were shot. You were dead, King," Conan points out.

"CIA, remember? I have access to shit you don't even know exists and that includes drugs that lower your heart rate enough to make you appear dead. I swallowed it after I was shot and hoped for the best. Of course, the bleeding out meant I almost really did die, but Half-pint got me out of there and took me to a private clinic where I had a doc on standby."

"I remember walking into the clubhouse and finding you

covered in blood with Gecko a few feet from you. It was Half-pint that checked for a pulse and said you were dead. It was Half-pint that dragged you from the room before coming back for Gecko. None of us blinked an eye because that's what Half-pint did. He was the cleanup guy," Diesel says wide-eyed.

"And he's dead because I got him involved."

61

Kat

"Okay, back up. I'm lost. You died. So why did you come back and where were you when all this stuff with Garrett went down?

"Well, I did have to recover from gunshot wounds." He laughs ruefully but sighs when nobody else does.

"I never had much to do with Garrett but he was a fuckup who progressively got worse. And yet they wouldn't pull him out, deeming him far too valuable."

He holds up his hand when I'm about to snap. "Not by me, sweetheart. That man should have been put down like a dog but he was very good at hiding and evading. So much so, the agency was able to look past his indiscretions as long as he did their bidding."

"Kermit thought he was doing the right thing bringing him in. He really did still have faith in the system. But Cohen got him out on a technicality."

"Cohen?"

"The guy who was Melly's handler. The one who replaced me and the one who orchestrated her death along with dozens of other undercover operatives."

"What the fuck?" I gasp.

"The girls Carnage were supposed to purchase? It was so they could track and trace where they were coming from and going to but we weren't going to save them, we were redistributing them."

The room seems to get smaller as we absorb his words.

"I went into this thinking I was making a difference and I did. I ruined more lives than I can count under the guise of being a good guy and I was blind to it all because I believed in a system that set me up to fail from the start."

"With you and Melly gone, so too was their plan. But then why come back? I'm not trying to be a dick here, but if you being gone kept Carnage safe, why come back?" Inigo asks. It's a valid question.

"I might have disappeared, but I did what ghosts do best. I haunt. I might not be with the agency anymore, but I'm not without resources. When you've had your fingers in as many pies as I have over the years, it's impossible not to make connections or to gather favors along the way. Now it's time to cash them in. I had no idea Garrett had a daughter or that he hurt her. Like I said before, not only were we not friends but both of us had covers to keep so nobody really knew the men beneath the masks.

"I was up to my neck in shit here but I heard what Bates had done and I knew Garrett had survived. The funny thing was, they couldn't pull Bates in for attempted murder without blowing Kermit's cover or leading a trail back to Garrett. That would place a target on his back and they had other plans for him."

"Like becoming chief of police," I say without thought.

"Exactly. Melly and I were already trained and had done undercover work before in the worst situations you can imagine. We knew what to expect, or we thought we did, but Garrett and Derek were fresh out of the academy. It made them easier to manipulate and mold into what they wanted. The difference between the two brothers was that one of them was a raging fucking psychopath."

"How did they miss that? I mean I understand them slipping through regular police, he was good at acting the part like all psychos are but with CIA involved, they were trained to spot the signs," Orion points out, making me look up at King whose head is bent, looking exhausted.

"They knew, didn't they? They chose him because of it, not in spite of it."

"He was the perfect man for them. He had a penchant for young girls and no moral compass stopping him from collecting them and sampling the merchandise. The girls were nobodies. Street kids, or from poorer homes, but most were trafficked from Russia and the Ukraine. They spoke little, if any,

English and even if they somehow managed to escape, what were they going to do? Call the police?"

"Honestly, this all sounds like something out of a movie. And some of it doesn't make sense, which given how all of this is fucked up, that's saying something. But you still haven't told us why you're back," Conan states.

"Because Carnage isn't getting the girls, the agency had to look elsewhere." King looks at Blade as his jaw locks tight.

"Bear, AKA Paul, and his brother David conveniently came into some money and purchased an apartment building."

"Fuck! All those empty apartments? They were for holding girls? That's why it was empty." Diesel groans.

"Kat and Pike were there before David and Paul took over or I doubt they would have leased you a place. But when Pike died, it suddenly made you a lot more interesting to them."

"Oh god, I'm gonna be sick." I nearly make it to the sink before I'm throwing up, thinking about all those poor girls and about how close I came to becoming one of them.

"Here." I look up when King hands me a toothbrush and toothpaste.

I take them and brush my teeth as the others continue to talk quietly.

"I'm sorry Kat, I should have thought of a better way to say it."

"No, I needed to know." We stand quietly while I brush and spit before he walks me back to the table.

Inigo opens his arms wide, so I climb up on his lap and let his arms wrap around me.

"You okay, Sunshine?" Conan asks softly, reaching out to stroke my hair as Blade looks on with concern in his eyes.

"I'm okay. Carry on."

"Sunshine—" Orion protests.

"Finish it. I can handle it."

"Alright, Kat." King nods before continuing. "All the apartments were soundproofed. It was the perfect set up until David fixated on you and Kermit killed him, drawing the attention of the media."

"Bear, er Paul, burned it down to get rid of the evidence." Diesel sighs.

"Now the agency is pissed. They want to hold someone accountable and it seems Carnage will make the perfect patsies. They need you gone. You've made your stance on trafficking known, and with Gemini controlling shit further afield, they're losing their footing."

"So instead of starting over somewhere else, they want to wipe us out and start over with a clean plate?" Orion concludes.

"Yeah, that's exactly it, Orion."

"So we strike first," Diesel growls, Conan agreeing with a grunt.

"For Cohen, it's personal and he makes Garrett look like a nun. He has resources like you wouldn't believe and he won't care who gets in his way. He'll ship the old ladies out to brothels after pumping them all full of drugs and he'll round up the kids and sell them all to the highest bidder. He will bring you to your knees and then he'll cut off your heads," King warns us.

"That's why Kat needed to be tied to Raven Souls." Orion looks at Blade and King who nod.

"Who the fuck is this Cohen guy?"

"He's the VP's nephew," King answers solemnly.

"VP? The VP of what?" Diesel stands up and starts pacing.

King looks at him grimly. "He's the nephew of the vice president of the United States of America."

62

Kat

To say things are strained right now would be an understatement. King is still mostly persona non grata at Carnage but he took it on the chin, masking the pain he felt for the loss of the club that was once his family.

"That the last one?"

I look up from my spot on the floor and shake my head at Blade. "You've been asking that since the first box." I grin.

"And one of these times when I ask, the answer will be yes." He grins back.

He scoops the box up, places a kiss on my head, and takes the box out to the truck.

"Hey."

I look over my shoulder at King's voice and take in the man

who leans against the counter like he doesn't have a care in the world.

He's in jeans and a black Henley today with heavy-duty biker boots, looking as handsome as ever with his serious blue eyes and silver hair.

"Hey yourself. Did you come to help me finish up? I've noticed the rest of my men have scattered in the wind."

He grins at that, those damn dimples making me melt.

"Conan and Inigo have taken Alex to collect more boxes and Blade conveniently just got a very important call."

I huff. "Of course he did."

Snagging the empty box closest to me, I sit it in front of me before ordering King around. "Well, don't just stand there, grab me one of those kitchen drawers."

He shakes his head at me, clearly not used to taking orders but he doesn't complain. He walks back over with a drawer in his arms and sits on the floor beside me.

"So," he starts.

I look at the unflappable man and see he looks, well, flappable.

"What's wrong? What is it?"

He slides his hand into my hair and slips his mouth over mine, kissing me unhurriedly as I melt into him. All thoughts of packing disappear along with everything else until he pulls away and leaves me breathless.

"I...um...I..."

King grins at my lack of speech until I shake the fog clear.

"I still can't believe I can do that now whenever I want," he whispers before kissing my forehead.

"I know, you're a lucky man." I wink. "I know it's weird, us taking it slow, but it's as much for the guys as it is for me. They need to be able to trust you again, King. Nothing is as important to them as me and Alex so it's gonna take time. I know we're all going to be living together and—" He places his finger over my lips to stop me from babbling.

"I can wait, I've already waited a lifetime. I've been so many people, lived so many lives, losing parts of the real me along the way but you, you strip back the darkness and give me nothing but—"

"Sunshine," I answer for him with a soft smile. I get that a lot.

Unable to hold his intense gaze, I dip my head and my eyes fall on the forgotten letter and photo I shoved in here the night I killed Chester.

Reaching in with a shaky hand, I lift the photo, ignoring the bloodstain in the corner, and stare at the man who helped me become a woman.

"He was a good man, Kat," King says softly, looking at the photograph in my hand.

"Yeah, he was the best."

Reaching for the letter, I open the blank envelope and pull the paper out from the inside.

I gasp, my hand covering my mouth when I recognize Alex's handwriting.

Sunshine

My gorgeous girl, I know that by the time you read this, I'll be gone. Doctors say I have an aggressive form of cancer and nothing they do has slowed its progress. God, you'll be so pissed when you read this, knowing I kept it from you but I've been given a year tops, and all I want to do is spend the last of my days with the woman I love. I don't want the end of my life to be tainted in sadness and regrets, I can't bear the thought of seeing the pain in your eyes. Maybe this makes me a coward, but I want you to remember me like this, as the man who was born with the sole purpose of loving you.

I want to tell you so many things but how do I put into words what you mean to me when there aren't enough words in the world to adequately explain how I feel. You are the best person I know, so full of love and kindness, don't lose that because of me. Don't let my death steal your light because I'll never forgive myself. I hope that by the time you read this, you'll be in the arms of another and I will have found the courage to tell you about the nature of Carnage and their old ladies. It's what drew me to them in the first place because I refuse to leave this earth knowing you're alone.

Let them in Sunshine, let them love you. You won't betray me by doing so. Loving you is an honor and a privilege I'm not sure I was ever really worthy of. Being with you, it's like magic. Somedays I have to pinch myself to know it's real. You always deserved better than the hand you were dealt, but you saw the good in everything, including me. You fell for me, a nobody punk ass boy and you turned him into a man.

I don't have much of a legacy to leave behind I'm afraid, my greatest treasure has always been you and even though I want you to live and love and grow round with babies, I'll keep a tiny piece of your heart for myself and take it with me.

You'll always be my girl, Sunshine, no matter what and one day, when you're old and gray and you've changed the world in all the ways you can, I'll be at our bench, waiting to carry you to the other side.

Love always

Alex.

"He was sick," I choke out, tears running down my face in an endless river as King pulls me to his chest and holds me while I sob.

I cry until I have no tears left before pulling away and looking up at King, noticing the look in his eye.

"You knew."

"I didn't know he was sick, Sunshine. Not until after." He blows out a breath before picking up the photo of Alex and me.

"Do you remember me telling you about my friend who was sick?" I nod, feeling numb and so fucking confused.

"He had a brain tumor. And much like Pike, there was nothing they could do to slow down its growth. As the tumor grew, it caused irreparable damage, changing the man I once knew into someone I barely recognized."

"Chester. Chester Froggett—Kermit—was your sick friend, wasn't he? Oh god, and I killed him."

"Hey," he grips my arms, "the man you shot was not Chester. He was already gone."

I nod, replaying that night in my head and Chester's whispered thank you as I set him free.

"Chester and Pike met by chance at a support group. Chester had been visiting Derek at the time and well, I don't know all the details, but I do know that Chester made a promise to Pike that he would look out for you and protect you when he was gone. The tumor screwed with that somehow and turned it into an obsession. Turning in Garrett started a domino effect he never saw coming, and when he saw you fall apart at Pike's funeral, something snapped."

"That's what you figured out that day in the park, wasn't it? It's why you left."

"You mentioned the people around you who had crossed you in some way dying and having a prospect on you."

"I always had a prospect on me."

"No darlin', you didn't. That's how we could meet so freely without me worrying about being outed."

"He was following me. The biker outside my apartment that night, being there at the bridge that fateful day—" I shake my head.

"Jesus. I can't take back what I did to him and even knowing, I'd still do it again if I had to, but the whole thing just makes me feel so sad."

"He's free now. No matter how it all played, you gave him peace."

The door slams open making me yelp as King dives in front of me.

Conan and Blade come barreling into the room, Alex held tightly in Blade's arms as Inigo storms inside, his cell pressed to his ear.

"I don't give a flying fuck, just find her," he yells, before throwing the cell across the room with a roar.

Blade rocks Alex, who starts crying, but I focus on Inigo, knowing Alex is in safe hands.

"Inigo? What's happened?" I question softly as I climb to my feet and approach him slowly.

He turns to look at me with wild eyes. "My niece Mercy and her friend were heading to her friend's parents for the weekend, but they never made it. Cops found the car abandoned on the side of the road, their luggage, handbags, ID, and cellphones still in the car. Both girls are missing."

I reach for him, but his eyes drift to King and he swallows hard.

"They found blood at the scene. A lot. Too much. It's started hasn't it?"

King stands and walks over to him with a nod, gripping Inigo's shoulder.

"We'll find her."

"The blood—"

"Won't be hers. She's the first pawn, she's too valuable to sacrifice just yet."

"Yet?" he snarls.

"We'll find her."

The question is, will we find her in time?

The End...for now.

Coming Soon

The Mercy of Demons: An Underestimated Novel Book six
https://books2read.com/mercyofdemons

EXCERPT OF RICOCHET BY CANDICE WRIGHT

Chapter One

Lying in the stillness of the dark room, I stare out into the stormy night sky. It's humid tonight. The open window lets in a balmy breeze that tickles my skin, but it doesn't warm me. Not when I can still feel the icy imprint of his hands on me. I take a deep breath, the scent of rain beckoning me outside with the promise of washing me clean. No more fingerprints or bruises or bite marks, all of them rinsed away by the downpour of crying skies, the heavens weeping for the girl who has no tears of her own left to cry.

I was naïve in thinking I would get a reprieve tonight. How silly to assume that burying my mother would grant me one night to grieve in solitude. I left the wake downstairs, walking up the staircase with heavy steps, hindered by the rustling fabric of the dress Clyde chose for me to wear. A fourteen-year-old walks into a funeral wearing a cocktail dress and a fake smile. It sounds like a bad joke, but this joke is my life.

I could hear the whispers as I sat in the hard-wooden chair, watching as they lowered my mother's white, flower-adorned coffin into the ground. Each shovel of dirt thrown over her casket echoed the mud being thrown over me. Nasty words scoring marks into my skin, made by catty women and perverted men who should have tried to help me. Instead, they cast me in the role of temptress and waited with bated breath for me to take my mother's place.

Not bothering to change after I made my escape, I kicked off my shoes and crawled onto my bed, the stupid dress billowing out around me as I grieved in private while hordes of fake mourners milled around downstairs drinking champagne and eating canapés.

It wasn't until later, when the crowd had thinned out a little and the voices that floated up from downstairs seemed fewer, that I realized my mistake.

Dresses made for easy access. Not that jeans stopped him, but psychologically I felt safer wearing them.

It didn't matter. I didn't fight back, didn't tell him no, or flinch when he told me with whiskey-laced breath how beautiful I was, because I knew it could be worse. He had crossed so many lines, but never the final one, the one I wasn't sure I would survive. So, to keep my virginity intact, I stopped fighting.

Maybe that made me complicit. Perhaps it made me a whore like the catty women below said about me. The ones who passed their judgments as they blew their rich sugar daddies and fucked their gardeners on the side.

But they had no clue what it was like to be me. Clyde had pulled me out of school under the guise of being homeschooled. It was a ruse so there was someone home to take care of Mama and someone around for Clyde to amuse himself with whenever the moment arose. I had lost the few friends I had, my brother was long gone, and now my mother, my last tie to the little girl I once was, is dead.

A bolt of jagged lightning illuminates the night sky just as I hear the telltale creak of someone stepping on the loose floorboard outside my room.

I tense, biting my lip as I hear the door open behind me for the second time tonight. I close my eyes at their approach, feigning sleep, forcing my body not to react to the cold fingers on my arm.

Even with a house full of people, I know it's him, his touch as familiar to me as my own, his icy, frigid skin mirroring the coldness of his heart. Fingertips tuck a strand of hair behind my ear, hovering for a moment before a cough from the doorway draws his attention.

"She's asleep?" the lightly accented voice asks. Italian, perhaps.

"Yes, so keep your voice down," Clyde replies, low and somber.

"And she is untouched?" the man persists, not lowering his voice at all.

I'd laugh at that if I weren't so terrified. I'm many things, but untouched is not one of them.

"I told you she was and she will remain so until I hand her over to you in the morning, but tonight G, she is still mine, so do not overstep," Clyde warns, his voice filled with anger.

"Maybe," the other man concedes, "but I paid for a virgin, and that's what I expect to receive. You can have your last night with her, but after that, forget she ever existed. Unlike you, I don't feel the need to trade in my toys every few years. I like to keep them until I break them."

Clyde sighs, stepping away from the bed, his heavy footsteps moving toward the door.

"Yes, G, I am well aware of the deal we made. Now let's finish our drinks. I'm being rude to my guests," he finishes, closing the door behind him.

I strain to listen over the sound of my wildly beating heart that threatens to crack my ribs.

I guess I know why he never crossed that line when he so happily crossed all the others. I wouldn't have been worth as much if he had broken me in.

The storm is raging now, both outside my window and in the darkest part of my mind. A scream builds within, rivaling any a banshee might make, but I swallow it down and bite my lip until I taste blood. The little girl inside me urges me to run, to push open the window and disappear into the night. But then what will happen to the little girl who comes after me?

Climbing from the bed, I grip my hands into fists. Nobody was there for me. They ignored my cries and turned their backs on me. I won't ever be the person who stands by and lets something like that happen, not if I can stop it.

I rip the dress from my body, tearing the fabric in the

process, and dump it in a pile on the bedroom floor. Rummaging through my dresser, I grab the first nightshirt I touch, pulling it over my head before grabbing my backpack from the back of my desk chair. I empty the contents on my desk. A cherry Chapstick makes its bid for freedom by rolling off the edge and landing on the carpet soundlessly. Walking on silent footsteps to the door, I pull it open gently, checking that the coast is clear, then step over the creaky floorboard and tiptoe down the dark hallway to Clyde's office at the end.

Pushing the handle down, I find the door unlocked like I knew I would. Clyde thinks he's untouchable. I'm going to show him how wrong he is.

I don't waste time as I move across the thick carpet beneath my feet, feeling oddly proud of myself for all the times I spied on Clyde. I must have always known deep down this day would come.

Lifting the picture of a forest landscape off the wall, I place it near my feet and focus on the safe hidden behind it.

0817, Mom's birthday.

I type it in, tensing when it beeps once, then I swing the door open.

The first thing I take is the money, ten stacks of cash tightly bundled together with rubber bands and shove them into the backpack. Next, I take the ledger filled with names and numbers. I don't know what any of it means, but something tells me this thing might be valuable. Finally, I take the item I came here for, the gun. It's heavier than I thought it would be, looking large and intimidating in my small hand, and yet, a wave of comfort washes over me. It doesn't matter how small I am, how weak I am; this thing evens the battlefield. I shove it into the backpack and close the safe, placing the picture back over it.

Leaving the room the same way I found it, I close the door behind me as voices saying their goodbyes drift up the stairs.

I head back to my room and remove the gun, shoving it under my pillow before grabbing items I'll need. I only pack the essentials I can carry—underwear, socks, toothbrush, a handful of toiletries, and three changes of clothes. There is no space in the backpack for anything else.

Opening the desk drawer, I lift out the tattered copy of *Chicken Little* and run my fingertips over the cover reverently. How I wished for a different life. Shoving it back in the drawer, I slam it closed.

The temperature had dropped, the howling wind blowing in the window, making the white gauzy curtain flutter as if it's dancing to music only it can hear. I pull the curtain closed before climbing under the comforter, the inky blackness of the night wrapping itself around me like a welcome friend.

And I wait.

It doesn't take long, the lure of spending his last night with me too strong for him to ignore any longer.

This time I don't pretend I'm asleep or ignore his presence like a ghostly specter. I turn to face him, watching as he flicks on the lamp and bathes the room with an eerie glow.

I watch him gaze around, his face sad as he takes in the pink and white polka dot wallpaper, the white gloss furniture, the bed, and the white bedding with tiny pink flowers. It's a bedroom fit for a princess, something I never aspired to be, but then this room isn't about me, it's all about Clyde.

"Hello, pretty girl," he whispers when his lust-filled eyes finally land on mine. "Daddy has a special night planned for us."

I don't answer him. I stare at the handsome face my mother loved. The strong jaw, sharp cheekbones, and twinkling bright blue eyes all add to his appeal, but it's just a mask to hide the monster beneath. But he's not the only one wearing a mask, and tonight he's not the only monster in my bedroom.

He removes his clothes, cufflinks first, popping the silver ovals on my nightstand. His white shirt is next, followed by his suit pants, his shoes, and his socks.

"Clothes off, pretty girl, you know I don't like to wait," he scolds lightly.

I sit up and pull my nightshirt over my head without protest, leaving me naked, my panties likely still in his jacket pocket where he shoved them after the first time he visited me tonight.

He smiles, a genuine one that lights up his entire face and makes the bile rush up the back of my throat, but I fight it down.

"So beautiful," he murmurs, sliding his boxers down to expose his hard length.

I hold my breath as he reaches out to twist a strand of my hair around his finger, my hand slipping under my pillow, my fingers wrapping around the handle of the gun.

See, Clyde is an evil man in the worst sense of the word. He doesn't just use his body to control mine; he turns my own against me, forcing my pleasure, reveling in my responses to his touch. He doesn't just make me hate him; he makes me hate myself.

For a long time, I thought it was my fault that I must have wanted it because good girls don't come when they are being assaulted. That's what he told me, that it's not rape when you like it. For the longest time, I believed him until I stumbled across a blog online written by a rape survivor. Her words changed something inside me, made me see that Clyde's words were just another way of hurting me, raping my mind right along with my body.

Well, it ends today.

"Lay back on the bed, legs spread," he orders, moving around to the end of the bed.

I do as he asks, moving on autopilot, my hand gripping the gun as he stares at me.

"What's going to happen to me now?" I ask, wanting to know what his lie will be.

"Hush now, that's for tomorrow. Tonight is all about pleasure." He smirks, climbing on the bed, kneeling between my legs.

"I know what you're planning on doing," I whisper, the words slipping out before I can stop them. "You won't get away with it, people will wonder where I am, they'll ask questions," I tell him as his large hand slides up my thigh, but we both know that's not true. Everyone I care about is gone.

"I forget how innocent you are sometimes, especially with a body like this. I'll tell people you ran away, but I doubt anyone will ask. Nobody will remember you, Vida, you're a ghost," he

Excerpt of Ricochet by Candice Wright

says lightly, as if he's talking about the weather. I think it might be his tone that snaps the last of my restraint.

"Funny you should say that." I pull the gun free from the pillow and point it at his head.

His eyes widen a fraction as his hand pauses on my thigh. I let my hate for this man fuel me and pull the trigger with zero hesitation.

My hand shakes, the noise sounding like a bomb that makes my ears feel like they are bleeding.

"I guess this makes us both ghosts now."

ALSO BY CANDICE WRIGHT

Also by Candice Wright

THE UNDERESTIMATED SERIES

The Queen of Carnage: An Underestimated Novel Book One

https://books2read.com/queenofcarnage

The Princess of Chaos: An Underestimated Novel Book Two

https://books2read.com/princessofchaos

The Reign of Kings: An Underestimated Novel Book Three

https://books2read.com/reignofkings

The Heir of Shadows: An Underestimated Novel Book Four

https://books2read.com/HeirofShadows

The Mercy of Demons: An Underestimated Novel Book 6

https://books2read.com/mercyofdemons

Ricochet (Underestimated Series Spin-off)

https://books2read.com/Ricochet

THE PHOENIX PROJECT DUET

From the Ashes: Book one

https://books2read.com/PhoenixAshes

From the Fire: Book Two

https://books2read.com/phoenixfire2

The Phoenix Project Collection

https://books2read.com/Phoenixcollection

Virtues of Sin: A Phoenix Project Novel

https://books2read.com/VirtuesofSyn

THE INHERITANCE SERIES

Rewriting yesterday

https://books2read.com/Rewritingyesterday

In this moment

https://books2read.com/Inthismoment

The Promise of tomorrow

https://books2read.com/Promiseoftomorrow

The Complete Inheritance Series Box Set

https://books2read.com/Inheritanceseries

THE FOUR HORSEWOMEN OF THE APOCALYPSE SERIES

The Pures

https://books2read.com/pures

SHARED WORLD PROJECTS

Cautious: An Everyday Heroes World Novel

https://books2read.com/Cautious

Hoax Husband: A Hero Club Novel

https://books2read.com/HoaxHusband

ACKNOWLEDGMENTS

Jodie-Leigh Plowman – Cover Magician.

Tanya Oemig – My incredible editor - AKA miracle worker.

Chantal Fleming — Proofreading Goddess.

My Beta Angels – You ladies are the bee's knees. I will never be able to tell you how much I love and appreciate everything you do for me.

Aspen & Catherine – My mighty Alpha's. There isn't enough words in the dictionary to express my gratitude for you.

Julia Murray — My amazing PA. We both know I'd never make it through the day without you.

My readers – You guys are everything to me. I am in awe of the love and support I have received. Thanks for taking a chance on me and on each of the books that I write.

Remember, If you enjoy it, please leave a review.

ABOUT THE AUTHOR

Candice is a romance writer who lives in the UK with her long-suffering partner and her three slightly unhinged children. As an avid reader herself, you will often find her curled up with a book from one of her favorite authors, drinking her body weight in coffee.

Made in the USA
Las Vegas, NV
08 May 2022